The Memory Chamber

Holly Cave

Quercus

First published in Great Britain in 2018 by Quercus
This edition published in 2018 by

Quercus Editions Ltd
Carmelite House
50 Victoria Embankment
London EC4Y 0DZ

An Hachette UK company

A CIP catalogue record for this book is available
from the British Library

PB ISBN 978 1 78648 537 3
EBOOK ISBN 978 1 78648 534 2

10 9 8 7 6 5 4 3 2 1

Typeset by CC Book Production

Printed and bound in Great Britain by Clays Ltd, Elcograf S.p.A.

For my Mummy-in-the-Oak-Tree

CHAPTER ONE

First of all, I tell the dying people my name. Then I offer them a seat on the sofa, next to me, and I pat the fabric in a way I hope is inviting. I do like the way I've set that up. I like the fact we are next to each other, on the same piece of furniture.

At first, some of my clients find it strange to sit so close to me. But towards the end of our time together, it makes it easier to reach out and touch them, offer them reassurance. By that point, a lot of them need that silent, lingering touch. It's part of the reason I take such good care of my hands. Although, having said that, it's rare I need to use moisturiser. I sometimes joke that my hands get worn soft from all the stroking of skin. I rub one over the other, inspecting the cuticles and the pink half-moons that sit above them. One or two of my nails always seem to grow faster than the others and the irregularity grates. I'd like to file them now but I don't have time.

I look out through the wide window of my office. My next client is approaching the front door of the clinic along the shrub-lined pathway. August sunlight flares across his face. It casts an artificial blush of health over the hair and tissue that's fading away from life. He fits the description I have in my file: male, thirty-six. Only five years older than me but old enough to die. How is that fair?

I find that most of my clients are late, so I'm often just sitting here, ready and waiting. Despite the micro-mechanical vibrations of the chips in their necks – the alarm which urges them onwards to their overdue appointment – I think they find it hard to push themselves through the clinic's doors. Doing so is an admission – an acceptance. Sometimes, if it's sunny, my clients will stop to look up at the building, or admire the plants and flowers. Men who I can't imagine have picked up a trowel in their whole lives will pause to rub the soft fuzz of a leaf between their fingers or will crouch down to inspect the buttercream petal of a spring primrose. Sometimes, they'll decide this is the perfect moment to make the call they've put off for weeks. To tell someone they love – or someone they have loved – the news. Even though the vibrating alert from the chip in the flesh of their neck is telling them, *You're late, you're late, you're late.* That's sentimentality for you.

But not this man. He's tall. He walks with strength and assurance, although his head tilts to one side, as if he's listening to the voice of a sprite perched upon his shoulder. His chin is tucked in and angled towards his collarbone. Anyone would judge him as handsome, I think, although it's hard to examine his face from here. I lose sight of him as he approaches the main entrance and I feel the familiar tumble of nervousness in my stomach. I glance down at the notes on my Codex. His name is Jarek Woods. He is dying as the result of a rare, aggressive brain tumour.

I would never consider entering a room unannounced, but

he doesn't knock. He is so tall he almost has to duck to fit under the door frame. And then I realise it's not that he's especially tall, but just that he walks that way. The tilt of his head leads the rest of his body into a slight left-leaning stoop. I've already seen his scans, so I know that this is the work of the tumour inside his brain. As I take in his broad, well-built stature, rust-coloured hair and calm green eyes, it's almost possible to forget the burden he must be bearing. But I feel it, as I do with every client. That never gets any easier.

'Hello, my name's Isobel.' His frank gaze catches me off guard. I feel myself take an extra breath and my voice drops in pitch. 'I'm your Heaven Architect.' It sounds curter than I intended and I berate myself, quickly enough that my small, carefully managed smile doesn't drop. It's important to look welcoming, but a beaming expression would give too much away about my enthusiasm for my job. No one wants to think I'm inspired by the idea of their death.

'I'm sorry I'm late.'

As his eyes meet mine, his grin fills the room. Something about him is familiar. His hair is damp and curls around the edges of his ears, clinging to the cartilage. He commands so much more space than any dying person I've ever met. The little equanimity I had fades, and I can't remember what to say next.

He shuts the door behind him. I watch him run his hand down the gap between the door and the architrave, checking that it's flush, before he comes towards me. Even in the face of death, we all concern ourselves with such minor matters. My clients ignore bucket lists to arrange their affairs, while I worry about whether I should open the door myself and close it behind them when they enter my room. When people leave it ajar, I feel like my chest is going to explode with agitation.

He pauses next to the sofa and seems to steady himself. His bold gaze drops to the carpet and a frown creeps across his forehead. He is more vulnerable than he first appears. He sits down and presses the base of his palm against his neck to switch off the alert emanating from his chip. Then he looks at me and grins again, relieved of the incessant, irritating vibration.

'I'm Jarek.' He extends his hand. 'Pleased to meet you.'

'And you.'

He leans forward to slip off his leather jacket and I see the lines of his collarbone sharpen as his shoulders rotate. The mottled grey marl of his T-shirt matches the freckles running down his arms.

'I thought your name might be pronounced differently.' I fight the temptation to alter the position of my hands, to avoid folding them into my chest. 'I thought it might be a silent *k*.' I try not to smile at my own vulnerability, pressing my lips together.

He shakes his head in a pretence of solemnity. 'There's nothing silent about me.'

I can't help but smile. 'Have you come far?'

'No – Maida Vale. Once, I'd have called it walking distance.' He knows he's talking in half-jokes. Sarcasm glides through his voice like a metallic thread through silk. Not like my own sarcasm can be, outside of this room: jagged and defiant.

I try to assess him as quickly as I can. It's difficult to be fully prepared and these first few moments are vital. Humans are unpredictable creatures – dying ones especially. I've seen it all, over the past ten years: a kaleidoscope of different reactions. Some of my clients can hardly speak. Some want me to hold them. The more self-assured men laugh and sometimes even flirt, grasping on to their dwindling chances. We are all so different, but I find myself wanting to act within the norms while being aware that there are none. I'm conscious that people like me are setting the traditions for this new rite of passage. And I can't escape the knowledge that Heaven Architects are not only revered but also reviled.

'What is with those crazies outside?' he asks. 'They can't be good for business.'

I sigh. 'The protesters? I apologise; they're usually moved on quickly.'

'I just don't get it,' he continues as he settles back into the sofa and focuses his gaze upon me. 'How could they think that what you guys do is anything less than commendable?'

I tilt my head to the side, fascinated at his naivety. 'Oh, plenty of people think that artificial Heavens are morally dubious.' Like Don, I think; like my mother.

'Well, hey.' He leans forward and rests his hand on the sofa, close to me but not quite touching. 'Don't listen to the doubters. I'm sure that what you do comes from the heart.'

As he speaks, I remember that what he says is my truth: my motivation to do this job was always emotional. I always believed it was the right thing to do, the kind thing to do.

'I asked around when I was first thinking of coming here,' he continues, wincing slightly as he pulls his hand back into his lap. 'And they say you're the best. But you're no-nonsense. Am I right?'

Despite his upbeat demeanour and the residual strength of his stature, there's no doubt that he's ill. His face is worn and his skin is sallow. Yet a boyish energy surrounds him. It seems to emanate into the room, happy to share itself out with whomsoever happens to meet it.

'Sounds pretty accurate,' I say, shrugging and pursing my lips. He probably expected me to act coy, but I know I'm good at what I do. Certainly, I'm the best at what I do in London, and this is what I take him to mean. That doesn't mean I'm good enough, though.

'You have glioblastoma. Is that right, Jarek?'

He bobs his head and twists his lips into a sad smile. 'We call it a brain tumour at home.'

'I'm sorry.' I have to focus in order not to stumble over the words. 'I hope your treatment is making you feel better.'

He shrugs. 'It's just bad luck that I got the one cancer they still can't cure.'

'Well, there's more than one,' I say. 'But I understand how you must feel. How has your treatment been going?'

'My consultant's ruled out any last-minute surgery, which I'm kind of relieved about in a way. I've had enough operations.' He runs his hand over his head, and I imagine that he's tracing the lines of his surgeries. 'Instead, he's injected a new PCL film, which should draw more of the cancer cells towards the cyclopamine cartridge. I can't say I feel any better, though.'

'You look well.'

He shakes his head and clasps his hands together, running his thumbs over each other. 'Whatever you say, Isobel. Beauty is in the eye of the beholder.'

I shy away from his gaze and place my Codex on the coffee table. I wave my hand and all my documents appear on the darkened glass. Jarek's notes materialise and the documents I need float to the top of the digital pile. After just a few weeks in my possession, this new system knows me, my voice and my gestures intimately. Its ability to predict my needs makes it well worth the investment, in my opinion. Plus, it sets our clinic even further apart from those others in London still relying on desktop computers and physical paperwork. I'm distracted from its impressiveness by a small smudge in the corner of the glass and rub at it with the base of my wrist. I should just clean this office myself.

Jarek rests his chin on his fist and leans forward over the table. 'You have the tiniest hands.'

I didn't notice him looking but he has turned his face from the notes and is smiling at me. He nibbles at the skin beside his thumbnail and a thick gold wedding band reflects the light from the window. I tuck my uneven nails away from sight, curling them into my fists. The knuckles push pink through my light brown skin.

'Have you done much research about artificial Heavens?' I ask him. Most people have, given the amount of cash they're spending.

'A bit. The general concepts, that kind of thing.'

'I'll give you an overview of what we'll be doing together, anyway. Just so you know, I'll be recording all our sessions in a format that prevents me or anyone else from editing them in any way. That said, I will have future access to them, as will your next of kin. I would think we'll have between five and eight two-hour sessions together, which for most people is enough time. Some people need more; some people need less. There's no judgement.' He lets me talk, punctuating my sentences with nods and murmurs of agreement. 'Do you have any questions before we begin?'

'No; let's get on with it.'

'This is the process.' I drag forward a diagram from the digital pile of documents on the coffee table. 'Over those sessions, we spend ten to twenty hours together, during which time I gather the information that helps me map out the backbone of your Heaven. We'll go through places, events, people, possessions, even your physical appearance. This is what we call the architecture. Once we're happy with that, I work privately on the balance of all those elements, forming them together into a cohesive whole that works and flows – a bit like the way the rooms in a house would. It's like creating doorways between memories; placing people into framed portraits on the wall; filling the garden with all the plants you love. There's a lot of creativity to that part of the process.'

'Heaven feng shui?'

'If you like.' I smile. I do like it. It conjures up a nice image of a neat, airy room where everything is in its place. I'll keep that expression for myself, I think. 'Then I send all the work I've done to our neurologist. I'm not yet sure who we've assigned to you but I'll find out and let you know. We work with a few and they're all excellent – at the top of their field. He or she will scan you at the lab and map what I've done on to the individual neurons. They try to find what I've requested – it's like a treasure hunt. Then they translate the activation patterns into digital data.'

'Will my tumour affect how easy it is to find everything?'

'It might take slightly longer than normal, that's all. Most of what they're looking for is in a few specific areas of the brain that process self-awareness, memory and emotion – the hippocampus, largely, as well as the cerebellum and possibly the amygdala, too, depending on what we need to find. If there are any issues, they'll let us know early on. After that, you'll have a further session with

8

me, in which you'll be able to see a visual simulation of your Heaven, and then one final appointment with the neurologist to ensure it's all good to go.'

I pause and let my voice fall lower, softer. 'In the event of your death, the tricky bit is that your neurologist will need to gather the cluster of neurons that encode your consciousness within a matter of hours. And when these so-called mirror neurons are extracted from your brain and connected up to the digital map of your Heaven in the lab—'

'Then voilà!' Jarek interrupts.

'Voilà.'

'You make it sound so straightforward.' The edges of his words are taut. I hear his unvoiced fears.

'You shouldn't have anything to worry about.'

Jarek drops his head, humming to himself, and then looks up again and raises his eyebrows. They are teasingly asking me to continue, as if he already knows the awkward topics that come next.

'Alongside all of this, there are legal procedures that we have to carry out. Firstly, I have to put in a request to see your criminal record so that we can confirm your eligibility.'

'Do I look like a serial killer?' He tries to frown but the warmth escapes through the corners of his eyes.

'Who am I to know?' I turn out my bottom lip and shrug. We meet each other's smile at the same moment and something fires up inside my brain: a new connection, or the chance of one. Or, at the very least, the possibility of one in another time, another place.

I realise he is still smiling at me with a warmth that would suggest we've known each other for years. He is waiting, patiently.

I tug on the threads of my thoughts and roll them back into the words I was going to say.

'But seriously, mass murder would definitely count you out. And any serious crime must be further assessed. Usually, anything involving extended prison time must go to a committee. But I'm sure you're clean. I haven't noticed any teardrop tattoos . . .'

'Oh, you have a sense of humour, too! We'll get on well.' His eyes are like searchlights now upon my face. I blink them away and drop my gaze to the coffee table.

'The other important thing at this stage is that double opt-in requires you to provide written or verbal agreement from any person, living or dead, that you wish to feature in your Heaven. We'll work together to create this list and then our legal team will make the necessary arrangements.'

Jarek raises a finger and it's the first time I notice him express genuine confusion. 'So, my mum, my sister . . .' He spreads his palms wide. 'They're out?'

'If they're no longer alive and there's no formal record of them agreeing to be included before their death, then I'm afraid so.' I swallow and my throat tightens. I never know how to soften that blow.

'Way to lighten the mood, Isobel!' He rubs at his temple with his fingertips. 'So, I'm an escaped mass murderer and now my family is forever dead to me?' He laughs before dropping his chin to his chest. 'They died years ago, before any of this was really possible,' he adds.

'I know it doesn't seem fair, especially in the case of family members, but it's important that we get two-way agreement. Those memories belong to them as much as they do to you.'

His smile fades and he rolls his head to the left, into the pain. I see the sadness in the furrows of his brow and it resonates in a corner of my own heart, tapping at the soreness there. We are both too young to have lost a parent. My mother will be in my Heaven. She agreed to that, at least.

'I do understand,' I hear myself saying.

He looks up at me from his hands. He's leaning forward and we're so close now. I can see the bright, wet squares of the windowpanes on his eyes. 'You do?'

I shouldn't carry on; it's too personal. But it seems too late to worry about that. 'I haven't seen my father since I was little, and my mother died six years ago. She wouldn't let me make her a Heaven. She didn't want one.'

I run my middle finger over the threaded arches of my brows and think of my mother, knees crossed on the living-room floor, pulling me towards her by my ear. As she set to work upon my thick, unruly eyebrows, she always muttered short phrases in Bengali — words I later learnt were swear words, the only ones she spoke in her native tongue. I think of her vanity for me every time I stand in front of the mirror, pulling the threads of silk across my own forehead. In my Heaven, we will relive the scene as adults, laughing as we weave each other into more beautiful versions of ourselves. I have just a few memories of my father that will feature in my Heaven. That's assuming I can even get in touch with him, of course.

'It's a personal decision, I suppose,' Jarek says. He raises his eyebrows, tugging up the skin from his nose and distorting the freckles that linger there. 'But that must have been hard for you. I'm so sorry.'

Briefly, it's as if I'm the client and he's the Architect. And it's like taking a sip of cool champagne, the bubbles bursting against the flesh of my mouth. Yet it's not right. I bite the inside of my lip as if to take back my words.

'There are things we can do about your mother and your sister,' I offer. 'We can find vaguer memories, not tagged with faces or locations, that are more than simply about emotions. There are ways of feeling the *presence* of people without actually featuring them.'

'Okay,' he says. 'That sounds good.'

'And this is definitely what you want?' I ask. 'You want me to make you a Heaven?' I realise as I speak that my voice is tinged with need. I am nervous that he'll have a last-minute change of heart. I've had clients walk away at this point before. I feel my senses winding down, turning inwards; I'm protecting myself.

'Is there an alternative?'

His voice is flat and I can't tell if it's a genuine question he's asking me.

'Well, are you religious?'

He shakes his head and purses his lips as if to hold back laughter.

'Then the alternative is . . .' I pause, searching fruitlessly for the right word. 'Oblivion.' It's dramatic, but it's true.

'I was kidding,' he says, batting my sincerity away with his hand. 'I've started to make some notes . . .' He checks one pocket, then the other, jiggling around on the sofa. I find myself smiling, relieved and thankful for his enthusiasm. Few clients are so stimulated by the idea, but this man gives the impression that little overwhelms him, even the idea of death. He hands me his Codex, and I scan through the jumbled bullet points. Then I glance at the time.

'We can try and make a start today.' My announcement is rewarded with an eager smile. 'First, it's important that you're trackable to us from this point on. We need to be able to find you as soon as possible . . .'

I listen to my voice trailing off, horrified. I find I can't say it. I can't look at him either. I put the Codex down on the table and he rolls it back into a tight scroll. *After you die. After you die.* The words run in circles behind my lips as I cross the room and fumble for the tracking kit in the drawer of my desk. Jarek is watching me. I know this not because I am looking at him, but because I can feel his eyes burning spots of heat into my cheeks. I clench my teeth and extract the kit and an unopened chip from the plastic box tucked inside. I rub my hands thoroughly with an antibacterial wipe and break the seal of the chip. I can feel him watching me as I load it into the gun.

'This is almost identical to the machine which fitted your main chip—'

'Oh, yes, back when I was sweet sixteen,' Jarek murmurs, closing his eyes and tipping his head back to the ceiling. 'Back when all this augmented reality stuff was just hitting the mainstream.'

'Me, too. And now nearly everyone's got one.'

I walk back towards him and perch on the edge of the coffee table. I always sit here. It helps me get a better angle.

'Although this will sit immediately below your existing chip, it won't interact with your Codex or stream any content to your eye lens,' I tell him. 'It's smaller, simpler; just a wafer of graphene that will allow us to locate you quickly and grab the bunch of neurons we need to activate your Heaven.' I swallow as I run my fingertip down from his jaw to the hollow in his neck. I can feel the small mass of his chip pressing into me with each of his heartbeats. I rub against the skin and feel the stubble that has grown there since this morning. As I bring the gun up with my other hand and position it against the spot I've chosen, I can feel his breath falling on my own neck. It sneaks beneath the collar of my shirt and slips down my spine.

I fire and the gun buries the tracking chip into his flesh with a small click.

'Ouch!'

I look at him in surprise.

'Only kidding.' He winks at me. 'I've had my skull cut open recently, remember.'

I laugh a little in relief as I bring my finger away from the entry point and dab on some wound gel to hold it closed.

'So, getting back to today, we could start by talking about some general ideas of what you'd like in terms of locations and settings.' I return the kit to my desk and wipe my hands. I walk back to the sofa and sit down beside him. I realise at the last moment that I'm too close. Some clients would shift slightly, awkwardly, but he stays put. I can hear his breath, heavy through his nostrils. I clasp my hands together over my knees.

'So, if my Heaven was a play, this would be the backdrops and the scenery?'

'Yeah, if you want to think of it like that. Although, remember that it will all be more fluid than you can imagine, because you'll experience your Heaven without the dimension of time.'

He frowns at me. They always do.

'We haven't really talked about the timelessness yet, but it's a key thing to bear in mind,' I add.

'Timelessness,' he echoes, considering it, turning the idea over. I watch the word sizzle in his mouth.

'So, essentially, nothing in your Heaven – in anyone's Heaven – operates within the dimension of time. Partly because we don't know how to encode it; partly because we wouldn't want to, anyway. Timelessness is a good thing. It allows me to create a finite series of events, scenes and memories that you'll never tire of. It makes them infinite; it makes *you* infinite. You'll experience sequences, orders to certain things, but you won't feel time passing.'

'It's hard to imagine,' he mumbles, raising his gaze to the window before rolling his chin to his left shoulder, as if he is retreating into his weakness. 'Time is all I hear about these days: estimates of how much longer I have left, how long a particular surgery will take. I wanted my eldest daughter to reach six before I died. In bed last night, I worked out how many days there are before her birthday. It'll be a miracle if I make it.'

I nod. I've never shied away from death and I prefer it when my clients open up rather than hide their feelings away. It's so much easier. I fight my natural tendency to reach out and touch him. I often squeeze a client's hand or place my hand on their arm. But the idea seems too intimate with him and I'm rendered uncomfortable, unbalanced on my seat.

'Sorry. I'd figured you were used to hearing people drone on about their own deaths,' he says, and I can feel his gaze upon me as I flush.

'I am; of course I am.' I speak more slowly, regulating my tone. He raises his eyebrows, asking me for more. 'It's just that not many of my clients are as young as you.'

'The facials must be working!' He yelps with laughter and uses his right hand to pull the skin taut over his cheek.

I smile and gesture towards him. 'See? No wrinkles!'

But he's already looking away, turning his head awkwardly about the room. 'What's that smell?' he asks. 'It's strangely familiar.'

'Oh, the ylang ylang?' I point to the little dish on the shelf above my desk. 'It shouldn't be strong; it's just a few drops. It's supposed to be calming.'

'And an aphrodisiac, I believe.' He grins and, although he smiles a lot, his expression is different this time; it dares me to respond and I feel a flush across my neck. I stare back down at my notes.

'It would be good if I could find out some more about you first,' I say. 'Whatever feels right. In your own words.'

It amazes me how people attack this request so differently. Many of my clients find they are inclined to define themselves by their disease. I anticipate that Jarek might be the same. He probably has whole conversations with people he's never met before about the rogue cells taking over his body, the blood–brain barrier, and the gold nanoparticles swirling around inside his skull. I watch him closely. I am waiting for that moment of connection. A tiny opening that will let me in.

'I'll tell you as much as you want to hear,' he says, sinking back into the sofa. There's a gentleness to his voice again, a succumbing. His arms are spread wide and he is open to me.

'I'll take as much as you're willing to share.' I find I'm almost whispering, leaning into him. My skin tingles as I correct myself, straightening my back and pushing stray stands of hair away from my face.

'I've just turned thirty-six. I live here in London with my

family, in a house that I'm not going to be able to get re-roofed before I die. I grew up overseas – my dad was in the army.'

'What was that like?'

And even before he replies, I spot the crack and the darkness slicing through the gleam of his armour.

'It's not a childhood I'd want anyone else to have,' he says, narrowing his eyes at me before looking down at his feet. 'My dad was . . . heavy-handed, shall we say. Either that or not around at all.'

I can hear the rancour dissolving the clean edges of his voice. Its barbs sink into my own feelings towards my father: the sadness and the unavoidable guilt that maybe it was me, somehow, that drove him away. Years of unspoken stories and heartache entwine in the space between us, linking us. I have to catch my breath before I speak.

'Family relationships are difficult.'

'Everyone's?'

'Well, no, but yours . . . and mine.'

I feel Jarek's gaze boring into me.

'And what do you do for a living?' I ask.

There's a pause before he replies, as if he's keen for me to reveal more. 'For now, I'm a journalist.' I wonder how on Earth that's managing to pay for my services. He has the tone of a private education and the aura of a man who hasn't ever worried about money. It must be in the family. That would explain how he has the cash to invest in creating a Heaven. 'But one day I'll be a famous actor.'

I laugh despite myself. He could have been an actor. He has the charisma. 'What kind of journalism?'

'Politics, home affairs. So, for God's sake, don't ask me about this war. I know nothing.' He rolls his eyes dramatically. Yes, he'd be a good showman. 'Oh, and my wife thinks it's the tumour's fault that our relationship is breaking down.' A guttural bitterness spreads through his voice and prickles at my skin. 'She thinks the cancer has changed me – changed my brain.'

'And has it?'

'No, no.' His head lolls forward so that his chin hits his chest before bouncing back up again. 'It's been failing for a long time now. We've both let things go.' He runs a fingertip over his eyelid and looks up at the ceiling.

I realise I've started to sit back and I correct myself, placing my elbows on my thighs and pressing them into the flesh. I find myself wondering what his wife is called. I imagine her names to alliterate. Perhaps she is Winnie or Winona. Or Willow. Willow Woods. She is pale skinned and beautiful, with long black hair and a razor-sharp parting down the centre of her scalp.

'My consultant has told me I've got a few months,' he continues. 'I don't believe him.' His eyes fix upon me then, and I can see they've tightened into what seems to be a determined sparkle.

'Good; you're optimistic.' I nod and pretend to make a note, looking away. A monsoon of laughter erupts from his chest. The force of it startles me and I feel my right hand creep towards the arm of the sofa. He's looking at me in surprise that I have judged him so poorly, shaking his head almost imperceptibly.

'You're kidding, right? I feel fucking awful.' He laughs through his words but I almost judder with his fear. The seconds roll by and I compose myself, doing what I was taught to do, while the voices inside my head jostle to be heard, screaming out questions.

I do not understand how it feels to be dying, but how can I ask? There will always be this chasm between myself and my clients.

I wait and I listen. Eventually, he gives himself over to the silence.

'I've given myself a month,' he says. 'I can hardly see out of my left eye anymore.'

'You might surprise yourself. I've had clients who have come here at death's door and recovered.'

'You say all the right things, Isobel. I'm so glad I chose you.' He reaches out and squeezes my shoulder. His face is serious, contemplative. His jaw is set hard. 'I don't want to die,' he murmurs, 'but I know you'll make me the most remarkable Heaven. I almost – almost – can't wait.' He presses his finger on to the exposed skin of my collarbone and I can't help but jump up from the sofa in surprise. I find myself walking towards the window and I lean for a moment into the glass, my nose almost against it, arms folded. I try to fight off the weight of his expectation, but it clings, shroud-like, around my shoulders.

'I'll do my very best,' I say.

'I know you will. It'll be even better than the real thing.'

'The real thing?'

I don't look around and I hear no response. It never fails to surprise me how many people admit to some kind of faith at this point; how they get here, to this office, with even the vaguest belief in a God-created world and some majestic, universal afterlife. I've dreamt about it before, of walking through the silvery gates of Heaven, led by a throng of angels. It's just one of those weird things – a psychological motif that's etched like a scar into my subconscious somewhere. In fact, dreaming is one of my problems; sometimes they feel so real they haunt me for days. Last week, I dreamt about Don, curled up like a newborn kitten in the palm of my hand, dying. I still can't take my mind away from the weakening flutter of his eyelids and his unspoken demand not to immortalise him. *I choose death. I choose death, in its entirety.* He hates what I do, I know he does. Just like my mother, he might love me, but he doubts what I do and he doubts me. It leaves me no room to doubt myself.

CHAPTER TWO

The day finishes in a way which is still, for now, unusual. My last client is called Clair and it is our final session together. She bounds into my room like a coiled spring, her excitement and nervous energy tangible.

'Clair!' I stand up from my sofa and we hug like old friends. The fact that she is not dying, at this moment in time, has somewhat altered the Architect–client relationship. 'How are you?'

'I'm good, thanks, Isobel. All ready now. I'm off to the Pacific next week!'

She's come straight from work and looks much more like an army officer than I've seen her look before. Yellow stripes flash at the shoulders of her storm-blue V-neck jumper. Her heeled ankle boots are gone, replaced with polished black military shoes. They are laced regimentally over her tiny feet.

'The real deal, hey?' she says, grinning and spreading her hands as she notices me appraising her.

'Wow – yes. And all this time I wondered if you were delusional and making it all up! Come, sit down.'

Clair sits on the edge of the sofa, as if ready to burst into action at any moment, and I seat myself beside her.

'Do you want to see it? Get a final flavour of what it'll be like?'

'Oh, yes!' She nods eagerly.

'Okay.' I take her left hand and guide it to an active area of the tabletop. 'Place your palm down here and don't move it. And close your eyes.'

Her eagerness fades to an expression that could almost be construed as impassive. I admire the intent slope of her cheekbones as her eyeballs dance around beneath the flimsy covering of skin. Clair knows that she is lucky to have this opportunity. The military are just starting to roll it out as an employment benefit. It is rewarding, refreshing, to create Heavens for people who wouldn't normally be able to afford it.

'This is only a visual taster, remember – a simulation. We can't put you into the real thing now, but remember that you would experience sounds, tastes, smells, touch and stronger, more immediate emotional responses.'

'So, you haven't seen it either?'

'I've seen what you can see, yes. But no more. It would be illegal for me to enter your Heaven, Clair, not to mention dangerous.'

'Yes . . .' Her words trail off and she brings the fingertips of her free hand to her mouth. I sense that she's not really listening to me.

'It might seem slightly disorganised or jumbled in this form,' I continue. 'And that's because you are viewing it with a sense of time. It's hard to explain, but as you already know, there is no sense of time passing in artificial Heavens.'

A rare hush descends on my office. People who are dying are usually so scared that they fill the void with words, tumbling over

22

themselves to say something, anything, boiling over in a palpable effort to disguise their imminent absence from the world. Clair is different. She knows she *could* die, of course she does. But, despite her chosen profession, she is still youthful enough to believe it might never happen. She had a child a few years ago; I've heard her plans after this next deployment. Unlike me, she doesn't believe this cold war is going to escalate. The risks are there – risks that feel like they're growing each day, if you choose to believe the journalists. I try to imagine her bubbly identity extinguished on a battlefield somewhere and find it impossible. No, I tell myself. She'll come back.

Clair's eyebrows rise and fall and, as the simulation runs on, her jaw slackens and her lips fall apart. Like Jarek, she is young. The nature of my work means that my clients are usually a lot older. And I like that, although a lot of the men and women I studied with at university can't get their heads around it. We operate with completely different outlooks. Most of them work in research now. They try to cure things. They treat minds and improve lives. They build new organs and optimise gene therapies. And I sit here letting life and death flow over me: a pebble in the river.

The unfairness of death is something I've thought more about, lately. My work doesn't desensitise me to it, as I once expected it would. What I do, day in, day out, is try to exert control over this most natural and most awful thing. And that control doesn't know where its remit ends. I can never do enough.

Clair snatches her hand away from the table and her blue eyes are gazing into mine, as if she finally realises that I've seen into her soul. I'm disturbed by her reaction.

'Are you all right? Was it what you expected?'

'It was . . .' she begins with a heavy voice, pausing to run her thumb over her bottom lip. 'It was amazing.'

'You didn't look for long.'

'I saw the birth of my daughter.' The wavering in her voice tells me that she is fighting back tears. 'It was like being there all over again. Like my memory of it, but stronger somehow.' She presses her hand into the middle of her chest. 'Gosh, I've never wanted to die before!' And she laughs at her own black humour. The Clair I've come to know is back in the room.

'Well, unlike many of my clients, I think you've got a good few years in you yet!' It's sarcasm, of course, and despite Clair biting her lip in mock concern, I worry afterwards whether she took it literally. For the first time in her short life, she has foreseen her death and I find myself wondering whether that can ever be right.

'Do you have any more questions for me?' I ask.

'No, no. I think we've covered it all before.'

'Then I just have to run through the final agreements with you. A verbal signature, if you will.'

She nods.

'Do you, Clair Petersen, agree that the details recorded here with your Heaven Architect, Isobel Argent of Oakley Associates, are used to constitute your artificial Heaven in the event of your death?'

'Yes.'

'And, as per the double opt-in agreement, do you grant access to said artificial Heaven to the twelve people recorded on this list?' I swivel the digital notes on the table's surface to face her. I glance at the names, my eyes tingling, as they always do, as I remember the stories, the love that they hold. Her tiny daughter, Joy Rosa Petersen; her husband, Reginald James Petersen; the woman she loved before him, Tally Elliott White. Her best friends, her parents . . . all the people that should never have to see her die. I hope that she'll live long enough to add more people to this list and expand the richness of her Heaven.

'Yes,' she says. 'Of course.'

'As you know, Clair, all the information you have provided me with is in the strictest confidence. I will not release any aspect of it unless I am required to do so by the law in the event of a criminal enquiry. Do you understand?'

'I do.'

'I see from your notes that your neurologist has already explained the situation with regards to gathering your mirror neurons?' I sound so businesslike that it makes me wince.

'You don't have to feel bad,' Clair says, smiling. 'It's not news to me that I could be blown to bits in the middle of nowhere. Dr Sorbonne said that you will do all that you can if the worst happens. I verbally signed the clause in the contract. If you can't get to me, you can't get to me. I know everyone would do their best.' She shrugs.

Clair knows that, if she is killed in battle, she will be lucky to ever see her Heaven. Her body would have to be retrieved and the medics would need to operate quickly to retrieve enough living mirror neurons from her cortex. Those cells would have to be transported back from the other side of the world within a day or two and safely delivered to the lab. Even though the programme is several years in, now, the Heaven-making process isn't yet optimised for those who don't die predictably, or close to home.

'And it says here you have a final meeting with Jess – Dr Sorbonne – tomorrow morning?' I ask her.

'Oh, yes: oh-eleven-hundred hours.' She smirks, knowing that I find reminders of her military background amusing.

'Great. She'll explain the upload process and you'll have to give your final consent to the surgery and storage of your tissue, your mirror neurons.' I find myself floundering, lost for words. By the time I usually reach this point with my clients, death is but days away or else constantly looming, clouding each minute of the life they have left. I must counter last-minute doubts and make assurances that they have done the right thing, as if I have never been surer of anything in my life.

'So, I guess I'll see you when you get back,' I say in the end.

'Of course.' She blows me a kiss from the doorway and I watch her leave the room. My thoughts gather behind my lips, tapping nervously, until I shape the questions into words.

'Clair?' My voice is so quiet that I'm surprised she even hears me, but her head pops back around, lips pursed quizzically. 'Is it as bad as they say?'

Her body reappears in its entirety and she leans against the end of the open door, resting back against her hands. 'Yeah, it's bad.' Her face is solemn. I've never heard her speak like this. 'We've had stand-offs like this before, just not as long-lasting, maybe. Although – trust me, Izzy – it is salvageable.' She almost smiles and then offers me a tiny salute. 'You keep doing what you're doing.'

And she's gone.

Salvageable. She seemed to choose that word so deliberately. Did she know the associations it has for me? In its medical context, it's the optimistic term used by jolly neurosurgeons as they try to make the best of a terrible situation. I can't help wondering if I'll ever see her again.

CHAPTER THREE

I push past the protesters on my way out of the office. There are a couple I don't recognise today, and I observe that these new recruits are younger than the rest of them. A tall, pale-eyed man threads wooden rosary beads through his fingers as he glares at me. A leaflet is thrust into my chest and I recognise the short, greying fingernails. It's always the same elderly lady who targets me. I feel her poke at my back as my hand stays fixed around the strap of my bag. The paper flutters to the floor.

'Let souls rise! Let souls rise!'

The younger ones bellow the words, but the men and women I recognise chant with far less agitation than the first day they started picketing us. Perhaps their enthusiasm is starting to wear thin. I let my gaze fall to the pavement as I cross the street. Caleb will have them moved along within minutes.

I arrive at the parlour less than an hour after leaving work. I had brought up the tattoo design from my Codex to my eye lens, casting it on to the pavement as I walked here. The elegant feathers had floated over the rough, grey ground, and I'd decided that I was happy with it.

Don will be returning to our flat now, wondering where I am. He's been away for a fortnight this time but it's gone quickly. I hope the negotiations went well. I've found that dating a Ministry of Defence consultant doesn't put you at ease. I feel guilty for being more concerned about what's happening with the war than I am for his own welfare.

He'll be aching with the tiredness that only a plane journey can bring. Every cell of his body will feel as though it's dried out. His airways will be lined with the germ-ridden breath of a few hundred other people. The thought of all that bacteria will make him feel shaky. To make things worse, his right arm will be aching from carrying the leather briefcase I bought him for his fortieth birthday. I like him because he won't feel let down by the lack of aromas escaping from the kitchen. I imagine the fondness with which he'll be rolling his eyes at this exact moment, as he takes a can out of the cupboard. Maybe there aren't even any cans left.

I hang my jacket over the back of a chair in the small down-stairs room, slip off my heels and settle myself on the bed. I look around the room, checking it as carefully as I did last time. It's still spotless. Brooke gestures for me to roll up my trouser leg.

'So, you wanna stick with the design we looked at last week?'
'Yeah.'

'I'm gonna freehand it,' she adds, before turning away from me. She leans over a table of instruments. Her pale flesh expands over the top of her jeans and I can see inked black tendrils curling around her spine. 'You don't wanna go any bigger, after all?' She looks over her shoulder to ask me this, resting the folds of her chin on her shoulder, eyebrows raised.

'No. I did think about it. But no.'

'Okay — your choice.'

I can tell she's disappointed, but the tattoo is for me. I don't want it to draw too much attention from other people.

I don't watch her get the equipment ready. Instead, I roll my head to the side and look at the array of inkings that cover the back wall. It's like a tapestry. The frames blend into the black paint and into each other. As I focus on each one, I am presented with a short holographic film of the tattoo's owner rolling up a sleeve, or lifting a top to expose the design on their body. An elderly lady sticks out her tongue as she tugs down the back of her trousers. I giggle as Brooke settles into her chair and wheels it towards me. I close my eyes because I don't want to see the contraption she's holding again.

'Yep, she was a character!'

I feel the cool tingle of Brooke wiping something over my ankle and I realise I'm holding my breath.

'Get ready for the pain!' she announces with glee.

I hum approval and fight against the nervous tension building in my foot, the toes squeezing against each other. She should realise that telling me it's going to hurt will only make it hurt more. I try to distract myself from the compulsion to pull my foot away by thinking of the day that has just passed. A typical day in so many ways: updating records, checking on dying clients, confirming access agreements, showing Clair a glimpse of her Heaven.

But the adrenalin pulses at my temples, fizzing behind my eyes. I bite down on my lip and clench my fists as the needle begins to buzz. My brain has ramped up the tension, already decided upon the fact that pain is imminent. When it comes, it's a bearable kind of pain, like the scratch of a jab to draw blood. You know it is for the best and, as the needle starts to gnaw at my skin, it's no more or less unpleasant than I expected.

During my training, the lecturer talked to us about the brain *preparing for death*, as if it was some kind of sentient being of its own: an alien in your body. It disturbed me for weeks, this idea. I kept dreaming about my brain walking up and down the stairs of my apartment building on cartoon-like legs, angry little fists pressed into the folds of grey matter where its hips might have been. I'd be inside my apartment, listening to it stomp around and bang on the door. But I wouldn't let it in.

I haven't had that dream for years.

The brain prepares for death. Perhaps, right now, Jarek's brain is beginning to accept its fate. Despite his fortitude, I could see that his eyes were resigned. I try to blink the image away but the green of his irises glimmer beneath my lids like bright lights stared at too long. The eyes close first. People who are dying sleep more and more as their metabolism fades. The brain shifts into a withdrawn, comatose state as it starts to let go. But it doesn't stop listening. Hearing is the last of the senses to go. I always wondered why. Why would we not save the last of our mental faculties for speech, or for clasping hands or kissing the cheeks of our loved ones? Now I'm a bit older, I can see why there's more value in listening. Most of my clients reach the point at which they have nothing more to say. The last session or two can sometimes verge on the awkward. We often cover old ground, review their Heavens one last time. And then we listen to the silence for a moment before their regrets begin to surface.

I've heard them all: the desire to see grandchildren grow up; the wish to have seen the South of France; the unfulfilled need to get arrested by the police and spend the night in a cell. Some are stranger than others. Some are laced with laughter to try to hide the unabridged honesty of the words. But I've realised over the years that all these wishes and regrets amount to the same thing: we always want more. We want to learn more and feel more, right up until that last breath. Our brains are desperate to gather what they can from our short lives. We are always listening, always hoping for something else.

Jarek's laugh breaks into my meditation, and as I feel the needle plunge into a new point near my ankle bone, a familiar sensation flickers between my thighs. Oh, no, no, no, Isobel, I think.

'Nearly done for today,' Brooke says, as if she's noticed my eyes opening.

Her voice grates more than the needle. It's as if she has broken some sort of sacred silence and I'm irritated. I feel like there must be pus or blood or at least some kind of cellular fluid leaking from my ankle on to the bed, but when I raise my head to look, all I can see is the outline of an angel emerging around my ankle bone.

I listen to the buzz of the needle, intermittent now as I imagine her filling in the finer details. A tattoo. Don will think I've lost my mind, but maybe I'll tell him that I've expanded it. *An angel?* he'll ask, his eyes wide.

Some people call me their angel, I'll say, laughing it off, placing my palms together in front of my chest, pouting and gazing skywards.

But it won't be the truth.

The angel isn't me. It isn't meant to be my clients' perception of me. It is a reminder of what I might be taking away from them.

CHAPTER FOUR

The rumbling rouses me and I refuse to open my eyes at first, willing myself back to sleep. My chip doesn't vibrate in warning, as I've set it up to do if a serious event occurs nearby. No emergency public announcement flashes across my vision or issues instructions directly into my ear canal. It's most likely a rubbish truck in the street outside. It's gone four a.m. I need to go back to sleep, I tell myself. But what if it's something else?

I'm out of the covers and the chill of the still bedroom air cloaks my body. I find myself opening the door on to the landing, where the window looks out over the back streets. The planes are shadows against the moonless night but I feel them in my chest as they cross overhead. They are so low. My heart rocks against my ribcage, out of sync with the shivering of my naked skin. The two motions disagree, forcing nausea up from my stomach. I stare at the sky open-mouthed, my fingertips pressed against the cold glass.

I must be imagining it. I must be dreaming.

I awaken to the clock digits, projected by my chip on to my eye lens. As my consciousness fades in, I realise a few hours have passed. I yawn and flex my feet, feeling the rawness of the tattoo on my lower leg as it rubs against the sheets. I realise I'm waking not to the artificial sunlight of my alarm, but to Don nuzzling my neck. For a moment, I succumb, stretching and then curling into his body, basking in his warmth. He only got back last night, but he'll be leaving again tomorrow. He's catching the train to the coast to see his ex-girlfriend and their kids. I should care, I know I should, but somehow it doesn't bother me. He kisses my cheek and I can feel the emerging stubble on his usually clean-shaven chin. I try to think of a reason to push him away and then I remember that I have a meeting today, first thing.

'I have a breakfast meeting.' I try to whisper but find that I'm unable to temper my voice amid my tiredness. It comes out almost like a shout and I think it disturbs me as much as it does him.

'All right, all right!' Don sighs. 'No time for just a . . . ?' He runs his hands over my bare belly, pressing the base of his hand into the hollow of my hip.

'No; I'm sorry, darling. Tonight, maybe, or tomorrow, before you go.'

He makes a grumbling noise and rolls away from me.

I tap him on the shoulder. 'I had a nightmare, I think, about these huge planes flying overhead. It seemed so real.'

'Oh, I'm sorry, honey.'

'Is something happening? Do you know anything?'

He turns back towards me, one eye open over the duvet. 'Don't worry,' he mumbles. 'It sounds worse in the media than it is. The U.S. Pacific Command reckon they've got it all in hand.'

'You trust the Americans?'

He rolls his eyes in response. He is always so evasive. As if telling me not to worry will make me think the event I fear less likely, rather than more so. I know he can't tell me what he does. I simply have to hope that if he had warning of something serious, he would make sure I was safe.

'I've got to get up,' I say. Sleeping naked offers the illusion of youth and cleanliness and feeling carefree, but it makes it so much harder to get up in the morning. I roll out of bed and stretch and jiggle on the spot, shaking my bed-rumpled curls of dark hair over my shoulders. I can feel Don's lascivious smile upon me as he watches. I zip around the bed, arms wrapped across my breasts to fend off the cold air. Before I open the door, I look back at him, wrapped up in the duvet to his chin. His eyes wander over my body, and a frown flickers over his face as he catches sight of the tattoo on my ankle. He won't voice his opinion on it again now because his eyes are being drawn to other things. I should feel lucky that, after four years, I have a man who still looks at me like this.

'You look beautiful this morning,' he says, so softly that I know he means it.

But beautiful things are never perfect.

On time is too late for me. I like to be early, and so I'm sitting in the sun-drenched meeting room at the back of the clinic before anyone else has arrived. There's no buzzing in my neck, no cues popping up in my vision from my lens. I feel content, alone here with my cooling coffee, wearing a freshly pressed grey trouser suit, and with my Codex unfurled in front of me. I soak in the cool, clear peace of the room, closing my eyes and letting the brightness of it colour my eyelids pink.

I undo my hair tie from the nape of my neck. I pull the tangled mass over one shoulder and tug my fingers through to the ends. I have no idea how it gets this unruly in a ponytail. This time, I plait it, pushing the braid back over my ear. I unbutton the collar of my shirt and brush the broken ends of hair from the lapels of my suit jacket. There's a loose thread raising itself like a charmed snake along the seam. This is my best jacket – the most expensive one I could afford. I fight the temptation to nip back to my office, take the small pair of scissors from the drawer under the coffee table and snip the thread away.

There's a polite knock at the door and the sudden noise jolts me. A granule of coffee falls from the edge of my cup on to the breast of my shirt. I grimace and blow it away. Only Harry would knock to join a meeting he'd been invited to. He enters, followed by Caleb and a woman I don't recognise.

Harry raises a hand in his characteristic greeting and grins. 'Morning, Isobel. This is Maya Denton. She's rolling out single opt-in for the States.'

'Hi.' I stand up and extend my hand across the meeting table. She takes it as limply as I offer it. I can't blame her for that. I can feel Caleb's eyes burning into me as he sits down. When will he learn that his demands have the opposite effect to the one he desires?

'It's a pleasure,' she drawls in a grainy Southern accent. 'I just wish these jet-lag drugs were more effective!'

I force a smile at her, taking my seat again and swirling the coffee around in the cup. I watch her arrange the feathery layers of her hair and straighten her wrap dress.

Caleb jumps back up. 'Can I get you a drink, Maya?' he asks, shooting me a look as he does so. As if it's my job to make coffee for other people.

'No, I'm all good, thanks, Caleb,' she replies, stifling a yawn. 'The pills should be better than caffeine!'

As I expected, Lela enters the room last, looking flustered. Her black hair curls haphazardly around her face and I can tell she's applied her deep red lipstick on the train. There's a small smudge beneath her nose, but it's too late to point it out to her now. Her disorganised state never fails to cheer me up in the mornings. It's a wonder that she has become the manager of anything, let alone the best Heaven architecture firm in the city.

'Morning, all!' she calls out with an air of unforced enthusiasm, closing the door behind her. No one pulls out a chair for her. They know by now that she doesn't sit.

'Maya! Caleb! Harry!' She flutters her fingers in a wave as she strolls across the room. 'Isobel.' She pauses to rest her hand on my shoulder and grins down at me with affection. She wanders around the table until her back is against the plain white wall. Sunlight flows down one side of her. She unfurls her Codex on the table and tucks in her shirt. I can see she isn't wearing a belt and I'm tempted to roll my eyes at her.

'Now, everyone,' she says, 'the lovely Maya has come all the way from California to be here with us. We're going to give her the weekend in London to settle in and then she'll be working with us as of next week.' She pauses and looks at us all in turn, as if she's expecting some kind of applause on behalf of Maya.

'So, Maya, you already know Caleb, our director. Harry, here, is our lead junior Architect, and this is Isobel, our longest-serving one.'

I incline my head and raise my eyebrows. It's the way she always introduces me: *longest-serving*. Perhaps it's only me that thinks this phrase lends a whiff of inferiority to my ten years here at Oakley. I think of all the words she could have used instead. *Most experienced* would have done. Lela has noticed me glaring at her and it has thrown her train of thought.

'Our longest-serving and our best,' she adds, smiling brightly at me. 'Perhaps even *the* best.'

'It's an honour, Isobel,' says Maya, tapping her fingers upon the table as if to emphasise her pleasure. 'I've heard a lot about you. Enough to know that you're an absolute asset to this company.'

I incline my head in way of appreciation, but Maya has already turned back to Lela, who is flicking through notes on her Codex.

'Now, Maya. Would you mind giving us a little bit of background about yourself and what we'll be working on implementing next week?'

'Sure.' Maya stands up and walks to the end of the table. 'As I'm sure you know, I direct Valhalla, based out of San Diego and Mumbai.' She runs her fingertips along the edge of the table and speaks slowly, carefully, directing her attention at each of us in turn. 'I think we've earned a good little reputation for ourselves over the years!'

Everyone apart from me dutifully acknowledges her with nods and hums of agreement as she purses her lips and flicks her long, blond hair back over her shoulders. Valhalla is the foremost Heaven architecture firm in the northern hemisphere. The MIT neuroscientists that originally developed the concept of engineered Heavens and founded the company, years ago, were quick to move across to the other side of the country. I can only imagine they wanted warmth, sunshine and scantily clad women in bikinis to go with their billions.

'What I'm mainly here to talk to you all about is the move to shift away from the double opt-in clause.'

This again. I clear my throat and take the last swig of my drink. 'For fuck's sake,' I mutter.

'Isobel!' says Lela. Caleb is flexing his jaw and furiously avoiding my gaze.

'Sorry, sorry.' I tut at myself and gesture at my shirt. 'Coffee.' I can feel her glaring at me as I rub at the spot where the stray grain of coffee fell from my cup on to the pristine fabric. 'Carry on, Maya.'

'Sure. So, the single opt-in clause. As you'll have no doubt heard, we've been successful in gathering support in the States. The bill has just been passed by the House of Representatives and we're hoping for the Senate to vote upon it in the next few months. There may be further amendments, but our lobbyist in the White House is convinced that we've got a good chance of getting it past the President. With any luck, single opt-in will be made statute by the end of this year and we'd like to see the U.K. follow suit.'

'And we're going along with this, are we?' I ask, directing my eyes towards Lela.

'We believe it's the right direction to move in, yes,' she replies, curtly. There's a pleading look in her eyes. 'If you have any concerns, Isobel, we can talk about them—'

'Yes, I have concerns!' I exclaim, cutting her off. 'Any individual should have the right not to be used in anyone else's Heaven. It's the only way the system can work, morally.' I can feel my pulse rising.

'But we're talking only about memories, recollections,' said Maya.

'No! That's simply not true. That does a disservice to what we do. I create far more than just memories for my clients.' I take a deep breath, trying to check my temper. 'And call me idealistic, but I believe that only truly loving relationships should meet the criteria. *Relationships*, with double opt-in.' I slap my hand against the table to mark my point.

'I have plenty of memories in here about my ex-husband.' Maya taps her head and pushes her shoulders back. She is admirably unruffled. 'Unluckily for me, they're stuck there. They are *my* memories; therefore, I have ownership of them. They don't belong to him, so why should he have any say whether he's in my Heaven?'

'Your choice of example somewhat evades the point.' I wait for her to challenge me but she waits, painting an image of calm across her face. 'Let me ask you this: would it be okay if a man could take memories of a child he has abused into his Heaven? Would it be acceptable to you if an unconvicted rapist could carry on attacking you again and again in his mind until the end of time? The current law is in place for a reason, Maya.'

'Isobel, that's enough.' Caleb's voice is quiet yet commanding. I let it sway me.

'I do understand what you're saying,' says Maya, angling her body towards me. She is trying to be gracious. 'We can discuss it further while I'm here, if you like.'

'Fine.'

Caleb swivels away from me to address the rest of the table.

'Isobel's personal opinions are a good reminder that the media isn't exactly onside with the idea of single opt-in,' he says. 'I mean, some remain entirely against artificial Heavens. Those idiots and their placards stood outside our front door still grab the odd headline.'

'Granted,' Maya says, bobbing her head. 'I'd say it's been quite an active campaign back home to get the media to highlight the positives of the change. In the States, far more so than here, anti-Heaven sentiment is generally quite strong. There's a hell of a lot of talk about lost souls!' Her laugh is tinny and I clench my jaw. With their money, Valhalla could bribe anyone.

'Lela,' says Caleb, 'we need to look at who in the media we can reach out to. Public influence is key.'

Lela twitches her lips in thought as I glare at her. 'There's James, at the *Mail*, and we've got close ties with a lot of bloggers.'

'Yeah, get me in for an interview or something.' Caleb is already moving on, flicking through his Codex. 'So, we'll need someone to arrange some more meetings next week with Maya to discuss all this further. And to draw up a list of points to discuss in advance. Harry?'

'I'll do it,' I say. 'It's fine. I know how it should be done.'

'No, Harry will do it.' Caleb speaks without looking up. Harry glances at me, pressing his lips together in apology, and scribbles a note into the air, recording it into his lens.

'I think we're nearly done here,' says Lela, rolling up her Codex. 'Caleb, is there anything you'd like to add?'

'Yes, sure.' Caleb stands up from his chair and plants his finger-tips on the table, leaning over it. Maya smiles at him, serenely. 'I know I've spoken to each of you individually about this over the last few weeks, but I just wanted to say that Valhalla continues to be interested in buying the company. I know this makes for an unsettling time as we proceed with negotiations, but I want to reassure you all that, if the merger does go through, nothing at Oakley will change.' He looks at each of us in turn and I almost believe him.

'Our jobs will be protected?' Harry asks, looking more closely at the table than at Caleb.

'Yes, of course. Oakley *is* its Architects.'

I try to pay attention to the rest of the meeting, but I feel too riled up. Finally, Maya stops droning and the meeting is drawn to a close. She leaves, flanked by Harry and Caleb, who both avoid looking at me as they leave the room.

'Izz?' Lela calls me as I'm walking out of the door. She's leaning against the floor-to-ceiling window, arms folded. She hates confrontation, so her tone only goes to show that she loves me really.

'Yep?'

'You're not going to get anywhere if you keep behaving like that, you know.'

I turn back, leaning against the door frame so that it presses between my shoulder blades. My hands find their way inside my pockets and I tilt back my head. I sigh. 'Enlighten me, Lela. Where do I want to *get* to?'

'Come on, Izzy; don't be like that with me. I'm speaking as your friend, not as your manager.'

'I know, and I'm saying that your point is irrelevant.'

'Sorry, I didn't mean to . . .'

I study her fallen face. The mid-morning light softens the strong nose and sharp cheekbones inherited from her Iranian father.

'Do I look upset?' I ask her, smiling. And I'm not, of course. Not with her, just at the system. A system that is starting to scare me.

Lela shakes her head and sighs as she walks towards me. She knows what will fix this. 'Wine after work?'

I turn and walk out of the door, giving her a thumbs-up over my shoulder. As I step into the lobby, she's already caught up with me. She squeezes my shoulders and squeals into my ear.

'Oh, hang on,' I say, spinning around to face her and thinking of my promise to Don. 'Sorry, I can't do tonight.'

She sticks out her bottom lip.

'I can do tomorrow, though.'

'Okay,' she says. She winks and I wink back.

I leave her in the lobby and I walk down the corridor, back towards my office, trailing my gaze over the Carrara marble tiles. I don't have much time for socialising, for friendships, but Lela's gentle presence always reassures me. Yet anger still simmers in my chest. I have got to know enough clients that I understand the delicacies of their situations. Double opt-in is a deal-breaker for me. If it's thrown out, I will not do this, I tell myself. I will not do this anymore.

When Caleb reaches out and touches my arm from the doorway of his office, I feel as though he's been listening to my thoughts.

'Come in, please, Isobel.' His voice is low and crisp. He glares and I realise how little he knows me because, if he did, he would understand that I'm easily riled for a fight. He would be best advised to play a gentler game, but Caleb isn't the kind of man to accept guidance. To look at, he's perfect with his smooth skin, leonine brown eyes and dark blond hair. I've seen him in the gym on occasion, forcing his way through chest presses with heavy grunts, and as a result he's sturdy: a brick wall that lets nothing in.

'To what do I owe this pleasure, I wonder, Cal?' I say as I move past him into the office and sit down on his deep green leather chair. I lean forward and place my elbows on his desk, folding my fingers together under my chin in defiance. He slams the door and looks as though he might scream in fury. It only serves to focus the anger in my belly into a tighter, more determined knot.

'What the hell do you think you're doing?' he demands, leaning over the table towards me.

'I'm telling you, telling her, what I think.' I force an artificial calm into my voice that I know will only serve to infuriate him further. 'You've told me before that you value my honesty.'

'Well, I don't remember saying that, but if I did, I must've been lying. I value your competence, Isobel, and quite frankly, that's about it.'

'My *competence*?' I'm astounded he could be so dismissive. 'I'm the best Architect in the country, and you know it.' I'm annoyed as soon as I say the words because I've exposed myself. I've let my emotions play upon my face. 'And if you're really going to sell Oakley to Valhalla – or anyone else, for that matter – I'm worth quite a lot to you, no?'

'Get out of my seat.' I feel his hand fasten around my elbow. I rarely feel fragile, but I look down and see that his thumb and middle finger meet on the inside of my arm. I stand opposite him, looking up into the strong lines of his face. His hand is still wrapped around my arm and I see a fleeting weakness in his expression as our bodies move closer. It's a thought I've had before. He *wants* me. I press my lips together as I think about this solid, powerful man being swayed by a small, slight woman like myself. I bet he likes to be dominated, stood over, hurt. I feel his fingers detach from my arm and I adjust the sleeve of my jacket, pulling it back to my wrist.

I grit my teeth. Here goes: 'I cannot support single opt-in. If it goes through, I'm out of here.'

He glares at me and I can only guess at the thoughts that battle inside his head. He can't afford to lose me; the clinic's excellent reputation – and, more importantly right now, its market value – are largely thanks to me. But the money, always the money. He always wants more clients, specifically rich ones lacking in morals – the sort of men who want to be able to have their ex-wives in their Heavens without their permission, so that they can do whatever they want with them. I think about the people I've known who might choose to feature me in their artificial afterlife and it makes me squirm. Although I wouldn't be there to experience it, it would be no less of a violation.

Caleb still hasn't spoken. He has nowhere to take this discussion. He was responding to his temper, as usual, by dragging me into his office.

'Is there anything else?' I ask.

'I won't let you destroy my business, Isobel,' he whispers, leaning so close to my face that I can feel his breath. If I was attracted to him, his strength of character would be desirable. He moves around me and sits down in his chair, leaning back and drawing one foot up to rest on his knee. 'Things are better than ever for us. The merger will be a good thing. And we reward you well, don't we? I don't understand what else you want.'

It's a change of tack and realise I prefer him angry to wheedling.

'I have enough to get by.' I'm dismissive, knowing full well that he can't afford to pay me any more than he already does. It's an excellent salary, more than I ever imagined I'd earn, and he knows that I do this job because I love it. I just try not to think about how much profit he skims off the top line. 'But I'm not like you, Cal. I actually care about what I do. I care about my clients and their families and their loved ones.'

He nods as if he understands, but I don't think he does. I'm not sure he has the capacity to understand love. I swallow the emotion that's rising in my throat and fold my arms before continuing. 'And I wonder what will happen if we officially go to war? If our troops stop sitting on the sidelines and take a military stand alongside Taiwan?'

He laughs. 'Then business will be booming!'

'I signed off my first soldier yesterday,' I tell him, although I'm sure he's already on top of my client list. 'And she was too young, too full of life to have to look at her death.' The wetness in my eyes surprises me and I have to blink it away.

'Too young to face death? Are you kidding, Isobel?' He never shortens my name. 'I know we're used to dealing with the old and the sick, but she's a *soldier*. I think they're well acquainted with the idea of dying.'

I know what he means and I can't explain why it upsets me so much. I think of the wonder that glowed from Clair's face as she exited the simulation. *It was amazing*, she said to me, and I recognise the strange feeling that's curled up behind my eyes as guilt. What if it's not amazing? What if her Heaven is lacking in something, devoid of some crucial factor that none of us has ever calculated for? Like all my clients, she trusts me completely and I am never completely sure if I am deserving of it. I don't experience the final product. That's the ultimate problem with this system.

'If we go to war – actually go to war, not more of this endless stand-off – then how will we cope? How will we keep up? She didn't ask me, but I can't even promise Clair that we would get to her body in time!' I'm working myself up, I know it, but the caged words fly out of me because I say them aloud so rarely. 'So many could die, so far away, and it'll be a huge mess. People will die and I don't understand how we can even begin to ensure we carry out our obligations to our existing clients, let alone all those others . . .'

'Isobel, Isobel.' His tone is comforting now and it's almost believable. 'You can't think like this. It might never happen, you know that.'

I nod.

'What does your government boyfriend say?' By asking the question, he's admitted his own fear.

'He's been away a lot. He's tells me what you've just told me – not to worry.'

Caleb lets his chin drop to his chest.

'Can I go?' I ask him, letting the irritation creep back into my voice. 'I have a client arriving soon.' I don't have to consult my notes to know that it's Jarek. It's as if I can sense him getting closer, placing his hands upon the copper handle of the front door and leaning his weight into it. I feel a slight dizziness descend.

'Yes,' Caleb sighs. 'Go. We'll speak to Maya about the single opt-in next week.'

CHAPTER FIVE

The second meeting is almost as important as the first. It's the point at which you leave social politeness behind and get stuck into the nitty-gritty of building a client's Heaven. It can be a tricky shift to negotiate.

I'm watching Jarek now, as he sits opposite me. It's lucky I make recordings of all our sessions because I'm trying to listen but my attention is drawn to his face. I'm focused on watching the interplay of emotions as he talks, as he tells me more about the highs of his life and his hopes for his Heaven. Like most of my clients, he is full of contradictions.

My fingers move from the string of small cream pearls around my neck to the matching drop earrings that I can feel pulling on my lobes. The skin there feels hot to the touch. Perhaps it's a reaction. I'm not used to wearing jewellery, but when I got dressed today I wanted to feel like a woman as well as an Architect.

A shadow seems to pass across his face and I almost turn to see if anything is blocking the window. His forehead creases and he stops speaking mid-sentence.

'You're in pain?' I find myself reaching out for his hand but the cool of his skin makes me recoil.

He nods. 'You don't have anything, do you? Any painkillers?'

'No, I'm sorry,' I say. 'Not here.'

'Not here?'

I'm reluctant to expand but I can see the torment etched on his face and it has latched on to my half-hidden meaning in desperation. 'Just at home, for personal use.'

'Serious strength ones? You need them?'

'I got hold of some opioids while my mother was ill. I'm not the bravest. The idea of being in pain and not being able to do anything about it unsettles me.'

Unsettled is, quite deliberately, not the right word. It terrifies me almost as much as Jarek's piercing gaze does now. I berate myself for sharing such personal information. 'I'm not licensed to dispense medication,' I add.

He hums in response and crosses his hands across his chest, squeezing his shoulders. I'm keen to move on and I turn my attention back to my notes on the coffee table, trying to remember what it was we were talking about.

'So, we've talked about your initial thoughts on imagery and settings,' I say. 'Another important thing we need to consider early on is emotions – what's in and what's out.' I'm eager to hear his reply. It's always interesting to find out what people think about this. Society is obsessed with happiness.

'Where to start?' He sucks in his breath and frowns. 'Depression, please. Some resentment and jealousy would be good. And perhaps a dash of insecurity.'

I hold my face still as I wait for him to crack. Two seconds pass before he launches a sparkling grin at me. But his eyes are challenging. I see the pride firing behind them. I can see that he won't ask me to explain what I mean, and I'm momentarily tempted not to. But I am not Isobel in this room. I am a Heaven Architect to a dying man. I must push my ego aside.

'Some people find it strange that I ask them about this.' I spread my hands and then lay them over my knees. *Not you, of course; we're talking hypothetically*, the gesture says. 'But imagine if you felt nothing but happiness all the time.' I purse my lips and narrow my eyes at him.

'Well, I guess I'd be pretty damn happy!' He taps the table definitively and then leans back into the sofa. There's something about the way he rests his cheekbone upon his fist and angles his gaze at me, rising to my bait. It transports me out of this office. We could be anywhere.

'But you wouldn't, would you? You'd almost be numb. True happiness is only cast from shadows in the same way that light is only framed by shade.'

'You want me to embrace my darkness?' he asks. 'Are you sure?' The half-smile doesn't leave his face and I feel like he's asking me so much more. I take a deep breath and the oxygen vibrates in my lungs.

'Yes,' I murmur. 'A little.'

Jarek rests his head back on the sofa as if he's a child settling down for a bedtime story.

'One way I do it is by giving people the *memory* of negative emotions,' I continue. 'It frames your experience without veiling it. You could select a particular memory, or choose the *feeling* of an emotion, unlinked to any experience. Both work.'

'What would *you* do?'

Here we are again, talking about me. I don't know how he turns the conversation around like this so smoothly. I consider his question but I cannot answer it. It feels as though we've left the office again and are somewhere else. It's like swimming in unfamiliar waters. I glance at the time.

'We're coming to the end of today's session,' I say, relieved. 'So, have a think about what I've just said and we can talk it through next time.'

He nods but I can see he's still deep in thought. His cheeks are pulled in, sharpening the line of his jaw. His lips are pressed into a pout. I stand and he dutifully follows me towards the door.

'Give the office a call if there's anything you want to discuss in the meantime.' I rebuke myself. We do not dish out our time for free at Oakley. Every minute is billed. But I am a planet in orbit, moving away from him, into winter. I don't want him to leave. His eyes meet mine and the pupils are wide and deep – sorrowful.

'You'd choose to experience a memory, right?' he asks and I wonder how he knows. 'Something sad?'

My thoughts spiral and I look away. It's too intimate a question, I know that. I hesitate, but it would be easier to just let the words come out. I am gripping the door handle, standing at the boundary of my professional life. I am almost not in my office. I am almost not his Architect.

'Your mother, right? You'd choose to remember her dying?'

My eyes snap back to his and he must know that he's right.

'I'm sorry, I shouldn't have brought that up.' His voice is soft and he lets several seconds pass in silence, resting his gaze on his shoes. They are scruffy in comparison to my freshly shined brogues. 'But I still don't really understand,' Jarek continues. 'Why wouldn't you only choose to remember the good times?'

'Because grief shapes the love that came before it.'

I am still wondering why he's closed his eyes when I feel his hand against my face. Perplexed, I stare back at his eyelids as his lips graze the corner of my mouth. He presses the pad of his thumb into the pillow of my cheek. My lips part into the silence but then he is whispering that he is sorry, the door is opening, and he is gone.

I should want to get back to Don as soon as possible, but I decide to walk home. It's over an hour from the clinic to our Earls Court apartment and it's a pleasant route if the weather's good. I usually skirt along the edge of Hyde Park and then cut through the residential back streets of Knightsbridge and South Kensington. I do it a lot in the summer, especially on days like this, when I need to clear my head. Once I'm in the park, the leaves absorb the chaos of the streets beyond its perimeter. There's always a stillness here. The breeze sweeps across my face. The sky is still bright and the air is clear but it's cool for a summer's evening. I tighten my cotton scarf around my neck.

When Maya finds me, I'm wandering down the eastern edge of the Serpentine, walking in the shadow of the café and trying not to think of Jarek's breath on my cheek.

'Isobel?' She's already beside me by the time she speaks. When I hear my name, it doesn't make me jump. I had already registered the awkward click of stiletto heels quickening behind me. She sounds out of breath. I smirk to myself as she presses her fingertips against the perspiration on the side of her forehead.

'Hello, Maya. Are you walking this way?' She can't fail to notice the resentment that rages below my forced politeness.

'Well, no, I wasn't, actually.' Her accent teases out the last word into five separate syllables. It's infuriating. 'You sure are a fast walker!'

My eyes shoot from my flat brogues to her patent courts and notice that it takes three-inch heels to bring her to the same height as me. She must be tiny because I'm not tall. I want to ask her what she's doing here, but resist. I can't bear for her to have any kind of control over me, so we walk in silence for a while as after-work joggers and mothers with prams pass by. I seek out glimpses of the glistening blue water from between the leaves of the trees to our right. I'm not eager to hear what she has to say.

'Ain't it pretty?' she says, as if we're both tourists here together, seeing it all for the first time.

'Wait 'til we come around the other side, when you can see the whole lake.'

'Listen, Izzy. Can I call you Izzy?' Her hand darts to my arm and I'm not feeling generous enough to give her much more than a shrug. Her forced friendliness grates on me. 'I'm sorry about how things went this morning, when we spoke about the single opt-in. I don't feel like we got off on the right foot and I feel kinda bad about it.'

'It's fine.'

'You're a tough cookie, I can see that. And you obviously have strong feelings about all that stuff.'

'Obviously.' I try but fail to keep the irritation from my voice. I stop and fold my arms as I turn to face her. 'Is this what you've come to talk to me about? Because I really don't want to discuss it in the office, let alone outside it.'

'No, it's not,' she says, casting her gaze around. She looks almost childlike, with her mouth drawn down in disappointment and the blonde waves bouncing around her shoulders. 'Shall we carry on walking?'

'Yes, please; I'd like to get home.' We're alone on the path now and, as she begins to speak again, I wonder whether she was waiting for such a moment.

'There was something else I – we – wanted to talk to you about.'

'"We"?'

'Valhalla, my firm, and a few other interested parties.'

'Okay.' I sigh the word out.

'It's kinda what you might call a job proposal.'

'You want me to work for you?' I laugh. 'Was it your twin sister in the meeting today? Did you not see that I'm a complete liability?' I'm only half joking.

'No.' She stops walking. 'I see that you're brilliant.'

I stop and turn towards her, raising my eyebrows. If I had more respect for her, I could take it as a compliment. 'According to Caleb, I'll effectively be working for you soon enough, anyway, if the buyout goes ahead.'

'I mean working for us directly, with a different remit.'

'A different remit?'

'There have been some . . . incidents.' Her pause before the last word fills me with a sense of dread. 'A few people we've made Heavens for in the past are under federal investigation.'

This captures my attention. 'After they're dead?'

'Ye-ah,' she drawls. 'They're under investigation for things they might've done while they were alive.'

'Like what? Murder?'

'Sure. And other stuff. Fraud, that kinda thing.'

'But these people must have had pretty clean records for Valhalla to create Heavens for them in the first place, right?' I ask. 'Or have you sunk to lower depths than I could have expected?'

She seems to bat away the insult with a flick of her hand. 'Clean records, yeah, of course. But that doesn't mean they haven't done wrong. There's new evidence in some of these cases. And the Feds want us to help gather more to support their investigations.'

'Fucking hell! The F.B.I.?' I snort with laughter and she shoots me a warning look. A man is walking around the corner towards us and I wait for him to pass by before continuing. 'And I guess they want you and your neurologists to break with the code of ethics and hand over all their records?'

'We already did that. They didn't find what they needed.'

I shake my head in disbelief. 'I don't know why I'm shocked.'

Maya is quiet for a few seconds and I can almost hear her thinking. She's changing tack. When she speaks, her voice is lower, more serious. 'They think these people did terrible things, Izzy. Murder, extortion, torture. If it's true, they don't deserve to be in the place they're in. Do they?'

I glance at her and her eyes are wide. I understand what Maya is saying, and my professional integrity tells me to cut the conversation off here, but I'm curious. We round the corner and the Serpentine opens up before us. I turn away from her, wandering off the path and through the grass, by the edge of the water. Maya follows me and I hold back a giggle as she teeters on heels that are sinking into the soil. Rollerbladers and cyclists swerve and jump on the far side of the lake – a lesson in elegance. Solar panels float like miniature icebergs in the water and ducks bob in the channels between them.

'The F.B.I. would create an artificial Hell if they could,' I say. I read too much into Maya's frown. 'Oh, no, don't tell me they want me to—'

'No, no, no.' She shakes her dainty head. 'God, no. They want to find a way of getting into the Heavens of these people remotely – interfacing with the memories to search for clues, to interact with the consciousness that remains.'

'Well, good luck with that, because it's impossible.'

'Then maybe I've misjudged you.' Maya stops walking and folds her arms, arching an eyebrow at me. I walk a few more paces before I turn back to her, sighing. There's no trace of the childishness in her face any longer. She's sucking in her cheeks and she's closing in on the only thing I care about: my professional pride. 'I didn't think the word *impossible* was in your vocabulary. You ought to come and see our labs.'

I think for a long while before answering, because I want to get the words right, for once.

'I don't give a shit about your ethical dilemmas and I have absolutely no interest in helping you. I'm not even flattered that you've asked me. The only thing I care about is my clients. I'm not going to agree to the single opt-in, and I'm certainly not going to agree to this. Go home.'

She stares at me, open-mouthed.

'You haven't misjudged me, Maya – you've underestimated me. I'm going to pretend this conversation never happened.'

I half expect her to totter after me as I turn on my heel and stride back to the path, but I've underestimated her, too. She's smart enough to recognise when she's lost a fight.

CHAPTER SIX

I'm still in my study at midnight when I hear the door open. I'm cross-legged, nestled amongst the embroidered kantha cushions of the sofa bed and surrounded by the papery cotton of my grandmother's antique quilt. An empty mug of hot chocolate sits inside the triangular gap formed by my folded legs. I look over my shoulder to see Don's head poking around the door. His eyes sparkle in the light of the candle on the table beside me as he steps into the room. The rest of him is shadowy against the inky blue walls. I'm sitting in silence and he raises his eyebrows so as not to break it. An invitation. I remember our conversation this morning and try not to sigh.

'I'm sorry, I need to spend a couple more hours on this,' I say, almost whispering, as if there is someone or something we're trying not to wake.

He stares back at me, arms folded, for what seems like an eternity before he speaks. 'Don't you ever think you should spend more time with real people instead of the memories of dying strangers?'

'I'm sorry?' I shift my body around so that I'm facing him.

After the last argument we had about my job, I'm surprised he would bring it up again.

'I'm trying to prevent a full-blown war in the Pacific and I seem to work less hours than you. And for what? Giving over-privileged people an artificial shot at redemption?'

'It might seem stupid to you, but it matters to them and it matters to me.' I try to keep my voice level. I'm in no mood for a fight.

'Forget dying. The irony is that you don't have a fucking *life*, Isobel. You hardly have any friends, and you never spend time with me. You barely see your sister and her family. Her kids probably don't even know who you are. And what gets me is that you treat all this like it's just a waiting room for something better. Well, it's not. This is it.' He opens his mouth to continue and then seems to change his mind. Making the most of my stunned silence, he leaves, slamming the door shut behind him.

I wince and rub my brow, dropping my chin to the springy softness of the quilt wrapped around me.

How long have we been like this? Four years ago, we were enjoying our first dates – the latest bar openings, virtual-reality adventures, soda and burgers at old-fashioned bowling lanes – always trying to outdo the other's choice of venue and activity in our inventiveness. I loved his company. We had fun. We didn't talk about work. He was a gentleman. He still is. And he's right. Now, we rarely see our mutual friends, the novelty of sharing a bed has faded and, if I'm totally honest, I can't remember why I love him. *If you ever did*, a voice whispers, coldly, cruelly at the back of my mind. I screw up my confusion and launch it towards the thought.

I stare at the door. I've lost my concentration and now I'm distracted by the door handle. I can see from here that it is stuck at an angle rather than lying horizontal. I can ignore it; it's fine. I turn back to what I was doing. It's behind me, out of sight now.

My notes on Jarek's Heaven and the recordings of our conversations are spread out on the glass in front of me. I've already started a list of people we'll need to get in contact with to get double opt-in approval. The name of his wife dances in front of me. *Sarah Woods*. I murmur it to myself. *Jarek and Sarah*. He's said very little about her, yet here she is, on this list: still such a huge part of his life. I feel the brush of his lips against the corner of mine and my skin bristles with something approximating jealousy. I push the sensation aside.

I've seen his criminal record, too, or rather the lack of it. He's been declared free to enter Heaven. It's not as easy for some. Convicted murderers, obviously, are automatically out. It's both company policy and the law, too, as it happens, although I sometimes wonder whether Caleb would abide by the law if he didn't agree with it. I don't think I'd be able to get into the mind of a psychopath, anyway. They would lead you down twisting alleys of memories, distort the truth, ask to relive the most awful things over and over again. I rely upon my clients' honesty. I'm not sure how lies would translate into Heaven; you would have to almost believe it yourself; it would have to become a false memory. There would probably be riots, though, if some of the stories got out. Don would be horrified if I was ever silly enough to tell him about them. Heaven architecture is still so new and for now, memories of immoral activity cannot be used as evidence. But one day soon, I would like to think that we will be able to offer our insights to courts and law enforcers. It's complicated though. I'd be happy to provide character references, or reveal the content of private conversations, if required. But Heavens shouldn't be open for inspection, even with a warrant. Once dead and enshrined in their afterlives, I feel that my clients should be untouchable.

But Jarek's record is clean, as I expected. I could have guessed from the openness of his face that he's never been arrested. There may be some complications in creating his Heaven because of his tumour, but his consultant is an excellent one. Jess will sort it out.

It's the creative side of things that I find harder to do at the clinic. I sometimes need to be in the comfort of this room, near the golden flicker of a jasmine-scented candle to start pulling it together. It's hard at first, but once you get started, it's instinctive work. Sometimes I'll go through all the notes repeatedly, thinking about them. It's like finding which piece to lay first in a jigsaw puzzle. You need to find something distinctive; something that sits somewhere in the middle of the board; something that links quite clearly to two or three other things. You don't always spot it straight away.

I flick through the written words, which have been automatically transcribed from our conversation earlier today. *My daughters are the love of my life.* I feel again the bizarre pang of envy that I felt when he spoke the words aloud. As before, I let the feeling wash over me while I concentrate on what I'm doing. They are the obvious place to start: his two children. He described each of their births in a lot of detail, which will make it easier for me and his neurologist to build the scene and extract the memories. I close my eyes and lean back, listening to our conversation this time, instead of reading the words.

'God, they're so beautiful,' he says. I can feel the sunshine of his smile even now. The volume is low so that it doesn't disturb Don. Now his words are softer, I find myself hanging on the lilt of each one. It's like a lullaby. My eyes are stinging with tiredness and I stifle a yawn.

'They both have this amazing hazel-coloured hair and it's so damn *shiny*, like they're tiny woodland animals or something. We called Helena our little Bambi when she was a baby.' He pauses, laughs. 'She had long legs for a toddler and these eyes straight out of Disney . . . She looks exactly like my wife. The same brown eyes.'

I pause the recording. Now I've heard it for a second time, I can hear the change in his voice even more clearly. How the warm contentedness of it suddenly switches. On a knife-edge. It's so sad, I think, that producing children together doesn't make people love each other forever. It should do. It should be like this ribbon of blood that doesn't tie you down but packages you all up together, like some perfect gift that keeps getting bigger and bigger through the generations. But it didn't work for my own parents, it apparently didn't work for Jarek's, and it hasn't worked for him, either. I guess love isn't the point of our selfish genes. I could fall pregnant tomorrow but it wouldn't make me . . . I let the thought extinguish itself in fear. The room seems colder and I pull the quilt around my shoulders.

I'm too distracted tonight; I can already tell that I'm not going to be able to get much done. I look up, through the open shutters to the cold, dark glass, and think of the war. I think of all the people who have far bigger issues to contend with than me. I can always find things to be angry at myself for and selfishness often comes top of the list. I crack. I stand up and walk over to the door, annoyed with myself, and lift the handle until it's straight again.

CHAPTER SEVEN

I wake early. I always do following a late night and broken sleep. My body gives up long before my mind does. I wash and dress in silence, trying not to wake Don. He's leaving again today but I'll send him a message later to say goodbye.

I grab a banana and slip out of the front door into the sunrise glow. It's long before rush hour and there's still a peace in the air. I look up and glimpse at the time, projected on to the hazy blue-white sky, and reflect upon the fact that this will always be a safe time to travel through London. A strike would come at the morning or evening peak to obliterate the most people.

The cab is waiting for me on the corner and its interior lights come on as I run my hand over the door and state my name. It recognises my voice and I hear the lock release. I slip into its warm cocoon and sink back into the seat as I give it my destination.

I doze for most of the twenty-minute journey. By the time I get out of the cab at the gates of the burial ground, the sun is already mounting its claim to the sky. After signing in, I walk along the path that's marked by young yew trees. The clipped grass is smooth underfoot and the path is straight enough that I can walk with my eyes closed for several seconds at a time. I prefer to listen to the trees rather than look at them. Today, the lightest of breezes stirs the leaves into whispers of old, crumbling tissue paper. You wouldn't want it to be silent here. The sound reminds everyone that life goes on.

Near the end of the path, I cut between the yews to the right and walk along the row of small wooden crosses and columns until I reach her spot. I never notice the upward growth of the sapling, but today it looks fuller. Its slim branches are heavy with green, heart-shaped leaves. I run my hand over the rough, silvery bark, letting my fingertips sink into the dark knots in the swelling trunk. I remember my sister and I planting it, laughing and crying together. Predictably, she wasn't as upset as I was that our mother didn't create a Heaven. We never argued about it, though. We never argue because she's the opposite of me: yielding and amenable. *It's her death, Isobel. She knows what she wants and that's all that matters.* That was six years ago. The tree is taller than me now, I realise. The passage of time seems so cruel.

I walk around the tree and kneel in front of it, pressing the flats of my hands into the grass. Now that my grandmother is too frail to accompany me, I don't do what I see others do. I don't chat, or leave flowers or tend to the tree. I just sit here for ten minutes or so, missing her. That is enough.

The grass is sun-scorched in places. It hasn't rained much this summer. I press the dried, faded blades between my fingers and remember my mother's fragile skin in those last days – against all odds, still a deep brown. If she had a Heaven, I could imagine her in it. I could sit here, breathing in the chlorophyll, and imagine everything about her. But a Heaven is not what she wanted.

Lately, I feel more aware than ever that my sadness and regret come from the fact that I wanted her to have a Heaven because it would make me feel better. I imagine her wobbling her head – neither a nod nor a shake – and laughing at me in that shrill titter of hers. *You're even more selfish than your sister, Isobel*, she would say.

She believed in an afterlife, I think. She just never voiced it aloud. I had grown up thinking she wasn't religious, but in her old age she'd made little shrines for the Hindu gods, on the bookshelves in the dining room. I found the little golden figures cute, surrounded by candles, slices of fruit and choice flowers cut from the garden. I didn't think too much more about them. Sometimes, in her last months, I would catch her praying. If she noticed me, she'd pull her frail hands apart and press them against the sheets. When I asked her outright why she didn't want me to make her a Heaven, she would avoid the question. *I don't want to talk about this silliness anymore, beti.* I sigh now, like I did back then, and rise to my feet.

Usually I head straight to work in the same cab, but today I have more time than usual, so I decide to stop for a coffee in the burial ground's café. I sit outside on one of the wooden picnic tables and look over the energising expanse of green, letting the trees throw their oxygen at me.

'Well, this is odd.' The voice creeps up behind me and, until I swivel around to see his face, I cannot place it. Jarek beams at me. He's holding hands with a little girl, who is looking up at him, demanding an explanation. I grip my paper coffee cup more tightly and the heat sears into my hand. The absence of any surprise on his face makes me wonder, somewhat irrationally, whether he knew he would find me here.

'Helena, this is my friend Isobel. Say hello.' He places his hand on his daughter's back and pushes her forward.

'Hello,' she says, playing with her long plait of hair. She meets my eyes only briefly.

'How old are you, Helena?'

'Five and a half.'

I glance back up at Jarek. I'm not good with kids.

'She's off school.' He rolls his eyes as he settles on to the bench opposite me. 'The last throes of chicken pox.'

Now he's said it, I can see the tiny, hardened blisters speckled over her forehead, beneath the wisps of brown hair.

'Why don't you go and see how high you can get on the swings?' He points to the small play park beyond the edge of the terrace and she scampers away.

Now that it's just the two of us, I allow myself to recall the sensation of his lips on the edge of my mouth. I feel my cheeks colour.

'This is strange, seeing you here.' I hesitate and end up using the phrase that I hear other people use here: 'Are you visiting someone?'

'My sister.' The honesty of his gaze draws me to him, sketching in the lines without words. 'She loved nature.' I watch his eyes flick towards the play park. 'And you?' he asks, looking back at me.

'My mother's buried here. I like to visit before work every so often. Did you lose your sister long ago?'

'Oh, it's been years now. She was killed in a collision when she was a teenager.'

'I'm sorry. That's awful.'

I notice that his eyes slope down slightly on the outside. The result is a little hangdog. It's endearing, I decide.

'I still miss her,' he adds. 'I wish she could've had the chance to have what I'm going to have.'

'Not everyone is lucky enough to get a Heaven. Time, money, circumstance – it all gets in the way.'

'Nice here, though, isn't it?'

I nod. I'm wondering why I mentioned money and I'm worried that he will ask me more about it. One of the protesters outside the clinic – a middle-aged man dressed in a shabby overcoat – once grabbed me by the collar with both his hands. *If what you do is so bloody fantastic, you should let everyone have a Heaven for free.* I can feel the mist of his saliva condensing on to my face now. All I could do was yell at him to let me go. Caleb called the police that time and I didn't see the man again. It upset me so much because the exclusivity of what we do is something that has always gnawed at me. Sometimes I can persuade Caleb to do some pro-bono work for some of the desperate people who write to us, but it's rare. I have to remind myself that I trained long and hard to get to where I am. It was expensive. I have to make a living. I change the afterlives of the people I can help. If they want it.

Jarek is watching his daughter on the swing. She's leaning forward, her legs dangling over the wood chips. She waves shyly in our direction.

'She seems in good spirits, considering,' I say.

'She's over the worst of it now.'

I think he's talking about the chicken pox. I had meant the situation: the fact that her father is dying.

'Coffee good?' he asks me.

I nod and bite the inside of my lip. I've never had a full conversation with a client outside of the clinic before. I know that Lela would tell me to politely excuse myself but I feel rooted to the spot, like the trees to their graves.

'I'm trying to use today to explain everything to Helena,' he says. 'She knows I'm dying, in her own way, and I want her to know she'll be in my Heaven.'

Perhaps he did follow my meaning, then. I glance back at the little girl. Her mouth is drawn into a line and she is staring down at her feet as she swings back and forth. It's a lacklustre effort and her sadness is painfully evident. I don't know enough about kids to have any suggestions.

'I think she's too young to understand how she can be both here and there at the same time,' he says.

'She doesn't understand that it's just memories of her in your Heaven?' I ask him.

'I think I've explained it all wrong from the outset. I'm going to have to start from scratch.' He pauses, rubbing at the stubble on his chin. The sound is like the rustle of the leaves. 'Do you need a lift back into the city?'

'No,' I lie. 'But thanks.'

'Really? I drive an Aston Martin.' It's not even an attempt to con me because he grins broadly as soon as the sentence is out. 'I wish.'

'Do you even drive?' I ask, raising my eyebrows.

He laughs and shakes his head. 'Of course not! Who does, these days?'

I'm not sure why he's still here and I don't know what to say next. We fall into silence as I realise that, without the giveaway laugh or smile, I'd believe anything he says.

'But, damn, what I would do for a 1965 DB5.' He closes his

eyes and rests his chin on his fist, dreamlike. 'I saw one once at a vintage motor show. Oyster paintwork, cream leather upholstery. The old boy who owned it let me sit inside. It was one of the most beautiful things I've ever seen.' His eyes pop open then and he looks at me with an intensity that knocks down the barrier I'm half-heartedly trying to put between us.

'You've got time,' I say. 'You could hire one – take it out for a spin.'

'You reckon they'd rent a car like that to a guy with a lapsed licence and a brain tumour?'

His tone invites me to smile with him. 'Well, then, we could still make it happen,' I find myself saying. 'I could put one in your Heaven.'

'Really? A fake memory?'

'Yeah, I've done it before.'

It can be done. It takes a lot of effort on my part, and I should charge more for it, but it's possible. Especially something material, something he's seen and touched. I realise that I don't want to backtrack on my offer. I'd like to do this for him.

'And could I drive it? Foot to the floor? Top down, full speed on an empty road?'

I smile encouragingly.

'Are there any limits to your powers, Miss Argent?'

I shake my head and he grins. He reaches out and places his hands over mine so that we're encircling the coffee cup. It feels like more. It feels like an embrace.

'Seriously, though, thank you for all you're doing. I'm so lucky that I found you.' His voice has dropped in pitch. It is gentle but resolute.

'Thanks, I'm glad you feel that way.' I shuffle back on the bench and slip my hands from beneath his. 'Sorry, I've got to go. I've got an early meeting,' I lie again.

'Do you have to?'

'Yes, sorry,' I say, as I gather up my bag from the top of the table.

He looks disappointed. 'I'll see you later this afternoon, anyway?'

I nod. 'Three p.m.'

I walk away through the café, before I'm tempted to look back at the figure of a dying man sitting alone at a picnic bench.

CHAPTER EIGHT

I'm just walking over to the sofa when I feel the vibration of an incoming call. I press my finger to my ear.

'Hello?'

'Izzy.' It's Lela, speaking in her clipped, business voice. It always makes me smile. 'I have your client, Mr Woods, on the line.'

I frown. He's supposed to be arriving for his session any minute now.

'Okay, put him through.' I look around for my Codex so that I can activate the video stream and we'll be able to see each other.

'Jarek?' I continue to cast my eyes around the room.

'Isobel, I'm so sorry. I can't make it today.' His voice is tight and his words run into each other. After he stops talking, deep, ragged breaths fill the silence.

'Oh?' I hear the disappointment cloud my voice. 'Are you all right?'

'I'm fine,' he snaps, pumping the words out like bullets. And then, as if he can see the bewilderment on my face, his voice softens. 'I just wanted to let you know.'

I run my fingers along the back of my chair and then decide to sit down. This obviously won't be a long call and I may as well stop looking for my Codex. I close my eyes and picture his face instead.

'Well, thanks for calling.' I pause because the erratic straining in his voice concerns me. 'Are you sure everything is okay?'

'I've just had an unexpected afternoon. That's all.'

There is silence for a while and I imagine him biting his lip, wondering how best to excuse himself from not just this meeting, but the entire process of creating his Heaven. I'm struck by a fear that he won't come back, that I won't ever see him again, and it shocks me.

'I was . . . I was looking forward to seeing you again.' I wince as I say it. I'm grasping for him and it must be obvious. I momentarily consider whether Lela monitors the phone lines. But it doesn't matter anymore. My embarrassment, my usual professionalism, is stifled by the realisation that he is slipping away from me even faster than he is dying. I wait for him to respond for what seems such a long time, I start to wonder whether he has hung up.

'The hours pass so slowly, don't they?' he says, eventually.

I look out of the window into the empty grounds and recall the memory of him walking up the path for our first meeting. The sunlight fell across his face. Today it is overcast and the threat of a storm presses against the glass. I circle my middle finger against my temple.

'I have a headache coming,' I tell him. 'So perhaps it's just as well. I'll see you next week, though?'

'I wouldn't miss it for the world.'

My shoulders soften in relief. 'I hope your day gets better.'

'I hope your headache clears up. Are they bad? Do you get them a lot?'

'No, not often.'

'Well, just promise me you'll get checked out if they get worse,' he says. 'Better safe than sorry.'

'Yeah,' I say, screwing up my eyes and wishing I hadn't mentioned it. I can be so thoughtless sometimes.

'Thanks for everything you've done so far, Isobel,' he says. 'You're very special.'

I smile then, shaking my head. 'No, I'm not.'

'You are. If it wasn't for you, I couldn't wait to be in my Heaven, away from my illness, away from the mess that is my life.' He laughs a little. 'That's an irony, isn't it?'

'You'll be untouchable in your Heaven, Jarek.' My voice wavers inside my throat, tied up with emotion.

'Untouchable?' He draws the words out, letting the syllables roll around his tongue. He sounds as though he is smiling.

'Absolutely. I promise.'

The day passes quickly. I manage to avoid both Maya and Caleb, and before I know it, I'm waiting for Lela on the street opposite the clinic. My last session ran over, but I know she'll be even later than me. She always is.

I stare across at the protesters. There are eight of them today, a new record. Their numbers have been bolstered by the arrival of a small plump woman, who grips on to the hand of a toddler. She has been glaring in my direction since she saw me leave the office. I feel too relaxed today to scowl back but I can feel her eyes on me. It would make more sense to wait around the corner for Lela, but

I'm intrigued by the spectacle. I like seeing the people passing by look up at the clinic in confusion, trying to figure out what all the fuss is about. A few push the leaflets into their pocket or bags but it's clear to anyone that they won't read them. I wonder what makes these protesters turn up every day. It seems like such a waste of life.

I slip off my jacket and step out from the shade of the lime tree, closing my eyes against the early evening haze. I hear the doors of the clinic slide apart and I open my eyes to watch Lela squeeze through the crowd. She dashes across the road through a gap in the traffic, looking sternly at me the whole time.

'Could you not have waited around the corner?' she says as she steps on to the pavement beside me.

I take in the disordered prettiness of her as she presses lipstick on with one hand and clasps her bucket bag in the other. It hangs open and, as she reaches out to me for a hug, make-up falls at my feet. I pick it up for her instead of opening my arms. I shovel everything back into the bag, pulling the drawstrings tight while she finishes applying her lipstick.

'Shall we go?' I ask.

She nods and shakes her black hair out, looping the coloured elastic around her wrist, where it joins several other hairbands.

'About the meeting, yesterday,' I begin, touching her arm.

'Forget it,' she says, abruptly, without looking at me. 'It's Friday. I've had to talk to that bloody woman all day and I'm as sick of her as you are. King's Arms or Chalet?'

'I don't mind.'

'Well, it's no contest for me. It's a fondue kinda day!' Lela laughs and pulls her bag over her shoulder so that she can link arms with me.

'Chalet it is, then.'

We walk in silence to the end of Wimpole Street as the cars roll past. It's a beautiful summer's evening and the Edwardian townhouses gleam in the golden light. We turn the corner and cut across the road to Chalet. Lela pulls open the rustic wooden door and pushes me inside before her, whispering over my shoulder as she does so.

'So, my management hat is off! Who's this handsome new client of yours?'

I glance back at her and roll my eyes.

Inside, it's already busy and we find a couple of barstools at the back of the main room. The air is thick with the aroma of molten cheese and evaporated alcohol.

'We'll be in a stupor within minutes,' I joke.

'Shall we order now?' Lela asks. She knows I'd rather knock back the wine, but she's right; I should eat, and Don isn't at home to cook something for me – although I always find packages of food in the freezer, labelled up with the ingredients and date, signed off with a kiss.

'Sure; shall we share one?'

She nods and I grab the attention of a passing waiter to order a fondue and a bottle of our favourite white wine, which appears within moments.

'How's Don?'

I shrug. 'You know – here and there. He works hard.'

'Almost as hard as you, I'd guess!' Lela grins. Even she recognises that what he does is more important, if there is a scale.

I look down at the table and wonder when it became a competition.

'Everything okay with you two?'

'Yeah, fine.' I cast my gaze around the bar, looking everywhere apart from at Lela's probing eyes. 'We just don't do anything together anymore. He keeps out of my business and I keep out of his. I'm not sure that's how it's supposed to be. Anyway, how's your lovely husband?'

Lela pauses and narrows her eyes at me before answering. I think she's deciding whether to press me further. 'Oh, he's fine,' she says eventually. 'Getting impatient for kids, though!'

'You're still not keen?'

'I just can't seem to summon up the enthusiasm, Izz. And the way the world is at the moment . . .' Lela plays with her earlobe, squashing and rolling it between the pads of her fingers.

She doesn't have to say any more. I know what she means because we've talked about it before, when the cold war against China started to heat up at the start of the year. She's too scared to bring a child into such an uncertain time in history. Perhaps we're prematurely concerned, but I'm sure we're not the only ones. Things are okay for now, perhaps, but the tension is mounting. I can see it in the faces of people on the streets. I can feel it ricochet through a crowd whenever there's a sudden loud noise or a siren.

'So . . . ?' Lela taps her nail on the table. She doesn't want our catch-up to be drowned in melancholy. 'Your client?'

'Lela! What about client confidentiality?'

'I'm not asking for details,' she says. Always so indignant. 'I just want you to admit that he's the sexiest client you've ever had!'

I laugh and lift the glass of wine to my lips, sucking it through my teeth and focusing on the bite of the alcohol at the back of my tongue.

'He's good-looking, I'll give you that.'

Lela realises that she's not going to be able to draw me further on the subject and her salacious grin fades. 'We've had some younger ones, recently, haven't we?'

I nod. 'It's sad. I find it hard to believe that there are still things we can't cure.'

'Yeah, it's tough.'

I think about how Jarek cracks jokes about dying, and how they only serve to heighten evidence of his own disbelief at what is happening to him. Older clients are so much more accepting, more grateful, about what I can achieve for them. And it's so much simpler to create their Heavens. They often just want the reality of their lives, as it comes. Perhaps they are old enough to have accepted that the rough comes with the smooth, experienced enough to have seen that life is defined by its contrasts, not by the moments of joy alone.

The half-light of the summer evening rolls into darkness as we gossip and drink ourselves silly. It always takes several glasses of wine before I can feel a fading in the tension that so defines me. The neatness unfurls and we splutter with laughter over the candle on our table. I stop caring that my shirt is getting flecked with splashes of wine and spots of grease. We're halfway through our third bottle when Lela falls over on the way back from the toilets and we decide it's time to go home. We order taxis before stumbling back out on to the street, pushing past the noisy queue of people still waiting to get in.

'There *is* something about him, you know,' I hear myself saying.

'Who?' Lela scrunches up her face in confusion and her eyes disappear into their sockets.

'My client, Jarek.'

'Oh, I know; I've watched you show him out. I've seen the way you look at him.'

My cheeks are already warm from the wine and the heat of the crowded restaurant, but I feel a fresh fever spreading through my face. Lela is perceptive – dangerously so. As our taxis pull up, I remember I've left my jacket over the chair inside.

'My jacket!' I call to Lela as I turn back inside.

By the time I return, a few moments later, she's already gone. I slip inside my taxi, feeling alone and drunk. My emotions are amped up now and I try to beat them down against the dopamine bouncing off the sides of my skull. I lean forward to speak my address into the dashboard before slumping back against the imitation-leather seats. As soon as I let myself relax, Jarek is in every particle of air in this dark space. I struggle to fill my lungs with the oxygen I need to fend him off. I know I can breathe, but I'm learning to breathe a new kind of substance. I'm choking on something quite wonderful.

I close my eyes and give myself over to it, to him. I take my memories from our two meetings, the time at the burial ground and today's brief chat, and caress my imagination over them, sculpting them into a fantasy. I run my hands though his hair, pull the pad of my thumb along his jaw. He towers above me and pulls me into him. I twist the wedding band on his finger and it falls to the floor.

My eyes flicker open, the cells of my retina grasping for something – anything – in the gloom. The display at the top of my vision tells me it's three a.m.

I feel it again, the gentle agitation against my jugular that woke me up. It's an urgent message. Something is wrong. And that usually means that someone has died.

I pull myself up from underneath the sheets, arranging them under my arms and plumping up the pillows behind me. I glance at the empty space beside me and smooth my hand over the creases in the pillow. I feel a sense of relief that Don doesn't have to see me like this. He hates it when I've had too much to drink.

I blink into the darkness, bracing myself. My head throbs but I'm still a little drunk. The nausea I'm expecting doesn't come. I lean back against the headboard and take a couple of deep breaths. Preparation is everything. I unfurl my Codex and there's the message: *Jarek*.

There's a part of me, still dozing, that's not surprised in the slightest at the tightening of my chest. My toes squeeze against each other and the cramp spreads through me. It tugs at my heart, where so few of my clients reach. He can't be dead. No, no, no. Not yet. Then I realise that the message is *from* him, not *about* him.

The two words call out at me, flickering with laughter: *You're awake!*

It's not a question. Of course it's not, because he's aware that by flagging his message as urgent, it's woken me up. An aggravated passion rattles in my belly as I talk, the words appearing as silent text on the screen. My voice scratches in my throat.

I thought someone had died.

Sorry . . .

The ellipsis flashes for a few seconds. I know before the rest of the sentence appears that this is his attempt at comedic timing.

. . . not yet!

I find myself running a fingertip over the words on the screen, feeling it buckle like skin with the pressure of my touch. I sink beneath the sheets again, waiting. Waiting for the reason a client would write to their Architect in the middle of the night.

I wanted to ask you something . . . I need to know what your Heaven is like.

I should decline. I should put my Codex down and go back to sleep. But 'need' is a word that's hard to ignore. It pulses in front of me, shimmering potently. Offering a transfer of power.

My life is so simple. I get up, I have breakfast. I wear almost the same outfit every day: a loose-fitting suit, with a crisp, white shirt tucked into the waistband of the trousers. Maybe a camisole underneath, if it's cool out. Matching underwear, obviously. Flats or low heels. Tinted lip balm, bronzer, eyeshadow, eyeliner and mascara. I go to work. I create things for people – meaning-ful things, comforting things. At least, I hope so. I talk to them about it. I write notes, I update my boss, I go to the occasional meeting. I come home. I go to bed with my boyfriend. I talk to my sister on the phone once a week. At the weekends, I work, clean the flat, listen to music, occasionally see friends. My life is ordered and yet, despite my fastidiousness, it remains inelegant. I don't need to start a battle; I already feel like I'm constantly at war with myself.

Please, I need to know.

It wouldn't be right. I'm lucky he can't hear the tone of my voice. I barely convince myself.

I've got all these ideas but I'm floundering. It would help me if I could see what someone else's Heaven was like.

That's normal. I'm here to help. In our sessions. I almost summon the willpower to roll my Codex shut but his next words appear almost immediately.

I don't think I've got long left.

'But my Heaven's not finished. I'm still creating it,' I whisper. As I watch the words appear, I know that this is a poor excuse. I should tell him that it's not appropriate for an Architect to share such details with her client. But who am I to keep it from him? I tell myself that Jarek is a dying man, a man that needs me. He is my responsibility now. I pull the Codex underneath the sheets with me and I whisper.

CHAPTER NINE

It's three days before I see him again and they drag. I have more nightmares. Planes and drones and shadowy soldiers trample through my sleeping mind. Sometimes Don doesn't come home at all and I wake up sweating, reaching out for him, before I remember that I'm stuck inside a bubble of my own turmoil. I am falling for a man – a married client – I barely know, and yet I feel like I need Don's reassurance. There's a residual attachment that won't fade. I worry about him. I worry about what will happen to us. And then the worry scatters into a sky of stars, beneath which I'm threaded into Jarek's limbs like a jigsaw.

Jarek has been with the neurologist. The first neurons of his memories have been patched into a computer; the integrity of his mind has been checked. The process is all so straightforward that it's easy to forget that Jarek is dying. He will be dead. His body will decay and he will forever be in a Heaven that doesn't even know my name. I can't think those thoughts without pushing my fingernails into my lip.

I wait for him now, my hands gripping the sofa. I'm torn and I feel like it's visible in every aspect of my appearance. I know I look exhausted. There are shadows under my eyes, yet I've swiped a hazy pink lipstick over my mouth. I dressed in a black lace basque this morning, but then I told myself I was going crazy and threw on a tired old suit that's too big for my frame over the top of it, but I put on heels instead of my flats. As I wait, his name appearing repeatedly – insistently – on the tip of my tongue, my hands move from the edge of the seat to my hair, unfurling it before I change my mind and scoop it back again to the nape of my neck.

All I can think is that I told him about my Heaven. But when he walks in, the words come more easily that I expected.

'Hello. How are you?'

'I'm tired.'

I didn't need him to tell me that. It's evident as soon as I look at him. 'Exhausted' is probably closer to the mark. Even the usual warmth of his smile falters against the sun streaming into my office.

'But you look beautiful, like you always do.' He says it slowly enough that I believe him. He doesn't lower his eyes and it's me that must look away. 'The sessions with Dr Sorbonne went well,' he continues, as I fight the flush from my cheeks. 'At least, I think they did.'

'She assures me they did.'

'She said that the car – the DB5 – is coming along nicely.'

'Yes, yes, I've been working on it today. I think it's looking really good.'

We talk and it's like the part of me that will enter my own Heaven one day is floating above me, looking down on us. We're sitting only inches apart and our heads are inclined towards each other. Our knees almost touch. I shuffle every so often as the bones of my basque dig into my ribs. One minute, I can't bear to look into his eyes, and seconds later, I'm not able to tear my gaze away again.

We go through more details about what he wants, how he wants his Heaven to look. He wants all the seasons, and the climbing frame he played on with his brothers when he was a child, and the memory of his mother washing him at the sink, cleansing his childhood scrapes of gravel and dirt. He wants to remember the first time he made love to a girl – even though he no longer knows her and so she'll be an anonymous figure, unable to opt in to his memories. But he will feel the heat of her body, the nerves and the elation. He will hear the nervous giggling afterwards. He wants to play rugby with his best friends (I can get their opt-in this week, I tell him), and eat the incomparable fillet steak he once had at a tiny restaurant in Florence, and sneak another sip of the warm cider that his grandfather used to brew in the cellar. He wants to remember playing with his sister in their youth, amongst the pine trees at the back of the family home – before their parents sent them off to separate boarding schools; before the accident. He wants to relive that big win at the blackjack table in Las Vegas and remember the night that he dropped acid with a stranger in Argentina. He wants – of course – to feel the love of the crowd around him as he danced his first dance at his wedding, and to watch the birth of each of his daughters. He ponders over the doomed love affairs of his younger years. Somehow the jealousy I feel becomes overwhelmed by his honesty. One girl is definitely in, and then out again, and his regrets mount, but he tells me he'll think about it and let me know.

'I'll get in touch with her, anyway,' I say. 'I'm sure she'll feel flattered.' My throat is dry and I realise I've drunk a whole glass of water in the space of a few minutes. Every so often, he clenches his jaw and his eyes harden, and I realise he's in pain.

'It hurts?' I ask him on the third occasion that I see him flinch.

'No one said dying was easy,' he replies, eyes shining through his feigned seriousness.

'No, but it's much easier than it used to be.'

'Yes, I know.' His expression closes down and his voice softens. 'But I'm getting bored with it. I'm ready to go. I'm ready to get out of here.'

And I want to shake him. I'm rendered selfish, caught up in the realisation that sitting with him here in my office is the most alive I've ever felt.

'You have to make the most of this time, Jarek.'

I can hear my tone suggesting more than the words I am speaking. I'm trying to tell him to throw caution to the wind. I am calling him to me. I am crazy. I have actually lost my mind, I think.

'Isobel?'

'You can call me Izzy. Izz.'

'You said that the timelessness of Heaven would make me feel free.'

'Yes, I did. It will,' I say, and I see that his hand is resting on my thigh above the knee. Did he really do that? How did he put it there without me noticing? I tense the muscle so that I don't shake. There is peace in the room for a minute or so. And I mean peace, rather than silence. It's an easy noiselessness, which consumes Jarek's need to crack jokes and absorbs my terror. It leaves only a soft pulsing current between us, that could also just be the blood rushing against my ear canal.

'How do you know?'

'How do I know? I know because it would, wouldn't it? The passing of time is the root of all our anxieties. We hate getting old; we rush around, trying to get everything done. We try to control the future by improving ourselves. If we could just live in the moment absolutely and completely . . . wouldn't that be perfect happiness?'

He is silent for some time. 'I've been thinking . . .' I can see his jaw work as he gnaws the inside of his cheek. 'I don't want my wife in my Heaven.'

'You don't?' I try to keep my voice level as my brain clouds with questions. I feel his voice, as if by osmosis, through my skin, but he is still my client. I am still his Architect.

'No, I don't.'

I try to mentally push myself away from him. I bring the Architect in me back to the forefront and let Isobel slide, protesting, to the back of my thoughts. There are many people who only want happier memories of their loved ones to appear to them after their deaths. But this is complete censorship. It will be tricky to separate out those memories, to erase her from his other recollections. I think of Don and the way he looks at me. As unlikely as it is, I know that if he decided to have a Heaven, he would want me in it. And I wonder, not for the first time, whether I would want to let him.

'Can I ask why?' It's barely a whisper.

'Why do you think?' His tone challenges me and I can't bear it. A weight of responsibility sinks over my shoulders, pinning me to the sofa. This is why you don't get too close to your clients.

I feel a perplexing panic rise like bile in my chest and I glance

89

at the clock. I've never finished a session early. I can't finish this session early. Can I? I struggle to hold my lips together. I imagine I look like a goldfish gasping for air, and stumble back from the caricature I've just created.

'I'm sorry, Jarek. I've just realised I have an appointment. I'll schedule you in again in a couple of days.' I jump across the words as if they are stepping stones in a stream, rising above the current. I grasp at my bag on the back of the door and fling it over my shoulder as I gesture him out of the room. He hasn't left the sofa, but has swivelled to face me in a kind of amused astonishment. I flush with embarrassment and find myself striding down the corridor. Out. Away. It's an intensified version of the feeling I often get after a long day in the office. It's the need to be alone, secluded from every other human voice in the world. When I'm like this, I can't even read a book or listen to music. It's all encompassing and it swallows my sanity into its depths.

I listen again to my mother, refusing to let me create her a Heaven, her raspy voice scratching at my heart. I hear Don's judgemental despair, holding me back from a sense of achievement. They have always judged what I do. I have never been good enough. Is what I do benevolent? Is it humane? Once, we just lived and we died, and now all these people are kneeling at my feet, expecting more, expecting everything. I can see them: Jarek, Clair, all the many, many clients I've had over the years.

I stride out through the doors to the building and I'm on the street, walking in a direction I never take. My trousers flap against the sensitive skin beneath my tattoo, catching on the scabs. The world around me blurs into a mindless meditation as I hear only the repeated fall of my feet on the pavement. I imagine the feathers of my angel's wings scabbing over and thickening into black, ugly scars that wind up my leg like earthworms looking for a place to burrow. The wind whips against my face and my hair loosens itself. I let it fly across my face and catch in the wetness of my eyes, almost wishing I could miss an uneven point in the pavement and stumble, falling, stopping myself by a self-imposed kind of violence before I can do anything more stupid.

And then, at the corner of the street, something does stop me. A vibration from my chip, a light flashing in my vision and a calm voice speaking directly into my ear canal.

'This is a drill,' the woman says. 'Please proceed immediately to your nearest place of shelter.'

She says it again while I'm still trying to process what's happening. Arrows appear in my vision, directing me back in the direction of the clinic. We have a safe room in the basement. Lela will be looking around, wondering where I am, nibbling at the skin around her fingernails.

'This is a drill,' the voice repeats.

Would they tell us if it was the real thing? If drones were swarming in the skies at this moment, would they want us to scream and scatter? Or would they want us to walk calmly and quietly towards shelter? I'm frozen to the spot by something that isn't quite fear or vulnerability. It's a sudden attack of hopelessness that crawls over me.

And then, before I can collapse in a heap, Jarek is there, grabbing my hand and spinning me towards him. I'm briefly terrified.

'I'm sorry; I can't help it.' His words reach me slowly, as if transmitted through water. 'I can't stop thinking about you.'

For a second, I know that I could lose everything. But then

he kisses me and the thought falls silent as the pressure of his lips seems to burst my eardrums. My grip on my perfectly structured world slips and shatters.

CHAPTER TEN

We walk down the stairs to the basement of the clinic. It's only when I reach for the door handle that I realise we've been holding hands the whole way. My palm tingles from the cold of the metal and I glance back at him as we enter the room. His cheeks are flushed from the jog, or perhaps from the kiss, and as I turn my attention to those awaiting us, I feel as if our intimacy is written across our faces in blood.

'Izzy, there you are!' I can see that Lela is forcing a wan smile through her worry. She doesn't hide her concerns as well as me. 'Tea?'

'Yes – yes, please.'

'And for you, Mr Woods?'

'Please.'

'I'm so sorry about this,' she says, as she turns to the machine. 'We still haven't decorated down here. It's on my list.'

'It's fine.' Jarek bats away her apology. 'It's . . . homely.'

And we all laugh, because of course it's a joke. A rather obvious one, but it breaks the awkward atmosphere. Caleb is sitting on the only chair in the room, chatting to Harry, who's leaning against the wall, hands in pockets. Maya is sitting on the floor in the corner, stockinged legs out in front of her, chatting to an older couple who I think are Harry's clients. I try not to let my gaze rest on her for too long. We haven't spoken again since she followed me on my walk home and I have no desire to continue the conversation. When I look away, I feel her eyes flick over me.

The room isn't tiny – you could fit five times as many people in here – but it is uncomfortable. There's no natural light, just a glow coming from a pair of copper floor-lamps, standing in opposite corners, like boxers in a ring. The walls are bare grey plaster and the old terracotta quarry tiles on the floor are cracked, unswept. I squint down at the area around my feet and realise with distaste that it's not just dusty but filthy. I feel my toes scrunch up inside my shoes. It smells dry and lifeless. It reminds me of my grandmother's disused garage, where my best friend and I used to hide for hours at a time until our voices were hoarse from the dry, granular air. We've only had to assemble in here once before and it didn't seem as bad then. I wonder how it can have got so dirty in the meantime.

Lela thrusts mugs of tea towards Jarek and me, and we both reach out at the same time. I feel his arm move against mine and I have to swallow down the nerves that sizzle in my chest. Lela is looking at me. I blink and look away but I can still feel her gaze on me and I wonder how she could have any idea what's happened.

Caleb stands up and offers his chair to Jarek. 'Do take a seat, Mr Woods.'

I watch Jarek refuse the offer and take the chair over to the couple in the corner. He bends to place it down for the lady and his body eclipses the lamp. A halo of light escapes around the fuzziness of his outline, softening the angles of his shoulders and the awkward jut of his hip. Caleb's eyes follow him, noting the rebuttal.

'Seriously, I do apologise for the inconvenience,' Caleb continues in his most charming tones, casting his voice around the room now more loudly than is necessary, given the space. 'I'm sure we'll be out of here soon.' He pushes back his shoulders, slaps his hand against Jarek's back and I'm embarrassed for us all. He feels threatened by him in such close quarters, I imagine. A young, handsome client with enough money to hire me as his Heaven Architect. No, Caleb wouldn't like that at all. It wouldn't even cross his mind to throw the fact that Jarek is dying into the equation.

'It's not a problem,' Jarek replies, sitting down with his back against the wall. He doesn't even dust the patch of floor first and I fight the urge to move him, to wipe the floor with my hand and clean off his trousers. I bite at my thumbnail as I think about it. I realise he's looking at me and smiling in a way that I can't decipher. It could be amusement, but I feel as if he's just looked right inside my head and scanned my thoughts. I can't bring myself to smile back, but I dare to look longer into the green of his eyes. I should feel powerful, standing over him, but I feel tiny. He raises the mug to his mouth and shakes his head as he looks away.

I sip my tea and can feel Lela's eyes switching between us, her lips pursed. I close my eyes but I imagine drones and bombers filling the skies over the office, so I open them again and begin to pace back and forth on my side of the door. I think I see Caleb tense his jaw.

'So, Jarek, I hear that your sessions with Isobel are going well?' Lela asks.

I glare at her but, all of a sudden, she won't look at me.

Jarek nods a few times and raises his eyebrows in what looks like approval. For a moment, I think that's the only answer she's

95

going to get, but then he opens his mouth. 'She's amazing,' he says. 'Even better than I expected her to be.'

I feel blood swarm to my cheeks and I drop my chin to my chest.

'It's quite claustrophobic in here, isn't it?' I say, running my fingertips down the edge of the closed door, counting the notches and imperfections in the woodwork.

'It could be better,' says Harry, and I silently thank him for helping me to change the topic. In the corner, Maya and the couple continue to speak in hushed tones. The rest of us are quiet for a few moments.

'This is the second drill this year,' Harry continues. 'That can't be a good thing.' His arms are folded and he's not speaking to any one of us in particular.

'I guess they just want to make sure we're . . .' Safe? Prepared? Protected? I struggle for the right word and Lela, Harry and Caleb all look at me, alert, because they know who Don is and what he does. They always think I know more than I do, which is next to nothing. Whatever I say now will make it sound as though things have escalated, as though a war being fought on the other side of the world is not quite so far away. 'I'm sure they just want to be prepared for every eventuality.' It sounds like something Don would say and, as I think of him, flicking my eyes towards Jarek, I'm surprised that I don't feel even a flutter of guilt.

'It does scare me,' says Lela. 'I feel like things are getting closer to home now. There could even be drones out there now, scanning our houses, our schools, our hospitals . . .' Her voice wavers and I'd like to hug her but I still feel wrapped in Jarek's scent, as if our kiss is visible on my skin if you look closely enough.

'No.' Jarek shakes his head. 'No, that won't happen. You'll all see out this war in safety. This country, our people . . . We're much stronger than we give ourselves credit for.' His voice is little more than a murmur and yet he commands the room. For the first time, even Maya stops talking to look at him. An expression approximating respect crosses Caleb's face. My lips part and something wells up inside me that I can barely acknowledge.

Several minutes pass before we each receive the same message on our eye lenses: *Drill complete. Thank you for your cooperation.*

'Well, thank goodness for that,' Maya drawls as she gets to her feet and thoroughly dusts herself off before helping up the couple she's been talking to. Everyone starts to file out, eager to leave. Lela pauses at the door and asks me to turn the lamps out before following the others up the stairs. I glance back into the room and Jarek is still pulling himself upright from the floor. He loses his balance and stumbles to the left. He places the flat of his hand against the wall to steady himself.

'The vision in my left eye is going,' he says, by way of explanation.

The tumour, I think, is sitting somewhere in there to the right of his skull, causing problems on his left. The brain works with opposites. Killing him in mirror image.

'I'm sorry,' I say, but it's not what I mean. I sound like I feel bad for him, but I don't. What impresses me is that he looks anything but weak. The tautness of his jaw is unapologetic and his body is still strong beneath the red T-shirt that clings to his frame. It's almost easy to convince myself that the diagnosis could be wrong. He could have months, perhaps years.

'Come on.' I'm still holding the heavy door open a fraction, waiting.

'The lights.' He turns one off and then the other. I can just about see him walking back towards me, but as I pull on the handle, his hand closes over mine. He pushes the door shut and the room is plunged into darkness. I clench my jaw and blink into the splotches of colour as my eyes adjust. He leans into me and I sink back against the wall.

'Jarek, we can't,' I say, without meaning it. 'They'll wonder where we are.'

He remains silent and kisses fall upon my neck as his fingers move to my shirt buttons. I manage to stifle the strange noise that bubbles in up my throat by pressing my lips together. I find my teeth closing around his earlobe.

'This is crazy,' I whisper into his ear. 'We can't do this.'

'Why not?' he asks me and I feel him pull away.

I have an answer. I do. I have a list of answers. But it's so long that my brain can't process it and already my body is yearning for him to press against me again. For a split second, it crosses my mind that he knows exactly what he is doing. It's a thought which almost illuminates the room. And then we are invisible to each other again. I rise on to my tiptoes and move my hands to the back of his neck, my thumbs tracing his jawline. I pull him towards me as I kiss him. The heat of his breath melts the boundaries between us as I swivel him around and push him up against the wall. The force with which I move surprises me. His lips change shape and I know that he is smiling.

'I'll tell you what's crazy,' he whispers as one hand slips inside my shirt and he runs his fingers down the bone of my basque. The other hand moves to the clasp of my trousers. 'It's crazy that I'm about to die and I'm feeling like this for the first time in my life.'

I don't know how much time passes. After just a few moments, it fails to matter. It crosses my mind that the timelessness of our encounter is ironic, given that we've already discussed the concept today. Heaven will be like this. It will be without time. Just a constant rolling of bliss, punctuated by subtle reminders that things are not always so perfect.

At the end, I fuss over myself in the darkness, pressing the backs of my hands against the fire of my cheeks, combing my fingers through my hair and retying it. I can feel the shock beginning to register, starting in my stomach and rippling outward. We arrange our clothes in silence. I feel the weight of dust and dirt upon them and I brush vigorously at the material. I only realise my hands are shaking when I go to fasten my belt. A fingertip glides down the side of my face.

I look at the door. I don't want to go beyond it. I can't bring myself to put my fingers upon the handle. I don't want to be the one to break the spell. Already, so little time is left for us.

'If you don't open this door, I never will,' he whispers.

I turn the handle and pull it towards me. Jarek tries to hold it but the door's weight leans on to his left side and I feel him stumble behind me, losing his balance and resting his hand upon my shoulder to steady himself.

'You okay?' I ask, turning around. He shrugs, embarrassed. I touch my own cheeks, soaking up the heat I find there and trying to wish it away before anyone else sees it. I walk up the spiral staircase with my hand running up the rail, Jarek's thumb resting upon it. I'm smiling at my feet. Smiling like a teenager. The light gets brighter as we rise. As we turn the last corner before the top, I know before I look up that Lela is waiting for us. She greets me with a stony stare. There's no pretence on her face. She has been there the whole time, waiting.

'Lela, look,' I begin, hoping that I can placate her with my words, hoping that I can distract her for long enough that this all somehow fades into the background. Jarek stands behind me. I feel his hand slip beneath my jacket and he lays his palm flat against the small of my back, over my shirt. The heat that is on him is partly mine and, as it sinks back into me, I start to feel incredulous at what has just happened.

'Good day, Mr Woods.' Lela ignores me. I sneak a glance up through my eyelashes at her face and see that the stern, thin lips of a moment ago are now forming a fake smile. 'We'll see you again soon. Isobel, could I see you in my office, please?'

Jarek and I look at each other and I imagine all the things he could be trying to tell me with his eyes. He can't say them now, but the unspoken words make him smoulder and his weaker left eye flickers at the lid. He reaches out for me and squeezes my forearm before he turns away. Lela doesn't see the way his hand lingers, the pads of his fingers stroking tiny circles on the thin skin of my wrist. A weaker woman than me might melt.

'Lela . . .' I sigh heavily. I know I can't be angry with her. She won't meet my eyes but I follow her down the corridor. I look back once and Jarek is watching us from the front door. He mouths something at me but I can't decipher it from here. I can't blame him for that. I think about smiling and waving, but do neither, before stepping into one of the side rooms. Lela closes the door behind me.

'Sit down,' she demands. Her voice is low but furious. Even though I stay standing in defiance, she sinks back into one of the chairs. I clench my teeth and look her in the face. It is etched with an anger that I didn't think her capable of.

'What in . . . ?' She shakes her head in despair and rubs at her forehead as if she would like to erase me from her brain. 'I'll put this politely: what the hell are you thinking?'

I shrug as if I'm a child in detention. I wonder whether there's any chance I can explain my way out of this, if there is an excuse I can give or a lie I can tell to make it all go away.

'I know I joked about it on Friday night,' she continues, 'but you can't take advantage of a client like that. Or let him take advantage of you.'

'Oh, for goodness' sake, Lela; nothing even happened.'

She raises her eyebrows and takes her time to run her eyes over me, looking for signs of the truth. I know she isn't stupid. She can see for herself, without noticing my smudged mascara, my reddened lips.

I sigh. I wouldn't allow anyone else to make me feel defeated. 'You shouldn't have waited for us,' I say.

'I stayed there because I was *protecting* you; can't you see that?' Her voice rises in volume with each word. 'I didn't want anyone else to realise! Now I'm thinking that maybe I should have knocked the fucking door down and pulled you both out of there!'

Lela doesn't usually swear. She hates confrontation. I remember when she had to sack a receptionist. She cried for a week.

I glimpse over my shoulder, through the frosted glass of the door, to check no one is out there, listening. 'I've fallen for him.'

Lela sits back in her chair and presses the base of her palms against her temples. 'No, you haven't, Izzy. After such a short time? It's lust. And you're being reckless.'

'Don't be stupid.' My veins fizz with the fear that she could keep us apart. 'I think I know the difference between love and lust, Lela.'

She rolls her eyes and I look away.

'How did he get into your head? Endless compliments? Offering you reassurance about all of this?' She gestures vaguely to the space around us. Her voice drops back to a whisper. 'Regardless, you can't be his Architect any longer, Izzy. You can't, and you won't. It would be wrong of me to let you. I'm reassigning him to Harry and I don't expect you to have any further contact with each other.'

'We're adults, Lela!' A fearful fury leaps into my chest and I slam my hand down on the table.

'He's *dying*, Isobel.' She spits the words out. 'He's vulnerable.' She looks at me as if she cannot believe my stupidity. I briefly see it for myself, like I've stared at a bright light for too long, the ghost of it appearing with each blink of my eyes. She opens her mouth to speak again, pausing as she thinks through her words. It's probably going to be the same advice she's given me a dozen times. *If only you would think before you speak, Izzy.*

'And *you're* vulnerable.' Her voice drops and she pushes a hand across the table towards mine.

'That's where you're wrong, Lela. Can I go now?'

She spreads her palms in defeat and I move towards the door.

'How many more times am I going to have to look out for you?' she asks.

'However many times it takes before you learn that you don't have to,' I say, and I slam the door behind me.

CHAPTER ELEVEN

Time passes in a blur. Don comes home for a couple of nights at a time before leaving again. I can't bring myself to look at him, let alone touch him, and I bury myself in work. I don't eat, which is usually a sign that I'm happy. This surprises me, because happiness is not what I feel. The emotions tumble like laundry in my belly, clean and warm. But it feels as if they are too big for me to process.

Lela signed me off for the rest of the week. I received a blunt message when I got home the night after the drill: *Don't come in until Monday.* I've never been the kind of person who spends all week longing for the weekend. I slept a lot. Yet I still felt drained. I hated not being in the office. I don't even know what Lela told Caleb. I suppose she said that I was sick. I wonder what excuse she gave him for transferring my client like that. She must have sworn Harry to complete client–patient confidentiality. I don't know, because she still hasn't spoken to me herself.

In the weeks since, I've been slinking into the office early, before anyone else arrives. And, like tonight, leaving sharply. I manage to get out of the office even earlier than usual. The evenings are already drawing in. Soon I'll be leaving work to meet him in wintery darkness. If he is still here when the last leaves have fallen.

When Jarek suggested we meet at his family home when I was off work, it seemed wrong. I found myself suggesting a hotel instead. *I have to see you*, he said. *It doesn't matter where.* Now that I'm reflecting on it, I realise my choice is even seedier. Just once, I told myself, and then we should call time on what was happening between us. But it's September already. I feel like we must make the most of how long we have left with each other.

I have an hour or so before I need to make my way to the hotel. As I peer at Jarek's house, across the street, I shift against the wall. Flakes from its crumbling surface slip under my collar and into my silk camisole. I don't expect to find him here. Right now, he'll still be in Harry's office, finalising the details of the memories he wants to feature in his Heaven. They will be starting the last stage of approval procedures and discussing the neurological process and its risks. Jarek and I have tried not to talk about his sessions with Harry. I think he knows it would drive me crazy not being able to take control of his Heaven. And I worry that Harry won't do a good enough job, although I'd never say that to Jarek.

I squint at an upper-floor window, framed by heavy swag curtains. A bedroom. I picture a silhouette of us in a shadowy embrace behind the glass. It's still what you'd call an affair. There's still Don, and there's still a marriage, even if it's in tatters.

Nor have I come here looking for Sarah, I tell myself. Drawing comparisons is dangerous territory. Yet there is a woman's figure in the lounge, picking up toys from the floor. From here, I can see little more than a short, sharp bob, and a pair of sunglasses hooked into a neckline. She disappears from view and then the front door opens. She pauses on the path, as if glancing at the time, and then heads down the street. Before I know it, I'm crossing the road to follow her. My brain is yelling at me to stop and turn around, but my curiosity pads boldly onwards.

Her dress swishes around her knees as she walks. I'm not close enough to tell for sure, but her long, pale calves suggest she is taller than me. She may even be the same height as Jarek. I push back my shoulders and lift my chin to rival her as best I can. We walk for several streets, turning a few corners until we reach the parade of shops beside the Tube station.

By the time I catch up with her, she is standing in front of a florist's shop, talking to a woman in a polka-dot apron. I stop a few feet away, staring at the funereal display of white carnations shaped into a heart, while I listen. My senses sharpen upon her; the post-work bustle fades into the periphery.

'Twelve, as usual, Sarah?' the woman asks her. 'Let me guess – just the white and purple ones?'

Sarah. Sarah Woods. Not the nanny or another relative. This is her. I swallow back the guilt that bubbles like lava at the back of my throat. I try to get a glimpse of her face, but I can only see her nose poking out from behind the bob of brown hair.

'No, you don't need to count them,' she says. 'Just a couple of bunches. They all look nice.'

The woman gathers the flowers from the bucket and swings open the door into the shop before turning back to her.

'Are you sure? I know how particular your husband is.'

'Those are fine, really.' Her words are clipped by irritation. I'm surprised. Jarek seems so laid-back. I find it hard to imagine he would care about a bunch of flowers.

I grab the nearest bouquet and follow them inside. I'm close enough that Sarah holds the door open for me without looking around. She smells of Turkish delight.

I stand at the back of the shop, casting my eyes over the rails of wrapping paper while the woman lays the anemones on the counter. I look down at the flowers which I've cradled like a baby in the crook of my arm: pink peonies with pure white centres. They are blowsy, their heads heavy with imprecise beauty. Something for a bride, really; not something to impose upon my minimalist flat. *Mine and Don's flat*, a voice inside my head reminds me.

I watch as the woman lays the stems in the middle of the brown paper. Her hands hover over them and she lifts her head to look Sarah in the face, as if she is about to speak. Her eyes catch mine.

'I won't be a moment, love,' she says, and she goes back to wrapping the blooms.

'Oh, no rush, really,' I say.

Sarah turns her head to look at me, smiling politely. And I notice for the first time that she's probably a few years younger than me – so ten years younger than Jarek.

'Those are gorgeous,' she says, pointing at the flowers in my arms and rotating her whole body to face me. 'Peonies?' She speaks as delicately as her appearance would suggest.

I nod. 'I think so.' My tongue feels too big for my mouth. Part of me wants to drop to my knees and beg forgiveness, but then I remind myself that their marriage was already failing before I came along. It's not my fault. Just like it's not my fault that he's dying.

For the first time, I look straight at her, head-on. She's all hips and bosom in her jersey dress, and she twiddles her hands together awkwardly over her stomach. I bet she was the girl at school that got teased for having to wear a bra at the age of eleven. I think of my petite, boyish frame, my narrow hips and the gentle swell of my chest. My tight, sharp lips and chin.

Sarah turns back to the woman. 'I'm so sorry, can I take a bunch of those instead, please?' she asks, pointing to my bunch.

'Er, yes, of course.' The woman doesn't seem to mind, pushing the anemones to the side of the counter. 'Let me just go and grab some.'

'You can have these,' I say, stepping forward and handing them to Sarah. She takes them, her lips parting in surprise. 'As lovely as they are, I was just thinking I was going to get something else instead.'

'Oh, okay, thank you.' Sarah hands the flowers to the woman before turning back to face me. 'Look at us, hey? Buying our own flowers.'

The woman tears a new sheet of brown paper from the roll and starts to wrap the peonies. The rustling almost drowns out Sarah's voice.

'Yeah,' I say with a shrug, returning her smile.

'That's a good sign,' the woman behind the counter says, her eyes wide, conspiratorial. 'It means your men haven't done anything they need to apologise for!'

We both laugh.

'Oh, yes, my husband was always in here, wasn't he?' Sarah jokes, her voice high. But I note the use of the past tense and, like me, the woman looks a little too long at Sarah's face. Perhaps she's embarrassed at her earlier mention of him. The meaning of her words is clear and it hangs like dirty laundry in the air between us.

'Well, I'm apologising to myself!' I say, blurting out the words to break the tension and avoid thinking too much about what she might mean. The woman laughs and Sarah raises her eyebrows as if to agree. As if to admit that she's also done wrong. She pays for the peonies and leaves, granting me a quick, shy smile as she walks past, to the door.

'Can I take these?' I ask the lady as I take Sarah's place at the counter, laying my hand over the discarded anemones.

She squints when she looks at me, and then nods in the direction of the closing door. 'Such a shame, that,' she says. 'I used to see him in here a lot. Handsome chap. He nearly bought up the whole shop, one day. A real romantic, you know?'

I bristle with envy and pride. *He's mine, now*, I want to tell her.

'Anything else, love?' she asks.

'No, that's all. Thank you.' I lean forward to present my chip to the payment receiver. The buzz of acceptance in my neck matches my excitement. It's time to meet Jarek.

Outside, I flag down an autocab and jump inside, breathlessly issuing directions. I can't get there fast enough, but it's as if the heat from my body is sinking through the car, making its tyres stick to the asphalt. Finally, we pull up outside the hotel and I push the mirage of Don to the back of my mind. This is another world — a crazy, temporary world that can only last so long. As long as Jarek lives.

I reach for the anemones as I'm getting out, but then hesitate. What if Jarek does only like the white and purple ones — six of each? I give them one last glance and leave them wilting on the hot leather seat.

I hear the door unlock as I lean into it and I knock before letting myself in. By design, I've never arrived first. It's my way of holding something back, I suppose. Just one of the many self-deluding ways I'm making it look as if I'm being dragged into this affair, rather than pulling it closer to my heart with every breath. I sigh at the empty room. By arriving on time, I've let my guard fall another notch lower.

I slip off my heels, place them side by side at the foot of the bed and run a fingertip over the wooden frame. It comes back clean. I like this place because it's always immaculate. Deciding to take a shower before Jarek arrives, I take off my clothes and hang them up in the wardrobe. There's a mirror inside the door. I stand on my tiptoes, push back my shoulders and try to find the angle at which I look most shapely. Giving up, I shake out my hair and pull it over my shoulders. It's getting long.

'Bathroom lights on.' I only murmur and they fade up. 'Shower on.'

The shower is instantly hot and I stand right beneath the head. I press my hands against the back wall above the controls and stretch out my shoulders. The tension is somewhat eased by the water, but it still tingles at my neck and down my spine. I know what's causing it. Guilt. Murky guilt, filling up the gaps between the bones like mucus. I push the thought away and fill my hands with shampoo. I massage my scalp and twist my hair into a rope around my neck.

I turn back around and flush the suds from my eyes before opening them. A dark shape. A face. A man. Adrenalin explodes behind my ribs and my scream must echo down the corridor.

Jarek creases up with laughter, enough that he stumbles and has to lean his forearms on the vanity.

'You bastard!' I cry.

He shakes his head by way of apology and wipes his eyes. He looks me up and down, before returning his eyes to mine through the glass of the shower screen. They narrow and the bright wall-lights glitter in his pupils. My breath starts to calm but speeds up again as, without speaking, he takes off his clothes and kicks them aside, pulling open the shower door and stepping inside with me. The steam fills my lungs as he wraps his arms around me. His muscles are softening; they don't hold me in a clamp like they did at first. Instead, we meld together like plasticine, slipping into each other's negative space. He kisses my lips, my face, my neck. The warm water works its way into my mouth and it softens the sharp ends of his stubble. The tension in my shoulders is forgotten.

He runs his nose down my body and kisses my belly. I hold on to his left arm because I know by now that he needs me to help him balance. So much of what we do together is this mutually understood, unspoken language. It's why it feels right. Jarek kneels before me and the water parts his hair where it is thinnest from his treatment. I lay my palms on his skull and trace the lines of the scars with my fingertips. Some are old, faded and pink. The newest line – his last, lost hope – remains defiant: raised and purple.

Afterwards, I help Jarek to the bed and he stretches out on his back. I sit down, facing away from him so I don't have to look at the water soaking into the bedspread from his towel.

'You like it here?' Jarek asks.

I hum approval and curl my bare toes into the plush carpet. The room is modern, with clean lines. He knows my taste.

'I've booked in for a few days, this time,' he says. 'I haven't got any more appointments for a while now, and I need some space.'

'But what if you feel ill? You'll be on your own.'

'I thought maybe you could stay, too.'

I curl one knee up on to the bed and twist around to face him. A fantasy bursts on to the stage of my imagination: we order room service; we don't get dressed; we take baths together each morning. The idea is tempting. I feel as though we are locked away from the world in here. If staying in this room would stop anyone from finding us, then maybe it could stop death, too.

'I can't,' I say, shaking my head and letting the wet strands of hair cling to my cheeks. Jarek clambers across the bed on his stomach and smooths them back behind my ears.

'You could,' he says. 'You're just choosing not to.'

Don's shadow has slunk under the door. I tighten the towel around my chest. I just don't want to think about him.

Jarek frowns as if he can read my thoughts. 'Will you stay with him? After I've gone?'

'Jarek, don't.'

While I'm sitting in this room, Don doesn't exist and Jarek isn't dying. Being with him is living in the moment – freely, joyfully. I do not make considerations, plans, judgements. I live and breathe him. And when I leave, our time together is like a daydream. But I must face reality; I know that. I must tell Don that things are over between us, but I'm more of a coward than I ever imagined. It's so much easier not to.

Jarek doesn't push me to answer but lets his towel fall to the floor and climbs awkwardly under the duvet. I arrange the pillows behind him, supporting his left side with an extra cushion. He winces and groans a little as his head bounces against the bedstead.

'Oh, sorry,' I say, kissing his forehead.

'My consultant gave me some new painkillers, but they're not really scratching the surface,' he says, rubbing his temples. 'I'm after oblivion-strength ones.' He chuckles under his breath. 'Do you think yours would do?'

The hint is heavy and yet I'm able to push it away — like I do the jealousy, the guilt, the confusion. Meanwhile, he watches me, his expression unreadable. I think of Sarah's kind face, and her words. *My husband was always in here, wasn't he?*

'How are things with you and your wife, Jarek?' My voice is oddly constricted; as I speak, I realise the question makes me sound as though I'm his Architect again.

Jarek flicks his eyes at me and beckons for me to curl up against his chest. I snuggle into his damp skin and rest my cheek against the hollow beneath his collarbone. I inhale the natural scent that's starting to come back through his pores. He's quiet for several seconds.

'Surely we don't have to talk about her?' He sounds as if he's talking to one of his children.

'I just keep thinking . . .' I can't finish the sentence because there's no way of explaining what goes through my head. Is this really an affair? Does she still love him? What if it's just his illness pushing them apart?

'How long have you known her for?' I ask, eventually. It seems a simple place to start.

'We've been together for eight years, married for five.'

I note that he's using the present tense and it's enough to make me slide my hand from his bare hip.

'Really? So, she must've been . . .' Sarah's soft face appears in my mind as I count backwards, working out how old I think she might have been. Surely not a teenager? As my eyes do their sums on the wall, I notice Jarek looking at me strangely. Of course, I've slipped up. I'm not supposed to know anything about her. But if there was a question, it fades quickly from his face and he kisses me on the tip of my nose. As his lips move on to mine, I'm almost distracted, but there's so much more I need to know. I pull my head back.

'What's she like?' She's womanly; she's beautiful. I know that.

Jarek tuts and closes his eyes, but the smile stays on his face. He knows there is no right answer.

'Is she very different from me?'

'Utterly,' he whispers. Delight sparkles in his eyes as he runs his thumb down my spine. I roll my eyes playfully and the questions finally leave my mind as his lips meet mine.

'Izz?'

I swallow the groan as he bites at my ear. 'Yes?'

'I can't die without you.' He pulls back from me to study my face. He squeezes my hand and I can only stare back, open-mouthed. I've always wondered how this would feel. Four years with Don and we've never discussed it. We never will.

'I'm in love with you. You must know that by now,' he says.

I feel the breath leave my lungs and wonder how I have been cheated out of meeting this man until this point in my life. The connection I feel to him casts the rest of it into the background – a fuzzy backdrop. This is real.

'I know,' I say. The words come out as the lightest of whispers. 'I love you, too.'

'I want you in my Heaven,' he adds, in case I haven't understood his meaning. But of course I have. I understand everything he says before he has even said it.

'And I want you in mine, too, when the time comes.'

'So, you'll send me the official documents to sign?' he asks. I nod and he pulls me back into him. I bury my face in his neck and we hug, tightly.

CHAPTER TWELVE

The following Friday, there's a staff meeting that I want to avoid. I excuse myself on the flimsy basis of an urgent appointment at the neurology labs. I haul myself out of bed a little later than usual, do a yoga session in the living room and make my way to the Francis Crick Institute in St Pancras. Jess has been pressing me to visit for months now, so I'm killing two birds with one stone.

'So, do you want to see Clair's simulations?' she asks me.

I nod, as I try to summon my usual enthusiasm for talking about work. My mind is full of Jarek.

'Are you all right, Isobel?' she says, in her soothing Irish lilt. 'You're in another world today!'

Jess always treats me like an old friend, even though we've only met a handful of times over the years. I'm envious of her openness and her natural warmth.

'Yeah, I'm fine. I'm just, you know, a bit under the weather.' I flap my fingers around my throat region, but I suspect that my acting is unconvincing.

'Well, I can tell that's not the entire truth, but I'll let you off,' she says, winking at me. I notice the dart of her eyes towards my stomach and I realise with a twist of embarrassment that she is wondering whether I'm pregnant. Oh, God. I'm wearing a loose top, so she wouldn't have noticed the beginnings of a bump, anyway. But what if I was? I find myself thinking. I wouldn't know it yet. And if I was pregnant, it would be Jarek's baby. I'd be carrying the baby of a dying man. A man I've fallen for.

Jess leads me across the corridor to the other side of the building. We enter the lab through a wide set of automatic doors and, as they slide open to let us in, my eyes drift to the inscription in the architrave above us. *Nos Sunt Electrica.*

'We are electric,' Jess calls back to me without turning around. She must have heard me pause in the entrance. Perhaps everybody looks at it and stops to work out what it means, like I just did. I find myself smiling as I quicken my pace to catch up with Jess's fast footsteps and the animated bounce of her curls. *We are electric.* The idea that we're all nothing more than a wet computer has always seemed magical to me. To others, it is depressing. To those of an older way of thinking, the people who still grasp on to the idea of a God, it is almost heretical. But to know that everything we are, every thought, emotion, memory, is no more than the arrangement of electrical activity in our brains – with a dash of chemical trickery here and there – never fails to inspire me. Evolution is a wonderful thing. Give me a few billion years, I used to think, and just see what I could do.

Jess stands in the middle of the large, dark room, waiting for me. The only light emanates from the pedestal in the centre of the black tiled floor, from which digital projections shimmer in a column of mist. I feel acutely aware of how far we are underground, inside a sealed chamber of dead peoples' memories. I walk to stand beside Jess and watch as she manipulates the data through the mist. The display hisses in the hush of the room.

'I can't believe I've never been down here.'

'Don't give me that, Izz,' she replies. 'I've invited you enough times!' She speaks without looking away from her projections. Her eyes are narrowed in concentration. She sorts through them, flicking from one to another, before selecting one square of light and enlarging it in front of her by pulling her hands apart.

'You might want to start spending more time here,' she adds. 'It's fireproof, bombproof, the works! Back-up power and life support if you need it, too.'

I look up at the ceiling, trying to imagine what reinforces it. 'I guess it has to be.'

'So, this room is where we find the basic details for each patient,' Jess explains. 'Anyone authorised to enter the Electric Lab can see where Clair's simulations are stored – room twenty-three – but they can't then enter unless . . .'

The mist flashes with a green light and, at the same time, I hear a click. Looking around, I realise that the walls of this circular room are lined with doors, and one of them has just unlocked.

'Unless they are me!' Jess whispers, and rests her hand on my shoulder to guide me in the direction of the unlocked door.

'What kind of biometrics does that system use?' I ask.

'A mixture. Voice recognition, iris recognition, blood-vessel patterns. I think it studies my biochemical fingerprint, too, as I use it. It's pretty advanced.'

Jess pushes open the black door and we move into a more brightly lit room. It's small, though – a few metres square. It is the opposite of the central room we have just left in that nothing is in the middle. Instead, everything is around the edge. A smooth, sloped panel runs at waist height from either side of the door, all around the walls. I fold my arms across my chest, feeling a bit claustrophobic.

'I'll try not to touch anything I shouldn't!' I joke.

'You could lie across it naked, Izz, and it wouldn't do anything! You're dead to this machine.'

It's not a pleasant thought, to be so powerless. I find myself running my fingertips over the featureless black panel in the hope that Jess is wrong, that maybe I can rouse something into life. Nothing happens. I think of the cemetery that my sister and I used to play in when we were kids. We used to run amongst the gravestones, ducking and hiding from each other, screaming with laughter. We were told off several times by mourners, and once by the vicar himself. But we were too young to understand what loss meant. The stones were ancient relics to us, not living memories for the visitors who wandered between them. I don't think we even got as far as realising that dead bodies were buried in the ground beneath our feet.

I become aware that Jess is muttering, either to herself or to the machine. She twirls her mass of brown hair back at the nape of her neck, letting the curls secure themselves to each other in a messy knot. The air smells so clean in here, almost completely without odour. I look around for vents but see none. Jess moves a few paces to the other side of the room and lays her fingers on the sloping surface of the panel. She runs a fingertip in small circles, as if feeling for a hidden texture, and taps twice. A cartridge pops out and unfurls into a small platform, the size of a fingernail.

'That's it,' announces Jess.

'What?'

'The only living part of the whole set-up.'

I peer closer, bending over the tiny platform. It's transparent and empty. 'There's nothing there, Jess.'

'Oh, no, of course not,' says Jess. 'Not yet. But one day – hopefully not any time soon – that'll be where I lay Clair Petersen to rest.'

'That's it?' Suddenly the room seems empty, soulless.

'Mirror neurons don't take up a lot of space, you know.'

Jess has already shown me the biology lab in this building. One of her latest research projects involves growing mirror neurons from a person's stem cells. If they could achieve that, then even someone blown up in a bomb could be put into their Heaven afterwards. Your brain could get smashed to bits and your mirror neurons would be safe and sound in a lab somewhere, ready to be connected to your Heaven. I think of Clair again. She has probably left already. She could be in the middle of the Pacific by now. I hope she's safe. Jess presses the cartridge into a small depression in the wall above the panel. I hear something click and a gentle hum fills the room.

'Look!' Jess says. She is standing back from the panel, near the middle of the room, grinning wildly at the upper half of the wall. I look back at her blankly. 'Ah, I forgot that you don't have the same eye lenses as me.' She retrieves a slim pair of glasses from a small box near the door and hands them to me. 'Here, put these on.'

I slip them on and follow her gaze towards the empty wall. But it isn't empty anymore; its shadows are flashing like a cityscape seen at night, from a distance. It is the most stunning form of augmented reality I have ever seen. Delicate pinpricks of light blink on and off in an indiscernible rhythm. As I look over them again, I see the lights not as office-block windows, but instead as speeded-up supernovae – whole galaxies disappearing from existence, counterpointed by gas clusters focusing into new stars.

'Aren't memories beautiful?' Jess whispers in my ear. I can't see her, because I'm wearing the glasses, but I nod, feeling the same reverence that I can detect in her voice.

'What *is* this?' I ask.

'It's the computer code of a single discrete memory. I can't tell you which one; this machine isn't designed to *show* us anything in a way we'd understand it. Heavens are supposed to be private, after all. This is the best visualisation of the code that we can see.'

'Created from reading the memories that Clair and I isolated together?'

'Yes, exactly. When Clair visited us, we spent hours mapping the memories you'd both discussed. We injected a chemical tag into her brain while she was in the M.R.I. scanner. Then we triggered the memories – the neurons – you requested and mapped the activation patterns into the binary code a computer understands.'

'We are electric,' I murmur. 'And then you overlay that with the Heaven architecture?'

'That's right. Before a client visits us for the last time, we spend a while translating the Architect's demands into the program, building in your side of things – like the intensity of certain memories; the desire for certain ones to be repeated more than others; the creative linking of one discrete snapshot to another so that it's as seamless as possible. We've done all that now. Clair's Heaven is here, all ready to go.'

I can hear from the tone of her voice that Jess is smiling with what I read to be pride and love for what she does. But as I watch the lights sway, I feel a profound melancholy take hold of me. As arresting as the dynamic patterns of lights are, they look minimalistic. A whole life, with all its richness, reduced to that.

'It's mesmerising. I wouldn't want to see more than this, though. No one should have windows into their Heaven – it'd be wrong.'

'I agree,' says Jess. 'But they're working on better visualisations, these days – ones which make it seem like you're watching a virtual-reality film. They're getting quite accurate.'

'Valhalla?' I ask.

'Spot on. I think they're trialling stuff out in India now – they've got quite a big operation out there because the regulators don't watch them as closely.'

'Maya asked me to go and work for them – off the record,' I say, thinking of Maya and our conversation by the Serpentine that evening. 'She told me they needed people to help get inside the Heavens of clients who were suspected of committing crimes – serious ones. I thought she was crazy at the time.'

Jess hums in what I take to be vague agreement. 'They seem unstoppable now.'

We continue to watch the visualisation for a while in silence, side by side. I think of someone else spying on my Heaven – the Heaven I haven't even created yet – and it makes me feel sick.

'Let me show you something else, something new I've just found,' she says, and Clair's lights disappear. I take off my glasses and watch Jess replace the cartridge where she got it from in the panel's surface. She taps again, in a different place this time, and another slim black cartridge appears. She seems to handle this one more carefully as she loads it into the receptacle in the wall.

'One of my clients?'

Jess shakes her head. 'Put your glasses back on.'

I do as she asks and the lights appear again, indistinguishable from Clair's simulation.

'Now, do you see the line of lights at the bottom of your vision?' Jess asks.

There's a chain of blinking lights, shaped into a wave. I only see the pattern after a few seconds, as I see them huddle together and expand, never moving far enough apart to be unrelated.

'What is it?'

'It's the focus for my next grant.' Her voice is animated with excitement. 'We think this is an extra memory. It's *linked* to the one we're seeing, but it's not something that the client and the Architect placed into this Heaven,' she explains, touching my arm before she lifts the glasses off my face. 'It's a ghost memory.'

'How did it get there?'

'I don't know, but most people I've studied so far seem to have them. I think – and I'm hoping to prove – that these are the fragments of very powerful memories – memories so strong that the brain has encoded them twice: once in the usual place – in memory-making neurons – and once again here, in the mirror neurons, in the seat of our consciousness.'

'So, you think these ghost memories slink into people's Heavens?'

'Yes.'

'Even after I've designed everything so carefully, my clients could experience unwelcome recollections?'

'Exactly.'

I feel my mouth fall open. The idea is incendiary. The one thing

I do, the single promise I make my clients is that I will create for them the Heaven they dream of, structured around the specific memories that they want to include. And yet, this innocuous-looking trace could make me an uninformed liar. Jess's words resonate inside my head: *powerful memories*.

'Could they be bad memories?'

Jess glances across at me and her expression says more than words could. I think of all the awful things that someone might not want to see again in their Heaven: pain, abuse, emotional turmoil. My stomach flips as I follow Jess back the way we came in. Her chatter about new staff and expansion plans for the Institute falls like summer rain over me. I can't take in anything else she says.

My eyes squint against the brightness as we emerge from the Electric Lab.

'I've got a break now,' Jess says. 'Do you have time for a coffee?'

I think of the time and it appears in my vision. I don't know why I bother because I don't have any plans anyway. 'Yes, why not?'

We walk out of the maze of rooms that make up the lab and join the walkway that slopes up to the glass-walled entrance hall. It should feel like a greenhouse in here but the tiny holes in the fabric of the building are open, letting the interior breathe fresh air.

'There's a Moroccan café a few doors down, if you fancy that?' Jess asks.

'Sure; sounds great.'

'They do great couscous, if you're hungry,' she adds.

Leaving the paved front garden of the lab, we walk down the street to a narrow red door between the buildings that I didn't notice on the way here. Jess knocks once and grins at me. A lady with bright teeth and gently curving eyebrows peeps out from behind the door. Without uttering a word, she beckons us within – not into a room or reception area, but to an open-air passageway that leads to a small, moss-covered courtyard. A quarter of it catches the sun and three tables covered with blue-and-white checked cloths sit empty, waiting for us. The lady gestures in their direction.

'Mint tea?' she asks us.

'Yes, please,' I say, and Jess nods her assent as we sit down at one of the small square tables. The air is warm and chaffinches titter around the feeding table in the centre of the courtyard. The warm autumn breeze flickers through the courtyard and I raise my eyes to the sky, always scouting, thinking of the drill several weeks earlier.

'So, how's Caleb these days?' she asks me. Her voice is cool, collected, but the look in her eyes betrays her emotions. I know what happened between them; she told me once. I remember her dropping it into a conversation at the end of a meeting at the clinic, out of the blue, as if she had to get it off her chest. *Well, the guy's a cad, but he* is *handsome*, I'd said. She'd laughed, as if I'd offered her forgiveness for having an affair with a married man. But I hadn't cared, in truth. If it was redemption she wanted, she should have asked someone else.

'He's . . .' I shrug.

'He's just Caleb?'

'Yeah, just the same old Cal,' I say, smiling. I think I know what she's asking me. She's asking me if he's still married. But for some reason I don't feel generous enough to tell her. Maybe because it's not what I think she'd like to hear. Maybe because I'm feeling short on kindness today, as if any hint of positive emotion has to be kept for myself.

The lady returns with a simple metal teapot in one hand and glass cups and saucers in the other. She lays them out neatly between us. As she leans over me to pour the tea, I smell a cheering blend of fresh mint and sugar.

'The clinic must be going well. We're getting more business from you than ever.' Jess picks up the bowl of syrup and adds some to her drink. As I watch it drizzle from the spoon, I think of the old days when you could still buy honey. When I was a little girl, my mother gave me the local stuff to help with my hay fever. I'd open the kitchen cupboard and ease off the lid, tipping it into my mouth straight from the jar. Jess pops the spoon in her mouth to suck off the last of the syrup. I can't stand it myself, all those chemicals.

'Yeah, I've been flat out. I probably need a holiday, but, y'know . . .'

'You don't take holidays.'

'That's simply not true.' I sip on my tea and look over the rim at Jess. I wink. When she smiles, her face is almost perfectly round, without even a hint of cheekbones. The soft symmetry of it makes her appear younger than she is. 'I think Caleb sees the risk of war as a rather convenient boost for the business.'

'That sounds like the man I know,' she says, placing the spoon back on the saucer. 'He hit me on two occasions – did I ever tell you that?' Another bombshell, casually slipped into conversation.

'Who? Cal?' I don't know why I ask this and sound so taken aback, because, as the thought sinks in, I realise that I'm not surprised at all. I've always known he was a bully. He hates

– absolutely hates – that he can't control me. And he despises me for not finding him attractive. I think of the verbal assault the other day in his office. He would have hit me if he thought he could get away with it.

'Wow, Jess. I don't know what to say.' I worry that my voice is loaded with pity. 'I'm so sorry. I'd like to say I'm surprised, but . . .'

'Yeah.' And that's it. 'I met Jarek again on Monday,' she continues. Her piercing grey eyes are on me, watching for my reaction.

'Oh, of course. I remember him saying he had another appointment lined up with you.' I can feel the blood rising in my cheeks, and I'm thankful that, after a long, hot summer, my skin is dark enough to hide it. My mother would never have let me get so tanned. I can hear her tutting in my mind.

'But he's Harry's client now.'

I can sense the hidden question behind the statement, but I can't think how to answer it. 'Yeah.'

Jess nods, her bottom lip upturned.

'How was he?' I dare to ask her.

'Not so good, if I'm honest,' Jess says. 'It's tragic. He seems nice.'

'Yes, he is.' I level my gaze at her, centring myself on the blunt line of her fringe, where the hairs have been tamed to align just above her brows.

'But his poor wife and kids.'

I lower my eyes to the table. Jess doesn't continue speaking and, when I look up, I realise she is looking at me, waiting for me to acknowledge her true meaning. She isn't talking about the fact that he is dying. She is talking about the fact that he doesn't love his wife anymore and he loves me instead. I shut my eyes for a few seconds. Perhaps it's written all over my face, seeping out through the gaps in my eyelashes. I'm irritated and I refuse to justify her with a response.

'I've been there, Isobel.' She reaches for my hand across the table. Her skin is warm, roughened by lab work. She blinks in the breeze that gusts between us and squints as the sunlight above is again released from behind a cloud. 'And it's no fun for anybody.'

'Well, it hardly matters now, does it?' My voice is barely a whisper. My words are sharp, angry. I feel Jess rest her hand upon mine, but my skin feels cooler rather than warmer as a result. I focus on that instead of the hot tears that are starting to coat my eyes.

'Things have changed, Isobel. You of all people should know that. We don't leave everything behind us when we die anymore. We take others with us.'

I'm not entirely sure what she means. If it's a warning, then it has come far too late, because I realise, with a nausea that folds me in half, that my Heaven will be nothing without him.

CHAPTER THIRTEEN

Jess's words linger in my mind for the rest of the day. I don't have any meetings and so I head straight home. I'm on the chaise longue, dozing in and out of a troubled sleep, when the buzzer to my apartment rings. The video link to the apartment's camera appears in my vision and, for a moment, I wonder if I'm still dreaming. 'Yes,' I murmur, to allow him in. I stumble to the door, arranging my hair as I go. How can I let him in here? Into our apartment? I'm still wondering as I open the door and watch him turn the corner of the stairs. We say nothing. He walks straight towards me – as straight as he can, given his worsening stagger – and wraps me in his arms. Another man might have kissed me first, but this is more intimate somehow. His emotions are stripped as he grips me to his body.

'I had to see you,' he whispers in my ear. He presses his lips against my forehead and, in an instant, nothing else matters. I pull him inside the apartment, pushing the warnings to the back of my mind.

It's still afternoon when I wake up, blinking my eyes. We're tangled together on the rug and sunlight floods the lounge. Jarek is lying with his back to me, and I raise myself on to one elbow and lean over to look at his face. He is so still that I'm surprised to find him wide awake. His eyes are staring at the wall and the sunbeams that slip over his head catch the edge of his eyelashes, making them glow amber. At first I think he's ignoring me and then I realise that it's his left eye I'm looking down at – the one affected by the tumour; the one which is losing its vision. I run my hand over his bare shoulder, feeling the heat of his skin, and he grins, rolling on to his back to look up at me.

'I'm sorry.' His words are punctuated by the trail of kisses he places on my neck. 'I couldn't resist.'

'There's no need to be sorry.' I lean down and kiss him in the hollow of his cheek. 'But how did you know where I live?'

Jarek smiles and rubs his nose against mine. 'You told me the building ages ago. I just tried every number until I got to yours. Hope I haven't annoyed your neighbours too much!'

I roll my eyes and grin back at him. Jarek flicks his eyes to the right, and I realise he is staring not at the wall, but at a pair of Don's shoes, tucked under the side of the sofa. I check the time. It's later than I thought. Don will be home in the next couple of hours. My stomach turns with nervousness – a reminder that I do, against appearances, care what other people think of me.

'He might be back soon,' I say. Mentioning Don aloud lets the guilt claw its way back beneath my skin. I sit up and hold my hand to my neck. 'I don't know how any of this happened,' I whisper.

I think of Jess and her disapproval, of Don and Sarah and their blissful ignorance. It sharpens my own self-loathing. I'm sitting on the floor of my apartment, for crying out loud, on a dust-filled rug. I suddenly feel quite exposed and reach out for my tunic, pulling it across my chest.

'Don't do that.' His voice is uncharacteristically pleading. He pulls the fabric down so that it pools at the top of my thighs. He runs one hand over my breast, trailing a line down to my belly button. His face is serious and it's as if I can see what he is thinking. He is a dying man, looking at a naked woman for perhaps the last time. I glance down at the boyishness of my body, and wish I had more to offer him. I look up and he clenches his jaw as he brings his eyes to meet mine.

'I'm in so much pain, Izz. I need it to be over now.'

I lean down and bury my face in his neck. 'You can't give up,' I whisper.

He pulls away and clasps his hands around my upper arms, holding me in front of him. 'I'm not giving up, Izz. I have a Heaven to go to.'

I feel my face screw up against the tears that threaten to drown me and, in this moment, I hate what I do. My fingers trace the outline of the angel above my ankle bone and I watch as Jarek's gaze falls upon it.

'But it's not real, Jarek! At best, it's a convincing illusion.'

'No, it's much more than that. What you do is amazing.'

'Is it?' My shoulders shake and I realise I'm crying. I expect him to console me but instead he watches me until I start to calm down. I sniff and wipe my eyes. I hope my mascara hasn't run. Vanity strikes us at the strangest moments.

'It may not be perfect, Izz,' he says, stroking my cheek, 'but it's the best I've got. *You're* the best I've got.'

I pull my knees to my chest and rest my chin on them, wrapping my hands around my feet. The nail of my big toe is chipped and I fight the urge to get up and grab the file from the bathroom.

'I'm sick of the pain,' he continues. 'It's constant now, the last few weeks. I've asked my consultant for help, but there's nothing else he can do. There's nothing else he can give me. It seems so ridiculous that we live in a society that can create Heavens but can't let people die.'

He's right. I'm still amazed that we haven't yet made assisted suicide legal. The bill is back in Parliament now, and this time it might go through. I've campaigned furiously for it in the past, but in the last couple of years I'd given up hope of it ever happening.

I realise that Jarek is seeking out my gaze, asking me something with his eyes. I don't want to process it, and I avoid looking at him, staring at my bare feet against the floor. I zero in on the contrast between the ebony wood and the pale brown of my nails.

'I'm going to die, Izz. I've come to terms with that, believe me. It's just a matter of how soon and how unpleasantly. I want to be at home; not at hospital, not in a hospice.'

I visualise the top shelf of the bathroom cabinet. The canister is still there, I imagine, tucked behind the multivitamins – unlabelled, full. I got hold of them years ago. Just in case, I told myself. Just in case something happened one day and I needed the end to come urgently. I should have given them to my mother weeks before she finally died.

It's the tight desperation behind Jarek's eyes that reminds me. It was our second meeting, I realise, when he first asked me for painkillers. *Not here*, I told him. *Just at home, for personal use.* He mentioned them again one time at the hotel. He knows I have them. I stare into his eyes, unwilling to believe what he wants me to do.

'You know what I'm asking you?'

He is dying and he wants me to help it happen on his own terms. I glance again at the time, because some sentimental part of me – the part that takes old print photographs and arranges them into albums; the part that buys useless trinkets just because they remind me of my childhood – wants to know how long it will take me to come to terms with this.

By the time I've made my decision, six minutes have passed. The human mind is quick to adapt.

When Don gets home in the middle of the night, I'm still in a daze. Somehow, that makes it easier to tell him that I don't love him anymore, that I'm so sorry but I think things are over between us. I haven't even showered. I imagine that he can detect the scent of another man on me, but I struggle to find the energy to care. My behaviour is repellent, I know, but I feel, for the first time in my life, that I have no control over it. And, in a strange way, that's empowering.

Don sits for a while next to me on the sofa, holding my hand, and for several minutes, I feel as if he is a client of mine. Then he unclasps his grip and gives my hand back to me, pressing it flat over my knee. He stares down at his palms, as if he is registering the idea that it's the last time he will touch me. Quietly, he tells me that he understands, and I have never been so grateful to have him in my life. Then he gets up and goes into the kitchen. And I feel a sorry surge of love for him that isn't quite pity.

CHAPTER FOURTEEN

Sleep comes fitfully. The minute I begin to drift off, I hear the planes again. On Saturday morning, I call my grandmother at the nursing home to check she doesn't mind me staying in her old flat for a while. She begins to launch an interrogation but quickly weakens. 'Of course, beti.'

Don tells me he'll move out for a few days so I can pack up my things. Before he goes, I tell him about the noises I hear at night and he glares at me with the closest approximation of contempt I've seen him muster.

'I could have kept you safe,' he says before he storms out of the flat.

As I fold my life into boxes, I think of Jarek. I think of him in my Heaven and I try to create memories that aren't there. I try to form images and sensations of us in all the places I've loved, at all the times in my life when I would have wanted him there. I try to imagine him at my mother's bedside, his arm around my shoulders. I picture him at my university prom, walking into the cloakroom at the exact moment my ex-boyfriend tried to put his hand up my skirt. Jarek would have punched him; he would have hit him squarely in the jaw. I try to imagine him younger: stronger, fuller in the face and with more tan to his skin, more freckles across his cheeks. I try but I don't succeed. My usual inventiveness is absent – stifled, perhaps, by fear. The Jarek that will be in my Heaven will be the only version of him I've ever known. A handful of stolen moments with a dying man; a man past his peak of youth and jaded by life, but still the most magnificent person I've ever met.

Sunday seems to pass me by. I spend it packing, hoping for another surprise visit, and listening out for drones and intruders.

I somehow get through Monday morning at work. Lela leaves me alone and I duck out of a further meeting with Maya and Caleb about the single opt-in clause. Not so long ago, this was my primary concern, but now it feels intangible, out of reach. Not worrying about it is freeing. It's like hanging a heavy winter coat back in the wardrobe on the first day of spring.

Just after lunchtime, there's a knock on the door of my office and Lela walks in without waiting for me to answer. Her eyes flit about and she bites her lip. We haven't had a proper conversation since she pulled me into her office after the drill. I glance up as she enters and then go back to rearranging the digital notes scattered across the surface of my desk. In the edge of my vision, I see her sit down on the sofa.

'Isobel, will you come and sit with me?' There's something about the words and the way she says them that gets my attention. It's compelling, hypnotic, yet as I stand and walk towards her, I'm thinking, No, no, no. She pats the fabric next to her, just as I do when I meet my clients. Just as I did when I first met Jarek. I sit down and fold my hands on my lap.

'Izzy, I'm so sorry.' She presses her lips together and places her hand between my shoulder blades. Her eyes are glassy, like the surface of a half-frozen lake. She's always been soft. 'Jarek passed away in the early hours of Saturday morning.'

My vision goes a little funny and I realise I'm nodding, and then I notice my cheeks feel sore and it's because I've pulled my face into a weird kind of exaggerated smile that's like a fence against the agony in my chest.

'I'm sorry it's taken time to tell you. Harry felt awkward. In the end, he thought it would be better coming from me.' She is looking at me carefully.

'Thank you,' I say, and my voice wobbles more than I expected it to. 'I knew that it would be soon, just not this soon.'

'We received the alert from his tracking chip and his sister called us shortly afterwards. He was found collapsed outside the hospital, but there was nothing more they could do. It was his time, Izzy.'

'His sister?' I ask, checking I've heard her correctly amid the shock. I think of the day I bumped into him at the burial ground. He was visiting her grave, wasn't he? The sister killed in a traffic accident as a teenager? The blunt force of the trauma starts to lead me off down these strange, spiralling pathways of questions before Lela's voice brings me back to the present.

'Harry said he'll send you over the forms for the double opt-in.'

She rubs her hand against my back. I nod. He must have had another sister.

'You knew he wanted you to be in his Heaven?' she asks.

I nod again, staring down at my hands, watching my fingers twitch together. I think of the digital document that Jarek signed before he left my apartment. It was ceremonial, this exchange of intent to be in each other's afterlives for eternity. The greatest of commitments made so easily – so much more powerful than a marriage would have been. Seemingly much more than his marriage was.

I look into Lela's face and I see something I interpret as guilt. Lela is driven by love. She's a romantic, an idealist. What she thought she saw between us was lust, but she was wrong. She knows that now. Lela is a good person. The best. She knows the truth when she sees it.

'He might be gone, but there's always more love, Isobel.'

Her words drift over me. I hear her sniffle back her tears, and am aware of the movement of her arm as she wipes at her eyes. She leans in to hug me. It's awkward because I must feel like a rock to her. Then she stands up and walks to the door. I don't watch her leave.

I wait until the door clicks shut and then I stand up and walk over to it, sliding the lock across and pressing my back against the wood. And then I don't care who hears me. A strangled series of sobs breaks free from my mouth as I slide down the door on to the floor. My mind turns to the memory of kissing him goodbye in the doorway of my flat on Friday afternoon. As much as I loved the sensation of him, I hated my lack of control. He was the one who had to pull away from me as I pressed the tablets into his hand. But I gave him what he wanted, I remind myself: a peaceful, pain-free death. I didn't think he would do it straight away. I thought – I convinced myself – that I would see him again. It was the only way to stay sane these past few days.

I curl up on the floor and run the nail of my index finger into the thin pile of the carpet. I feel my lips slump against the fibres.

I close my eyes and remember lying like this against the shrunken body of my mother.

The nurses let me lie like that for two hours before rousing me. There were no flowers at her bedside in those last weeks, apart from a tiny, potted patio rose. *If you love a flower, don't pick it up*, was one of my mother's favourite proverbs – the words of an Indian guru I've forgotten the name of. She never once bought cut flowers. The pot plant was covered with tiny buds, I remember. I thought they would open before she died but they waited until a week later, when I finally took it outside and placed it on the balcony. They were waiting for the sun, those tiny yellow petals. They weren't concerned with death.

I lie on the carpet against my door for longer than I should, reminding myself that love is not about possession but about appreciation – knowledge that now feels like the greatest gift my mother ever gave me.

CHAPTER FIFTEEN

Brooke is less gentle on my second, much overdue visit. She asks me what's taken so long and I just tell her that I've been busy. The needle dives into my flesh, gouging valleys in my calf. I watch her face this time. I like the way she sticks her tongue out, running the silver piercing back and forth over her top lip. In a strange way, it's hypnotising.

'It stings more because I'm shading the feathers in,' Brooke says, reading my thoughts. 'Before, I was using one needle. Today, I'm using three.'

'Thanks. That makes me feel *so* much better.'

Although I'm being sarcastic, the discomfort is a kind of relief. At first, I felt so numb that the packing and moving was enough to calm me. I managed to take comfort in slotting my belongings neatly back into the same boxes I used when I moved in with Don. A weak gratitude fills me that I live so frugally, at times like this. One trip across London in an on-demand autovan and it was done. I spent yesterday evening cleaning my grandmother's flat. Not washing away dirt and the detritus of life – the last tenants left months ago – but scrubbing at the stench of absence and neglect.

That night, beneath the fresh but damp bed sheets, loneliness weighed me down.

The depth of my sleep surprised me, but the pain must have thickened overnight because I awoke in anguish. I knew where to come and I was right. Finally, it has an outlet. It seeps through my skin and joins the tattoo needle, mixing with the ink to mark me. My angel had no identity when I chose it. Now, regardless of whether I wanted it to, it has taken on a personality – *his* personality. It was faceless, but I now know that I will always see him in its outline.

The needle changes tempo and I swallow a squeal. I see Brooke grin out of the corner of my eye. Sadistic bitch. The discomfort is stirring up the anger that buzzes over the surface of my skin. I squeeze my hands into fists, crushing my thumbs. I hope Jarek didn't feel any pain towards the end. He wouldn't have done if he took the pills I gave him. He would have sunk into a warm, soothing haze. He would have even felt high. I feel bad for thinking it, but I hope he thought of me as he slipped away. I know that he must have thought of his children. He would have thought about the many wonderful things that had filled his life – things I know nothing about. I am filled with a sudden bitterness.

Funerals don't interest me. They're for the dead, not for the living. But I wonder whether his body will be cremated. If so, who will have his ashes, and where will they spread them? I think I would know where to take them – to the parkland he used to play in as a child, overlooking the fields. But it doesn't matter now. Sentimentality is a distraction from the truth. The main thing is that Jarek's emotions, sensations and memories are bundled up together in Jess's lab.

I turn my thoughts back to the mirror neurons. I imagine Jess transferring the cluster of cells on to the plate and sliding the cartridge back into its concealed slot, never to be disturbed again in that high-security, lead-lined lab, so far beneath our feet. By now, his mirror neurons – surgically extracted from his brain – would have granted his memories consciousness: the neurons that fired as he watched me reach out to touch him, the neurons that fired as he returned the gesture.

It's a spellbinding shift in perspective that these tiny cells can achieve, driving an innate kind of virtual reality. They allow us to see ourselves in other people, in other animals, even. That magic is what makes us human. These neurons, these magical threads of life that we once thought only managed our feelings of empathy and our understanding of others, are the key to it all. A discovery made by a long-dead scientist while I was just a child. A discovery that shaped the rest of my life, my career. A discovery that there was, beyond doubt, no soul to speak of, nothing besides the electrical activity in our brains, creating a sense of self, a consciousness, for each of us. Jarek would be alive again in his Heaven. In the Heaven I created for him.

Brooke pushes a tissue into my hand and I realise there are tears rolling from my eyes on to the bed beneath me. I feel the wetness pooling in my ears and shake my head in shame. I hate crying in front of other people.

'I'm sorry,' I say. 'It's not the pain.'

'No, I know,' she says, without looking at me. Her mouth is pulled into a tight line. I was expecting a jibe, but I am starting to realise that other people can see into me at the moment, able to see and feel exactly what I'm up against. Even Don dealt with me quite gently, given the circumstances.

'My kid brother has just flown out to the Pacific,' Brooke says. 'It's his first deployment.'

'I'm sure he'll be fine. Our troops know what they're doing.' I find that I don't even think about my words before I say them, because that's what we're told, day in and day out. Thoughtless reassurance is rife.

'You reckon? The first day he got there, he told me it was complete chaos.'

I don't need to know this, I think. Perhaps I'm too used to Don's calming confidence. Perhaps he was hiding much more from me than I ever imagined. I catch Brooke's eyes and I think she senses my misgivings.

I hear a click over the whine of the needle and then there is pain-free silence. Brooke stands back and then crouches down. She tilts her head one way and then the other as she studies her handiwork. She makes a cluck of appreciation and then turns away to sterilise her equipment at the sink.

'Have a look!' she calls. 'It's finished.'

I let her wrap my ankle and calf in a fresh film before I've looked at it. Her words of guidance on aftercare sink into the background as I realise that at least Jarek won't see this war, and at least I have no children that will have to try to live through it and face its aftermath, whatever that might be. And I think, not for the first time, that I ought to get around to finishing my own Heaven sometime soon.

As I stride down the street, I let the news headlines flash across my vision. The persistent clamour of thoughts and demands in my head fades to a dull ache. There's something meditative about the cool autumn air and the buzz of mid-morning activity, and I find myself walking without direction, not raising my eyes from my feet. This kind of peace is rare for me – and unexpected, given the circumstances.

I walk until I'm gazing up at the curving roof of the Francis Crick Institute from Brill Place. It seems like weeks rather than days since I was last here to meet Jess. The small courtyard at the back of the Institute is empty and I sit down on one of the benches beneath the lime trees, buttoning up my coat and drawing my bag on to my lap.

He's in there, somewhere. I drop my eyes to the grass that borders the edge of the building. Down there, beneath the ground. Deep in the foundations, where he's safe. I stare into the green and feel the mindlessness overtake me again as I readjust to the new surroundings, my brainwaves dampening to a soothing hum.

'Morning, Isobel,' says a voice behind me, and I swivel around in surprise to see a man I don't recognise standing behind me, one hand resting on the back of the bench. I cast a cursory gaze around the courtyard and note that we are on our own. I check the zip is closed on my bag and feel my toes clench inside my shoes. The tattoo stings afresh.

'May I join you?' the man asks.

'It's not my bench.' I look up at the windows of the Institute, seeking the reassurance of onlookers.

I hear him sigh under his breath as he moves to sit down. Like me, he's quite slim. He probably only stands a little taller than I do. And I bet he's no fighter. He nests his delicate fingers together in his lap. The nails are neatly clipped and the beds are a soft pink against the black of his skin. I glance at his face; he's tight-lipped, looking down at the ground. I can picture, now, Jarek's almost permanent smile. I think of how my sarcasm always made him laugh and am overcome by an even stronger sense of needing to be alone.

'I'm sorry for your loss, Isobel.' He leans forward to rest his elbows on his knees, flicking his eyes in my direction, as if he is shy. I feel my heart start to pump faster. I scan his body for clues but there's little to give anything away. He's wearing a thin, finely knitted black sweater that's pulled back from his wrists. His arms are stronger than I first assumed, despite his stature. I can see the interweaving contours of muscles. The trousers he's wearing look remarkably like a pair of my own: loosely tailored with an almost invisible grey check. No jewellery. And I'm quite certain I've never met him before. But what about in the bar, with Lela, perhaps, that Friday after work? I'd had a few drinks. That was the night I admitted to myself that I'd fallen for Jarek. And now he is gone.

I look again at the man's face for the slightest hint of recognition, but find nothing.

'Do I know you?' I ask, coolly.

'D.C.I. Lyden,' he says, in a voice that sounds as though it should be accompanied by a soft smile, even though his lips return to being pursed. At the same time, he pulls out a slim wallet from his pocket and flicks it open. A fancy emblem shines on one side and, on the other, a photo stares sternly at me from beneath the blue words *Metropolitan Police*. It's unusual to see something printed on card and a childish impulse in me wants to reach out and touch it.

In what seems like an afterthought, he stretches out his hand towards me and I take it. He shakes my hand twice, firmly enough that he doesn't feel the tremors spreading through my fingers. 'Daniel,' he says, with the passing hint of a smile.

'How do you know my name?' I ask, narrowing my eyes. My initial thought was that he was younger than me, but the lines beneath his eyes and the shades of darkness that lie within them tell of several more years in this world. He still looks too young to be a detective chief inspector.

'It's my job to know your name.'

My heart stumbles over its beats. I think of the pills I gave Jarek. The pills that we told ourselves were to ease his final hours, but, in truth, would have brought the end much sooner than would have otherwise been expected. This man is here to arrest me. I fight the urge to fold my arms in upon myself, and place my hands over my thighs, rearranging the sharp creases of my trousers so that they run perfectly over the centre of each knee.

'How did you know where to find me?' I ask, trying to hold my voice steady but realising, too late, that it is spiked with a challenging note.

'It's my job to find people.'

'Ah, well, now we're really getting somewhere.'

'Lela and Caleb said I might find you here.'

I stand up and pull the strap of my bag over my shoulder. The adrenalin has kicked in. 'Look, it's been lovely chatting, but I've got to—'

'No, Isobel, you need to sit down,' he says, and I feel like I see a flicker of genuine concern in his eyes before his gaze falls again to the paving slabs beneath our feet. He pats the bench next to him and I feel a strange sense of role reversal. I wonder if he works with Don, if he has been hurt, or worse. But, no, telling me that he's sorry for my loss means that he must be here to talk about Jarek. I perch with resentment on the edge of the bench, feeling the adrenalin rise.

'Jarek's wife was found dead by her mother on Friday night.' As he finishes the sentence, his eyes meet mine for the first time. They are like searchlights through a dark night, fixing upon their target.

'What?' The air needed to form the word barely leaves my throat and my voice tangles somewhere between an exclamation and a whisper. I feel my mouth fall apart and my tongue pull back from my teeth. The back of my throat closes. I see her smooth, round face, and her bright eyes, remembering how she smiled at me in the flower shop. Time slows down as my brain struggles to think through the implications of what this man is saying.

'You weren't aware of her death?' he asks. He doesn't blink and the golden brown of his irises remains full as his eyelids pull closer together. I can feel him trying to read me. He's good at it because, suddenly, I feel naked. I think back to Helena on the swing, her round little face veiled with bewilderment as she tried to work out why her daddy was leaving her. And now she and her younger sister had lost their mother, too. Both under six years old and orphaned. My heart sharpens its beat with sadness for them.

'Of course not. I haven't seen Jarek since . . .' I trail off because I remember that he wasn't mine, that we were doing something wrong. Jarek's words ring in my ears: *My wife thinks it's the tumour's fault that our relationship is breaking down.*

'That was my next question. Since when?' he asks.

I pull myself upright and twist my upper body towards him. My voice shakes. 'Did she kill herself?'

He looks at me for what feels like a long while before replying. 'No, we don't think so. We believe she was murdered.'

I press my hand tightly over my mouth and stare at my shoes, letting the blood rush to my face. I again think of her flushed cheeks, so full of life, of the little girls, and then some self-protective mechanism tries to push the thoughts away as quickly as they came. A question appears and I find myself asking it before I've thought of the right words or decided whether I want the answer: 'How . . . ?'

I glance at him and then drop my eyes to my lap. I can tell that he's watching my face and I know from the pause that he is sighing, but I can hardly hear the long, soft exhalation.

'Whoever killed her had access to the family house. The attack happened in the kitchen, we think in the early evening. The primary cause of death was asphyxiation.'

I can't help but stare at him then. I feel my eyes widening against my better judgement. A few silent seconds sink through me.

'After Sarah was found, the police put an immediate call out to locate Jarek,' he adds, as if reviewing the crime-scene report aloud. 'He was found collapsed outside the Wellington Hospital, just over a mile away.'

I nod. I already knew that. I turn my thoughts back towards Sarah. 'Would it have been over quickly?' I ask, biting my lip. He looks away, across the courtyard, and I sense that he isn't going to say any more.

Those little girls . . .

'Isobel.' His voice quietly demands my attention. 'Isobel, Sarah was murdered on Friday evening. We can't be sure of where

Jarek was at the time of the murder. When did you last see Mr Woods?'

I feel the weight of the detective's attention on me. It's unyielding now, pushing my shoulders down like extra gravity. He shifts along the bench so that he is closer to me and drops his face so that I can see him on the edge of my vision.

'Earlier that afternoon,' I whisper. 'At my apartment.'

'At what time?'

'I don't know. It was a few hours, mid-afternoon. I'd finished work early. It was still light.'

'What did you do afterwards? Did you go anywhere?'

'No, nothing. I just stayed at home.'

'Alone?'

'Yes, alone.' I pause. 'My boyfriend got home at midnight, maybe one o'clock.'

I struggle to lift my head, but I do, at last. As the shock starts to settle down, I begin to think that, if he asks me any more questions, I should probably ask to see a lawyer and make sure the conversation is being officially recorded. I am desperate to be back in the safety of my office. I want to be the one offering reassurance. I hate feeling so exposed.

'Why are you here?' I ask.

He opens his mouth once and then closes it again, pressing his lips together. I ask myself why he's hesitating. 'Jarek is a suspect,' he says, eventually.

I stand up from the bench and fold my arms, staring down at him. 'You're being ridiculous!' I try to check my anger as it rumbles up from my stomach. 'Jarek? A murderer? Don't be stupid.'

'Most homicides are carried out by family members, and we know the killer had access to the house.' His voice is measured; he must have used these words so many times before. 'We can't account for where he was at the time of murder, but we know he was nearby.'

'Is it possible that someone could have broken in? Stolen a key?' I can feel a ferocity building in me, and the hairs on my arms rising despite the warmth in the air.

The detective shakes his head. 'There's no evidence for that, Isobel.'

'He adored those little girls. It *destroyed* him that he wasn't going to be there for them. There's no way he would've taken their mother from them as well.'

'Perhaps he didn't do it, Isobel, but if so, we need to find a way of counting him out.'

'He's fucking dead.' Tears spring to my eyes, hot and moist. I clench my jaw to hold them back.

'With all due respect, he wasn't dead last Friday.'

'I don't have to stand here and listen to this.' My body turns even before I've finished speaking, the last words lost to the air between us and the Institute.

'No, you don't,' he says, his voice as soft and level as when he first arrived in the courtyard. There's no sense of urgency, no fear that he will lose the battle. 'But if you loved him, if you love him, you're the only person who can prove him innocent.'

I'm already several steps away but I turn back to face him. 'What do you mean?'

'You know as well as I do, Isobel. Convicted murderers don't get Heavens.' He shrugs, spreading his palms to the sky as if he feels bad about it. 'At least, my whole unit spends its time trying to ensure that's the case.'

I tuck my fingers into my collar and feel the cool of my nails against the skin of my neck. He's right, of course. Beyond all reasonable doubt and they'd switch Jarek's Heaven off in a heartbeat. 'But why do you need me? I wasn't with him on Friday night. I wish I was, but I wasn't. I'm no alibi.'

'I know.' He pauses to let the power of his words sink in.

I frown at him. 'So, what is it you think I can do?' I let the irritation mesh through my words.

'We want to look back at what happened, to find a window into that night, in their house.'

'This is ludicrous; Jarek would never—'

'Sarah had started making a Heaven, but she hadn't finished it. She wasn't in a rush because she wasn't expecting to die any time soon. But Jarek *does* have one – one that *you* helped to make. And if he did something, perhaps something incredibly violent, then it's the kind of powerful memory that could be hidden in there somewhere.'

'I'm sorry – what?' I frown, thinking of Jess's whispered words to me in the Electric Lab, just a few days ago. I see the excitement in her eyes as her finger traced the pale, undulating lights at the bottom of the display. *It's a ghost memory.*

'The only memories in his Heaven are the ones I put there. Maybe a few by my colleague, Harry. He didn't mention any desire to murder his own wife to me, Inspector Lyden.'

'Then perhaps Dr Sorbonne hasn't shared her recent findings with you?' he asks, inclining his head towards the Institute. I can tell he already knows the answer. 'She thinks a memory as powerful as murder could creep into someone's Heaven. It makes a lot of sense, when you think about it.'

'Encoded twice, I know,' I mutter, running my thumbnail over my bottom teeth. Bad memories.

'Encoded twice,' he agrees, nodding his head and bringing his fingertips together to form a bridge. 'Once in the normal neurons, once in the mirror neurons.'

'And you've spoken to Jess about Sarah's death because . . . ?' I'm stunned. I didn't get the impression that she'd shared her theory with anyone else outside the lab.

'We're starting to work with Heaven neurologists and we're building better relationships with firms like your own, here and overseas. Caleb and I have been in touch for a while now. My colleagues are working on tighter regulations to ensure convicts don't get Heavens – and, increasingly, my role involves revoking them from people who shouldn't have got them in the first place.'

'You rip down Heavens?' I feel fear pulse in my chest for Jarek; his safe world is suddenly rendered fragile.

'Very few so far, but when necessary, yes.' The tip of his tongue plays at the edge of his lip. 'The exploration of ghost memories is a new path for us, however. And that's why I'm here.'

I stare back at him, feeling the air rush over my lips as I breathe rapidly, heavily. He's toying with me, waiting for my mind to catch up with his.

'We can't work out what these traces are saying from the outside.' His words echo my thoughts.

'Wait.' I hear disbelief bouncing through my voice like laughter, tricking me into smiling. 'You want me to put myself on the line and go into his Heaven somehow? Raid and ransack the delicate assembly of neurons and memories without any kind of warrant?'

'You may know that there are new visualisation techniques in development. They think that it's now possible to immerse a living person into another's Heaven. You'd go in, experience it, see what happens. I know the circumstances are unfortunate, but this is an opportunity, Isobel.'

'No – no, it's not. With respect, you simply can't do that; it's not right to force your way into someone's Heaven.'

'I've come to you, Isobel, because this is a unique situation. You feature in Jarek's Heaven, but you also happen to be an Architect. So ethically investigating ghost memories could be possible for the first time.' He clasps his hands together, still making no motion to move from his position on the bench.

'You're kidding me, right?' I try to laugh it off, but my mind is racing. No. There must be another way. There are the simulations I use for my clients, but they are too tightly programmed, too limited. Why couldn't Jess translate these ghost traces back from the digital data into thought? There must be some way she can do it.

'I'll be blunt. We haven't tried to do this before. As far as I know, no one has. We would be setting a precedent and, quite frankly, there's no one else we can ask to take the risk.'

'Apply through the correct protocol and I will have to tell you what is featured in the architecture of his Heaven!' I shout, knowing what I'm saying is immaterial.

As I stride away, squeezing my hands into a ball at my chest, it strikes me that I get scared too easily. I walked out of my office and away from Jarek that first afternoon he kissed me. I turn my back on things that disturb me. I walk away from arguments with the last word, but they remain unresolved.

I hear Daniel's steady footsteps following me, crunching over the gravel. I reach the gate that leads out to the street and his hand closes around the metal bars at the same time mine does. I feel his hand on my shoulder as he twists me around to face him. He does it without force, but I feel corralled.

'We thought you might want to do it.'

'Well, I'm sorry to disappoint you.'

'I can't make you do this, Isobel. But don't you want to know what happened to Sarah?'

'I don't need to know *anything*. Jarek did not murder his wife.'

His face is close to me now. We are even more similar in height than I thought. He stares at me but says nothing, trying to capitalise on the silence. It feels heavy with things he wants to say and can't.

'Wait a minute.' I lift my hand from the railing and point towards him. 'Is this in any way linked to the Valhalla thing?' I rest one finger over my lips, curling the rest under my chin as I lean back against the gate. 'Not so long ago, Maya Denton asked me if I'd be willing to help the F.B.I. force their way into the Heavens of suspected criminals. Then I hear they're working on advanced visualisations in some out-of-the-way lab . . . and now this?' I shake my head, a grin of disbelief on my face. 'It seems an awful coincidence.'

Daniel licks his lips and nods. 'I'm a detective, not an employee of Valhalla. But we've been working closely with them for a while now, and the technology to do it is closer than is widely known, Isobel. You've got two choices. You can carry on with your day-to-day life in your small-time clinic, believing you're helping all those affluent, vulnerable—'

'I'm sorry – *believing* I'm helping the vulnerable?'

'You're no angel, Isobel,' he says, and I don't miss the fact that he gestures towards my left ankle. He can't see the tattoo, so how does he know it's there? 'You can carry on with your blinkered life, or you can start confronting the fact that the concept of artificial Heavens is a flawed one.'

I feel as though he's hit me in the stomach, undoing every reassurance that Jarek gave me. My feet are rooted to the spot in rage, as I struggle to control the ragged edges of my breathing. He swings open the gate and saunters down the passageway, disappearing amongst the people on the street beyond.

CHAPTER SIXTEEN

Three weeks later

At first, I'd turned down Maya's offer to fly us first class, but Lela talked me out of my stubbornness. As I stretch out in the comfort of my bed, an empty glass of champagne beside me, I can't help but feel relieved. The journey passes quickly after I knock back the anti-jet-lag drugs and put my head down. I hadn't realised that Lela doesn't like flying. She tells me afterwards that she didn't sleep for a second. I feel bad, wondering how I'd not been aware of her discomfort. I'm lucky she's here with me. She's using up precious holiday time, abandoning her family and eluding Caleb to escort me to a country she has no desire to visit.

But I've given up everything. Everything I've ever worked for. Everything I've ever wanted. My career, my home, Jarek – even Don, who won't fully let me go. I spoke with him a few days before I left London. I was packing my bag when his face started to shimmer on and off in my vision. I had ignored him until then, but that time I took the call. He asked me if I had got everything I needed from the flat. Did I want the coffee machine? I said no. I told him I was going to India and I couldn't tell him why. It was a strange role-reversal that made him laugh sadly. *You shouldn't, you know,* he said. *India's asking for trouble, rolling those nukes out. And China won't hold back.* I let anxiety grip me momentarily and then let it go. This is something I've only recently learnt to do. He wished me well and urged me to stay in touch. I might.

We stumble out of the plane and down the steps. I breathe the damp, early morning air into my nostrils and let its monsoon heat settle in my chest. Lela blows kisses and waves like Jackie Onassis, to nobody in particular. It's a private tradition of hers, she tells me, as I giggle. Time and again on that journey – cab to airport, plane to Mumbai, car to hotel – I remember Lela's words: *There is always more love, Isobel.* I look at her and I see it.

One of the Taj Mahal Palace's sleek cars collects us from the airport. The journey takes about an hour. At home, it would be much less, but private vehicles still seem to be popular here and the roads are busy. For a while, we trail an enormous truck carrying chickens. Its brightly painted sides puff with creamy white feathers every time it brakes. The traffic reminds me of being a little girl, sitting in the back seat and watching my father drive. I look out of the window at the men and women gripping their steering wheels. I watch in fascination as their imprecise senses try to take in the chaos around them and fail. The unfamiliar, bestial honking of horns is the soundtrack to our journey.

As we sweep around the curve of the bridge over Mahim Bay, Lela squeezes my hand. The skyline of Mumbai solidifies out of the morning fog, rising like a series of termite mounds in the distance. I don't recognise it. So much has changed in twenty-two years and my memory is poor. I count the years on my fingers, checking my maths. It seems impossible that it was that long ago that my mother, father, sister and I embarked on our last family holiday together to visit my relatives. There was a fight – a big one. My parents' relationship fell apart soon afterwards and we never came back. All the aunts and uncles and cousins I had here in India were never heard from again and nor did we return to see them. It occurs to me now that they probably frowned upon my parents ending their marriage. I will never know if divorce made my mother any happier. And I still wonder whether it was her long, solid wall of emotion that drove my father away. She was always so impenetrable, so frustratingly constant. *How's your mum, these days?* people would ask. *Is she coping on her own?* No one ever asked how she coped while she was still with him.

The bridge's cables flash past, punctuating my vision like the flicker of an old black and white movie. If only we got to deal with life one frame at a time.

The car delivers us to the steps of the hotel. I had almost been expecting it, after the aeroplane treatment, but the gilded lobby still impresses me with its unapologetic grandeur. My mother had always wanted to stay here. We check in and Lela lets the rudimentary bellboy android carry her bags to her room. She is a picture of exhaustion as she waves at me and tells me she'll see me after she's slept. But I have somewhere to be.

After a quick shower and a change of clothes in my suite, I catch a taxi from Colaba into Churchgate. These self-driving autocabs are still yellow and black, I note, just like the old cabs had been. I watch others zip past. They weave through the traffic amongst electric rickshaws, bicycles and pedestrians, like eager bumblebees. After a while, I curl sleepily into the corner of the pod, which lies in shadow as it zips through the traffic. Despite the air conditioning, it takes me a while to cool down from the thick, humid midday heat. The threat of rain still lingers in the air and, despite the cloud cover, it must be over thirty degrees outside. I close my eyes and try not to think about what tomorrow will bring.

A few minutes later, the cab pulls to a halt beside the green expanse of the Oval Maidan and I let the cab's sensor scan my chip for payment before I scramble out, back into the heat. I barely register the fare because I already know that every rupee I spend will be reimbursed by Valhalla. Until I'd walked into my hotel suite – Maya's choice – this idea had made me feel a little uncomfortable, but it's hard to turn down such luxury when I'm taking so big a risk with my health, with my life. I'm already dancing with the devil.

I weave through a crowd of men gathered at the entrance of the park. In their midst, I realise they are tiffin-wallahs, hastily preparing their boxes of food for the local office workers and chatting noisily in what my eye lens tells me is Marathi. They clear a path for me, smiling politely without breaking the tempo of their conversations. I look at their faces, lined and darkened by hours beneath the sun. They could even be the same men I'd seen plying their trade when I was last here.

I walk into the park through the tall black gates and it's easy enough to find D.C.I. Lyden from the main path. He is dressed all in black, silhouetted against the backdrop of young cricketers clad in white cotton. He inclines his head in recognition as I approach.

'Cricket? Really? I thought you had something interesting to show me,' I say as I close the last few steps between us.

I notice a slight dimple appear in his cheek. That small

movement of his mouth is the closest I've got to a smile from him in the few weeks I've known him, yet his hands stay in the depths of his pockets.

'Who doesn't love cricket?'

'Sure, it's so . . .' I raise my eyebrows. 'So riveting.' I stand beside him at the edge of the grass. Despite my sarcasm, I watch with veiled interest as the bowler pitches. It's fast, true – and then we hear the thwack of leather against willow. Daniel hums in what I take to be admiration as the ball spins venomously towards the edge of the pitch.

'Thanks for coming.'

I assume he means my journey to Mumbai, rather than the cricket match, and I shrug. He already knows I'm not doing this for him; I've made that quite clear.

'We could've just caught up in the hotel but I thought it would be good for you to get some fresh air,' he adds, gesturing to the scene around us. The thin fabric of his long-sleeved T-shirt clings to his body, creasing around the sinewy muscles of his shoulders. I can feel sweat tickling at my temples and my lip, but his face is smooth and matt.

'I'm guessing what we're doing is illegal back home?'

'I'd call it a grey area,' he replies, staring down at the grass. He speaks, as he always does, in a low voice, even though there are no people within hearing distance.

'It's lucky that Valhalla have a clinic here, then.' I let the sarcasm roll around my mouth, unabashed. Daniel ignores me, switching his gaze back towards the match.

'How have you been?' he asks, as if we are old friends. 'How was the journey?' I note again what a good detective he must be.

He slips into the spaces beside people, between people, with such effortless ease. And I almost let him.

'I've been okay,' I say. 'First class was *very* me.'

'You're ready for tomorrow?' he asks. 'Valhalla's suite in the hospital, at nine a.m.?'

'Yes. And bring nothing with me, I know.'

'It's great – what you're doing.' As soon as he looks at the glower on my face, he knows it's the wrong thing to have said.

'Great for who? Valhalla? This must be *such* a convenient case for them,' I say. 'And Maya doesn't even have to get her hands dirty because I'm doing all the hard work for her.'

I think of my conversation with her in the park when she asked me to work with them on forcing a way into the Heavens of suspected criminals. *I didn't think the word* impossible *was in your vocabulary.* Her challenge has never left me.

'It looks like she's getting what she wanted, after all.'

I realise how petulant I sound when I notice the slight shake of Daniel's head.

'I know you're not doing this for them.'

Although his voice has a questioning tone, I know he won't delve any deeper. And I don't need to trouble him with my reasons. Since I made the decision to do this, I haven't even mentioned them to myself. Yet, now, they flood my mind. Released from their hiding places, they rush through my head again and crowd between my temples.

Because I need to see Jarek again, because the possibility of it is keeping me awake at night.

Because I have nothing else left to do. Because, without this, I am useless.

Because why not? Oblivion has never felt more tempting.

Because no one else has ever done what I'm going to do. The part of me that can't stand to see a speck of coffee on a white shirt needs to see much more than a basic simulation of the Heaven that I've created; I need to experience it in its fullest sense. I hear Don's doubts and the words of my mother and the protesters louder than ever and I let them speak for me. Because it's easier that way, isn't it? To let someone else criticise you, rather than criticising yourself. To let them bear the brunt of your anger. How do you know you're doing the right thing for these people? How do you know you're creating something heavenly at all?

I will know soon.

And the overarching reason: because it's my responsibility to prove Jarek is innocent and to let him rest in peace, his memory uncorrupted in the minds of those who still live.

I glance at Daniel. 'You still think it was Jarek?'

'A clearer picture is emerging of what happened that evening,' he murmurs. 'The D.N.A. results have been fully evaluated—'

'You do, don't you?' I cut him off. 'You think it was him. If you're so sure, if all your evidence is so fucking helpful, why am I even here?'

He levels his gaze at me, always so cool in response to my fire. 'My team are still conducting interviews, pursuing leads. It's not a closed case, Isobel.' He looks me in the eyes for the first time since I arrived. He stares, as if he's deliberately trying not to blink.

I look past him and wish, again, that I knew where Jarek had gone after leaving my apartment that Friday afternoon. He only left because Don was coming home; otherwise, he would have stayed, wouldn't he?

'Any more questions?' Daniel asks. He clasps his hands together behind his back and stares down at the grass as if he's preparing for an onslaught.

Who killed her? Who killed Sarah? That's the only question I have. It wasn't me and it wasn't Jarek. So, what about Caleb? What about Maya? She wanted me here, doing these experiments for them, and Caleb is her sociopathic lapdog. And after all, Sarah's murder has got them exactly what Valhalla wanted.

'So, you do have other suspects?' I ask.

'We're fully evaluating the possibilities, but I'm not at liberty to tell you any more than that.'

'You can't even tell me if you're investigating anyone else?'

He sighs, relents. 'At this stage, yes, but it's probably best I don't discuss that with you.' I try to read something, anything, from the deep golden brown of his eyes and his pursed lips. He's no Hollywood action hero. His gentleness must make it easy to hide his insecurities.

'Come on, Daniel. Who?'

'It's more artistic than I expected,' he says suddenly, and I wonder what he's talking about until I realise he is looking down, not at the grass, but at the ink swirling around my bare ankle. He crouches down to take a closer look, his expression unreadable, and I squeeze my toes together in discomfort.

'I hate it,' I say.

'Why?'

'When we first met, you told me I was living a blinkered life, and now I don't know who I am anymore.' It feels as if the thought has been dragged from my head and woven in words. 'I guess I thought the angel represented me in some way. But now I don't know. Maybe it's . . .'

'Jarek?'

I shrug. 'Maybe.'

Daniel exhales heavily and shakes his head. 'Your world is so damn idealistic.'

I start to fold my arms but he closes his hand around my wrist as he stands back up. 'No one's an angel, Isobel.' The forcefulness of his voice matches his grip.

Daniel's words echo in my ears as he walks away. I stand there for a while on my own, the searing Indian sun cutting through the trees of the Maidan, dappling beams of light on to my face.

The following morning, the spotlights above me cast a similar pattern, whirling and throbbing against my eyelids. The clinical emptiness of the room buzzes around me and I close my eyes against its prying brightness, feeling the awareness of complete loss ripple through me so acutely that it stings at my temples. Some days are worse than others, I've found. The room is cold and I feel the tang of metal on my tongue.

'Isobel?' a voice murmurs, as if through water.

I try to respond but my mouth doesn't seem to move and I feel myself falling back into my dream. I can't remember where I am, but it's so much easier there. If I just close my eyes and—

'Isobel,' the voice says, more sharply, more urgently. I feel a hand against my face. 'You need to wake up, sweetheart!'

Lela – it's Lela. For her, I open my eyes.

'Hi,' I say automatically, and as I register the scratchiness of my voice, I remember where I am. I'm not at home. I had to move out. I'm not even in London. I'm in India. I'm in Valhalla's private hospital suite.

'You're all right?' Lela asks. 'You know what's going on?'

I nod and Lela exhales heavily, shakily, in a way that reminds me that this procedure was not without its risks.

When I agreed to this, I already knew that Valhalla's neuroscientists wouldn't be launching me straight into Jarek's Heaven simulation. They're too nervous. Today was just to check that my body managed under the general anaesthetic — given that I've never had one — and to identify the memories needed for my Heaven. It's the last procedure each of my clients goes through with their neurologist before their death — although, for them, it would be done while they remained conscious. The chemical tag would have filtered through my brain to help Valhalla's team trigger the neurons carrying the memories I've requested. Jess will have the activation patterns. My Heaven will become digital, backed up multiple times. In case something goes wrong with the next experiment.

'It went okay?' I ask Lela, blinking and looking around the room as it gradually comes back into focus. It's quiet, bare.

'Yeah, I think it did. Your vital signs looked good under the sedation, and the M.R.I. scan seemed straightforward. You weren't under for long, really. Maybe an hour.'

'You spoke to Jess?'

'Yep; she watched everything from London. She says hello, by the way. Her team has the readouts now, so I think they're working on everything. They'll need a couple of days to save it all safely at the Institute.'

'Great.'

I'm reassured that the memories I've put into my Heaven – like jewels into a trinket box – are now in safe hands. Otherwise, I could have risked the most precious moments of my life being lost forever. But something could still go wrong. My mirror neurons – my very consciousness – cannot be copied, cannot be digitised. I know the risks. I've been through them a hundred times now and, every single time, I've amazed myself with my continuing affirmation that I will do this. The chances of me dying in this hospital bed are low. And yet the repercussions are worse than death. As this series of experiments progresses, the risk that my self-awareness – my very being – could be corrupted, or irrevocably wiped out, increases. I would be the worst kind of vegetable: a fully functioning body with a completely absent mind. I would be like the androids that scuttle around department stores and factories. I would be a ghost.

I struggle to lift myself and Lela fusses around me, rearranging the pillows behind my back and supporting my shoulders as I shift my position on the bed. The room looks as if it is designed to match the iciness of the air conditioning. White walls, floors and ceiling; sleek chrome fixtures. Out of the small, square window, I can see that we're a few storeys up, and I can see the cloudless blue sky, hazy with heat, and the top of a clock tower, its finely wrought lines offset by the swaying palm leaves.

'Where is everyone? I thought half the world was in here when I went under.'

'It was a bit crazy, wasn't it? The anaesthetist is around somewhere, and a couple of nurses, but everyone else has gone. Maya was delighted with it all.'

'Oh, good.'

'Come on, Isobel. As much as I hate the idea of you doing this, it's really going to transform the field. We're going to learn so much from this.'

'*Valhalla* is going to learn so much from this. Besides, I'm not here to transform the field. I'm here to prove Jarek's innocence.'

'Still.' Lela's meaning is swallowed as she turns away from me and walks over to the window.

'When I saw Daniel yesterday, he told me that there are other suspects. That's good, isn't it?'

I hear Lela hum a response. We're silent for a while and I watch her, resting her elbows upon the ledge and gazing out. I can tell that she's not admiring the view over Churchgate; she's thinking. She always thinks so loudly. She clinks her top and bottom incisors together repeatedly and I bite my tongue to prevent myself from telling her to stop it.

'Are you sure you want to do this, Izzy?' she asks, without turning around. 'You can still change your mind.'

I consider her words for a moment or two – I do. My mind is still heavy with anaesthetic; my thoughts move as slowly as syrup over the back of a spoon. But I know the answer. She doesn't need to hear me say it; she already knows the answer, too. I need to prove he didn't do it. Even if it's the last thing I do. I nod.

'I know I don't need to ask you all this, but you've read through all the consent forms, haven't you? You've gone through it all properly?'

'Of course I have, Lela.'

She stops clinking her teeth and we fall into a companionable silence. I've noticed over the past few weeks that these brief vacuums of activity seem to draw out my grief. I swallow and raise my tongue to the roof of my mouth to try to stop the anguish from escaping, but it slinks out some other way – through my skin and my ears and my eyes – and spreads to the sides of the room. It clings to the walls, trapping me inside it, making me feel smaller than I already am. I want Lela to ask me how it feels. I want someone else to say his name, to remind me that it's not all in my own head, but I know that she won't.

'Well, okay,' she says, walking back towards the bed. 'I'll leave you to get some rest. And eat – *please*, eat. You're thin.' She squeezes my fingers and then pushes the fruit bowl on the bedside table closer to my pillow. The cloying smell of warm banana wafts into my nostrils and turns my stomach.

I know I've lost weight, but on the way to the hospital this morning, I saw women balancing on ankles bonier than my own. I wanted to give food to the children whose ribs I could see from across the street. They looked at me like they recognised me. Being half Indian has never been a major part of my adult life, but now I'm here I feel as though I'm a part of something, despite this country's harsh realities.

'They said they'd drop you back at the hotel later,' calls Lela from the doorway. 'Give me a shout when you're ready for an enormous, carb-laden dinner. I'm in twelve-oh-four.'

I watch her leave, her tall, curvaceous figure bobbing out of the room. She looks lovely out of her office clothes. The loose linens gathered at her waist with a narrow woven belt suit her. It is so kind of her to be here for me. I don't remember asking her to come, but she was always going to. She would have hated having to tell Caleb where she was going to spend her vacation. He was still fuming.

I resigned perfectly. I contacted all my clients first. I organised my things the day before, taking them to my grandmother's flat and sorting them in labelled boxes in the wardrobe of her spare room. I worked all day, arranged for messages to be sent out to colleagues for an hour after my departure and then knocked on the door of Caleb's office.

I stare out of the window into the sky and replay the rush of blood to my cheeks as I made my announcement. It was short, well prepared, suitably vague. It left no room for comeback. For the first time, Caleb was speechless. I closed my life to him and to the clinic. I've walked away from other things before. But never my work. In all likelihood, there is no going back.

Time has flown. Before I walked out of Oakley Associates forever, I spent all day, every day, working at the clinic, and then every night working on my Heaven, first in my grandmother's old bedroom, then in my office and then hours and hours – late nights and early mornings – spent with Jess in her room beside the Electric Lab.

If nothing else, I know that my Heaven is the most beautiful one I've ever created. It should make me happy but I feel a slight guilt in saving that brilliance for myself. In fairness, it's the first time I could be so accurate. I have always tried to understand other people – their whims, their motivation, the complexity of their sins – but I've always had to read them in my own language. Each of us is an island. Even between Jarek and I – even though I know in my heart that he couldn't commit murder – there lies an ocean.

My Heaven is carefully considered, made of the thoughts and ideas I've had every day since the start of my training as an Architect but had put off again and again. It is honest, threaded with things I wouldn't tell another living soul, coded and layered so that even Jess will never see it in its totality. There are features drawn from my imagination rather than from memory, things I always wanted and never got. A kiss from the boy I met on my first solo trip abroad. A world without war on the horizon. My Heaven is drenched in my favourite colours and imbued with the scents of happiness: cut grass, freshly chopped basil, the sweetly fading jasmine on my mother's balcony, Jarek's eau de cologne. In the glimpses I've had of it in Jess's simulations, it has been everything a Heaven should be. I almost can't wait to see it.

CHAPTER SEVENTEEN

There are no windows down here in the basement. Chinese jets flew over Delhi yesterday and they are still skirting around Indian airspace, asserting themselves. I've been moved down here from my airy private room on the third floor for my own safety.

Don was right about the dangers. Maya told me earlier this morning that Taiwan has called for British, American and Indian support. The British Prime Minister released a statement yesterday that said she supports Taiwan's right to independence from China. The cold war in the Pacific isn't as cold as it was before I left England. I think of Clair and I think of my tattooist's little brother out there, disconcertingly close to that big red button.

But I'm safe here, according to Maya and the Valhalla doctors, under concrete and steel nanocomposite. If anything happens while I'm under, they shouldn't have to move me. My anaesthetist wears a serious expression as she reads the stream of data coming from the temporary tattoo on the inside of my elbow. Her facial expressions look exaggerated, as if she's overcompensating for the fact I'm watching her every move from here on the bed. Hunger rolls around in my stomach like a marble. Now that I can't eat, I'm hungry. The irony riles me.

'Can I have some water?' I ask. She shakes her head without apology. I feel as though she's been briefed to say as little to me as possible.

'Surely she can have a sip?' Lela asks, half rising from her chair.

The anaesthetist tuts and moves her head in a way that reminds me of my mother – a half-nod, half-shake. My sister still does it sometimes. Lela looks at me and shrugs, before watching the anaesthetist as she lifts the glass of water to my lips.

This is the next stage. It's Valhalla's chance to test out their visualisation technology by studying my Heaven. I was all for attempting to go straight into Jarek's Heaven but Maya wants to be sure of the accuracy before going any further into the unknown. The technology is more advanced than the starry lights I saw in Jess's lab. They're hoping for something closer to the simulation I show my clients in our last appointment together, but coupled up with readouts on brain activity, emotional state, heart rate and so on. It feels invasive. And not only in a physical way. I've been assured that only the necessary members of the healthcare team will view it. My Heaven isn't supposed to be mass entertainment.

They will knock me out cold. They will drill holes in my skull and insert deep brain-stimulation probes into the region of the brain containing my mirror neurons. Then they will activate my Heaven program and it should be just like the real thing. Except I'll be alive.

I will have no sense of time passing, but they won't keep me under for more than five or six hours, Maya told me last night. It's still unclear how time will translate between Heaven and reality. I will see Jarek, but it will only be my version of him. He will be an amalgamation of my memories. Nothing more than a convincing illusion of the real man, at best.

I watch the anaesthetist pull a holographic up from the surface of a side table to my right. She twists it in mid-air, swapping the image between a numerical data stream and a glowing map of what must be my body. My vital stats are all there, I imagine. She arranges it so that the green-blue light lies at an angle, sloping into the table, and then she leaves, closing the door behind her.

'She's friendly,' Lela says, and I grin back at her, rolling my eyes.

'Yeah, she's bursting with reassurance.'

'I bet you've pissed her off. How many times have you asked her to change the sheets?'

I feign annoyance, narrowing my eyes in Lela's direction. 'Only once, and only because she'd spilt my blood all over the bed.'

I glance at the drip running into the vein on the back of my hand, where crusty remnants of blood encircle the cannula.

'You're a drama queen. Really? Only once?'

'I asked her once and I asked the nurse once,' I admit.

A frown flickers across Lela's face and she forces the messy strands of hair back behind her ears. 'Do you want me to stay here with you?' she asks.

I hesitate from declining the offer as I look up at her.

'Perhaps I could pop in a couple of times to check on you? If I'm allowed.'

'That sounds good.'

'Do you know who will be here for it?'

'Yes; the lovely lady who just left, another doctor who I met yesterday afternoon, and Maya was going to send someone over from Valhalla to oversee things, but now she's put her big girl shoes on and is coming herself.'

'I think she's scared of you!'

'I think she senses I'm not her biggest fan.' I think about our conversation that evening in the park. I've never told Lela about that. 'But she said she thought I'd at least feel more comfortable with someone I've already met.'

I feel the temporary tattoo deliver three sharp pulses to the skin of my arm. The sedative has been released. The anaesthetist pokes her head around the door. At least, I assume it's her. Her voice doesn't quite seem to filter through to me. It catches unevenly on the thinning air in the room. She sounds wonky, like the notes of a long-disused piano.

'One minute,' I think I hear her say.

Lela nods and blows me a kiss. It ripples towards me and I can feel it settle, veil-like, over my face.

'It won't be perfect, will it?' I surprise myself as I hear the words spoken aloud. I thought I was only thinking them. Things are starting to blur, yet I don't have the wherewithal to panic.

'It'll be beautiful, Izzy.'

'See you on the other side,' I say, in a sudden moment of clarity, as a younger version of Lela, holding a carafe of wine, dances into my vision.

'Oh, yes, of course!' She grins as she remembers that she's in my Heaven. 'Tell me I say hi.'

The footpaths of my Heaven are lined with blackberry bushes. The seasons change – I always loved the alterations in the air and the cyclic fluctuation of the sun – but the blackberries are always there, waiting to be picked. Each one is so ripe with juice that they threaten to burst the moment I touch them. I can smell the deep red, sun-ripened sugar. Juniper and Olive weave their tiger-like stripes through the undergrowth at my feet. I can hear them purr and I can feel the softness of their kitten fur on my cheek. They roll and play as if they've met before, as if they've been getting to know each other for all these years, waiting for me to arrive. Every so often, I catch the back of my hand on a thorn as I extract my arm from the depths of the brambles and it sears a bloody scratch into my skin. A momentary pain to make the sweetness even more gratifying. I press a berry into my mouth and let it melt – still warm with sunlight – on to my tongue, filling my mouth with the smooth wine-like flavours and a closing tang. I gaze down at my hands in quiet amazement. They are rippled with the purple juice, which gathers in the lines that crisscross my palms, and, unlike in life, I don't feel the nagging impulse to wash them clean.

My Heaven, like all others, is timeless. I see the changes to patterns around me but I have no sense of how quickly any of it is happening.

For an undefined moment, I feel the full heat of the summer sun prickling against my back as I lie in the freshly mowed parkland of my childhood. I watch the traffic jam of ants picking their way through the carpet of grass. Each antenna is delicately sensing, reaching, exploring. The whir of the mower resonates in my belly and the smell of the bleeding grass fills my nostrils. With it come deeper, vaguer flashbacks of school sports days and summer holidays. I'm listening to my baby sister giggle as she tickles my neck.

Then it shifts to the cool, overcast day of my graduation. I feel the coarse texture of the certificate in my hand and the teasing threat of rain upon the bulbs of my cheeks. There's a smile upon my face that spreads through me. I'm surrounded by people but I don't see their faces and it doesn't matter. I feel their companionship, I know some of them meant something to me once, but this moment is about me.

I'm at my desk alone, in the clinic, notes scattered before me. I'm sorting through them with the peace that only my work was ever able to deliver. The memory is silent but my Heaven is filled with the calm of concentration that comes with me challenging myself, pushing my brain to its limits. I can feel the concave exclusion of every other concern as I work. The room is rich with a rosy sense of fulfilment.

I clink glasses with Lela in one of our favourite bars and it rings merrily in my ears. I hear her laugh – her beautiful, uncontrolled, carefree laugh – and it warms me. That warmth becomes the complex, spicy scent of family Christmases. I pick out the aromas one by one: cloves, cinnamon, orange, five spice, star anise, chocolate, ginger, my sister's rum-muddled mulled wine.

I feel a hug from my grandfather, the side of my face against the whisky-scented pillow of his stomach, with the foresight that it will be the last time we share the same room without sadness. I dance with my mother to my favourite song, almost carrying her frail body around the bedroom in which she spent her last months.

I run, naked, into the Pacific with my best friend from college. The moon is high in the sky. I'm screaming so hard with laughter that it seems like my ribs will crack, and the cold is shrinking me, squeezing me into a tiny packet of elation.

And I see Jarek, his weakening form curled into mine on the

floor of my apartment, the late afternoon sun turning his hair into strands of light. The images of him and the emotions that filter through me seem to have more dimensions than they did in life. I hear the lilt of his voice, punctuated with sarcasm. *You have the tiniest hands*, he says, resting his chin on his fist and leaning forward over a table. I watch him looking at me as he nibbles the skin beside his thumbnail.

These episodic memories are more recent, perhaps, and so more heavily ingrained. He is undiluted. I see him again, as if for the first time, as he walks into my office, his shoulders strong but his chin hunched down into his chest. It blurs into a vision of me running my fingers through his hair, rubbing my cheek against the stubble of his neck. *I can't die without you, Izz*. His eyes are as green as I remember from life. Maybe greener. My memories like to exaggerate. *I want to ask you something*, say the words shimmering in my vision. *I want to know what your Heaven is like*. We whoop with delight as we drive down an empty highway. It's the one piece of my Heaven in which he's young and healthy, driving a convertible at top speed: a 1965 Aston Martin DB5 – his choice. The glow of a summer sun bounces off the bonnet. My Heaven is loaded with the knowledge that I created this false memory for us – because I'm that good at what I do. I throw my hands into the air as he pulls around a corner and feel the pride and sense of achievement flood through me. He kisses me – an event that now has no place in time but is tagged with the knowledge that it is our first kiss. I feel the grip of his hand in mine, knowing it is him without looking back and then letting myself be pulled into his body. The scene loops over and over again so that I notice new details every time: small details lodged in the background of the memory, such as the bronze buttons on his jacket, the way the wind pushes back his hair from his forehead, the brief sensation of almost slipping on an uneven paving slab. *If you don't open this door, I never will.*

There's no anxiety, no fear. No compulsion to achieve anything. Just a beautiful, quiet observance. Jarek was right to believe in me. I was right to believe in myself. The timelessness of Heaven makes me feel free.

CHAPTER EIGHTEEN

Chowpatty Beach glitters with children playing with pocket holograms on the sands. I'm sitting on the sea wall, drinking in the bliss of being alone in the early evening light. The coconut scent of sticky, melting kulfi spreads from the food stalls behind me, and the residual heat of the day lies like a stole around my shoulders. Every few minutes, a lady or a small child prods me with a bony finger to ask for money or to try to sell me something, but I shake my head without speaking. They usually return my half-smile and go on their way. I already know that Daniel won't tap me on the shoulder when he arrives. He will sit next to me and match my gaze out to sea.

'I don't have to go back,' I murmur, imagining myself once more in the soothing folds of my Heaven.

I hear Jarek's voice in my ear: *Go back where?* It's easy to forget, momentarily, that Jarek and I no longer share the same world. The barrier between us pains me.

I have had a few days to recover from the first proper intervention. The visualisations worked beautifully, they told me, gathered around the bed with dewy eyes, bubbling with an excitement I didn't yet feel. Even the stern-faced anaesthetist squeezed my hand and raised it from the bed triumphantly, with a grin plastered across her face.

For some reason, instead of running the bath this morning, I washed on the floor of the separate wet room. The chambermaid looked shocked to find me cross-legged on the tiles, pouring soapy water over myself with a bucket. I hadn't even heard her knock. The sedatives were powerful, the anaesthetist had said. I might not feel myself for a while. But I don't think I was still half-tranquillised, sitting there in my own world, stripped bare. The truth is that I feel as though I'm suffering from some kind of mental hangover, as if I can't quite disentangle my entire self from my Heaven. What if it's seeping into my reality, its fingertips reaching out into my brain? I should find these thoughts disturbing, but my mind is clearer than it's been for years. I could almost forget that I'm involved in a murder investigation.

My Heaven was sweeter than I could have imagined. I'm lost inside it, even now. There's Jarek, yes, but it's like there's another me still in it, reaching out and begging me to join her. *We'd have so much fun*. She's the best version of me, the side that catches me off guard in the mirror some days, and I think, Oh, I can be quite pretty, sometimes. She lives for the present, lives for the love that surrounds her, treasures and relives memories without becoming sentimental. She smiles at the right time, always says the right thing, even *thinks* the right thing, because, in a way, Heaven is just a well-rehearsed play. But I'm only seeing it that way now that the curtains are closed and the lights are down. When I'm submerged in it, when I'm *her*, it's as if that perfection is natural. It's intoxicating. It's affecting me even now I'm removed from it.

It's like taking a drug, I think, letting my memories roll to the night I snorted bluestone with my college friends, on the beach, in Brighton. The world seemed so perfect, yet we could have drowned laughing.

Daniel arrives as I predicted, settling himself quietly beside me. He waits for me to start the conversation with a patience that I find admirable. I let him wait for a couple of minutes, testing him.

'It went well,' I say eventually, keen to preserve the sentimental workings of my thoughts. I'll stick to business.

'So Maya tells me,' he says, with a slight nod of his head. 'How was it?'

'Oh, I had a ball!' I roll my eyes and clap my hands, feeling the trapped pocket of air burst out through the gaps.

'Seriously,' he says, frowning. 'How does it feel? Going under?'

'You've never had an operation?' I ask. He shrugs his shoulders. 'You don't feel a thing. They rub the tattoo on to your skin with some alcohol, the general anaesthetic activates itself at a set time, you get drowsy and that's it. And then you wake up.'

I glance at him but he doesn't move. He sits like a Buddha, cross-legged on the wall, with the palms of his hands pressed against each other in his lap. He's exactly the kind of guy I can imagine doing yoga: svelte and agile, comfortable with himself. It's easy to forget who he really is. I'm sure he's strong, confrontational, and lethal when he needs to be. The stun gun clipped into the back of his trousers fits that profile.

'So, I'm back in tomorrow,' I add.

'The next bit is trickier, as you know.' It sounds like a warning.

'Trickier?' I raise my eyebrows. 'It's not a computer game, Daniel.'

'Has Maya explained it?'

'In her own way.'

I note the slight twitch at the edge of his mouth. Maybe he finds her as annoying as I do.

'And you know the risks?' he asks.

We look at each other. His expression is impossible to read. I go through it in my head. They do the same thing all over again, but this time they run Jarek's Heaven simulation into my brain instead of mine. My consciousness goes into his Heaven. Or, at least, that's the idea.

'It doesn't seem so long ago that you were trying to talk me into this,' I remind him.

'It wasn't.'

I look back out to the horizon. 'So, have you got any other bombshells for me?'

'I watched the visualisations of you in your Heaven.'

I cast my eyes over his form, blurring now into the twilight.

'I wasn't sure if you knew about that,' he adds, his eyes meeting mine.

'You watched,' I repeat back to him. 'Not only Maya, but you did, too. That's not in the consent forms! And it's fucking creepy!'

I think of Daniel standing in the room as Jarek and I made love on the floor of my living room and imagine him studying my face as we kissed for the first time. I think of him watching me dancing with my mother. Although it had already occurred to me that something like this would happen, it's still a shock.

He shifts ever so slightly towards me. 'I only watched a bit. It was rough — blurred in places and delayed — it wasn't perfect. Not nearly as good as the ones you use with your clients.'

I start nodding and find I can't stop until the anger bubbles back down to a simmer. This detective is good. Oh, he's good.

And then: 'I'm sorry, Isobel, that so much of this is out of your control.'

I glance at him disbelievingly as he stares down at his hands, and I find that I could almost laugh. 'What do you even mean? What else haven't they told me?'

'I needed to see it for myself,' Daniel says. 'I need to be sure that what we see in Jarek's Heaven – if we see anything at all – is reliable, is meaningful.'

Now it's my turn to stare out to sea as he tries to decipher my expression.

'I don't even know why the visualisations are so important! No one trusts me to do this on my own? No one believes that I'll report back? You think I'll lie about what I see? About what he says to me? Is that it?'

It all seems ever so clear now and I'm mystified by how I could have thought it would be any other way. I've been so engrossed in the process, in seeing Jarek again, that I'd forgotten I'm being manipulated like a pawn.

'I didn't have to tell you,' he says, and it's this which really gets to me. I turn to face him and I can feel the anger rippling across my face, making my lips tremble.

'Oh, great. You were just supposed to keep me completely in the dark? Fantastic. Thanks.'

'Well, I'm telling you now. And I'm telling you that this is the way it will be. I'm doing my job. I'm trying to solve a crime. I'll watch again tomorrow, and the time after that, and every time we do this until we've got what we need.' His voice is harder now;

there is a tone of warning threaded through it and I find myself asking whether I really have any choice anymore.

'What the fuck am I doing?' I murmur to myself, and it's enough to almost tip the balance of my emotions towards vulnerability. I'm angry with myself for letting the details slip past me, but there's no way I'm going to let this happen without all the legal formalities in place. I claw the emerging tears away from my eyes with the tentacles of fury rising at the back of my mouth. I agreed to do this. I want to prove that Jarek is innocent. It's like a resurrection. Jarek *was* dead; he was innocent. And now that I've been with him, smelt him, touched him, it's as if he is alive again. He *is* innocent. I underline the thought. He is innocent. I raise my gaze to the horizon, still radiating the remnants of the sunset. It's nearly time to go.

'Your other suspects,' I ask. 'Are you getting warmer?'

Daniel ignores me and swings his legs back around over the wall so that he's facing in the opposite direction. He places his feet on the pavement and presses his palms into the stone of the sea wall, preparing to stand up.

'Maybe,' he says. I lock my eyes on to his face, fixed in perfect profile. 'As I'm sure you're well aware, Jarek and Sarah's relationship was a troubled one. He wasn't the only party who was being unfaithful.'

'Really?' My heart reaches up out of my chest and grasps at this vindication – this beam of hope. 'Sarah was having an affair?'

'I've got to go,' he says, standing up. 'And you need a good night's sleep.' He turns back towards me briefly, and touches his fingers to his temple in a mock salute before walking away.

'And we'll do the proper paperwork in the morning,' I call after him. 'I want a list of who is able to watch the simulations.'

But, in truth, my concerns are already almost forgotten. Sarah had been seeing someone else. Someone who could have turned violent. Someone who could have quite easily walked into her house and strangled her. I walk back to the hotel lighter, as some of the fear, and some of the residual guilt, vaporises into the night air.

CHAPTER NINETEEN

I lie back in the hospital bed that's fast becoming my second home and consider the tumult of emotions in my belly. Maya fusses around me, tucking the sheets in at my feet as fast as I can kick them free.

'You understand?' She has asked me this on so many occasions that I believe my answer less and less every time. Today, they will run Jarek's Heaven through my brain.

'Yes, of course I do.' I've made sure it's all formally signed, too, I think, restraining myself from winding her up by saying it aloud.

'You sure are a brave woman, Isobel,' says Maya, half smiling at me.

'For what? Letting you and your cronies see my Heaven?' I see Daniel look up from his Codex.

'Yeah, that.' She gestures across my body, under the sheets. 'This.'

'I don't mind,' I say, 'so long as you don't screw it up.'

Maya is trying to soften me but, instead, her voice makes me bristle. I comfort myself by thinking about last night's conversation with Daniel. His reluctance to share details of this new

189

suspect must be meaningful. Perhaps because his suspicion is shifting towards this man – Sarah's lover – instead of Jarek. Jarek's warm smile appears in my mind and then the shadow of a strange man ripples over the surface of his face, eclipsing it. I work through Daniel's possible reasoning. If Jarek is no longer the prime suspect, Daniel wouldn't let on, because he and Valhalla want me to do these experiments regardless. And I find I'm happy to. Despite the risks, I want to slip back into that mesmerising coma again and again.

Although today will be different. The room has been re-arranged appropriately. The lights are turned down to allow the staff to see the array of projections on the back wall. Valhalla's visualisations will map my brainwaves against both my Heaven and Jarek's Heaven. Maya is optimistic that I'll be able to slip into his Heaven, and that they'll get a fairly accurate picture of what I'm seeing, hearing and feeling.

She and Daniel have suggested that I could try to talk to Jarek, in the hope of triggering a ghost memory. They hope I will see something – a flicker of a clue, maybe, about what happened that evening – but I'm convinced that I won't.

I remember when Daniel first approached me, outside the Institute. He spoke then of Jess's research, of the mirror neurons and the ghost memories. He knows, he *must* know, that what we're doing today only has the tiniest chance of success. I just don't believe anyone would be able to get far enough into someone else's Heaven. I'm sure they'd only ever see the record of memories created by the Architect. And that's assuming Jess is right about ghost memories. After all, I didn't see any in my own Heaven.

Still, I'm happy to play the game, if that's what it is. I'm happy to take one step at a time. And I want to get it right.

The anaesthetist rubs the tattoo on to my inner arm and it tickles at the skin.

'You look like some kind of addict,' Daniel says, and pulls back the corner of his lips into that rare half-smile of his. I've noticed that he's the kind of man who only finds his own dark jokes amusing. I see what he means: my arms are pockmarked with the remnants of old anaesthetic tattoos. They are running out of places to put the new ones so that they'll stick. But he has no idea how close to a drug my Heaven is. I don't point this out. I make a different joke.

'I *have* been washing.'

If Lela had been allowed into the room for today's procedure, she'd laugh out loud at this. She knows me well enough to know that I've spent hours soaking in the bath of my suite. I've spent minutes upon minutes scrubbing at my skin with every cleaning instrument available to try and get rid of the glue. Would Jarek have expected this behaviour of me, too? Did he know me that well? I consider the question for a while, but the mention of his name in my mind brings with it the fresh capacity for tears. I turn away from it. I'll see him soon enough.

As the drowsiness begins to envelop me, the number of people in the room seems to increase. The anaesthetist floats somewhere to my left and, as the seconds tick by, she seems to double and then triple. White coats surround me. Maya stands statue-like in the corner, and there's Daniel, standing with his arms folded, at the end of my bed. He's said little to me since signing the forms this morning. His lips are twisted to the side. I can tell that he's annoyed with himself for being honest with me, for revealing more than he intended to. He slipped up. Perhaps he's not as good a D.C.I. as I first thought.

I close my eyes, urging oblivion on. There's only one place I want to be: with Jarek and in the flashes of brilliance that have been my life. I forget the questions I must ask and let the smile spread across my face.

We're back in the convertible and, this time, we're driving through a rainstorm. I'm being launched straight into an artificial memory that I created – the only one Jarek and I share – and yet it feels so real to me. I recognise every detail: the scent of wet leather; the grey-purple of the sky, interrupted by patches of bright blue; the warm, clean droplets falling into my mouth as I throw back my head and laugh. My legs are tucked beneath me, or nestled under Jarek's thighs, or hooked over the door. I look like a student again; my calves are thicker, rounded by late-night parties and fast food. *I love you, I love you, I love you.* We both say it – sometimes whispered into an ear, sometimes shouted out for all to hear on the road ahead. It's pelting down for a reason that Jarek and I both agreed upon: life isn't all sunshine and cloudless skies. There's an inherent childishness in baring yourself to the elements. I'm drenched to the bone and I don't care. Soaking up the words and the rain, I admire the rainbow, which frames the stretch of road before us. I wonder why I haven't put more of them in my own Heaven. There should always be a rainbow, I think, in a distant bit of my brain that isn't part of this artificial memory.

And then, suddenly, I am Jarek. I'm running across a rugby field, wet with mud and pulsing with adrenalin and the anticipation of victory, the ball clasped to my chest. It feels like the kind of virtual-reality experience you can do in shopping centres.

A wave crashes over me and spins me into a free fall from an aeroplane, which blinks in and out of my vision as I plummet. I dance with Jarek's sister in the family lounge, teaching her to waltz. The chiffon folds of her ball gown feel stiff under his fingers – my fingers. I'm racing through memories. Why should I make it easy for Valhalla? They can't touch me if I don't stop.

My own memories appear again. Warm water churns around my ankles and splashes upwards over my skin. I feel myself waiting for friends. I glimpse faces I know I should recognise, but I don't.

And then I'm in the basement safe-room with Jarek. We cover each other in kisses, and the brightness of the blood beneath our skin almost gives colour to the darkness. But I feel trapped. I remember why I am here and suddenly the basement looks a lot like an interrogation room. My feet seem to sink into the floor and I feel myself pull back from one of Jarek's kisses.

That never happened.

This is a new reality.

I stare into Jarek's face, wondering what will happen next. His damp lips stay parted; his green eyes, glassy. He looks dead. He *is* dead. I groan in frustration and slam balled fists into his chest. He doesn't even stumble. He is like a passive hologram – a dummy. I sink to my knees and press my hands into the floor. I care that my open shirt is dragging in the dirt but I'm too angry to do anything about it.

I've never felt claustrophobia before but it hits me now in the centre of my chest and I realise there are no buttons I can press to take me out of this illusion; no tubes I can rip from my arms. I feel as though I'm strapped to a bed and then wonder if I really am, if that's what they do with me when I go under. Every neuroticism I've ever had collides in my mind and I pull myself up, throwing myself at the wall in a blind panic, hammering my fists, screaming. Let me out, let me out, let me out. The panic rises and falls over me and I tremble beneath it. My throat can't decide whether to bring up the contents of last night's dinner or just close itself off. Like Sarah, I am choking.

This isn't going to work, I think. I already knew it wouldn't work. Why didn't I tell them to stop wasting everyone's time?

Jarek would comfort me if this was real, but he is frozen to the spot, looking through me. I try to take deep breaths and I feel a cool scrape against the inside of my arm. I stop shaking and the nausea fades. They've tranquillised me. I roll up the indignation and bury it for later. I try, the only way I know how, to do what I was sent here to do.

'Did you love your wife, Jarek?' I ask, turning back to him, grasping his shoulders. He smiles and then his face retreats into blankness again. The world I created spins around us as I realise that, if he can answer this, I can reach the full extent of Jarek, hidden there somewhere in the Heaven I made for him. I'm clasping at straws, I know I am, because this man in front of me isn't Jarek as he really was. He's a man we've pieced together from his memories.

'Did you love your wife?' I shout this time, begging him to answer me, shaking him by the shoulders and sending my own tremors into him like poison arrows.

'You have to tell me, Jarek!' I slam my fists into his chest and he stumbles back to avoid losing his balance. Our eyes meet and I detect confusion floating over his face. I realise he has responded. Not with a memory, but with something else.

'Jarek?' I clasp him to me, wrapping my arms right around him, squeezing my body into his. But the moment is lost. He stands there, immobile, and I let my tears soak into his shirt. Just let it be over.

I feel Lela grip my hand, the short, sharp edges of her nails pushing into my palm.

'Isobel? Isobel? Are you okay?' a voice says in my ear, and I realise it's not Lela, but Daniel leaning over me. Darkness surrounds him, the side of his face lit only by the holograms at the bedside. His eyebrows are drawn together in concern and the flecks of hazel in the deep brown of his irises seem to glow. The movement behind him doesn't come into focus at first, but after a few seconds, I realise the people in the room are turned away from me, moving from readout to hologram and back again. Their voices chatter and clatter off the walls.

'You're awake,' he says. His voice is soft and level. 'You're fine.' He smiles in what looks like genuine relief. A real smile.

I open my eyes fully at him and tense my stomach muscles as I pull my head up towards his ear.

'I'm not fucking fine,' I whisper, clipping each word into an assault.

'I'm sorry,' he says, and his startled expression suggests he means it. 'They were almost there – you were part of Jarek's Heaven for a moment – but then they lost it again.'

Maya appears next to him, looking just as concerned. 'I'm sorry; it's much harder than we thought, Isobel.'

'If you can't figure it out,' I bark, switching my gaze and my venom towards her, 'then let *me* do it.'

CHAPTER TWENTY

'First of all,' I tell them. 'If we're going to carry on doing this, I need a way of getting out of there because, let me tell you, having a panic attack isn't much fun.'

The three of us – Daniel, Maya and I – are sitting around a small bistro table at the back of a Parsi café. I refused to have the meeting in the labs. I'm spending enough time in there already. Maya's eyes are darting around us and she shifts about on her chair. She thinks we're going to be bombed by a drone at any moment. I look at her face and I can see myself, in a half-dream, staring out of the window in the middle of the night, imagining planes swooping overhead. I spent so many nights like that. But I feel different now, like the grief has locked me into a transparent box that numbs not just me, but my surroundings, too, making me untouchable. The fear can't reach me.

I stifle a yawn. I slept so deeply last night that I am finding it hard to wake up – which reminds me: 'And I didn't give anyone authority to tranquillise me.'

'No, and I am so sorry about that, Isobel.' Maya glances out of the corner of her eye at Daniel. 'But we're still trying to figure out what works.' She pauses, as if considering her words. Then she leans forward, dropping her voice. 'You knew when you agreed to this that it was experimental.'

'Have you had this kind of attack before?' Daniel asks, eyes narrowed.

I feel like he'll have a whole dossier on me by the end of this. I think about lying, but it won't help my cause. 'Yeah, a few times. And I can handle them. But no more tranquillisers,' I say firmly, and they nod.

No one has touched the plate of turmeric-laced potatoes in the middle of the table. People chatter around us. Outside, it's a bright morning and you can taste the humidity in the air. Taxis and rickshaws fly past and I watch the charcoal tandoor smoke rise from a fish stall across the street. I turn my attention back to Maya. I'd like to see her do it. I'd like to see her agree to be put to sleep in a room full of strangers and let everyone watch her innermost fantasies play out.

'What *is* awesome is that we managed to link your consciousness so quickly into Jarek's simulation,' she says. 'And there was something – what seemed like a moment of connection between your Heavens – right at the end.'

'It wasn't much of a Heaven by that stage, but, yes, point taken.'

Attempting to ignore the fact that she's talking to me like she would a child, I reach out and take a potato from the plate. It's still hot and I try not to screw up my face as it scalds the top of my mouth. The taste of ginger tingles down the side of my tongue and I wonder why food doesn't feature more in my Heaven. I'll have to make a list of things to add when this is all finished.

'We just couldn't quite keep it there,' Maya continues. 'And we couldn't get him to respond to you.'

'Should I have been more deeply immersed? I felt the needle of the tranquilliser.'

Maya seems to ignore me.

'Before I went under, I felt sure he wouldn't be able to see me,' I say. 'But when I was in there, it felt strange that he didn't.'

I note that Daniel has largely remained quiet. Not just quiet, but preoccupied. Right now, he's staring down at his foot, folded across his knee. As if he knows I'm looking at him, he pulls his head up, meeting my eyes.

'So, now we've got to figure out either how we can truly connect with Jarek, or how to get deep enough into his Heaven to see a ghost memory,' he says, and I feel like he's completely missed my point. I want to carry on telling him about how it felt, and have the detective in him listen to me in that intent way he is trained to listen: as if he's being told the secrets of the universe.

'I guess we hoped that there would be a reaction of some kind to a new event in his Heaven,' says Maya. 'That's what Jess and our team said was a possibility – that his Heaven program would respond in some way – especially to something so close to what's already featured in his Heaven and to a person that he . . . cares for.' She stumbles over the last few words and I'm surprised that I feel rather sorry for her. It's an awkward situation to discuss. We all know he was married. We all know what kind of woman I am. I realise it can't be easy for her to say it aloud.

'But it didn't work,' Daniel interjects, perhaps sensing the unease. 'So, do we have any other ideas?'

'Well, there are a couple of things that the guys back at Valhalla thought we could try . . .' Maya begins.

I shake my head. 'Jarek's mirror neurons,' I say. 'To go deeper, we need his consciousness. We need to see the real him.'

Maya nods in agreement without taking her eyes from mine.

I take a deep breath and sit back in my chair. 'We need to talk to Jess about this. I'm not prepared to do anything – anything at all – that might endanger Jarek.'

'Or you, for that matter,' says Daniel.

I glance at him. It feels as if his role in this is changing. He is becoming more like my guardian. I decide to try to slink through this chink in his armour.

'Have your team tracked him down yet? The guy Sarah was seeing?'

Daniel sighs and Maya studies him as he responds. 'He's being questioned, yes.'

'Let's get back to the issue at hand, shall we?' Maya begins. 'What about if—'

'Why should I even carry on with all this?' I say, cutting her off. 'I know Jarek didn't do it, and now there's this new lead—'

'Jarek is still a primary suspect,' Daniel says, not letting me finish.

'You're wrong.'

'Prove it,' he fires back in a voice I imagine he usually reserves for the interrogation room.

I press the heels of my hands into my forehead. 'Ideas are no good,' I say, without moving my hands from my face. 'I want a solution that's going to work, first time. And Jess is the person to do that. Everything that's left of him is in her lab. She's the only person I – we – can trust.'

My words are final; they both know I'm right. I'm glad I don't have to carry on talking. A fresh grief has sprung out of nowhere and is throbbing in my throat.

'London is over five hours behind us,' says Daniel. 'We'll have to call her this afternoon.'

I look for the time in my eye lens. 'Two o'clock. I'll try her at two – from my room. I'll patch you both in.'

The power is back in my hands and neither of them seems to query it.

I turn up the air conditioning in my suite, pour myself a glass of water and settle on to the chaise longue at the end of the bed. Feeling drowsy, I gulp back the water. I press my middle finger against the opening of my ear canal. 'Call the office of Jess Sorbonne,' I whisper. I wait for it to connect. 'Copy in Daniel Lyden and Maya Denton.'

A male voice answers. I tell him my name and ask for Jess. I activate the hologram viewer on my Codex and position it on the window ledge opposite me. 'One moment, madam.'

'Isobel?' A watery gleam in my vision becomes Jess. She's grinning. 'How was it, you intrepid explorer?'

'My Heaven? It surprised me, Jess.' I pause, teasing her. 'It's phenomenal.'

'And how are you?' she asks, her voice more serious.

'I'm okay. You?'

'Fine; I've no complaints.'

'I've got Daniel and Maya copied in.' Even if they're not listening live, they'll get the audio file.

'Okay. So, I hear things didn't go to plan yesterday?'

'No.' I resist telling her the whole story. I don't want to sound petulant. 'Jarek didn't respond to me at all.'

'That's because it's just his Heaven simulation, not his actual consciousness. It's not really Jarek.' Her tone is a little sharper than I would have expected.

'So, what's next? How can I get deeper? How can I get him to react to me?'

I'm testing her, waiting to see if she has also come to the same conclusion as me.

'It's more a question of *if*, Isobel,' she says, slowly. 'I did tell Valhalla this.'

There's a suggestion in her voice – a blame. I raise my eyebrows and hope that Maya is listening, wriggling awkwardly in her seat.

'If,' I repeat.

'You know as well as I do that this is all theory. It's an experimental procedure. I felt confident that we could get you to wake up inside your own Heaven, but to wake up in his? That's another question entirely.' Her words hang in the sterile, air-conditioned environment of my hotel room.

'And the answer to the question involves Jarek's mirror neurons, right?' I scratch my fingernails into the velvet of the chaise longue.

Jess sighs and looks away. 'If there was a way of doing it, then – yes – it's possible that there would be some kind of natural reaction in his mirror neurons to seeing you, and you might be able to get further into his Heaven.'

'If you could connect my consciousness with Jarek's somehow?'

'Yes, if we could do that. We think love is one of the experiential clusters of emotions that is encoded into the mirror neurons – encoded twice. Connecting your mirror neurons to Jarek's might evoke a deeper level of consciousness – one not specifically written into his Heaven, but that is responsive. Responsive to you.'

I swallow my embarrassment. I feel unclean – more like a mistress than ever before.

'You don't sound sure, Jess. How do we do it?'

'I . . . I really don't know.' It's a marked hesitation and, in that drawn-out second, I realise what I've got myself into: something incredibly dangerous.

'You do know.' I stand up and brush down my trousers as if the deep creases in the linen are going to disappear under my hands. As I pace the small area at the end of the bed, I look over at the hologram of Jess. Her face shows concern. After having built my Heaven together, she is well acquainted with my doggedness.

'So Jarek's Heaven is pre-programmed – finite – which is no good to us. We need a better chance of identifying and visualising the ghost memories that you believe are backed up in his mirror neurons, right?'

Jess nods slowly.

'A part of me must find the part of him that's hidden inside that bunch of cells in your lab,' I continue. 'And the only way to do that is physically, not digitally.'

'Correct.'

'So, what if you just throw my mirror neurons in with his? Let them react to each other; let our consciousness bind together?' I feel slightly breathless and, as soon as I finish speaking, I realise that this is not just a possible solution – it is the only solution. I watch Jess closely as she looks away from the camera. The hologram isn't perfect. Only the bounce of her curls gives away the fact that she's ever so slightly shaking her head.

'Jess?'

'You're right.' She turns back towards me and a look of resignation flutters across her pale features. She spreads her hands. 'I knew you'd be right.'

'Didn't Daniel ask you to do this from the beginning?'

She meets my eyes but says nothing. We are both silent as I wonder what to ask next.

'Can it be done?' I ask.

She takes a while to respond and, when she does, she doesn't meet my eyes but mutters into her chest. 'I don't know.'

'Come on, Jess. You *know* you can do this. How? And how soon?'

'I'd have to come to India, bringing Jarek's neurons with me. And then we'd have to insert probes into your brain, tap right on to your mirror neurons from your brain, connect them directly to his somehow . . . run some artificial synapses between them, or something.'

'So why the hesitation?'

'I've never done that with a living person before and no one there will have done, either. I can't tell you how much of a risk it would be. I don't even know if it'd work. And the ethics of it trouble me. Jarek doesn't get a say in this.'

'But we agreed to allow each other into our Heavens.' I know that I sound like a sullen child. 'I have access.'

'It's dodgy ground, Isobel.'

'I don't care. I don't care about the risks. As long as his Heaven is still safe, I'll do anything.'

Anything? I repeat in my head. Would I really do anything to prove Jarek innocent?

'We're getting away from my point. I'm more worried about *you*, Isobel, not him.'

'I'm not afraid of dying, Jess,' I say, my voice thick.

'Yes, you are. Everybody is.'

'But I've seen Heaven.' I grin, knowing how cheesy it sounds.

She shakes her head. 'The nature of intrusive brain surgery and heavy, lengthy sedation aside, I've no idea how your neurons will react with Jarek's. There's no way of knowing whether they will be altered by the process in any way. There's no way of knowing whether they'll remain fully functional. And those neurons are all we have of your mind – of *you*, Isobel.'

It's my turn to fall silent.

'We might lose you completely. You'd be a piece of meat on an operating table, Izzy,' she says, her pitch rising. 'Your body would live, breathe, but you? You'd be gone.'

CHAPTER TWENTY-ONE

I wake in pitch black to a knock on the door of my hotel room. I glance at the time. It's one a.m. I'm warm, despite the air conditioning, fully dressed and curled up on the bed. There's another knock and I struggle up to go and answer it. The brightness of the corridor washes over me, silhouetting Daniel's slender frame.

'I can't ask you to do this,' he says. 'I didn't realise what it would involve.'

'I did,' I mutter. And it's almost true. I've already thrown everything away to be here: my relationship, my home, my job, my career. There's nothing of me left. Right now, I feel as if I want to sleep until my body has had enough of this life. 'Now, if you'll excuse me.' I try to close the door but he slides his foot into the room. His shoe butts into my big toe.

'I'm concerned about your mental state, Isobel.'

'My mental state? You think I'm *crazy*?' I move towards him, letting the light fall upon my face.

He looks at me, his face bursting with rationality. He glances up and down the corridor. 'I'm not forcing you to stay here. No one is.'

I don't speak. I clamp my teeth together and stare back at him, resolute.

'Let me get you home,' he whispers.

'This might be your investigation, but I bet you're in far too deep, now, Daniel. Aren't you?'

'For Christ's sake, Isobel!' He hits the door frame with his fist, but not before I see him flinch. As I take a small step backwards, I think of the way he behaves in the presence of Maya and the Valhalla team. I replay the subservient nods and acquiescing hand gestures in my mind and know I am right. Valhalla are pushing this forward, not him.

When he raises his head again, his composure has returned. 'I'm sorry; I shouldn't have snapped.'

'It's okay,' I find myself saying. 'Look, do you want to see if the bar is still open?'

We wander down the elegant staircase that sweeps from the guest rooms to the public areas of the hotel and make our way into the Harbour Bar. The seating area is mainly empty, but a few large groups of people, dressed in suits and cocktail dresses, are gathered against the white marble bar, chatting and laughing. I spy a gap and squeeze in, as Daniel follows me. I lean forward to catch the bartender's eye.

'I'll have a whisky, please; whatever's good.' My eyes scan the extensive selection copied in multiple images behind the mirrored bar.

Daniel pokes me in the side with his finger. 'You're not supposed to drink before the operation, are you?' he asks.

'Why did you agree to come for a drink with me if you're going to be pernickety?'

Daniel rolls his eyes. Something about the way he does it reminds me of myself. I pinch my thumb and index finger together. 'Just a teensy bit. Room eleven nineteen,' I tell the bartender. 'And my colleague here will have . . . ?'

'Tonic water, please.'

'No, seriously, what do you want?'

'I don't drink,' Daniel says, smiling at the bartender and avoiding my stern gaze. The bartender waggles his head.

'Wow.' I wish Lela was standing next to me instead. I could go upstairs and wake her. She wouldn't mind, once she'd woken up. We'd share a bottle of wine. We'd laugh. We'd forget about why we were here. But then I remember that I need to mine Daniel for information on the case, and I turn my attention back to him.

'So, does your work always bring you to such exotic destinations?' I ask him.

'I've been to India a few times, actually. I used to work on hacking investigations.' He always speaks so quietly. We stand beside each other, watching the bartender prepare our drinks.

'Should we have the ice?' I ask Daniel, under my breath.

'I've just told you not to have a drink before undergoing tomorrow's procedure and you're asking me about ice?'

'But will it be full of bacteria?'

'What year do you think this is – 2003?' He smirks. 'Have you been brushing your teeth with bottled water, too?'

I shoot a disapproving glance his way. The smile is for himself because he knows he's right, but he's focused on the display behind the bar. It's showing the latest news broadcast on some international channel. *British Navy denies laying mines in South China Sea.*

'I don't know why we're getting involved,' I mutter.

'Because that's what we do.'

'My boyfriend – my ex – is an M.o.D. consultant. But all I know is that it's all a complete mess. Everyone's getting involved. It's got every element for another world war.'

Our drinks are pushed towards us and I take a deep gulp. The sharp spiciness numbs the back of my throat. I wish it could numb me all over. I would stay at the bar, but Daniel walks away and takes a seat on one of the leather banquettes beneath the picture windows. I sit down beside him and watch as he crushes the crescent of lime against the inside of the glass with his thumb.

'Are we going to add *neurotic* to your list of personality traits?' he asks me.

'There's a list?'

He taps the side of his head. 'There's always a list.'

'And who are we calling neurotic?'

He glances at me and inclines his head. 'Touché.'

I twist to look out through the glass, cupping my hands around my eyes to block out the reflections. The Gateway of India is regal in the darkness, lit by golden uplights. Tourists and hawkers still flock around the feet of the arch. Beyond it, the lights atop boat masts bob in the deep blue darkness, reminding me of the visualisation of Clair's Heaven in the Electric Lab. The walls of the harbour fade into the sea and the sea fades into the sky. Even in here, I'm sure that I can taste the salt in the air.

'You know what I'm going to ask you,' I say, turning back around. I hook my nail over the rim of my glass and raise my eyes to his.

'The investigation.' He almost smiles. 'You want me to tell you that someone other than your beloved Jarek savaged and squeezed the life out of the woman he once loved.'

I'm not accustomed to Daniel speaking with such emotion and his words shake me. I open my mouth but the questions have vanished.

'You really want to know what happened? You want to know what we know?' Daniel's voice is hushed, unhurried. It scares me. 'Someone let themselves into that house while Sarah was preparing dinner. They put on a pair of gloves and compressed her throat for several minutes until she was unconscious and brain dead. It was done weakly, slowly – without skill. She would have been in excruciating pain. Blood vessels in her eyes and face popped. Her larynx was crushed. Then the perpetrator forced a barrel-load of drugs down her crushed windpipe with the handle of a wooden spoon, just in case she wasn't quite gone. Is that enough information for you?'

I tear my eyes away from his and look over the dark water of the harbour. 'Jarek wasn't strong enough to do that,' I say. It comes out as a whisper.

'Oh, you'd be surprised how easy it is.'

'So, who else could've done it?'

'It's a very short list, Isobel.'

'Comprising?'

He shakes his head then and leans back in his seat.

I push back my shoulders. 'So how long have you been tracking down cold-blooded murderers?' I ask before taking another gulp of whisky.

He unfolds his arms and swirls his drink around. The ice clinks against the glass.

'Are we not talking about work anymore?' I ask.

'No, we're not.'

'What *are* we allowed to talk about, then?'

'Anything else you like: art, politics, philosophy . . . any medical issues you're concerned about.' I notice that I can rarely see his teeth when he smiles. He's always so guarded. I knock back the last of my drink and hold my glass aloft, signalling for another. Daniel wraps his hand around the glass and lowers it to the table, shaking his head at the bartender.

'If I can't have another drink, can we at least talk fashion, then?'

He rolls his eyes at me.

'Can I ask why you have seven versions of the same top?' I want to reach out and rub the finely knitted black fabric between my fingertips, but I don't. Instead, I run my fingernail over a scratch on the wooden table in front of us, gauging its depth.

'You like things to be perfect, don't you?' he asks, swivelling around to face me.

'Doesn't everyone?'

He sticks out his bottom lip and shakes his head. 'I'm surprised that a perfectionist would like getting drunk. I'm especially surprised that a perfectionist would get a tattoo.' He gestures towards my ankle where the feathers of ink are covered by the baggy linen of my trousers.

'Why?'

'Because why would you physically – permanently – mark something that's already exactly as it should be?'

'Are you saying I'm perfect, Inspector Lyden?' I purse my lips in mock-flirtation but his seriousness remains steadfast. 'Am I an angel?' I pull at my trousers from the knee and twist my foot to show him the tattoo.

He bends forward and lowers his head to inspect it. He twists his lips to one side. 'Why an angel?' he asks.

'I was . . .' I pause. I'm not even sure anymore. I look out of the window. 'When I got it done, I was worried, I think. Worried that what I was doing for people wasn't good enough, or the right thing.' I tug back the linen and press my index finger over a wing. I know he agrees.

'Everyone says you're excellent at your job, Isobel.'

I look at Daniel closely and wonder who 'everyone' is. How many people has he asked about me?

'As I've already told you,' I say, letting the fabric fall, 'I hate it.'

'No; it's nice.' He's polite, if nothing else.

'I'm going to bed.' As I stand up, I can feel the whisky run down the blood vessels from my knees into my feet. I can feel him watching me as I make my way out of the bar.

When I get back to my room, Lela is sitting on the floor outside my door.

'You silly woman!' I grin and pull her to her feet. 'What are you doing?'

'I couldn't sleep. I wandered down here and saw the light shining from under your door.' At first, seeing her is a relief from Daniel's intensity, but then I realise that she's glaring at me. 'You shouldn't be drinking,' she adds.

'I've been downstairs, but I wasn't drinking.' As perceptive as Lela is, she often ignores my little white lies. I stare into the door lock and it clicks open.

'Can I come in for a bit?' she asks.

I glance at the time and then I look at her, nibbling at the skin of her thumb. 'Can we talk in the morning, before I go in?'

'I just need to know if you're all right.' She looks at me intently for a few seconds, her head cocked to one side. 'I'm fine, if you are.'

I take her by the shoulders. 'I'm all right, Lela. I'm fine.'

She pulls me into a hug. 'I'm sorry for what you're going through.' Her voice is warm and muffled in the hollow of my neck.

'They killed Sarah while she was making dinner,' I whisper after a few seconds. 'Daniel said she would've been in a lot of pain.'

Lela pulls away from me, clasping her hands to my shoulders. 'Is that who you were with? What's his game, telling you things like that?'

I shrug.

She sighs. 'I'm sorry I couldn't be there for the last procedure,' she says. 'They told me there's too much going on, now, that I'd get in the way.'

'I know. I'll ask Maya again, if you like, tomorrow. She might change her mind,' I say. I reach out and flick away the last particles of mascara from underneath her eye. I should tell her that I do wish she could be there, that she makes me feel stronger simply by her presence in a room. But I don't. Partly because I need to reassure her that I'll be fine. Partly because it's easier not to.

'Go on!' I say. 'Get a good night's sleep and I'll see you in the morning. The next procedure is in a matter of hours.'

'Which is exactly why you shouldn't be drinking whisky.'

I sigh and turn my head away, gazing down the empty corridor.

She stares at me, her expression unreadable. 'What changed, Isobel?'

I look back at her and I feel the honesty between us, the complete acceptance of each other. Ten years of friendship and she has always understood me. I hesitate, searching for the true answer, for the reason I turned my perfectly ordered life upside down.

'I found somebody who believed in me.'

Her face tips forward, her lips downturned. 'Night, Izzy.' She blows me a kiss and turns away. It's only as I look at the slope of her shoulders as she retreats down the corridor that I realise that what I said has hurt her. She has always believed in me.

I close the door and stumble out of my clothes, leaving a trail of them behind me. I'm fuzzy with alcohol and, I suppose, the remnants of anaesthetic. I manage to work a toothbrush around my teeth without turning on the bathroom light. For once, I ignore the bottle of mineral water and drop my head into the sink, letting the tap fill my mouth before swilling and spitting. I crawl into bed and lie awake for a few minutes, flat on my back. I imagine Jess packing for the trip and think about the runaway train I've put into motion. It is gathering speed. In eight hours, my body will be forced into a coma while my Heaven — the memories and hopes and dreams I've worked on day and night for the past few weeks — will be activated. And then, my consciousness will meet Jarek's consciousness. We'll be together again in a way that I can't yet conceive. It *should* work. But even if nothing goes wrong, it will still feel a little bit like dying.

CHAPTER TWENTY-TWO

The previous times I've launched myself off this precipice and into the chasm that awaits, I've felt quite calm. It's a case in point that I've never thought in terms as dramatic as that analogy before. But, today, my nerves are fizzing in my extremities. My stomach is complaining of hunger. Even having Jess here doesn't seem to have helped. She is shaving away patches of my hair with a silent dignity that asks me to trust her. Her cool fingertips press lightly into my skull and the skin of my face.

'I'll ask you one last time,' she whispers, her voice hovering somewhere above the top of my head. 'Are you sure?' I stare into the white cotton of her lab coat and remain silent. She takes her hands from me and stands back, crouching to look at me. Her eyes are calm grey pools. Her dark hair is scraped back from her face so that it almost looks straight, and I notice, for the first time, silvery white hairs springing out from the severe centre parting. Perhaps she's older than I thought. She gives me time. She waits with a patience that I'd like to test. I blink back at her.

'I know it's important we get this right, but I'll try to keep it as short as possible, Izzy,' she says. She moves around me, checking wires and displays and pushing the bedside table away in order to tuck the drip alongside me. I feel her fingers catch on the dips between my ribs.

'I'm aware you haven't been eating well.' Like Lela, she is always finding new ways to tell me off.

Jess inclines her head in the direction of the anaesthetist. It's a man today. He has a kinder face than the woman he replaces. He approaches and runs a smooth finger over the inside of my arm, feeling for the vein and deciding where to place the new anaesthetic tattoo.

'How long?' I murmur, running my eyes over Lela, Daniel and Maya, who are all standing at the back of the room. Maya agreed to let Lela in at the last moment, with a little persuasion. She had to rush down here from the hotel, so she's not wearing a scrap of make-up and her hair isn't brushed. It makes her look younger – closer to the age she was when I met her on my first day at Oakley Associates. That was years ago now. I smile at her and make a little wave without lifting my hand from the bed. She waves back, her face frozen with what I assume is worry.

Beside her, Daniel and Maya are turned away from me with their heads bent together. Maya is talking with a whispered ferocity, accompanied by sharp hand gestures. I start to lose interest in what they might be talking about and I'm not even sure what I've just asked Jess.

'The surgery will take the most time – cutting through your skull, inserting all the probes, getting them to the right spot and connecting up the artificial synapses. I think that will take quite a lot of fine-tuning to get right. So, the prep alone could be four, maybe five hours.' Jess's words almost run into each other, she's talking so fast. I sense that she is nervous. 'Then we'll activate your Heaven and link your mirror neurons up to Jarek's.'

'And you'll have an idea, quite quickly, if it's working?'

She crouches by my side and folds her arms on the bed, level with my chest. 'Yeah, hopefully, like we discussed, your consciousness will then overlay your Heaven and help shape it. Your mirror neurons should quickly fill the gaps – make assumptions – to tie your Heavens together into a cohesive whole. It's like with vision: our brain can fall for optical tricks and illusions because it's so keen to make a full picture. It takes shortcuts.'

Her matter-of-fact tone fades and the real Jess smiles gently at me. 'I'll stay with you between the surgical procedures. I'll watch you.' She glances over her shoulder. 'Lela, too.'

'What will happen to me?' I ask, and try to raise my arm to point at the side of my head, but it won't move. Emotions sweep through me so quickly that I can't even identify them. I feel water coating my eyes, blurring the last of my vision as they sink closed.

'I will do this perfectly,' she says. 'I will make sure those synapses and neurons of yours remain unchanged. Everything will be as it should be, I promise.' She pauses and I wonder if she thinks I'm already gone. 'I can explain it to you, Izzy, but I can't understand it for you,' she whispers.

The last thing I hear as I'm going under, clutching on to reality, is what sounds like the scream of a siren. Every other sense has blackened, but my ears register it as I slip away. It crashes rhythmically into the corners of the room as they close in around me. It is the colour of danger and it smells of fear.

*

I lie face down in the grass, breathing in the aroma of chlorophyll and feeling the sun heat the cotton shirt on my back. My sister is doing the same and we are giggling at ourselves hysterically. My belly is full and the birdsong is loud in the trees. Now we're collecting blackberries from the hedgerows and I look at my hands. They are black and blue and dirty, laced with scratches, beaded with blood. Where my sister was, my cats now purr, looking out at me from within the bases of the brambles. I crouch down and I'm in my childhood home, rolling on the rug. Olive is a kitten and she paws at me with her pink velvet pads, her huge eyes watching my every move. I hear my sister's disembodied giggle and the rustle of damp autumn wind through a hedgerow. Juniper and Olive mew at me, asking for their dinner.

Then it all blends and blurs and sharpens into a crackle that is more tactile than noise. It tugs at me and it feels like my body is being altered by it. I look down at the palms of my hands and, as I'm studying the lines and the bands of my rings, the edges of me shatter. A white noise thunders through me and I remember that I can't get out. Pulling out of this too fast would be more dangerous than seeing it through. I'm screaming and laughing and my lungs feel like they will explode. I'm spinning and falling through rooms and vehicles and sky, feeling that it should be making me sick, but it's only mentally confusing, rather than physically disorienting.

I'm on Jarek's rugby field again, surrounded by mud-splattered men. A mist of sweat rises to envelop us and I feel nothing but pure elation. My legs are strong and sturdy beneath me and I'm running through pine trees, being chased by my kid sister. I laugh because I always win. I'm cradling a tiny baby and she is screaming through her gummy mouth. She is pink and purple and white and hairless. It's wonderful, it's beautiful, and yet I'm weeping. We're running along a cliff top and, somehow, I know that the little girl ahead of me is the same child as the baby. She glances back at me and laughs, her brown hair covering her face, and it makes my heart sing. A shadowy figure runs beside me and I know that it's Jarek's wife. But Jarek has no idea who it is. He didn't want her in his Heaven, but he wanted this memory. So, she's there, but without identity, fading into the background. Yet there's an underlying sense of darkness that has no time or place or meaning. It makes me gag and I close my eyes to it.

'Izz.' Jarek's voice is raspy in my ear. I'm spinning into his arms as he yanks me towards him. Everything inside me feels broken and healed at the same time. But then he kisses me and the world falls silent as the pressure of his lips seems to burst my eardrums. I can't feel the paving slabs beneath my feet but I know they are there, struggling to hold me upright as I melt into his embrace. Our first kiss. The only kiss I ever need to remember.

We're in the basement safe-room again. I can't look. I'm too scared that I'm imagining it. Because, if he's talking to me like this, as he would have done in life, it's real. We may not be in this building or in these bodies or in these clothes, but our minds are real.

Against all odds, it has worked. Jess is a genius.

'Are you okay?' Jarek asks and I gasp as he runs his hand over my back.

'Yes.' It sounds like a question, I realise. Because I'm not quite okay – of course I'm not. And I find myself wondering for the first time how much of my time with Jarek was spent being honest.

'I'm dead, aren't I? This is my Heaven?' Confusion dances

across his face and I remember that he has no idea – no idea at all.

I nod my head apologetically, until I realise he's grinning.

'You *are* the best, Izz. What you've done is incredible. Incredible.' He smiles, and I know with a rush of emotion that this is, without doubt, the man I love, not some figment of my imagination.

'Are you dead?' he asks me, and I almost laugh, but shake it away.

'No.' He doesn't need to ask me to explain, the questions are written all over his face. 'It's complicated.'

'Of course it is!'

I expect him to grab at me playfully or latch his mouth on to my neck and trail kisses up to my ear, but he doesn't. I almost lean into him with desire, but then I find myself wondering how well Daniel and Maya can see this scene and I hold back. I realise I haven't planned what I'm going to say at this point. I never considered that I was going to have to interrogate him. I wait for him to ask me why I'm here, and how, but he doesn't. We sit facing each other, our hands in our laps. I want to be somewhere else in our Heavens. I want to be free but I know that I'm not.

'Did you love your wife?' I stare into his eyes, half expecting him to freeze up again but imploring him to answer me at the same time.

'My wife?' He shakes his head, knitting his brows. His eyes wander, searching for something that isn't there. The memories that feature in his Heaven are limited and she is not in them, it's obvious. But Daniel's words enter my mind: *If he did something, perhaps something incredibly violent, then it's the kind of powerful memory that could be hidden in there somewhere.* Somewhere in his mirror neurons – the cells that are making it possible for us to have this conversation.

'You were married, Jarek. She was the mother of your children.'

'Oh.' He frowns. 'Then why isn't she in my Heaven?'

I ignore his question. 'When you died . . .' I choke on my words, feeling his absence anew, despite the magic that places him here, a simulation of flesh and blood, in front of me. 'She was found dead, too. She was murdered.'

'Oh my God.' His mouth falls open and he stares at me, eyes wide.

I find it hard to continue, but then I think of the darkness that I felt when I was experiencing his Heaven. I saw it, I felt it, what feels like mere moments ago. I think of Daniel's calm, rational insistence. I think of the urgent, passionate force Jarek pressed upon me in life. Could his anger be as highly charged? And although it is half swallowed and broken, just enough doubt enters my mind to utter the words: 'Did you kill her?'

'*Kill* her?' he scoffs.

'You can tell me,' I find myself saying. 'I just need to know. I won't tell anyone.' The words slink out and disappear into the dim corners of the room.

'I can't even remember having a wife, Isobel. All I remember is you!' He clings to me and kisses my ear. I note that it's the first time he's done so. 'Even if I *had* murdered her, how would I remember it here, in my Heaven?'

'They think . . .' I begin, and I realise that I should have said 'I'. I scan his face but find no sign that he noticed. 'Your mirror neurons – the part of you that lives on in the lab, encoding your consciousness – that's what's allowing us to have this conversation. I think that some memories can be stored there, too. Memories with strong emotional resonance.'

'Like love?' he asks.

'Yes, like love,' I reply. 'But also like hate.'

He stands up and drops his hands to his sides.

'I understand what you're saying, Izz. But don't you know that I would never have done anything like that?'

'Of course; of course I do.'

'Then why do you even have to ask?'

I shake my head. Now I'm here, I have no idea why. I'm so far away from myself that my memory is failing me. What made me agree to all of this? Was it that I wanted to see my own Heaven? Was it that I wanted to see Jarek again, by any way possible? Can I really have been so blindly driven by love? Yes, yes, yes. Did I also need to see what I've spent my life dedicated to creating? Did I need to rediscover some lost belief in the ethics of my profession? Yes, oh, yes.

'Because it's up to me to prove you didn't do it. I'm trying to find a way to demonstrate your innocence.'

I let him pull me up and squeeze me tightly to his chest. I feel the love permeating through my clothes and I know from his silence that he had nothing to do with Sarah's death. He didn't kill her and there is no memory to be found that says otherwise.

He kisses my nose and I realise that, when I leave him, my job is done. I will be finished with all of this. The probes will come out of my brain, our mirror neurons will be disconnected and that will be it. Even my Heaven, when I do die, won't be able to replicate this strange reality. We won't be able to make any more moments together. We don't have a future together. All we have is old memories and beautiful lies of our own making. The panic spreads through my chest, quickly, aggressively. I can't go, I can't go, I can't go.

'I don't want to go back,' I whisper into his Adam's apple, blindly hoping that no one watching me in the simulation will hear. 'I want to stay here with you.'

'I'll be here, Izz, when you're ready.' He tilts my chin up towards his face. His jaw is clenched and I think I see tears gathering at the corners of his eyes. 'But you have a life to live first.'

'I don't; I don't have a life.'

'Don't be silly.'

And then, for a snippet of a moment, the decisive clip of scissors through a thread. Everything trembles. Jarek is looking around him, as if recovering his balance, and I know that he felt it, too. And then it happens again, for longer. It's a silent scream that rips through the basement and my body fractures. It's like when I'm flicking through documents too quickly in my office and they judder as they struggle to catch up with the movement of my finger. Or when I look for the time in my eye lens when I'm jogging and it shifts awkwardly. Tremors convulse our world. And then it's back to how it was before.

'What was that?' asks Jarek, and I see him trying to disguise his fear. He presses his hand against the wall.

'Just a glitch?' It's a brave face I present him with. On the inside, I wait for bricks to fall and dust to explode around us, but I hear nothing. It's gone again. I place my hand upon the door handle.

And then I'm thrown to the ground. Instead of scraping the

base of my hands against concrete slabs, I'm looking out over the azure sea in the Cinque Terre. It's a scene from my Heaven I haven't experienced before. But it's not right. The view is beneath me, beneath my hands and knees, dropping away from where the floor should be. I'm suspended, as if on glass. It's all out of context and I can smell cut grass, invading my nostrils with the aggression of burning hair. I can see Jarek is standing with his back flush against a wall, as if gravity is forcing him against it, as if he's on an accelerating roller coaster. I can almost see the distortion of the g-force in his cheeks. I look around me and a door stands on its own in the centre of the room, ajar. My cat, Juniper, lies on the vertical face of the door and, when she opens her mouth to mewl at me, what comes out is the soft rock music my mother and I used to dance to. I feel suddenly, violently sick.

'Jarek! Jarek!' I call and his eyes meet mine. 'Something's going wrong!'

'Is it you? Because you've come in here?' It stings like an accusation, but he seems to correct himself, stumbling over and crouching beside me, steadying himself with one hand. The veins at his neck and temples are engorged with blood. His eyes are wide and his mouth is pulled back, as if with pain.

'We need to try to move. Maybe this part of the Heaven simulation is corrupted,' I say. My thoughts try to catch up with my words. Something could have damaged this part of our neurons, I think, in the physical location in which our consciousness is currently active and connected. Maybe elsewhere in this cluster of neurons keeping me alive there is refuge.

'Okay, let's go!' Jarek grabs my hand and helps me up. I struggle to connect my vision with thoughts, and thoughts with actions.

Leave ... The door ... What is a door? I look aimlessly at the different objects that are slipping in and out of my vision. I seem to stroke them with my fingertips before letting them float onward. One of these things is a door, but which one? And why do I need a door, anyway? I might say these things, but I also might just think them. I can feel Jarek shake me hard by the shoulders but it doesn't reach me. I am numb and in pain simultaneously. I can't laugh or cry or scream or ... I let him gather me in his arms and carry me up the stairs, out of the basement, and then in the next moment we're running and the world is dying around us.

A blur of colours and a cacophony of sounds ripple around my head. Everything is rich with texture. One moment it rubs lambswool-soft on my neck and the next it catches like needles. I look for the blackberry bushes but they are not there. My emotions, too, are scattered. I veer from horror that pumps and spits in my veins to a discordant easiness – not quite contentment, more an absence of feeling: the quiet acceptance of dementia. There is no time for a panic attack.

'When do we stop?' asks Jarek, without looking at me.

Before I can reply, I see a mirage glimmering before us. It waits for us. It becomes our target. Around it, the world takes shape. It's the literal light at the end of this tunnel.

'Jarek!' I point at it with my free hand and squint. It's the convertible. The paintwork gleams oyster. The doors are open and maybe, just maybe, that's the grumble of the engine I can hear. We rush ever closer, I see the highway stretching out beyond it and I feel my feet falling on tarmac. It swallows the sound of my fear.

Jarek grins at me, jubilant. 'Keep going!' he says, although I'm not breathless. I know I should be, but I don't feel the physicality of it. It's an incomplete illusion.

'You can drive,' I say. My eye catches the sunlight reflecting off the silver back plate of the car and, as it hits my retina, the ground falls away. It's as if a chasm has opened in the middle of the road. It's like a photograph has been torn in two and then awkwardly pieced back together. In places, it sticks, it almost works, and in others the two sides are so far apart as to be unrecognisable as the same image. I manage to pull myself to a halt only just in time, my toes teetering at the edge, my arms wheeling to keep my balance. There is no opportunity to scream or swear or exclaim.

But Jarek is heavier than me, and taller. The thrust behind his sprint is stronger and harder to stop. He keeps on going and it's too late to change it. I watch as he plunges forward and then feel myself falling again. He drops over the edge, if that's what it is, or could be perceived to be, and pulls me down with him. But I'm behind him and I collapse into the road, my breasts crushing back into my ribcage and my chin hitting the ground. I expect to taste blood, but nothing comes. He's hanging, clinging on somehow, and he's screaming at me – screaming at me to hoist him back up. I can't see the lower half of his body; it has been sliced off in the darkness. He wants me to save him. I feel that I could, but I choose not to try.

I let go and I push myself up, folding my empty hands around my own neck as I listen to his fading scream.

CHAPTER TWENTY-THREE

I'm horizontal and I'm shooting forwards, feet first. White coats flutter alongside me. I hear screams and I smell the metallic earthiness of blood. I'm inside, but the air I'm breathing isn't indoor air; it's laced with dirt and smoke and pavement. My eyes flicker shut.

I open them again and we're outside, definitely outside. I'm still moving and Jess is beside me, walking quickly but with a hand spread flat upon my chest. 'It's okay, it's okay,' she says. She repeats it over and over again and I'm not sure if she's talking to me or talking to herself. The words run into each other and, in her Irish accent, it starts to sound like a song. There's shouting all around and traffic thunders about us.

The third time I come around, it's like waking up from a bad dream. Nausea rolls in my belly and my lips feel dry and cracked. I don't open my eyes until I've composed myself. I remember my conversation with Jarek. I remember the chasm and the visions I've just had. I expect the clean white sterility of the hospital room to confront me, but I am mistaken. I am somewhere else. My hand slips away from my abdomen and hits the floor. I'm lying on a sofa. Three people sit on chairs pulled into a semicircle around me. As I look at each of them in turn, I can see the relief on their faces.

'Isobel!' one of the women exclaims. She drops forward on to her knees and places her hand upon my face. Her frizzy hair tickles my neck and I resist the impulse to push her away. The other woman rises to stand over us and presses something cold against my chest, bringing a tube to her ear. There is a gash through the pale skin of her forehead and her hair is dirtied with ash. The man they are with is silent. He sits forward on his chair, his fingers forming a bridge. His eyes leave my face and turn away to gaze out of the window at the greying sky.

'Isobel, do you know who I am?' asks the woman who is standing up. She pushes my hair back from my face and I feel her nails scratch the backs of my ears. It doesn't hurt, but I wince.

I hear the man speak. 'Don't push her. It's too soon. We need her to rest.'

Yes, I say to myself, I need to rest, and I let my eyes fall shut.

Darkness. Only shapes and outlines are visible. I'm covered in material which scratches at my neck, like the woman with the frizzy hair. Lela. That was Lela. I sense movement beside me and see it's the man. We are alone, it seems. He's sitting there with his elbows resting on his knees. He doesn't look like he's moved since I last saw him. The air smells stale and I wonder how long I've been lying here. Maybe that smell is me. I don't know if he notices the half-opening of my eyes.

'I'm so sorry,' he whispers, just loud enough for me to hear.

I struggle to remember his name. The first thing I remember is that I don't trust him.

'Daniel,' I murmur. I wish I could stay awake to watch him watch me, but I dissolve back into sleep.

'You need to eat,' a female voice orders and a spicy aroma wafts under my nose. I can feel my body being hauled up to a sitting position and the soup is tipped towards me before I can respond. A warming tomato broth meets my lips. I take a few sips and then the woman presses the mug into my hands. I look up at her. Jess. I think she must be able to tell that I recognise her, because she breaks into a smile. A row of tiny stitches forms a bloody line above her eyebrow. Then she walks over to the window and I observe her profile as she talks. She wriggles her small, upturned nose when she's thinking, I remember, and I watch for it.

'There was an explosion,' she says. 'Chinese terrorists got into the hospital, I think. We thought we were safe down there, but part of the ceiling ruptured and rubble fell in, on to all my lab stuff.' She glances over at me and I nod for her to continue. 'That's what went wrong – in your Heaven, I mean. I think there was a tiny amount of physical damage to your mirror neurons. And then we had to work fast to get everything disconnected.' She watches me, tipping her head to her shoulder. 'We had to get out of there and I've never done it before, let alone done it so quickly. I was convinced that I'd damaged you permanently, but I think you're okay.'

'I feel all right. It sounds like you did well.'

She nods a couple of times and starts to continue speaking, but is interrupted by the opening of the door. It's Daniel.

'You can have a couple of minutes,' Jess says with irritation, pressing the back of her hand to the wound on her forehead. 'No more.' She leaves the room and closes the door behind her.

Daniel comes closer to me, pulling a chair with him, and sits down.

'Where are we, then?' I ask.

'Valhalla's offices – luckily everything is largely intact here. It was the best place we could think to come.'

'Where's Lela?'

I am met with silence and the dropping of his gaze.

'She's gone,' Daniel says.

'She can't have gone already; I saw her earlier.'

Daniel shakes his head and glances over at the door.

'She was here; you were all here,' I say.

There is more silence and my words gather momentum in the vacuum.

'She spoke to me, Daniel. She was here. Why can't you remember? I'm not imagining things – I'm not.'

'I think you might be, Isobel.' He pulls his chair forward and rests his hand on my forearm. I try to remember if that's the first time he's touched me. He feels warm, even through the shawl that covers me. I gape at him. I can't imagine what he means.

'What happened in there?' he asks, frowning. He draws his hand away. 'Why did you let Jarek fall?'

'I . . .' I grasp at words. I was expecting an answer, not a question. 'I . . . We . . . I don't know. I don't know what happened, why it happened.' I pause, my mind is still heavy and my thought processes are moving through treacle. 'Oh, God; is he all right?'

'Jarek's neurons sustained a similar level of damage to your own – a tiny area of physical corruption. But Jess thinks that they are pretty much intact and, like yours, the area may even heal. Jess will reinstate his Heaven when she returns to London.'

I think of him, absolutely dead. Right now, he's not even in a simulation of life and I feel desperately sad. I cradle the mug of hot soup against my heart.

'I didn't do the damage, did I? When I . . . ?'

'No; and actually, by that point, your Heavens had probably separated. I think the chasm only appeared in your own Heaven.' He pauses and sits back in his chair, folding his arms. When he speaks, his voice is lower, firmer. It searches through me. 'I thought you loved him? I thought that's why you were doing all this?'

'Of course I loved him! I still do! How could you even ask me that?'

'Because I can't get my head around why you wouldn't have saved him. Why didn't you try to haul him back up? It doesn't make sense.'

'I was scared, I guess.'

'No,' he says, dipping his chin decisively. 'No, you weren't.' He is in control and I am stripped bare. He saw it all. 'You just let go,' he continues. 'Some people might call that psychopathic.'

'People like you, you mean?' It's the best comeback I can think of. I cannot believe that he's using this to make assumptions about my feelings for Jarek.

He raises his eyebrows and cocks his head by way of a response.

'I've done what you wanted me to do,' I say, sullenly. 'And you saw what I saw: there was nothing – no hint, no clue that he hurt Sarah, or even wanted to.'

Daniel remains still, pressing his index finger to his lips. He is waiting for me to say more. An uncomfortable sensation flickers through my chest as I remember running along the cliff top in

Jarek's Heaven, next to the faceless figure that I knew was Sarah. I recall the bitterness, the simmering anger that, having lived it, now almost feels like my own. And, indeed, what I was seeing and experiencing was so confusing that perhaps that emotion was my own; perhaps it was jealousy. That is the only thing I could tell Daniel that he might not have noticed from watching the simulation. But I don't voice it. It was only a *feeling*, after all. As my hesitation persists, there is a knock at the door and Jess reappears. The concern written across her face tells me that she has been standing right outside this whole time, listening.

'That's it, Daniel. She needs to rest tonight.' She had been looking at me, but now she directs her gaze at him. 'We all do.'

He sighs and stands up, pulling his sleeves back from his wrists.

'Wait. You never finished telling me where Lela is.'

Daniel looks at Jess and, in that moment, I know. She's gone. Nausea crashes through me and I press my hands to my mouth to keep it inside me.

Jess walks over and sits beside me, slipping her arm around me. 'Lela's dead, Isobel. I'm so, so sorry.'

'No, no, no,' I mumble into my hand. I can feel the blood leave my face as I shake my head.

'She was hit by falling rubble on the way over here from the hospital.'

'It's my fault,' I murmur. 'If I hadn't come here . . .'

I think about our conversation outside my room last night. I was too tired to talk to her properly. I feel the lashing of guilt against the walls of my heart, and I know they will never heal over.

'It was her decision to come here, Izzy, no one else's.'

'It was supposed to be safe in that lab. Valhalla are meant to be looking after us.'

I clamp my hands over my collarbone to quell the hiccup-like contractions that are spreading through my chest. All I can think is that I wish it had been me instead. It should have been me.

'It was over very quickly,' Jess says, her voice growing quieter. 'We carried her body here and Caleb is paying to have it repatriated privately tomorrow. And I have her mirror neurons intact, all ready to go. She will be in her Heaven as soon as I can get back to London.'

What now? I ask myself. What now?

Jess pulls me into her body and wraps her arms about me as I cry. I cry for a long, long time.

CHAPTER TWENTY-FOUR

I've dozed through a day and two nights, through nightmares and jagged awakenings. Jess keeps coming to check on me. She takes measurements and looks at readouts in holograms that pop up beside me. She pushes my eyelids apart and shines a bright light inside. She does this a lot, but she seems satisfied. Jess tries to make me smile, but all I can see when I look at her is Lela and I feel like my lips might be broken forever because I can only hold them closed and taut.

My chip has marked me as safe on my social networks. I think my sister calls a couple of times, but Jess speaks to her. I watch the news a lot, until the stinging in my temples sharpens into a shower of sparkling pain. Much of it is the global reaction to the drone strike here. It's strange to see it on my Codex when I've lived through it, almost unaware. The scenes of smoking rubble and the remnants of clothes torn from victims at the point of impact seem a world away from here. Looking out of the window, you'd never know this building was in the same city in which close to a thousand people have lost their lives — one of whom is Lela. All I can see are the formal gardens at the front of the offices, a large car park and then Powai Lake beyond. Valhalla's offices face north, away from the carnage.

In my waking moments, when I'm not fixated upon the latest broadcast or thinking about Lela – the smudge of her red lipstick, her conspiratorial laugh – or about her forgiveness, I imagine myself somewhere else. I can sometimes manage to sink into a daydream so deep that time starts to slip and slide, and I'm walking amongst blackberry bushes, hand in hand with Jarek. But not now. Right now, I'm the most awake I've been since going under for the final procedure. It feels like months ago.

I finger the metal studs in my scalp, just in case Jess has pulled them out in my sleep without me knowing. But they're still there, handcuffing me to an experience that fills me with the darkest emotions. It's a strange feeling to be inside an office, on a sofa, while the world is carrying on around me. But then reality has lost its appeal. I feel like it's forever damaged – dirtied by the events which have enveloped me. I didn't think I was capable of more grief, but it turns out that I am. While before it hung like fog at the edges of my vision, now it consumes me like a physical force, weighing me down. A smoky grey silt appears to thread through everything in this room, like a virus; it dampens down colour and scent. Even the nourishing soups and spicy curries that Jess tempts me with are losing their appeal.

I push off the shawl that's wrapped tightly around me and pull myself to my feet. Sickness sloshes in my belly. Leaving the room, I trudge in the opposite direction to the toilet and in search of Jess. I listen for her voice, but this floor of the building seems completely deserted. I step into the elevator and drop down to the first floor. I stare at myself in the mirrored interior and wipe the smudges of mascara away from beneath my eyes. It doesn't shift. I lean closer and realise the silt is there, too, lurking beneath my skin.

The doors open and I seem to be in the functional part of the building. Men and women are waiting for the lift and I walk past them into a small glass atrium that frames the lake. I feel their eyes upon me as I brush past. So, this is the greatest Heaven architecture firm in the world. It certainly makes our clinic look like small fry. I know from the buttons inside the lift that there are four floors. Hundreds of people must work here. Large projections are displaying local news reports. A holographic Valhalla logo is suspended in mid-air in the centre of the ceiling. The gilded gates that frame the company's title sit upon silvery clouds that seem to shift and swirl. The atrium is buzzing. Beyond the people milling back and forth, I spot the figure of Jess. I wonder whether it's her, at first, because she's not wearing her lab coat. She's wearing blue jeans and a navy shirt, and her hair is loose. She's leaning against the window, talking to someone on her Codex, and she's twisting a curl of hair through her fingers. She doesn't see me approach until I slide my back up against the glass, raising my fingers in a small wave. Her mouth drops open in surprise and she grips me by the shoulder.

'Okay, darling,' she says. 'I'll see you soon. I love you.' She rolls up her Codex and slips it into her back pocket. 'Izzy! What are you doing up? Are you okay?'

'I want these gone.' I gesture to the metal plugs in my scalp.

'I know, I know. I want to take them out, too, but Valhalla didn't want me to just yet.'

'C'mon, Jess. Screw them. Please, can you do it now?'

'I need the right equipment. I can't just yank them out; you'd haemorrhage all over the floor.'

I roll my eyes because I know she's exaggerating.

'There – that's almost the Isobel I know and love.'

And I frown. Because why would she make such a throwaway comment? Who could possibly love me? I need to go back to my Heaven – not Jarek's Heaven, not some bizarre limbo between the two, but mine – the only place I have any control over; the only place that I will be able to be happy again. I am done with this.

'Listen.' Jess grabs my hand and pulls me closer to her. 'Caleb is here.'

'Caleb? What the hell?'

'I've no idea. He says he came to make sure Lela's body was repatriated properly, but I'm . . . suspicious.' Her eyes dart around, beyond me, scanning the atrium.

'What? You think he's come to murder me?' My sarcasm is barbed. I know I sound quarrelsome, but Jess seems to ignore it.

'Well, he's pissed off, certainly. But . . .' She pauses and twists her lips to one side of her mouth, shaking her head. 'I know him; I know he's up to something.'

I study her face as she thinks, her gaze slipping off into the distance, over the lake. If Caleb had ever hit me, I would have killed him. I would have scratched his eyes out. At least, the old Isobel would have. This one would probably just shrug and walk away with blood dripping from her lip. I follow Jess's gaze out of the window and look down at the entrance area below. A gleaming red car pulls up and Caleb steps out of the back seat. And out of the other side appears Daniel, wearing a suit jacket rather than his usual dark sweater. It makes him look taller. I watch him unbutton it as he walks around the back of the vehicle.

'Jess.' I elbow her in the ribs and nod down at the car.

'I didn't even know Daniel had left,' she says, pursing her lips.

Jess is too magnanimous to hate Caleb, I think, whereas I would make it a defining point of my character. Perhaps part of her still loves him, but how could you love someone who'd done something as awful as that?

We watch them enter the building together and disappear from view.

'They'll be coming up here,' she says. 'Come with me.'

We move away from the window to the side of the atrium, where a few rows of benches and reading pods are clustered. The area is busy and we sink down on a bench towards the back. I'm pleased to be sitting because my chest is already tight from fatigue. Caleb and Daniel appear from the lift at the far side of the atrium and walk with purpose towards a petite, blonde woman. It's Maya. She goes with them and, together, they swiftly disappear out of view.

Jess rubs her finger over her lips for a few moments, deep in thought. 'Come on.' She doesn't wait for me to follow her. She almost jogs across the floor and I must move my heavy limbs quickly to keep up with her. As we turn into the corridor, the three of them are reaching its end, chatting animatedly. They turn right. Jess stops in her tracks.

'Okay, they must be going to Maya's office. Let's give it a minute or two. Let me think.'

And we stand there, awkwardly, in the middle of the corridor. Jess drums her fingers against the wall. A woman pushes past me, muttering something in Hindi. I blink away the automatic translation and move to lean against the wall. I feel quite drained, even from this small amount of activity.

'We can try to get into the meeting room next door,' Jess murmurs. 'We might be able to hear them from there.'

'Surely you don't want to spy on them?'

Jess pretends she hasn't heard me. We walk together to the end of the corridor and cautiously move around the corner. There's no sign of them.

'In here,' Jess whispers, pointing at a door to our right.

At that moment, it swings inwards and I gasp in surprise. People flood out, smiling and chatting, clutching tiny mugs containing dregs of chai. A meeting must have just finished. They flow past us and we are forced back against the wall. A man in a suit is the last to leave and he nods at us, pushing the door back so that it stays open behind him. Jess grants him a sparkling smile as we slip inside.

'This is insane,' I whisper, as we sink down to the floor, our backs against the wall.

Jess says nothing, but shoots me a warning look. As the people disperse from outside the door, the room falls quiet and I start to hear the muffled murmur of voices. I glance at Jess and she nods, her brow furrowed in concentration. *That's them*, she mouths and taps lightly on her ears. *I want my stethoscope!*

I smile and shrug. As the sounds from outside fade completely, their voices become clearer. We lean our heads against the wall and I close my eyes in concentration.

'She's always seemed fractious,' I hear Maya say. 'She's threatened me before.'

I can't hear what Daniel replies but I can tell that it's definitely him and that he's asking a question.

'To muddy Oakley's name, to make the business look bad,' says Caleb.

I open my eyes and look at Jess, pointing a finger to my own chest. *Me?*

Maya says something about a meeting but I can't make her words out fully. She's talking about that meeting, about the single opt-in discussion, when I first met her.

Caleb interrupts her. His voice is deeper; it carries further through the wall. 'And you'd never know where you were with her. In between all this, she'd always flirt with me. It was inappropriate at best, and I'm married – it made me uncomfortable.'

I nearly punch the wall in rage. How dare he?

Jess grips my wrist and brings her finger to her lips. *Listen.*

There are footsteps which seem to move closer to us, presumably towards Caleb. This time, I hear Daniel speak more clearly. 'Personally, I've had doubts all along. For a start,' he says, 'she's a slight woman. Our forensics team still seems to think that Mrs Woods was strangled by a person bigger than herself.'

'Come on. Coupled with the D.N.A., I think we have enough evidence now, don't you?' It's Maya's voice, high and sharp over the vowels.

D.N.A.? I mouth at Jess.

'I'll ask you one more time,' says Daniel. 'You really believe she could have done this?'

'Yes.'

'Yes.'

I think of our conversation that night on the sea wall overlooking Chowpatty Beach. *I'm sorry, Isobel, that so much of this is out of your control*, Daniel had said. I didn't know what he meant, but now I think I do. Have I really been a suspect all along? Did Daniel deceive me to get me to come here and do Valhalla's experiments, even though they were preparing to arrest me?

I press my hand against the base of my neck and shake my head in disbelief at Jess.

She looks quite composed, almost as if this is what she had expected to hear. She jerks her head towards the door. *Go.*

We rise and run out of the room and back the way we've come, flitting around people until we're in the atrium again. I'm breathless and my heart thuds against the walls of my chest, overwhelming my jumbled thoughts.

Jess takes my hand and pulls me into the lift. 'Isobel, listen to me. You need to go back to your hotel, now. Take out some cash, not too much, and go somewhere, anywhere.'

'What do you mean?'

'They're going to arrest you, Izz, and once they've done that . . .' Her voice trails off as the doors close and the lift sinks.

'But it's ridiculous. What would my motivation be to kill the wife of a dying man?'

'I don't know.' Jess sighs and tips her head back, staring up at the ceiling of the lift. 'I don't know. Plain old jealousy?'

'But I didn't do it; I didn't kill her!' I whisper. There is a man and woman in the lift with us and they are looking right at us now. 'How could they think . . . ?'

'Valhalla are powerful. Caleb is powerful. And you heard them mention D.N.A. evidence. If this is what they want . . .'

'Caleb just *lied* to a detective about me! He wants Daniel to believe I killed Sarah.' I stumble over my words because I can't believe what is happening. 'Why?'

'I don't know, but, trust me, you've just got to get out of here. You've got to buy me some time to figure this all out.'

The lift doors open and we move around the couple from the lift as they kiss each other. We walk across another glass atrium, through the automatic doors and out into the glaring sunshine. I follow Jess blindly as I clench my fists and imagine pounding them into Caleb's face. We've never been close, but I can't think why he would betray me like this. There must be a reason. I can't trust anyone anymore, especially not anyone as ruthless as him.

'I'm flying to London tonight to take Jarek's and Lela's mirror neurons back to the lab,' Jess says. She looks around and moves in the direction of the taxi rank. 'I'll play it cool; I'll tell them that you wanted a few days away on your own. Go to the station and get a bus or a train out of here.'

She pushes me into the back of a cab and leans over me to let the sensor scan her chip. She unbuttons her top pocket and cash flutters into my lap. I open my mouth to speak but nothing comes out.

'Please, Isobel, just do it,' she says, and slams the door shut. She's back inside the building before we've even pulled away.

CHAPTER TWENTY-FIVE

If only Lela could have come with me, I think. 'Where are you going?' she would have asked, eyes wide. 'Haven't you told them?' If she was still here, she'd stand up for me; she'd stop them doing anything. I make a mental note to write to her husband.

While her absence has left me bereft, I have gained the ability to lie to whomever I wish. When the receptionist asks me where I am heading next, I don't hesitate for a moment. 'Delhi,' I tell her. 'I'm going to Delhi. They can find me there, if they want.'

I leave against an overcast sky, catching a taxi to Chhatrapati Shivaji Terminus to seek out the first bus I can find that isn't heading north towards Delhi. I take a wad of cash out of the A.T.M. at the station and then I run from bus to bus through the drizzle, not daring to pause to look over my shoulder. If anyone has followed me, they will catch me; I don't need to waste time worrying too much about it. I soon realise that the more modern, driverless vehicles are locked to those without a ticket. I switch to targeting the most decrepit buses, begging for a seat from whomever is behind the wheel. Wet to the bone, I hammer on the door of a half-empty one as it is pulling away from its stand, placing my hands together in prayer to plead with the driver. It is only when I've paid that I ask him where we were going. He laughs at me, a deep, guttural laugh, as if to say, *Crazy foreigner.* 'You are lucky today,' he says. 'You are going to the beach!'

I sleep for a few hours and wake up almost dry. Outside, the world is dark and it feels as though we are weaving down a mountainside. We have left Mumbai far behind. I lean into the cracked window and focus on the contours of the road ahead, illuminated by the headlights, so that I don't get sick. The air conditioning seems to have stopped working and I'm squeezed next to a butterball of a man who crushes me with every nauseating turn of the bus. He chews betel leaf incessantly. Every so often, he spits it out into a small sandwich bag that he ties back up and pushes into the depths of his pocket. For hours upon hours, I wait for the red, saliva-thickened juice to escape from it and soak through his thin trousers on to my thigh. And while I wait, I breathe deeply, trying to calm myself, and I think about Daniel, Caleb and Maya's conversation.

I try to be logical. I know I didn't kill Sarah. Therefore, Caleb and Maya should have no reason to believe that I did it. Nor should they really care. But they do. They care a lot, because it sounded as though they were trying to frame me. I take several more breaths, pushing my nails into my palms. The last thing Maya cared so much about was bringing me here, to India, to take advantage of my unique position to trial Valhalla's new technologies. I hear her voice again, forceful, insistent: *I think we have enough evidence now, don't you?* I bite my lip, mentally backtracking. What puts people on the attack? Fear; always fear. The idea of ghost memories must terrify both Oakley and Valhalla. If proof of them was found, and it got out into the public domain, their empires would be shattered. No one would want a Heaven. They'd be sued – destroyed. Daniel's team are on the trail, and I've been tantalisingly close to spotting them for myself. So, would sending me down for murder stop me talking? Would it nullify my opinion if rumours ever surfaced? Would it throw Daniel and his team off the scent? And, most disturbingly, if they could stoop so low as to falsely accuse me, would they have had any qualms about committing the murder themselves?

By the time I clamber down the steps into Anjuna's dust, I am dehydrated and physically drained and I wish I had taken a train instead. The bus drops me in a car park that couldn't possibly be any closer to the cliff edge. Electric charging points line its perimeter. Motorbikes and rickshaws jostle for room, watched over by donkeys and goats. I stop for a few moments to gather my thoughts. I unwrap the cotton scarf from my head and flatten and fold it again, lying it back over the bare patches of scalp with the metal rings lodged in their centre. I find myself gazing down over the rust-red rocks to the ocean below. Even in the warmth of the mid-morning sun, its confident light catching the crests of the waves, I feel a magnetic darkness drag me down.

I look at a few rooms around Anjuna before I find myself on the far edge of the village, wandering through an unmarked back gate into the sandy gardens of the Ocean Pearl Guest House. I choose a small, private bungalow with a veranda out front, paying for three nights in advance. The smiling owner hands me a fresh coconut as a welcome gift, and I gratefully accept. His skin is marbled by vitiligo but I try not to stare and he tries not to stare back at me in return. The heat of the midday sun presses down on me and I walk straight from the sand into the cool of my room. Lying down on the bed, I fall asleep until early evening, when I'm woken by a call from Daniel. I let the Codex ring out, knowing that he could use it to pinpoint my location.

Now, I'm sitting on the wicker chair by the front door of my bungalow. The noises screeching from beneath me suggest that it's not supposed to be a rocking chair. Yet, as I push my toes away from the warm tiles of the deck, it rocks nonetheless. Clouds of evening insects and mosquitoes storm about me. The last time I was in India, I remember obsessively taking my anti-malarial at the same time each morning and our mother coating our bare skin with a pungent liquid every evening. How different it was then. Thankfully, the days of malaria are long gone. Another deadly disease wiped from the face of the planet. We're ticking them off, one by one.

I close my eyes and imagine Jess sitting on the plane, her lab case containing the living remains of Lela and Jarek upon her lap. Perhaps it doesn't stay in the cabin with her. Maybe it goes in some special, secure hold. I don't know. I find it harder than ever to believe that people are dead longer than they are alive. When I really consider how fleeting life is, it's little wonder that I fell for Jarek so quickly, so completely; it becomes less surprising that just a handful of shared connections – an abusive, absent father; the loss of a loved mother and a sister; a crisis of self-doubt and a willingness to cure it – would be enough to ignite a love affair in the face of death.

Locusts chatter in the dune grasses and the sky is painting itself in hues of pink and orange as the sun sinks behind the tall palm trees that camouflage my view of the ocean. This part of Goa is like a time capsule. It feels as if this place has been here for decades, unchanged. I could be a hippy here, I think. I could go off-grid and hide away from the world, selling necklaces on the seashore, subsisting on stolen bananas, cheap tarka dhal and puri. But even that idea seems too fraught with difficulty. I turn my thoughts away and slip my fingertips beneath my headscarf, running them over the circles of stubble surrounding the metal plugs. I rub at the edge of one, where I find a rough patch. And I rub and rub until I feel a strange sensation in my fingertip. It's only when I pull my hand away and bring the tip of my finger close to my face that I realise it's bleeding.

I run through a tick list of symptoms in my head: anxiety, hopelessness, fatigue. But this isn't really a depression, I think. It's an absence – an absence of any emotion whatsoever. I find it hard now, as I sit here, to even think about myself. I can watch the tiny bats swoop and flit; I can find a certain contentment in the sound of the sea washing the distant shoreline. But me? I am done with myself. I am a vessel that has been emptied and I have nothing with which to fill it again. All I can do is save Jarek. Maybe I can figure out who killed Sarah and why. Maybe I can make them pay for what they've done to me, Jarek and Lela.

Slowly, I begin to drift off to sleep on the chair, with my feet dangling over the tiles.

A gentle vibration in my ear canal wakes me up, alerting me to an incoming call. I blink into the pitch black, disoriented. And then the smell of sweat and seawater reminds me where I am. As I sit up, I see that the moon has sunk behind the palm trees. I glance at the time in my vision. Half past one. I unfurl my Codex from the wicker side table and see that it's Don. I think twice before answering.

'Hello,' I say cautiously. I don't activate the visual link, and lie back again, closing my eyes. He wouldn't be able to see me, anyway.

'Isobel, where are you?' His tone is piercing, probing. It makes me realise that I shouldn't be answering any calls. I can't let anyone find me.

'Hi, Don, and how are you?'

'This isn't the time for your sarcasm. I'm worried about you.'

I don't reply. It's much cooler out here now. I ought to go inside, but I have to concentrate on this first.

'Caleb messaged me a couple of hours ago, saying you'd gone missing, saying he needed to find you.'

'Well, he doesn't need to find me.'

'He said it made things look worse for you, disappearing like this.'

I had wondered that myself, but Jess had seemed so sure. I'm not capable of making my own decisions at the moment.

'Lela died,' I say quietly. 'In the drone strike.'

'I know; I'm so sorry, Isobel.' His voice has mellowed back to the one I remember – deep and rich. And, for a moment, I wish he was here in person. I know that he would hold me tight and make me feel better without saying a word. He knows me. He's one of the few people left who do.

'What's going on?' Don asks, his voice swinging back at me in a tone so firm that it demands an answer.

'Jarek – my client – his wife was murdered. Strangled in her own home. I think . . . I think I'm a suspect.' Talk about cutting a long story short. There is silence on the line, but not from shock. Don is never shocked. Instead, he is thinking, and the emotionless void in my chest is overwhelmed with relief that he has got in touch. There is a reason he called. He will know what to do. He will help me.

'When did it happen? The murder?' he asks.

I run through my conversations with Daniel again in my head, summoning the details in full before I answer. And then I realise how easy it is to remember the date, because it was the same day I last saw Jarek. 'It was a Friday evening back in mid-September. The same night that we called things off.'

'The night *you* called things off,' he says, and I recoil at the hurt strung through his words. There's nothing I can say, so I wait, again, for his thoughts to process.

'I got back to the flat at—'

'Late,' I interrupt. 'It was late.'

'No.' Assurance infuses his words, demanding my silence. 'No, it wasn't that late. I think your mind's playing tricks. I got home at – what? Five? Six p.m.?'

Of course. He's giving me an alibi. And he's doing it in such a gracious way that not only do I not have to acknowledge it, or even thank him, but it is credible if the call is ever logged and listened to. He is making it plausible. A Ministry of Defence consultant is always going to be believable. I almost believe him now. I press my fingers into my cheeks. I could cry that he is doing this for me, but I can't help but wonder why he would be so nice to me. After everything that happened, he would be within his rights to . . . And my chest tightens. What if he had found out about Jarck and I? Isn't it probable that a man who specialises in gathering intelligence would've known? Wouldn't that have driven him crazy with jealousy, to know that I had made love to another man in our flat? And, just hours later, Sarah was dead.

I let my hand slip across my mouth and blow my naivety out through the gaps in my fingers. What if this call isn't about providing me with an alibi, but about giving himself one, too?

'Yes, yes, you're right,' I say, trying not to let my voice waver. 'It was around five.'

'I hope you're okay, Izz.' His tone is softer again – his outside-work mode.

'I hope *you're* okay.' I know what he's going to say next and I wish he wouldn't say it.

'I love you, you know that?'

'Yes. Yes, I know.'

Part of me wishes I could love him. Everything else forgotten. Part of me wishes that I could fly home and walk back into our old flat to find him polishing his shoes at the kitchen table. This could be such an easy exchange: an alibi in return for affection. But all that is dead and buried, and the part of me that is left trusts no one.

And I wonder whether the damage to my mirror neurons has done something to me – whether it's wiped out my ability to love – because all I feel is an emptiness that grates behind my ribs and hums in my ears. As I move inside the dishevelled bungalow to its straw-filled bed and tuck the thin sheets around me, it's the only lullaby I have.

CHAPTER TWENTY-SIX

I spend hours wandering up and down the beach and staring out at the ocean. I almost feel normal, in a way – if I don't dwell on Lela and Jarek, and the people who have betrayed me; if I forget the fear for a moment and try not to look for signs of recognition in the eyes of every person I pass.

To distract myself, I look repeatedly for the love inside my brain and, while I find the grief that results from love, and the memory of love, the love itself no longer feels like a tangible thing. I feel broken.

I walk along the beach most days, all the way to the headland and back. I'm careful, I suppose, in my own way. I don't stop for a drink or meal in the same place twice. I don't make conversation. I ignore the repeated calls from Daniel and unknown contacts. I don't do anything to draw attention to myself. Luckily, there are lots of cafés and bars dotted along the edge of the sands. I got drunk on one of my first days here, on a fast succession of distractingly fruity, free-poured cocktails. I'm not doing that again. It sent me into a morose downward spiral that only sleep could clear. Often, I buy a coconut from the beach vendors and sit right at the edge of the waves, sipping on the clean freshness of the milk before catching the vendor on their return and asking them to split it open with their machete so that I can scrape at the flesh inside. I watch them attack the coconut with a practised strike and again find myself wondering, if I didn't do it, and Jarek didn't do it, then who did? Who killed Sarah? Her lover? Could it even have been Don, seeking revenge of some kind? Could Maya and Caleb want me silenced, after everything I've seen? Could one of them have arranged the murder in the first place, to make me desperate to prove Jarek's innocence, to get me here, taking part in their experiments?

One afternoon, I let a girl on the beach decorate my feet with henna. She paints the prettiest, most intricate patterns, down to tiny swirls around my toenails and many-petalled flowers between each knuckle. She adorns me with toe rings and anklets, in an effort to get me to spend more money. She clips earrings on to my lobes and holds up a hand mirror so that I can admire myself.

'Pretty,' she says.

I look back at the woman in the mirror and wonder when it was that I last properly looked at myself. I don't see pretty. I never did. But I do see gaunt shadows on the face I was once so well acquainted with. I look tired and dehydrated. But that isn't it. My eyes are dishevelled. Stray hairs have roughened the once-perfect arches of my brows. My skin is less clean, less cared for. I've never seen my hair wrapped in a headscarf like this, let alone one that's been reused for days in a row and has become an excuse for not washing my hair.

The girl takes away the mirror to slip it back into her bag and I look down at myself. I would never have let a stranger decorate my body with cheap metal a few weeks ago. I would never have worn anything that wasn't tailored and grey, black or white, and now I'm dressed in an orange crocheted tunic and baggy cream elasticated trousers that I once would have thought a dirty colour. I am changed; there is no doubt. Yet the change has not brought peace. I am more alone than ever and the arguments that rage inside my head are louder.

'What is this?' the girl asks, in impeccable English, pointing at my tattoo. She looks at me with shy eyes beneath thick lashes.

'It's an angel.'

I smile at the confusion in her face. It's as if she hasn't heard of one before.

'They have wings,' I say, tracing the outline. 'They live in Heaven and carry out God's wishes.'

'Really?' Her brown eyes widen.

I feel bad. 'No; no, they're just make-believe.'

She smiles, relieved. 'Hopefully I'll make enough money this week,' she says, settling down beside me and mimicking my position by resting her elbows on her knees. 'And then I'll be able to take my brother to school with me next month.'

I look at her with veiled cynicism. She wants me to buy this anklet – the most expensive one – that she insists is made from silver and inlaid with lapis lazuli. I can see that it's nickel and glass, but I can't bring myself to tell her this.

'Do you like school?' I ask.

She nods vigorously. English is her favourite, she tells me. She likes her teacher, and one day she wants to travel the world. We sit together for a while in a friendly silence and then she asks me again if I'd like the anklet. I tell her to ask me again tomorrow, which she seems satisfied with, and she skips away down the beach, her boxed-up shop jangling against her childish hips.

The next morning, I wake early and find a spool of cotton in the bedside drawer. I settle in the shard of sunlight that cuts through the small window and thread out the stray hairs on my shins. I'd like to do my eyebrows but the only mirror is fixed to the wall in the dark bathroom. I stretch out my legs and note how I look more like my mother every day. I eat pineapple on the porch and file my nails with a beaded glass file I bought on the beach a couple of days ago. When Jess calls, I find that I have the strength to wipe the juice from my chin and talk to her.

'Hello,' I say, while I'm still unfurling my Codex. 'How are you?'

'I'm fine.' Then: 'You sound brighter.'

Maybe I do; I'm not sure. The hologram viewer kicks in and I see Jess, leaning forward on her elbows.

'I wanted to try and catch you before I go to bed,' she says. 'Are you safe?'

'No, probably not.'

Jess ignores my sarcasm. 'Seriously. Can your Codex be tracked?'

'I got a guy to disable that shortly after I upgraded last year,' I explain, pursing my lips. 'But I did wonder whether there's still a way the police could track it, if they really wanted to. I don't know.'

'Okay, we'll keep this brief. You look well, though. No after effects from the operations?'

I think of the spongy darkness pressing in on me and filling the gaps between my thoughts. 'Nothing I can think of,' I say.

'So, Daniel has had you down as a suspect all along,' she says.

I'm still surprised, I suppose. I thought he liked me. It always seemed like he was making allowances for me. He is the one who talked me into going on this ridiculous errand. Fresh anger bristles across my skin.

'And now Caleb and Maya have turned against you, too. Together, they're even more powerful. Oakley Associates and Valhalla are one and the same now. They're signing the paperwork today. The rumours are that Valhalla got Oakley for a bargain, in the end.'

'Oh.' I fall quiet, looking past the image of Jess to the sparkling sea beyond. It's a distant world, that meeting about the single opt-in, being told off by Lela, fighting with Maya and Caleb. 'I have an alibi, though.'

'That's fantastic! Who?'

'Don. He called me a few days ago.'

'Great. That's great.' She sounds unconvinced, but it's good to have her company. Seeing her makes me realise how lonely I've been. She squints at me. 'You do know *how* she was killed, right?'

I nod in response. I don't feel inclined to drag myself back through the details, especially if Jess already knows them.

'So, you know that she was strangled and then drugged, just for good measure, perhaps to ensure death before a quick getaway.' She pauses, nibbling at her lip. 'What were your thoughts on the high-strength opioids?' Jess levels her gaze at me again, and her jaw tightens. It takes me a few seconds to process what she is saying.

'Opioids?' I feel a knot of nerves unfurl itself from its hiding place, deep behind my ribs.

'Daniel didn't tell you that detail, huh?'

I shake my head, my eyes fixed on her face.

'Where would the murderer have got his hands on pills like that, Isobel?' Jess asks. Her voice wavers. I don't need to offer her a response. Perceptive as ever, she is already convinced of where those pills came from.

'An alibi is good,' Jess continues, 'but it's not enough. This and the D.N.A. evidence we heard them mention? I don't know any more about that, but it looks bad for you, Isobel.'

'I know; I know it does.' I can hardly hear my own voice and I have to look away from the display. I haven't been forced to admit it to myself before and the breath falls out of me like I've been punched in the solar plexus.

'So, we need to uncover evidence that he did it . . . given that nobody else seems to be bothering.'

'You think it was a man?'

Jess sighs heavily. 'Come on, Izzy. I think we both know it must've been Jarek.'

I stare back at her, resolute.

'What did he tell you?' she asks. 'Did he say he hated her? Had she done something to hurt him? I need something to look for.'

My eyes zigzag across the hologram of her face, searching for a part of it that I can believe in.

'Who else would've done it, Izz? Who else?' Her accent deepens and her voice rises like hot air, swirling around me. I feel dizzy.

'Not him.'

'So, who did?' She's swallowing back her anger now but her derision is clear and sudden, like the day when she warned me about my relationship with Jarek. The memory of her words resonates in my temples. *We don't leave everything behind us when we die anymore. We take others with us.* 'You think a stranger found their way into her house and then murdered her with a packet of pills that they happened to find in the bathroom cabinet? Pills that were once yours?' she continues.

'Maybe someone else knew about them,' I mumble. 'Daniel told me that Sarah had been seeing someone. He might have been to the house before; he might have seen them.'

'Really? That's interesting. I just wonder what the motivation would have been. The details of the murder make it seem pre-planned, not a hot-headed mistake. And wouldn't they have found some of his D.N.A. at the scene?'

'We don't know that they didn't. And what about Caleb? He has access to the same drugs dispensary as me. He could've got the same pills.'

'Does that really seem even vaguely likely to you?'

'If we're talking about what's likely, what would Jarek's motivation have been, Jess? He was already dying, himself. Why on Earth would he kill his wife?'

Jess shrugs. 'Any number of reasons.'

'I think we need to consider Caleb and Valhalla. Maya wanted me here, doing this, helping them. And Sarah's murder achieved that. If it's a motivation we're looking for . . .' I can hear my voice rising with desperation.

'Well, I don't know much about Valhalla, but Caleb is nasty, Isobel, you know that.' She pauses and sighs. 'On a personal level, I'd say he's furious that you walked out on him. And from a business point of view, you're dangerous to them now, confidentiality agreement or no confidentiality agreement.'

'See, I thought this, too,' I agree. 'If you or I went on the public record talking about ghost memories . . .'

Jess nods, looking away from the camera for a few moments. 'They'd be finished.' I realise that she, too, is treading on dangerous ground. 'Although Daniel's team knows about the possibility of ghost memories, too. If they were found, they'd want to use them in criminal trials. It would all come out then, wouldn't it?'

'Maybe,' I say. It's hard to know I'm thinking straight when I feel so paranoid. 'That could be why they're keeping him so close. They want to control what he knows, what he does with the information he gets access to.'

'We're getting off track.' Jess sounds exasperated. 'I can't do anything to examine anyone else's motives, Isobel. I can only look at Jarek's.'

I look past her again, back to the shoreline and the steadily rising sun.

'You really loved him, didn't you?' Jess speaks calmly again, recovering herself.

I nod because it's all I can do. Anything else will wipe me out. I realise that not once has Jess asked me outright if I did it. She trusts me and I take a huge amount of comfort in that. But how could she possibly think that Jarek did it? She met him so many times. She scanned his brain; she created the simulations of his Heaven. She would have seen his easy smile, listened to his jokes, admired his lack of self-pity, his calm strength, and talked to him about his love for his daughters.

'I'd better go,' I say.

'Just quickly: I know you'll be disappointed, but I thought you might want to know that single opt-in was approved by the Council on Bioethics last week. With their endorsement, I think it'll slip through Parliament quickly.' I watch Jess shake her head. She feels the same way about it as I do. 'Things are going to change.'

I hang up and feel the sigh reverberate through my body. I let the tension spread and settle, while the self-recriminations rise to the surface. I walked away from the clinic when I should have stayed to fight against the roll-out of single opt-in. I could have made a difference but I gave up when it really mattered. I get up and walk down to the beach through the dappled light cast by the palm trees.

Jess is right. Things will change now. People will be able to put whomever they want in their Heavens, without that person's permission. I imagine that most of my old clients, now long gone, would have been excited by the thought of including a Hollywood actor or a teenage crush. Almost innocent. But the slippery ethics of it are unavoidable. Single opt-in derails the sanctity of Heaven and other laws will swiftly follow, no doubt. Valhalla and the law-enforcement agencies will get their wish of being able to root through the mental realms of strangers. What they've just made me do will be outdated. It's likely that, soon, anyone will be able to rifle through Jarek's Heaven. I push his name away as I hear it emerge inside my head. I cannot engage with it now.

I reach the ocean and stand on the shoreline, letting the shallow waves lap at my feet. The water is still cold with night and I squint down at the tiny white shells rolling helplessly over my toes. Things could have been so different. If single opt-in had been approved earlier and the other rules relaxed, we may not have had to come all the way to India to get into Jarek's Heaven.

What we did would have been far less of a grey area than what Daniel described that day on the Maidan. A roomful of people prying into Jarek's Heaven from the safety of London would have been little more than a technicality. They might not have needed me at all. Lela would be alive.

I stand there, contemplating an early morning swim in my clothes until the sand reaches my mid-shin. Then I turn and wander back towards my bungalow. If I can, I think I might go back to sleep for a while.

The little girl is waiting for me near the gate to the guest house. Today she is dressed in a bright purple cotton dress with frills at the hem and neck, but I recognise the lopsided smile and her narrow shoulders. As I get closer, I see that the anklet is dangling from her index finger, and a cheeky giggle erupts from her.

'Oh, hello,' I say. 'Who are you?'

She giggles again, her whole face bursting with delight at my joke. I ruffle my hand through the hair on the top of her head.

'Hello, lady. Do you still like this?'

'Yes, I do.'

Without hesitating, she kneels in the sand and fastens it around my ankle before I can change my mind. I wait for her to get up again, but she's staring at the angel.

'Why did you have a picture of something that isn't real?' she asks. She looks up at me and her cheeks are pulled in, making the bones stand out beneath her eyes. There's a seriousness to her face, as if she somehow knows what it means to me.

'I chose something that's not real because I didn't know what to believe anymore.'

She nods as if this makes perfect sense and stands up, casually slipping her tiny, dry hand into mine. 'Do you know what to believe now?'

I lose myself in the open innocence of her face. I feel a thrust of something in my chest that swirls upwards, a warmth which rises to the very top of my head. And then I realise: what I'm feeling isn't the loss of my capacity to love; it's an explosion of my capacity to doubt.

CHAPTER TWENTY-SEVEN

I'm in the village, sitting in a restaurant that commands an addictive view over Anjuna's rocky cliffs and the ocean below. As I eat, I watch the local fishermen haul in their catch on to the beach, far below me. I can't make out their faces, but their bare backs are slick with effort and I feel guilty for sitting here under the shaded tarpaulin.

Jess's latest message blinks on the screen of my Codex: *Are you there, Izzy?*

I wave at the screen and the word *hello* automatically appears.

I'm running low on rupees and this restaurant's cheap, so I've been here a few days in a row. The charming elderly owner seems to be feeding me up despite my poverty, tempting me with aromatic fish curries and elaborate ice-cream sundaes sprinkled with dried flakes of banana and coconut. When I arrived an hour or so ago, he poked me in the ribs, nodding with satisfaction that his concoctions are filling out the gaps between my bones.

On the beach, children are playing at the edge of the nets, trying to grab fish caught in the outer reaches. The fishermen swat them away like flies.

When I glance back at my Codex, another message is waiting for me: *On my way into meeting. Will call properly later. Need to tell you something.*

I reply immediately: *What?*

I lean closer to the screen. I don't blink. But she doesn't reply within a few seconds, so I turn my attention back to finishing up my masala dosa while I wonder what news she could have. I've got better at eating without cutlery. It's meditative, the action of tearing the pancake between the fingers of my right hand and then sweeping it around the plate again and again, until it's clean.

Found something in Jarek's Heaven. Hang in there. It's going to be okay.

My mouth falls open.

'It's a great view,' says a man's voice, over my shoulder. A voice I recognise. A voice I'd been listening for in every shop, on every turn of the path for the past week.

I yank my Codex into my chest and shut my eyes. The reality is that I nearly choke on the last piece of dosa, but I purse my lips and swallow repeatedly until I've found some composure and raised my defences.

Daniel pulls out a chair right beside me and sits down without even looking at my face to double check that it's me. I look around, narrowing my eyes at the owner, who is standing awkwardly near the kitchen door. He must have fallen under Daniel's charm as well as mine. I notice that there are two Indian policemen standing by the entrance, notable by their drab khaki uniform. They see me look over at them but they remain expressionless. With podgy arms folded over their guts, they look like glorified bouncers.

'I can see why you came here,' Daniel adds.

'I got on the first bus that would take me. This isn't a holiday.'
I refuse to be the one to try to make eye contact first. I watch the fishermen and silently note that their day is suddenly looking a lot better than mine.

'Why did you think you had to run away?' he asks, resting his cheek on to his fist so that he's looking at me. He appears to find it – find me – amusing.

'I don't know. Why do you think that I killed Sarah?'

At that moment, the owner appears beside me to clear my plate. I shoot him an accusatory glare and I don't know if it's that or the nature of our conversation that makes him scuttle away with empty hands.

'There are people that think you did, yes.' He spreads his hands on to the table now and it is deliberate body language, of course. He's telling me that all his cards are on the table and that I can trust him. I feel nothing of the sort.

'Not you? You haven't thought it right from the beginning?'

His head wobbles in a response that gives little away. His time in India is starting to reflect in him.

'Jess and I heard you talking in Maya's office – the three of you.'

'You weren't supposed to.'

'No shit.'

He sighs. 'It hasn't helped your case, to try and disappear like this.'

'I have an alibi,' I tell him.

'You do? That's good.' His eyes seem to match the genuineness of his voice.

The fishermen are gathering up the nets now. It's like a dance as they move in their practised routine, skipping around the edges and meeting in the middle to bring them first into a snake-like tube and then into a coil. More locals gather on the sidelines; the children continue to dart over the nets and the adults wave their hands around, haggling for lunch. I think of the message from Jess and wonder desperately what it could mean.

'Interesting conversation?' Daniel gestures at the Codex nestled against my stomach. It's the supercilious tone which gets me. I furl the screen into a scroll and present it to him. As his hand opens to take it, I fling it across the table and out over the cliff edge.

Daniel bites his cheek and shakes his head, fighting back a smile. 'Have you finished?' he asks, gesturing to my gleaming plate, a warm grin upon his face.

'Not quite.'

'Come on, Isobel. We really do have to go now.'

I think about making another joke, but one glance at his face stops me. The smile is gone; he won't meet my eyes. There are two of him and it's evident that he's torn between them. Or perhaps he knows that he can't make me play his game.

'Are you arresting me?' I push my plate away and lean back in my chair as I twist slightly to face him.

He looks beyond me. 'I'd rather not.'

'Do you have an international warrant? Filled out all the forms on the journey down here, did you?' I'm guessing. I bet he hasn't. I bet he's relying on me being compliant. His eyes flash at me and I know I'm right.

'I could ask these men to arrest you.' He gestures to the officers who are still standing waiting beside the entrance. 'They're not too worried about paperwork, given the right incentives.'

'Oh, yeah,' I snort. 'You? Mr Straight?'

Daniel stands up at that and leans over me, resting his hands on the arms of my flimsy plastic chair. I feel it start to buckle with his weight. His shadow covers me completely.

'I'm telling you, this isn't the time for games. You come back to London with me now, or you stay here in a cell until I have filled in the forms and got the warrants that you think are so important.'

I stay seated, looking up at him. I almost want to laugh, it's so ridiculous.

'I don't want to force you, Isobel.' He speaks too softly for anyone around us to hear. He reaches for my forearm and I resist for a second, which lasts longer than thinking through my available options. I must believe that Jess will come through for me.

I let him ease me up out of the chair. Once upon a time, I would have kicked him in the shins and run, and I very nearly tell him so. He leads me out of the restaurant, weaving between the tables. I let my spare hand trail over the backs of chairs as we go. The owner watches us, standing still, arms by his side, next to the serving station. He nods at me, half smiles.

'Thanks for the sundaes,' I say.

The Indian officers nod politely and let us walk past them before following, their heads bowed. We walk out of the palm-leaf festooned doorway and Daniel turns to go up the hill.

'I have things in my room,' I say to him.

He pauses, possibly to look at the time. 'We don't have long, but okay.'

I hear him say something to the policemen and they head up the hill. Daniel and I start walking in the opposite direction, and I lead him this time, through the stalls that close in around us, and the patter of the sellers. The smell of cinnamon wafts at us from a gloomy passageway. I glance down it, into the jumbled network of cobbled paths. We duck beneath the silky ceilings of the sari shop and I feel that I'm almost free of him. I slip ahead, pushing the fringed tassels of sarongs and shawls apart. I could run, but I don't.

'Is it much further?' Daniel asks.

'No,' I call over my shoulder. 'Just around the bend.'

We break free of the stalls and the path opens out into the heat of the day. Sand mixes with the dust inside my sandals. We turn left on to the road and then veer around the corner to the Ocean View.

Daniel places his hand on the peeling paint of the gatepost. 'I'll wait here.'

I walk through the sandy gardens dotted with patches of grass. I try to commit it all to memory: the scent of the sea, the ladies selling fruit from the tops of their heads, and the tall, dense copse of palm trees that partially obscures the view down to the sea. I let myself into my room and look around. I already have my bag and into it I add my main toiletries from around the sink. I push in a few items of clothing, but most of it was cheap. England will be too cold now for this thin cotton. It's already late October. I count. Jarek has been gone for six weeks.

I get down on my knees and look under the bed. I pull the pillows off the mattress. I need to hurry, I know, but I can't find what I'm really looking for. The window ledge is bare, as is the wooden side table. I sweep my hands over the inlaid mother-of-pearl flowers. I check the bathroom again. As I'm about to leave, my heart heavy, I see that what I'm looking for is hooked over the door handle. I clip the already-dulling metal around my ankle. I smile as I walk out and close the door behind me. For a few moments, I stand on the porch, squinting in the direction of the beach. I'm looking for the diminutive figure and listening for the tinny rattle of jewellery. I hate not saying goodbye. There are too many people I haven't been able to say goodbye to recently. I wait for a few moments, unrewarded. My throat tightens and I feel the tickle of tears on my eyes. I fold my mouth into a sad smile and blow a kiss out at nothing, out at the shifting sand and the rolling ocean beyond it.

I turn away and walk back to meet Daniel. The owner waves at me energetically from his own porch as I get close to the gate.

'I need to settle up,' I call to Daniel.

'Already done,' he says, shaking his head and wiping the flakes of old paint from his hands.

The car journey to Goa International Airport takes about an hour. Daniel sits in the front with one of the local policemen while I remain silent in the back, next to the other one. I stare out at India and wonder if I will miss it. I think I will. Daniel takes sporadic calls and hums along to the radio. I note that he sings along to the same songs I would, if I wasn't too busy being furious. I see Jess's message flashing across my vision. *Found something in Jarek's Heaven.* She was looking for ghost memories, so what has she found? *It's going to be okay.* Okay for me? For Jarek? For both of us?

The car guides us to the entrance of the airport and then Daniel takes over the controls to deliver us to a drop-off point. Two officers appear from a small building and open the doors of the car to let us out. Daniel exchanges pleasantries with one, while the other watches me. She looks angry, as if she wants to reach out and punch me. It's as if she knew Sarah. *I'm innocent*, I want to tell her. *I didn't even do it.* She is still watching when Daniel slips a slim wire handcuff around my wrist, fixing himself to me.

'I'm sorry,' he says. 'It's just protocol. It's switched off – it can't shock you.'

The only good thing about it all is that we get fast-tracked through security, and seats in premium economy. We don't talk much. Daniel tries to make light-hearted small talk every so often and I grumble at him, letting it taper off each time.

I wake up in darkness. I can only hear snoring, the shuffle of warm bodies under blankets and the muted hum of the engines. In places, the odd spotlight shines down upon a seat. Daniel is peering into my face and I sense that he has woken me up deliberately. I sit up straight, embarrassed and angered by the idea that I might have been resting my head against his shoulder. Sleeping with the enemy.

'This is the only time we can safely talk,' he whispers. 'I'm supposed to record every conversation I have with you.'

I stare back at him, letting my lip curl at what feels like a poor attempt at coercion.

'Anything I do say may be given in evidence, I'd imagine.' I am sullen. I'm not going to be tricked again by his smoothness.

'Look, I'm not going to sit here and say whether I think you did or didn't do it,' Daniel replies. 'But you need to be prepared.'

He pauses as an air steward walks past, and looks around before continuing to talk. I wait until his attention has turned back to me before pointedly rolling my head away from him. I stare into the beige abyss of the closed porthole. I wait for his reprimand, but it doesn't come.

'You might have an alibi, Isobel, but alibis can fall down in court. Quite easily. Sarah was murdered with opioid drugs that we can prove came from you. Your D.N.A. was found on the canister, on her body.'

'What D.N.A.? I never even met her.' The unnecessary lie thickens in my chest.

'Strands of your hair were retrieved from her throat.'

'What?' I jerk my head back around. 'How?'

Daniel shrugs. He is silent for a few seconds, to let the implication of his words sink in. It sounds bad, I realise that. My hairs must have still been on Jarek. They must have been transferred on to her somehow, into her, before she was killed.

'So, you came and found me after that,' I say. 'But why the talking me into this ridiculous experiment? If you thought it was me all along, why did you make me put my own life on the line to try and prove *him* guilty?' I try to temper my voice but I notice the man in front shift and roll his head. Daniel cautions me with his eyes. 'None of that sounds ethical,' I continue. 'Scrap that; none of it sounds *legal*.'

'It's complicated.'

'Compulsive lying does tend to complicate things.'

'You need to get a good lawyer,' Daniel says, before dropping his voice even lower and leaning in closer to me. He smells sweet, like vanilla. 'Valhalla are dangerous, Isobel. I think they've wanted to do this for a long time, but they haven't had the excuse. This was perfect. It was handed to them on a plate. Think about it: a Heaven Architect – one that's against them rolling out single opt-in, no less – becomes romantically involved with one of her clients before his wife is murdered. That's a gift.'

'Maya wanted me to help them do this right from the start. She came to me and asked me to work with them and the F.B.I. to figure out how to scrutinise the Heavens of people accused of serious crimes. I shot her down.' I stop for a few seconds, letting my thoughts straighten themselves out inside my head. 'They haven't just set me up, Daniel. Someone from Valhalla killed Sarah so that I'd leave and Oakley's market price would fall. They knew that I'd come to India and look at ghost memories for them, just like they wanted from the beginning. Have you thought about that?'

'Yes, I have thought about that,' he says, calmly. 'I know Valhalla can be ruthless at times, but it seems a bit far-fetched, don't you think?'

'Oh, yes, because powerful corporations are always squeaky clean and ethical,' I snap. 'They've used me and now they want me gone.'

My mind is reeling. I think back to entering Jarek's Heaven, being stuck in the basement room with him; his glassy stare, my panic attack. There was nothing, nothing to suggest he did anything to hurt Sarah – or that I did. I console myself with the fact that their little experiment didn't prove anything. It didn't prove that you could look into people's Heavens and successfully uncover the deepest secrets of their soul. It only showed them how you *might* do it. I realise I'm not as angry as I expect. Once, I would have rattled with it, audibly and visibly. I would have made a scene. But I've been worn down around the edges by sorrow and love and everything in between.

'Besides, I didn't find anything on Jarek, did I? After all that, I found nothing.'

He glances at me briefly, before turning away. Uh oh.

'I shouldn't be telling you this.' He sighs heavily. 'Think about when you were in Jarek's Heaven, when you were running along the cliff and experiencing it all through his eyes. Sarah's face was invisible because he didn't want her there. But you knew it was her, didn't you?'

I fight back the discomfort to think about it again, dragging it up from the bottom of all my memories from that strange, in-between world. It has sunk below all the others, I realise, as if it's been trying to hide itself. Or because it is weighed down with dread.

'We saw the bitterness towards her, Isobel; it appeared in the simulation and in the readouts. We saw the anger.'

'I was living out Jarek's Heaven. Most of those thoughts, those feelings were his. They weren't mine.'

'I know.' Daniel is still refusing to look at me. 'It looked confused, admittedly. But it didn't look good either. Especially not when we'd already found yours and Jarek's D.N.A. on Sarah's body.'

'You *really* think it was me?' I narrow my eyes at him and place my hand on top of his — accusatory, yet pleading; angry, yet cajoling. He doesn't speak for a very long time and I don't take my eyes off his face for a second of it.

'I think it was one of you.'

CHAPTER TWENTY-EIGHT

It is dull grey outside when the Metropolitan Police car picks us up from the airport, but there's a tiny gap in the cloud through which I can see a patch of ochre-tinted light. It is early morning, but it looks more like late dusk, or a tropical storm in London. I am staring up at it, trying to decipher the clouds from the sky, when Daniel opens the door for me and simultaneously reads me the caution: 'I'm arresting you on suspicion of the murder of Sarah Woods. You do not have to say anything, but it may harm your defence if you do not mention when questioned something which you later rely on in court. Anything you do say may be given in evidence.'

The words rattle around my head as we travel to the police station. The unfairness of them stings and yet I have this strange sensation that it was always coming to me, all along. I have made so many bad decisions; it's the least I deserve.

Daniel guides me to the end of a corridor filled with stale air. It's cold down here and I'm shivering. My arms are wrapped around myself and I'm too tired to be angry. I look at each one of the closed cell doors but tear my eyes away before I can see through the grate. I want to be able to pretend that it's just me down here; that I'm just staying in a terrible hotel for a night.

'I got you a good one,' he says, opening the door to a cell and gesturing to the four bare walls. A felt blanket covers a bed in the corner. I can't tell if he's joking. 'Step inside.'

We walk in together and he gestures for me to lift my shirt away from my trousers. 'No belt? No jewellery?'

I shake my head before I remember.

'Oh, wait.' I sit on the bed and unclasp the anklet, running my thumb over the cobalt blue glass before handing it to him along with my shoulder bag. 'Look after it,' I tell him.

In return, he hands me the rolled-up ball of fabric he's been holding. 'To keep you warm.'

I hold it out in front of me. It's a baggy woollen jumper. It looks as if it was hand-knitted for someone.

'You took the jet-lag pills on the plane?' he asks.

I nod and sit down upon the hard bed, wondering what time it is but not bothering to look.

'Get some sleep.' He walks out of the door and locks it behind him. 'We'll be interviewing you in a few hours,' he says through the grate. 'You'll need to call a lawyer when you wake up.'

I hear the click of a switch and the room falls into darkness. It stops me from inspecting my surroundings too closely for dirt. Now I might sleep. I unwrap the jumper in my lap and pull it over my head. It reeks of damp cupboards and kindness. Loosening the blanket from where it's been tucked in around the thin mattress, I pull it over myself, right over my head, as I lie down. No light reaches me now and I feel my body heat start to gather in the air pockets around me. I close my eyes.

CHAPTER TWENTY-NINE

It takes me a while to realise that the metallic clanging is the sound of a fist upon the door. I hear it swing open and I twist around. I feel as though I've only just dropped off to sleep.

'You have the right to legal representation,' the woman says. She's dressed in a long suede skirt and a purple sweater that rides up over her belly. She looks me over. 'Would you like to call your lawyer?'

'I don't have a lawyer,' I mutter.

The woman sighs. 'Fine. Do you want to speak to our duty solicitor?' she asks, folding her arms.

I struggle out from under the restraints of the tangled blanket and pull my hands out from the voluminous sleeves of the borrowed jumper. I rub my hands over my face and tuck my hair behind my ears. I hear the woman sigh again.

'I guess so, yes,' I say.

'I'll send him down,' she mutters over her shoulder as she leaves, slamming the door behind her.

The room is square and scantily furnished, unsettling in its perfect symmetry. There are no windows, only a sky-blue carpet and cloud-white walls covered in dirty scuff-marks. I sit next to the duty solicitor on an uncomfortable bench, drawn up to the small table. He's a very tall, very thin man. Even sitting next to me, his head towers above mine. In a flat voice, he tells me I should get a lawyer and then say nothing at all. 'You seem like a feisty young woman, Ms Argent. I suggest that you attempt to keep that in check. Just for the next hour or so.'

I pretend to acquiesce. I fold my hands in my lap and imagine that the room smells of jasmine and star anise, not the stench of decaying carpet tiles splashed with evaporated milk. A stranger enters the room. He's big, in every sense of the word, and dark haired. Hair covers his head like a helmet and creeps down his forearms. He looks like a human that's been recreated from a child's felt-tip drawing. His shirt strains around his armpits, and it's only when he sits down that I realise Daniel is behind him. I almost smile, but then remember that he's the worst kind of traitor. Daniel undoes the button on his jacket and settles himself down on the chair, avoiding my gaze. I watch as the man fiddles with some outdated recording equipment fitted into a panel on the surface of the table. I think, longingly, of my state-of-the-art table in my old office. I spent a weekend playing with it when it first arrived, learning how to activate simulations and access documents.

'Where were you on the evening of Friday the sixteenth of September?' the stranger asks, flatly. His voice is as heavy as his brow.

I at least expected an introduction and open my mouth to say so, but I can feel the gaze of the solicitor bore into the side of my head. He must have seen people like me screw this up before.

'No comment,' I say dutifully.

'Really? You've got no idea where you were?'

I think of Don, my alibi, and decide that it seems plain stupid not to answer simple questions with a straightforward response. 'I was at home,' I say, 'in my apartment.' I speak in an imitation of Don's natural confidence. 'I was with my boyfriend at the time.' I know Don will be true to his word. I hope they can believe him and that he doesn't turn out to be in two places at the same time. He is cleverer than that, surely. I can almost hear the solicitor groan.

'No. Comment,' he whispers in my ear.

'Was he with you between six p.m. and seven p.m., would you say?' the officer asks, unfurling his Codex and angling it away from me.

'Yes, definitely.' I watch Daniel. He's resting one foot over his knee, and his hands on his calf. His head is so far drooped down that I can't even tell if his eyes are open. Is he, too, pleading for me to shut up? It crosses my mind that I have known Daniel for almost as long as I knew Jarek. Is this what would have happened if Jarek and I had known each other for longer? Would one of us have eventually betrayed the other in some way? Did that short, sweet, dizzying couple of months leave no room for the truth?

'What were you doing that evening?'

The questions are so thick in my own head that I barely have room to process any more.

'I don't know; I can't remember,' I mutter. 'It was quite a long time ago now.' But not that long. Six weeks. It seems both more and less time than that. On the one hand, it doesn't seem enough to contain the things that have happened since. But then so much can happen so quickly.

'Nothing springs to mind?'

I shake my head. This is why you say *No comment*, I think. Because then, when you really don't have a comment, you avoid sounding like a complete idiot. Or a liar.

'You don't remember *anything*?' he asks, raising his eyebrows in forced disbelief. 'You know that you were at home but you don't recall a single thing that happened that night?' He leans forward on the table, eyes focused upon me.

I try to swallow my rising emotions back, but the unnecessary aggression in his face provokes me. 'Oh, yes – wait – I remember! We were teaching our neighbours how to samba, naked. Or was that the night that we were swinging from the chandeliers? I have such an exciting life, officer, that it's hard to think.'

The interviewer sucks in his cheeks and glances across at Daniel.

'Sorry,' I say. 'I mean, no comment.'

'Wait.' Daniel waves his hand over the recording panel. It's the first word I've heard him speak. His colleague frowns and, at the same time, he nods. Daniel walks around the table, rubbing his chin. He crouches in front of me.

'I don't think you did it, Isobel,' he whispers into my ear. His voice shivers with anger. 'Is that what you needed to hear? For God's sake, help me out here. Help yourself out.' He speaks so quietly that I can barely make out his words. Afterwards, I wonder if I heard them correctly at all. He walks around the table and sits back down. His colleague watches him the entire time, his head moving like the second hand on an expensive antique watch.

'Would you like to take over?' the man asks, his voice tight and accompanied with a sharp jut of the head.

I look at Daniel, and I see what looks like confusion flickering across his face. It's as if he doesn't want to do it.

'I don't think . . .' he begins, scratching his cheek. But then he must feel my gaze upon him because he looks up at me and I silently tell him, *Yes, go on. I will behave. I will be good.* I finally realise the allowances he's made for me – the exceptions, the generosities – despite the fact I was a suspect all along. And I've thrown them all back in his face.

'Okay, Ms Argent.' He clears his throat and pulls his chair closer to the table so that he can lean his forearms on to it. He glances down at the Codex that's tilted towards him. 'You are a Heaven Architect by profession, correct?'

'No comment.'

'It's our understanding that the husband of the victim, Jarek Woods, was one of your clients?'

'No comment.'

Daniel doesn't need to look back at the Codex to know the next question. He knows it. I know it. But he seems to struggle.

'You were also in a sexual relationship with Mr Woods, weren't you?' Now the words are out, they sound more like an accusation than I expected. The straightness of his face masks some hidden undercurrent. It's like anger, pricking at the hairs on my arms. Or jealousy.

'No comment.' My voice wavers. The other cop and the solicitor have faded away. It's only Daniel and me in the room now.

'Describe what happened on the afternoon of Friday, September sixteenth, when Mr Woods came to your apartment.' His voice has steadied. It's as if he's on autopilot. As he strengthens, I can feel myself breaking. I feel as though cracks are appearing in my skull around the metal plugs.

'No comment.'

'You had sex?'

'No comment.'

Daniel looks at the Codex again, where I presume the notes are, and then glances at his colleague. The man shrugs and turns his hands outward slightly. *This is your interview now*, he seems to say.

'Do you believe that Mr Woods was still having a sexual relationship with his wife up until the time of her death?'

I try to swallow back the dryness in my throat. I stare into Daniel's eyes. They are wide open. Neither eyelid flickers.

'No,' I say.

'What makes you think that? Does the idea make you angry?'

'No comment.' I try to say it as levelly as possible, but at best it's a tortured whisper. I am behaving. I am doing what I was told. Not for me, but for Daniel. And now he's taunting me with these questions.

I know that he wasn't having sex with Sarah. *Because he was angry with her, and he was jealous*, a tiny voice inside me whispers. The emotions I felt reverberate through me in that scene on the cliff top did not belong to me. They did not belong to me. They were his. They were all his. Jarek's hateful anger and his bitter resentment focused on the shadowy figure that he couldn't quite identify.

As I sit here, at my lowest ebb, in a cold London interrogation room, shivering beneath the bright lights, a new memory rises to the surface. It's one I haven't been able to admit I even noticed before. In Jarek's body, occupying Jarek's mind, I watched my little daughter running ahead and I looked at my wife and I thought, Now, I could do it now and no one would know.

'My client is entitled to a break,' the solicitor whines. I almost jump; I'd forgotten he was there.

Daniel sighs heavily and sits back from the table.

'One more minute,' the first cop grunts as he looks down at the recording equipment. 'How far was Mr and Mrs Woods' house from your apartment? How long did it take you to walk there?' He is rubbing his thumb along his middle finger and I can hear the friction of his skin echo in my ears. It makes me want to smack his hand on to the table.

'No comment,' I say, although I'm asking myself again what I did know about Jarek. It strikes me that I heard so many of his memories and stories from his past that perhaps I missed the fact the man sitting beside me was little more than a stranger.

'Would you care to tell us why you think your D.N.A. might have been found on the body of Mrs Woods?' he continues, clearly relishing the detail. 'Do you have any thoughts on why your hairs were extracted from the back of her oesophagus?'

'No comment,' I say firmly, my strength returning at the craziness of the questions.

'I'd like you to take a look at this document, please, Ms Argent.' He swivels the Codex around to face me. It's words, only words.

'What is it?' I murmur.

Daniel presses his lips together and I see the gentlest shake of his head.

'Oh, I'm glad you're taking an interest at last!' his colleague continues. 'These are transcripts taken from Mr Woods' audio diary, which he seems to have recorded regularly from the time of his diagnosis right up until his death. Would you care to, say, read this sentence aloud?' He leans over, angling the display back slightly so he can also see it.

I stare back at him dumbly.

'No? Okay, D.C.I. Lyden will read it out to you.' He hands the Codex over to Daniel. 'How about the entry dated Thursday the fifteenth, there.' He jabs at it with his stubby little finger.

Daniel hesitates in taking the device. I watch him swallow and clench his jaw.

'"Well, what do you know?"' he begins. '"It only turns out that I was wrong for once in my too-short life. I know we've had our differences, but I'm starting to see that this fucking illness has clouded my brain."'

I fight back the tears at the sound of Jarek's words in Daniel's voice. Jarek's light tone is missing, but I can hear it nonetheless; I place his exclamation marks where Daniel only allows serious full stops. I want to close my eyes and escape with these words, let them transform me. But they are not the words I want to hear, not the words I expect to hear.

'"Perhaps Sarah should be in my Heaven. We're a family and I owe her that, after everything. I just bloody hope that I haven't realised too late and that there's still time for Harry to change things."' Daniel flicks his eyes up at me. I'm not sure what he must see in my face, if he sees anything at all.

'"It's Isobel I've got to think about really. Maybe I should be honest. Maybe I owe it to her to explain that our affair has been a mistake. Although she won't take it well. What a fucking mess."'

I imagine the cool calm of his laughter. I know it was there. A mistake, a mistake. The word stabs at my heart.

He did come and see me that next day, of course. *I had to see you,* he had whispered in my ear. He came to make love to me. He came to ask for something for the pain – something strong enough to end it once and for all. He did not come to tell me that he'd been wrong, that he loved her and not me. Nothing of the sort.

'Time, gentlemen,' the solicitor says, breaking through the spell that's seeping out from my brain like weighted ink into the blood of every throbbing vein, artery and tiny capillary. He and the officer push back their chairs without hesitation while Daniel and I stare at each other, dazed.

The solicitor helps manoeuvre me out of the interview room. He sits me down on a bench in the corridor and disappears, muttering something about fetching me some water. I think he can see as well as I can that I need something stronger. I need oblivion. I grip at the edges of the bench. My knuckles are white.

I sip at the water that has appeared next to me. It tastes white, like the rest of the world. I feel the familiar panic rising from my legs. It's a tingle at first, like pins and needles, until I remember what it means and it starts to stab at me, then, because I've looked it in the face and acknowledged it.

If I freak out now, they'll lock me back in that cell. They'll tie me down and they'll never let me out. I hear footsteps and I see Daniel striding down the corridor towards me. I feel myself harden. The walls that Jarek broke down are back up and the very thought of a man consoling me is enough to snap me out of it. I breathe in and out, slowly, as heavily as I dare. I fake a smile.

'Hello, Daniel.' And as soon as I've said it, I'm fully aware that I sound completely and utterly mad.

He looks down into my face, his forehead wrinkled in concern.

He doesn't ask me if I'm okay; he doesn't say anything at all. And I see something pale unfurling behind his eyes that is the last thing I want to see right now: a thing I never want a part of again.

'Come on; we're getting out of here.' There is an urgency in his voice, as if he hasn't yet seen his own flag of surrender.

I sit, unmoving, looking past him to the blank wall behind. I think about saying lots of things. I think about asking him what the point would be of going anywhere; I think of asking him to help me tease apart the barbed thoughts tearing through my mind. I could accept the idea that Valhalla may have framed me. It's in keeping with my opinion of them, and of Maya. But what if they haven't?

'The diary,' I murmur. 'Do you think it's the truth?'

Daniel shakes his head, with what looks like sadness. 'Just before their deaths, I think Sarah had kicked him out for good. But I can't be sure – their families say nothing had been mentioned to them.'

If Jarek deliberately wrote a diary that was the opposite of what he thought and felt, then how did I figure in his life at all? I try to block out my doubts. Is it possible that Jarek did it? That he framed me so perfectly? Could his diary be an elaborate lie, designed to burden me with a motive? It's the only possible explanation, and it reverberates in every cell of my body. *He used you; he set you up; he never loved you.* The lengths he would have gone to in order to cover his tracks blindside me. He let me be part of his Heaven so that I would be so utterly won over by him, in order that a jury would look at me and see a scorned, husband-stealing mistress, not an innocent bystander. Did Jarek also come that afternoon to tear hairs from my head as we clung to each other? Did he come to collect the pills and set everything up perfectly? If it's true, if this is what he's done, then I am lost.

The shock grounds my feet to the floor so that they feel like they'll never move again. The questions collide and rebound in no particular order. I want to cut every one out of me, or scream them out. I want them gone. I want my mind to be vacant. And I must be insane because I'm still yearning to be in my Heaven with a man who may well have been a liar and a psychopath; a man who has taken everything from me, and who could have murdered his wife.

I think of collapsing into Daniel's arms and crying. But apparently there's a part of me that still has some fight left, because what I actually do is tell him, 'There's only one place I'll let you take me.'

CHAPTER THIRTY

'You're still under arrest,' Daniel says as we climb into the police car. 'Now, unless someone applies for an extension, we have twenty-four hours in which to either charge you or release you. I'd prefer it to be the latter.'

I stare at him. 'Why?'

'Jess twisted my arm,' he says, before telling the vehicle to take us to the Francis Crick Institute, Midland Road. The warm glow of the dashboard lights on this dull, rainy London morning matches my relief to be out of the station. The car moves cautiously down the narrow streets. We pause at the junction and, through the rain that clings and then falls down the glass, one of the shop window displays catches my eye. A robot is arranging cut pieces of fabric on to a mannequin, the sections forming the shape of a suit jacket. It moves back and forth over one shoulder as I watch it, seemingly checking the measurement, once, twice, three times. There's no room for error. Daniel was like a robot, reading Jarek's diary, trying to say those words without attributing emotion to them. He was trying to save me, but nothing could have made it sound colder.

'I'm sorry,' he says abruptly, from the seat in front of me. I almost wonder if I was thinking aloud. 'Jarek's diary probably came as a shock. I wanted to get straight to—'

'It's okay,' I say, cutting him off. I look back at the robot, which is still moving backwards and forwards across the body of the mannequin as we pull out from the junction and turn left on to Regent Street.

The streets in this part of London are filled with Lela. We used to come Christmas shopping together here. I remember being younger, starting out at Oakley, and Lela taking me under her wing. She brought me somewhere near here, tucked away, to buy the new Codex that I would use for work. As the car turns right and passes by the black beams of Liberty, I remember how we would go in on each of our birthdays and choose something tiny as a present from the other one, just so that we could get the regal purple bag, embossed with gold. I crane my neck to seek out the gilded ship on the edge of the roof. Lela was the one who had pointed it out to me. I'd never lifted my eyes high enough before to notice it. *It's the Mayflower*, she'd told me. Now I imagine tiny golden people aboard it, sailing towards freedom.

The car pushes on through the light mid-morning traffic and I notice familiar corners where I remember saying goodbye to her for the evening. The car stops in traffic, right outside the Palladium, and the theatre's gleaming array of light bulbs reminds me of the shows we saw together there. I remember joking about how perfectly her lipstick matched the red carpet beneath our feet, as we skipped up the steps for the first time. I can't recall what we saw, but it was terrible — so bad that we giggled all the way through it and got told off by the couple behind us. I miss her; I will always miss her. I grasp on to the veracity of the love we had for each other. I wasn't wrong about that.

We're not far, here, from Wimpole Street, and Oakley Associates. And beyond that is the corner of the street where Jarek first kissed me – pulled me towards him with what seemed like lust, but in hindsight might have been an entirely different type of need. My breath steams up the window so that I lose sight of what's beyond it. I could rub it away with my hand but instead I rest my head against the glass and close my eyes. These streets are filled with a life that is no longer mine.

'How are you feeling?' Daniel asks, but there's no reply I can give. He clears his throat and lets the question dissipate.

'Didn't your mate want to come with us?' I ask.

'He did, yes, but I told him we wouldn't be long.'

'If Jess has some evidence, something she wants to show you, why are you bringing me?' I ask. 'Shouldn't you have left me behind?'

Daniel twists right around in his seat. 'Jess wants you to do another experiment, Isobel,' he says, meeting my eyes. 'Do this, and we could have everything we need to close this case.'

My teeth click together and my stomach drops.

He stares at my face for a few seconds and then turns back around and I can only see part of the back of his head. 'Can't you see that I'm trying to help you? I'm tearing the pages out of the rulebook for this – for you.'

'You *arrested* me! You have put me through hell!' I explode. But even I know that there's not as much fire behind my voice as there should be. As much as I am angry with others, I am furious with myself for my own stupidity and for ever agreeing to get involved. The blame is mine; it does not lie with him. If he had never asked me to do what I've done, then I would never have seen my own Heaven. I would never have met Jarek one last time. I whisper the last thought quietly in my own head, barely letting myself acknowledge that I've created it. And then I recognise a sensation rising through the resentment. It's a survival instinct, a force for good: the drive to prove myself innocent. It finally takes over, pushing everything else aside. It is all that matters now.

'I had to arrest you, Isobel. This is out of my hands now.'

I watch the way the neat, manicured curves of his nails are scratching at the armrest. I don't make a sound. I look out of the window again, watching the trees at the edge of the park ruffling their reddening leaves.

'I have been breaking the rules since the day I met you,' he says. His voice is so quiet that it's barely audible over the traffic and I wonder whether he meant for me to hear him speak at all.

Jess is waiting for us outside the Institute, at the top of the slope outside the atrium. She stands still, arms folded, as we approach through the paved courtyard, weaving around the shrubs. She looks older than I remember; perhaps she is tired. Because of me? I wonder. I look up at the building's glass walls and curving roof. Around that corner is where Daniel first found me and saw that the passion of love and subsequent grief had opened me right up. I am not that vulnerable anymore, I say to myself. I say it silently to Daniel, too, challenging him with my eyes.

Jess is completely passive until we reach her and then she throws her arms around me and crushes me against her. I feel so weak suddenly that I worry I will collapse. I hold her awkwardly with one hand.

'Shall we?' she says.

Jess leads us inside and we walk up the sloping glass walkway. Last time I was here, it was warm and sunny outside – a typical mid-September London day – and the glass had breathed. Today it is cold, and the glass is closed, insulating us against the threatening winter. So much has changed.

'Are we going to the Electric Lab?' I ask quietly.

'Yes,' Daniel says. Then, to Jess: 'Tell her what you told me.'

Jess strides ahead, leading us from the walkway and down a corridor that feels familiar, but probably looks like every other corridor in this building. She glances back at me and I see excitement, a tumult of possibilities, dancing in her eyes.

'We never really found what we were looking for in Jarek's Heaven, did we? You never found it.' Her voice moves as quickly as her feet. She knows we don't have long.

I shake my head. 'Just the—'

'Just the scene on the cliff,' she says, nodding. 'Those vague emotions—'

'That were his,' I say, forcefully, to both her and Daniel.

'I know.' Jess looks directly at me. 'I know they were his.'

That lifts me. I let myself relax a little. I let myself hope. Jess is the kind of woman you want on your side: sweet, friendly, but when push comes to shove, hard as nails.

We enter a lift and Jess touches the button at the bottom of the display, letting it scan across her eye before the doors close and the lift drops. The three of us are silent. I feel the same sensation that I felt when I got off the bus and stood above Anjuna's ragged cliffs: that I could fall and that would be preferable to any other option. There would be a safety in it – a safety in sinking into the pit of this building and never leaving.

The lift doors open and Daniel and I follow Jess as she takes a sharp left and then walks through a wide pair of metal doors. They slide open as she approaches and make a noise that I didn't notice the first time – a welcoming beep – as if they are pleased to see her. Daniel hangs back and pauses slightly to read the inscription that I know is above them.

'We are electric,' I say, over my shoulder.

The three of us move into the heart of the room, gathering around the pedestal and its misty projections. *Lela* – I suddenly realise.

'She's here?' I ask Jess. 'She's safe?' I look around into the veiled walls of the circular room, seeking out the telltale seams of the doors that I know line it. In one of them is what remains of Lela. In one of them is what remains of Jarek. So many of my former clients are in here somewhere, their last functioning cells living out lives that were never really theirs, existing in Heavens which might, it seems, be clouded in part by the shadows of reality. Now this place seems like a prison. Sealed, inescapable: a memory chamber.

I promised my clients perfection and I didn't deliver. They could be locked inside worlds which taunt them with their strongest recollections – emotionally turbocharged memories living a double life inside their mirror neurons. Memories not only of the best moments, but also of the worst. The darknesses that we hide, I think.

'I can't remember which room,' Jess says, 'but, yes, Lela's

neurons are safe and sound. I've been monitoring her Heaven for ghost memories, but so far, nothing. It looks stable.'

Stable. Is that the most my clients can hope for? And yet I feel the familiar drug-like tug of my Heaven. I know it's not possible, but it's as if I can sense my proximity to it. I am so close to where I can access it. The serotonin receptors hammer like pneumatic drills. But if Jarek killed Sarah, then it is all ruined. My Heaven will be a falsehood, lying in rubble inside my skull, sharp and jagged, cutting at the edges of every emotion. It would all need rebuilding, I think automatically, before wondering whether the scrap heap is where it should stay.

'We don't have much time,' says Daniel, softly, trying not to look overawed by the display that twists and swirls into rainbows under Jess's fingertips. The light dances over his face and it looks like hope. I can't find myself able to hate him, or even dislike him. I turn my gaze towards Jess. I already have a sense of what they are asking me to do and I am almost prepared. There is a strength in my heart, in this place, with these people – both alive and dead.

'I wasn't prepared before, Izzy,' she says in that beautiful Irish lilt that makes it impossible not to warm to her. 'They didn't give me time. We hoped . . .'

'I know, you hoped it would work,' I reply. 'And it almost did.'

'But since I flew back from India, I've been looking – looking more closely. You remember when you first came here, when I showed you the trace of the mirror neuron . . . ?'

I nod, but she's already turned her attention to what's in front of her. I listen to the suspended water droplets hiss and hum. The mist flashes with a green light and a door behind Daniel clicks into life. Jess waves us towards it and holds open the door as we walk in.

Wordlessly, she places a fingertip on the dark surface of the panel that wraps around the room, and taps. She takes the tiny cartridge which appears and presses it into the shallow cavity in the wall above the panel. As the machine begins to hum, she takes two slim pairs of glasses from her lab coat and hands them to us, pointing at the wall. I slip them on and see the dark blankness transformed once more into the augmented-reality panorama of flashing lights – pinpricks in a star cloth. I try to follow one point of light as it shoots across my field of vision, bumping into others, spinning and dancing with them before moving on. Despite these encounters, it's alone, really; always alone.

'Wow,' murmurs Daniel, beside me. 'These are memories?'

'It's a more basic representation of the brainwave data than what we saw in India,' says Jess. 'This is just what we use on a day-to-day basis to check a Heaven is functioning properly – a way of looking in from the outside without needing any type of formal access.'

She moves in front of the lights, breaking my train of thought.

'Remember, Izz, here?' She points towards the bottom of the display, at around her own knee height, and traces a wave of light that shakes and trembles but is remarkably steady, compared to the rest of the vision.

'A ghost memory?'

Jess nods and moves her hand further up, running her fingertip along a separate pair of intertwined lines. 'Three.'

I nod and try to swallow, but something feels lodged in my throat. 'This is Jarek's Heaven, isn't it?' I ask.

'Yes.'

I'm taken by surprise by the burst of fury that grips me. It cuts

300

through my own words. I imagine the convertible crash, taking us both up in a fireball; I imagine chasms ripping through the rugby field. I imagine taking him by the throat in the basement room and throwing him against the door. I tear the glasses from my face and hurl them at the lights, at the memories I so lovingly crafted into shape.

'We need you to look at it more closely, Izzy,' Jess says.

I stand there, shaking, and feel Daniel put his hand on my shoulder. It's awkward, as though he's about to push me into the back of a police car, rather than offering me comfort. Jess calmly retrieves the pieces of the glasses and puts them back into her pocket. She is frowning and I can see the telltale puckering where her forehead was cut open in the attack on the hospital. I look around the room, at the invisible outlines of the cartridges that I know are buried in the black, featureless panel.

'One of *you* can do it. I want nothing to do with it.' I can't conceal the fear that pulls at my voice. Jess hears it. She comes to face me and runs her fingertips over my head, letting them catch on the metal plugs that I have almost forgotten are there. I know that this ghost memory is my salvation. I know that there are a thousand logical reasons why I have to do it and they can't. This is just one of them.

'We don't have much time, Izz,' she says, apologetically.

Jess leads us back upstairs to her lab. I've been in it once before. It's a complete contrast to the sleek dimness of the Electric Lab. We walk down the aisle that runs through the middle of it. Men and women are hunched over microscopes and other unidentifiable pieces of equipment, which seem to be scattered randomly across every surface. Nervousness fizzes at my lips and my fingertips, but the calming odour of disinfectant, that familiar lab smell, fills my nostrils. I breathe it in deeply. It always transports me back to my undergrad degree and the contentment of knowing that I was going to spend a whole afternoon somewhere so clean. My obsessions were much worse back then, I remember. A few people are clustered around a projection which shows some highly magnified neurons. They are engaged in urgent discussion – an argument, maybe – and their voices rise clearly above the soft hum of machinery and the otherwise hushed chatter that fills the lab.

'Luke,' Jess calls to one of the men in the group. 'Is it all set up?'

He raises his hand to acknowledge her. 'Yep – room five.' I feel his eyes linger on me as we walk on. My story must be the most salacious gossip they've heard for a while. If Valhalla and the investigative forces of our countries get their way, they'll be dealing with a lot more than this. There will be someone here every few days, sneaking a glimpse into the brain of a possible fraudster, hacker or murderer. I briefly reconsider whether that would be such a bad thing.

Jess beckons us down an aisle towards the end of the huge lab, through a door into a small room, into which is squeezed a sofa, a desk with an office chair, and a window. Behind the desk is a white metal door with the number five embossed into the centre. Jess gestures for us to sit on the sofa and closes the door we entered through. She leans back against the desk, holding its edges with her hands. As with the lab outside, I feel comfortable in here. But it reminds me of my own office back at Oakley and how irretrievable it is to me.

Daniel sits forward on the edge of the sofa and assumes his

listening pose: fingers pressing into a bridge, his forearms rested on his knees. I notice the characteristic wave of one of my hairs ruining the lapel of his jacket and fight the urge to pick it off. I look away again, at Jess, thinking of those brown waves of mine threaded down the back of Sarah's throat, tickling and scratching at its dry, terrified surface.

Jess rests her eyes upon me and I remember that, for the moment, I have a new purpose. It's one that will kill me or save me.

'So,' she begins, allowing a few seconds for us to fully focus on what she's about to say. 'I looked first at the mirror neurons that were activated in Valhalla's lab when you were in that cliff scene. That seemed to be the closest we could get to any potential lead because, although Jarek didn't recognise Sarah, it looked as if he had an emotional response to her.'

She pauses and tucks her hair behind her ears. It slips forward again almost as soon as she starts talking.

'I believe that those emotions we noted – what seemed to be anger, perhaps a kind of frustration – are his, Isobel, I do. But it's hard to disentangle them from you in the simulation. So, we have to find something else, something more.'

I feel myself leaning forward.

'Three of Jarek's mirror neurons were activated at that cliff scene. We examined them more closely and we did find a couple of ghost memories.' She turns towards Daniel, reminding him for clarity: 'Encoded once in the brain's normal neurons and once again in the mirror neurons.'

He nods; I nod.

'And in the third mirror neuron, we found a third ghost memory, on its own – the one I just showed you, lower down on the visualisation. This one was completely different in its intensity. Something huge.' Her voice is growing more animated. She's almost grinning in excitement. 'If these memories were measured like an earthquake, the first ones would be a four, maybe a five on the Richter scale. Enough to cause some localised damage around the epicentre, maybe a few fatalities.' She pauses for effect. 'But the third one? That would be an eight or a nine. A rare event and one causing widespread, long-lasting devastation. The kind you'd hear about on the international news.'

'You think that memory is the murder?' I realise that it's the first time I've really acknowledged it aloud; the first time I've truly admitted my willingness to believe it. But I am more than willing – I am desperate.

'It could be,' she says. 'And as for those first, less intense memories – well, they're anyone's guess at this stage, but they're clearly of major importance to Jarek. All I'd say is that the fact they were activated at the cliff scene, in the presence of Sarah, suggests they may be related in some way to the murder.'

Jess finishes and signals that she's come to the end by resting her hands on to her thighs and dropping her gaze to the floor. I can see, more than ever, the tiredness etched into her face. I know her well enough to be sure that she has lived in this lab since coming back from Mumbai. She has lived and breathed the diagnostics of Jarek's Heaven until she knows every detail. She is my saviour and I feel a rush of affection for her. She has always had my back. I remember her warning to me in the café around the corner. She could see me falling, reeling. She sees it now.

'And you need me again, to see all of this.' I hardly hear my own voice. It's not even a question. We all know why we're here now.

'We're going to have to connect your mirror neurons again. Ironically, putting all of your consciousness in with all of Jarek's is the only way that we can separate out what's your memory and what's his, so that we can have two separate brainwave readouts, two separate visualisations,' says Jess. 'Otherwise, it'll be like the data we have from the cliff scene: controversial, and open to being misread.'

'Last time . . .' I begin, the words faltering as soon as they form in my mouth. 'Last time, my mirror neurons were almost destroyed. Last time, Lela died.' Spoken aloud, the fact horrifies me afresh.

I see Jess look at Daniel. 'This won't be like last time. I can't honestly tell you this is low risk, but we're safer here than in Mumbai.'

'And I can't confront Jarek. I can't go in there and speak to him.'

'We'll only be running those ghost memories of Jarek's into your brain. Nothing else. No Heaven. What I think will happen is that, because you'll be experiencing a specific memory, it'll be like watching a movie. After all, this isn't the Heaven you created for him and you're not in it.'

'Then can't anyone look at them? Why me?'

'Because you're all ready to go, Isobel,' Jess says, touching the tips of her fingers to the fuzzy patches of scalp around the metal plugs in my skull. 'And because I think you might need to see this for yourself.'

I sigh and drop my gaze. I stare at my hands, turning them over and inspecting them. Would anyone really believe that these slim, bony fingers could kill another person? Would a jury not see that these hands were built for comforting people in their time of need, or pulling a thread delicately across an eyebrow? I could take my chances, I think. I could argue my case. I have Don as my alibi: strong, capable Don. He would look great in court. A Ministry of Defence consultant? They'd love him.

'Is it even legal to do this here?' I ask, looking first at Jess, then at Daniel. 'There was a reason we all flew to Mumbai, wasn't there?'

'Like I said, it's not really Jarek's Heaven we're looking at. I'll tell people I found this accidentally, during my research.'

I'm scared, but my head moves. It's nodding.

'It's all set up,' she continues. 'It's all ready to go. I've got Jarek's neurons primed in the right places. I promise we'll get you in and out as quickly as possible. Straight from one memory to the next.'

Here we go, I say to myself, as we all get up and walk out of the office into lab number five.

CHAPTER THIRTY-ONE

It's all a little ad hoc. I'm not lying on a hospital bed, or indeed any kind of bed, but on the cold, hard lab bench. I'm fully clothed, but the woolly jumper is off and I'm down to my T-shirt. There's no sheet to cover me. Despite Daniel's concerns, comfort isn't a major issue for me. I'll be out of it, soon enough. I'll be somewhere else entirely. It's warm in here, though, perhaps from the equipment that surrounds me, buzzing with electricity and boxing me in. Like a body in a coffin, I think. I am so thirsty, so hungry. It's all clean, though – at least, it looks like it is. I cast my eyes around once more. Perhaps, thinking about it again, it's a bit too messy in here to be truly clean. I turn my eyes back to the ceiling, trying not to think about it.

Luke, the researcher from the lab, is apparently my anaesthetist, making it four of us in this tiny room. Five, if you count Jarek. Jess already had the cartridge here, set up. She must have brought it with her from the Electric Lab without me noticing. I saw it, almost accidentally, as she opened it up and started linking it to her equipment. I try to stop myself from thinking about the fact that my mirror neurons will be physically linked to his again. It turns my stomach into a sickening mixture of fury and fragility.

'As the most impartial person we've got on hand, Luke is going to keep a written and audio-visual record of the process,' says Jess.

Luke inclines his head and holds up his Codex.

I look again at the screens and equipment around me. A lot of it looks familiar. 'Valhalla gave you authority to use their simulation software?' I ask her.

'Of course they did,' Jess says. I detect a note of despondency in her voice. 'They want me to solve all their problems – find a way of preventing ghost memories from getting into people's Heavens.'

'Or find a way to cover it up,' Daniel says.

I stare at him open-mouthed in surprise that he could be more cynical than me. Jess raises her eyebrows and turns away, and it's in that moment that I fully realise what these ghost memories could mean. They could mean the total collapse of the industry. No more Heavens. After all, who would want one?

I watch Jess as Luke rubs an anaesthetic tattoo on the inside of my elbow. She moves from machine to machine, her shoulders hunched, and I wonder what lengths Valhalla, Caleb and all the other Heaven architecture firms would go to in order to save their businesses. I think I know the answer. Jess would walk away, but there are many more like her who wouldn't.

I look up at the LEDs that fill the ceiling and watch them first seem to brighten and then dim, as Jess closes the curtains and then turns them down so that she can pull up the simulations at the back of the room. The drugs fill my veins and they calm the last of the fight in me. The tenderness is soothed. I am resigned. I am sinking. As my eyes fall shut, I am thinking about the excitement that filled me last time as I prepared to see Jarek in my Heaven. This time, it is completely different. I am standing on a headland, my toes curled over the edge. I'm watching the waves crash on the red, jagged rocks below me and my insides are too paralysed to care what happens next.

I'm straight into it. My cats don't purr at my legs. I don't play with my sister or dance with my mother. I don't reach out to pick ripe blackberries beneath the red of an autumn sun. My Heaven is bypassed completely. It feels different, just as Jess said it would.

I'm walking into a house, through a side door, it seems. As the scene around me starts to crystallise, I realise that I'm behind Jarek. I recognise his rusty hair atop those broad shoulders. He walks tall, with purpose – not with the weakening inclination to the left that he had while I knew him. That stoop lent him valuable vulnerability. I'm just watching his memory, but I feel as though he will spot me at any moment. I stay behind a doorway and let him move on into what I think is the kitchen. I remain with my back to the wall and listen to him walk around. He is still wearing his shoes, but he is moving very quietly, deliberately so; I can barely make out what he is doing. It's then that I realise I can't hear anything at all. This ghost memory is silent. And now I see that my view of it has never fully crystallised. The edges of my vision fade into blank white space where there should be a wall or a ceiling or an item of furniture. It's like tunnel vision. This memory doesn't have the touch of my work; it's rough and worn. It's been buried for too long to be perfect. It hasn't been shaped and coaxed back into life by the architecture of Heaven. Something more primal lurks here.

I remember why I am here. I am going to see something that changes Jarek forever. That is the only reason this memory exists, copied into the very depths of his consciousness. I swallow and steel myself. I let my heart thud against the walls of my chest, let its rhythm attempt to calm me. But it's uneven and speeds up; it's putting up my defences and getting me ready to run.

From the ghostly silence, noise appears. There is a thump from above my head, from upstairs, swiftly followed by laughter. High and joyful: a woman's laughter. Jarek rushes out from the kitchen and I am sure that he'll see me then, standing right there behind the door frame, but he looks straight through me. The rules are different here, I remember; this ghost memory has never met me. We aren't in the Aston Martin, or in the basement room or my apartment. We are together but separate, and I am relieved.

I hear the taunting tinkle of laughter again. It is the only sound, other than my own heartbeat, yet it's as if I can hear his mind working. It's rolling into a different gear, setting itself up for something it's never known.

For a moment, I wonder which of the memories I am in. I can see that he is younger here and it is long before the glioblastoma took hold. This ghost memory must date back several years. Jarek is standing stock-still. His face is calm. His hands are hanging at his sides, fingers flexed, feet shoulder-width apart on the glossy wooden floor. He is reflected in it. I look down and notice that I am not.

There is a sudden flash of movement and Jarek rushes past me. I don't want to follow him but I know that I must. I take comfort in the fact that I am invisible. As Jarek tiptoes up the stairs, I remain a few steps behind, staring at the spot where his shirt is tucked into his belted suit trousers. I let myself admire his body; it belongs to a man a few years younger than the one I knew, stronger, perhaps happier, and momentarily I let myself imagine meeting *this* Jarek and wonder how different things would have been.

He stops halfway up, dropping his gaze as if concentrating on the sounds coming from the room to the right of us. I can't see what's beyond. I can only see the stairs and the door, and the landing outside it. Silent white noise supports it all. As Jarek creeps up the final few steps, the emotions start to take hold of me. Like that scene on the cliff, there is a growing sense of tension in the air. This time, I don't feel it as if it were mine, but I sense it, as if it's radiating from the back of his neck. I start to feel fear for whoever is inside the room, but that emotion is all mine.

We move along the landing and a musky, flowery fragrance invades my senses. It's seeping out from around the door frame like smoke. I recognise it; I used to burn an oil that smelt like this to sweeten the air of my apartment when I lived alone. It's ylang ylang. Don couldn't bear it; I had to throw it away when we first moved in together. *But it's an aphrodisiac*, I told him, teasingly, as I tried to persuade him to let the oil burner stay. *Men like me don't need an aphrodisiac*, he said, sweeping me up in his arms and carrying me to the bedroom. I smile. It's a happy memory. Scent forms the strongest memories.

I realise now that I also kept the oil in my office at Oakley – a few drops in a dish as a soothing background scent. Jarek commented upon it on our first meeting. Did it remind him of this memory I'm in now? Did it incite anger in him from the moment I met him?

Jarek's hand is on the doorknob, gripping tightly, so that his knuckles are pale, fading into the paintwork around them. I edge forward until I'm standing almost directly behind him. I know I have to give Jess and Daniel the best chance to capture what happens next.

I suppose I expect Jarek to fling the door open widely, dramatically. But he does the opposite. He turns the knob so slowly that I can barely notice the movement, despite the fact I'm staring at it. He must know more about what he is going to see than I do, although I have an idea that is rapidly sharpening in my mind. Perhaps our thoughts and emotions are moving together again: two parallel streams meeting briefly before separating once more. I fight to pull us apart, closing off my mind as the door cracks open. He cannot implicate me in death, having already succeeded in life.

I cannot see beyond him. His body fills the tiny opening of the door. *Open it!* I want to scream. *Open it!* I want to push him. I need to see what's inside. Jess needs to see what's inside. Otherwise, they can't save me. Otherwise, I am lost.

The climax is calm. Jarek's hand loosens from the knob and drops to his side as he straightens up. I stay standing behind him, to his left, but I can see it all as the door slowly swings open. The bed stands directly opposite us, against the wall. It is surrounded by uncertainty that is coloured a pale pinky-red, rather than the pure white around the stairs and the landing. It is the colour of love and of fury.

Sex toys are scattered across the crumpled bed. I look at each one in turn, as he must have done. I involuntarily feel a pang of pity for him then. The injustice of it is palpable. The couple are standing in an embrace. Their curves wrap and diffuse into each other. It's the flame-haired woman who notices him first. Even her hair is redder than his, artificially bright and looping in tousled clumps around her shoulders. Her mouth falls open and I watch as her hand tightens on the back of the other figure: a warning – far too late.

The soft brown hair trembles at her waist and Sarah slowly looks around, fearful eyes flicking over her shoulder in our direction. I feel my mouth fall open for a different reason to Jarek: she is truly beautiful. The top of her nose catches the sunlight streaming in from a window I can't see. Her lips are pressed together, but they are still full and tinged red from passion. She has the body of a woman, not a girl, but she is young – perhaps in her early twenties. In a less incriminating situation, you might call her statuesque, but she shrinks under his gaze. Part of me feels as though I should look away, but I stare at the dimples at the base of her back and feel envy rise at the sinuous curve of her hip and, as she turns further, the heavy fullness of her breasts. She is so different from me. Did Jarek even find me attractive? Was I nothing more than convenient?

I feel embarrassed but I hold my head up into the rich silence that hangs in the air between the four of us. Sarah's hands drop from the woman's shoulders to her sides and the red-haired woman starts to pick up her clothes from the floor. I watch, transfixed, as she pulls on a sweater without bothering to put on her bra first, stuffing her undergarments into a bag instead.

'I'm sorry,' Sarah says, her voice hushed in shock, her eyes upon her husband. 'I'm so sorry, Jarek.' Her face is fragmented by a tangle of emotions and her heavily made-up eyes slant downwards, wide and glassy, like a doll's.

'Come on, Sarah; you don't have to put up with his shit.' The woman spits her words out. 'You can't play his games anymore.' Her free hand is outstretched, but Sarah's feet are anchored to the floor and she drops her eyes apologetically.

The woman's voice softens. 'This isn't what love looks like.' She stares at Sarah a little longer before shaking her head in defeat. She turns and sharpens her gaze into Jarek's face and her eyes blaze with defiance as she pushes past us, still half dressed and dishevelled.

I move because I don't want to find out if she will walk straight through me. I see Jarek clutch at her arm fiercely, forcing her close to his chest. She smells as if she has spent hours in this room, with the ylang ylang and with Sarah.

'I will kill you if you come back here,' he whispers ferociously in her ear. His fingers make craters into her forearm and she winces under their pressure before he lets her go. I hear her jog down the stairs and out of the house, slamming the front door violently behind her. It is the first loud noise that this memory holds and it makes me shudder.

Jarek falls upon Sarah then. I stand in the doorway, my hand pressed against my mouth, as I watch him rampage. He approaches her in what is like a sprint, but only covers a few metres of space. She cowers, her hands at the sides of her head. I watch helplessly as he raises the flat of his hand and brings it flying across her face. My heart recoils with the sound it makes, sharp and damp, upon her cheek. It knocks her on to the bed and a flicker of nausea hits my belly. I realise I have never seen anyone this angry before; I have never myself felt this degree of fury. The anger I feel towards Jarek is only just beginning to drag at my ankles, an emotion that's slowly growing into life. It's not the flaring, dagger-like madness that grips him here.

I take a step backwards. I can hardly bear to watch, but I know that I have no choice.

'How could you do that to me? After everything I've done for you!' The words pummel her alongside his fists. I clench my teeth and remind myself that this is all in the past. The memory is fractured by adrenalin. I don't always see it from my perspective; my consciousness can't always arrange itself properly according to Jarek's thoughts. It can't always make the necessary adjustments. I see the splatter of tiny droplets of blood against white linen. I get a glimpse of Jarek's fist buried in her hazel hair, as if it's right in front of me, rather than across the room. I never know what is coming next and the shock fills me, detaches me from what I'm seeing; it has to, otherwise I'd run screaming.

'Why do you always push me to this, Sarah?'

I watch him undo his belt with unease. I wait for him to whip it across her bare body, over that soft, pale skin, but he drops it to the floor with his trousers. I could vomit. The bile rises in the back of my throat and both my hands cover my mouth to push it back. This is the moment that Jarek snaps and they both break. He forces himself into her with a grim determination. I have let this man run his hands tenderly through my hair and I would never have known he was capable of this.

I stop hearing anything but the creak of the bed. I wonder if Sarah really was wordless, really was completely silent during this awful encounter. Was she so unsurprised by it? Had this treatment become a way of life for her? Perhaps Jarek didn't hear her through the blood that pumped and screamed at his temples. It goes on for so long that eventually I know I have seen enough. The barbarity of a few seconds would have been enough. I close my eyes; I wish I had closed them sooner and count my heartbeats until they soften and slow.

Fragments appear. Discordant slices of a story I recognise, combined with ones I don't. I open the door to Jarek. It is afternoon and the sun streaks in through the living-room window on to his hair. He looks surprised to see me in my own apartment. As I grasp at them, the memories slip and slide through my fingertips.

I don't remember opening my eyes, but I'm standing on a sun-bathed street, looking at the display outside a florist's shop. The image is framed like a picture against a blank wall. I jump when I realise Jarek is standing right beside me, almost touching me because his body leans that way, stooping to the left. It is the Jarek I know. From his other side, I see a tiny hand reach out and point at the flowers. It is Helena, his daughter. She tugs him forward, and I feel it, too.

'These, Daddy; these ones!' She's pointing at the bucket full of anemones, their black centres focused upon us like angry eyes.

Jarek folds his arms and smiles. 'Do you think Mummy will be pleased?'

Helena turns back towards him, her plait swinging over her shoulder, and nods insistently. As she turns her face upwards into the sun, I notice the scabs that dot her forehead. Chicken pox, I think. It is the same day I saw them at the burial ground. It is the same day that Jarek called to cancel our appointment, minutes before it was due to begin.

'Do you think they will make Mummy let me into her Heaven?'

Helena frowns, confused. 'Yes,' she says, uncertainly.

I look at Jarek's face and try to read it. He's grinning at his daughter, but his words unsettle me. I'm confused. Had Sarah refused to grant Jarek access to her Heaven?

A lady emerges from the shop and offers to wrap the anemones. He pulls out the stems I know he will: six white, six purple. I think of Sarah that day in the shop, choosing the random bunches and then swapping them for my peonies. She was slipping out from under his control, striking out alone. *Look at us, hey? Buying our own flowers.*

He pays and they move on down the street. I walk slightly behind them, sheltered from the crowds in the wake of Jarek's awkward gait. I reach out tentatively as a woman walks past. My hand doesn't catch on her jacket; it passes right through as if she is a mirage. Or as if I am.

'We don't have much time, but shall we go and play spy on Mummy?' Jarek says to Helena. I can hear him as clearly as if he's whispering directly into my ear. Helena nods with excitement.

'Tell me what you know, Agent Helena,' he says. He pulls her closer to him and crouches down in the middle of the street, dropping the bunch of flowers on to the pavement.

'She said she was taking Eden to playgroup,' Helena says, hopefully. Her eyebrows lift towards her father and I see her eagerness to please him. I remember being like that.

'Well, that'll be over now, but maybe she's somewhere nearby. Shall we track her chip?'

'Mummy doesn't like that.'

'Doesn't she? Well, if it makes her sad, we don't have to tell her, do we?'

Helena shakes her head and time must skip forward because, all of a sudden, we're in the chill of a shaded avenue.

'Here,' murmurs Jarek, looking across the road. There's a small coffee shop a few doors further up that he settles his gaze upon. From here, I can see a few people are sitting at the bistro tables outside, but not Sarah and their daughter.

'Stay close,' Jarek says, and I nod before I remember he's talking to Helena. 'We're going in.'

There's something creepy about the way he's making this a game, and I feel complicit as we move so that we're directly opposite the coffee shop. Jarek pulls Helena into his legs as they slip behind an autocab stop. I look, as they do, through the scratched screen of plastic, over the traffic, to the wide window of the café. There, at the first table on the left, sits Sarah. Their youngest daughter is sitting happily on her lap and beside her is a man, whose head is tipped back in laughter when we first see him. As the man brings his head back level, he rakes one hand through his blond hair and places his other hand over Sarah's.

It could just be a friendly touch. But the man's hand stays there, atop Sarah's, and although we are across the street, I'm sure that I can see their fingers entwine. Perhaps I am wrong. Perhaps Jarek is wrong.

I hear him take a sharp intake of breath and it sounds as if it comes from inside my own throat.

'Ow, Daddy!' Helena squeals. I think he is holding her hand too tightly. I can feel him trembling beside me.

'Do you know him, Helena?'

She shakes her head vehemently.

I study his face. A clenched jaw betrays his fury. His squinted eyes are sharp with focus, observing every detail of the scene. He is taking the time to absorb this man's face, his clothes, his demeanour. I guess that he hasn't seen him before. He must also see Sarah's tight, guarded smile. It is, I think, a smile that will change when Jarek is gone and she is finally free. I remember what Daniel said about the possibility that she had already decided to end their marriage. Maybe she has already walked away. Maybe that's why Jarek was talking about Sarah not letting him into her Heaven.

'Can we go and play with Mummy and Eden and their friend?' Helena's voice is bright, eager.

Their friend. I think this is what does it. The man in that coffee shop will not just be part of Sarah's life after Jarek is gone, he will be part of their daughters' lives, too. When Jarek dies – soon, so soon – that man will also meet Helena. That man will take Jarek's place in their family. He will replace him. To Jarek, this man poses an even greater threat than the woman he found in his bedroom.

'I've told you before,' Jarek says, his voice brittle. 'Mummy doesn't want to play with Daddy anymore.'

My mouth falls open and I look back across the road at Sarah's face. She is laughing, now, her defences down. Daniel was right. She had already left him.

I watch with sadness as Jarek shakily lifts his fingertip to his ear canal. He is about to call the clinic. In a few seconds, he will be talking to me, telling me that he can't come to our session because he's had an unexpected afternoon. I am about to tell him that I was looking forward to seeing him, with an unmistakeable desire in my voice. I am about to tell him he will be untouchable in his Heaven. I *promise* him. Unknowingly, I convince him that everything he wants to do is okay. I give him strength. I plant a seed in his mind.

CHAPTER THIRTY-TWO

My guilt becomes silence. And it's a silence the like of which I've never known. It is a true void, an absence of everything. I don't even hear my own body anymore, shifting beneath clothing or rising and falling as the tissues that form me adjust and expand and contract. I am only thought. Only my mind is left and even that lies in this state of enforced meditation.

For those few moments, as Jess takes my connections apart and links me up to the neuron containing Jarek's third and final ghost memory, the nothingness takes hold. There is no beauty; there is no darkness. It isn't either terrifying or uplifting, but there is *something* in it. There is peace. Before I open my eyes into the new memory, I somehow know I'll see either blinding whiteness or pure jet black. As it turns out, it is strangely both. Like an optical illusion, the void that surrounds me – that *is* me – fades from one to the other as I absorb it.

Momentarily, I am Jarek, clasping my hand around a canister of pills. I stare at my hand, scared the simulation will show the wrong thing. But I'm looking at a man's hand, too big to be mine. I look like I'm wearing a glove that's dotted with freckles and trimmed with thick hairs, which creep up from my wrist, sprouting across the pale skin. I shake that memory away. The black–white void flickers back and then I'm plunged into something new, as clear and real as the scene I was in before.

I'm standing behind him on an escalator that rises out of the belly of a Tube station. I can't see much, save for the metal grooves of the moving steps and Jarek's back, a few steps ahead. I know it's a London Underground station by the smell: the tight, swirling scent of trapped bodies and human heat, the damp aroma of rain clinging to old tiles and the staleness of air that stays too long beneath the streets.

Jarek walks out through the scanners and one flashes against his face. Not for me; I slip through unnoticed. I glance up at the red, white and blue sign. *Maida Vale Station*, it reads proudly, against the antique red tiles of the building. As he strides lopsidedly forward, on to the street, I'm surprised by the darkness of the sky and the flicker of the street lights. It is late. If this is the day he came to my apartment and I gave him the pills, then he left long ago. As he flaps his overcoat, about to button it up, my nostrils catch the waft of alcohol that flares around him. He pulls a hood up over his head; that won't disguise the distinctive lumber of his disease-induced gait. Even without seeing his face, I know that it is gaunt now; his shoulders have lost the strength they had before, when he threw the furious energy of his weight upon Sarah in their bedroom.

We cross the road. He doesn't walk fast. I almost fall over my feet in an effort to stay behind him. His stoop is worse than I remember. At the top of the avenue, he stops to rest against a tree. He leans into it; a sorry sight. I watch his shoulders rise and fall. He presses one hand to the left side of his head, wincing, and we both look up at the sliver of moon that decorates the muddy sky.

If this is the night – the Friday night that Sarah dies – then Jarek himself is dead within hours. I wonder how he had the strength to make love to me that afternoon. Not passion, perhaps, but desperation: a need to bring his plan to fruition. I would never have known.

Pedestrians pass me – pass right through me. This must be what it's like to be a ghost. Part of me – a larger part than I might admit – wants to go and hold him. I know that I can't; it's not possible. He wouldn't even see me or hear me; this is like watching a film. I tell myself no and hold my feet firm on the pavement. Eventually, he heaves himself forward up the street.

As I dutifully follow, the weight of the night starts to press down upon me. It's as if I can feel the tension coil and spring from the muscles that remain on Jarek's back. His hands are thrust deep into his coat, his head is bowed and, if you didn't know he was dying from a vicious brain tumour, you would think that he was drunk. Perhaps he is. He veers to the left and then corrects himself again and again as we walk down the street. I start to recognise the neighbourhood. I remember waiting here, hoping to catch a glimpse of Sarah. Little did I know that she had already called an end to their marriage. *Such a shame, that*, the florist had said to me. *I used to see him in here a lot*.

Jarek pauses again, resting his hand upon the wrought iron gatepost of his house. My stomach tightens and twists. He looks up and down the street, straight through me, and I feel a wash of sadness, or possibly regret, seeping from his eyes. We seek out the moon once more, caught in the bare branches of the lime tree above our heads, before going inside.

I slip in the door behind him and watch as he hangs up his keys on a little hook, draping his coat over them and taking out the canister from the pocket. He pushes it deep into the pocket of his trousers.

Victorian tiles shine at my feet. A framed picture hangs to my left. Although it is blurry to me, long forgotten, I can tell from the flash of white, charcoal grey and pink that it's a wedding photograph. The wide stairs flare open as they meet the hallway. A pair of small, purple shoes sits neatly on the bottom step. A child's shoes. I tune in my hearing as Jarek does, listening out for the sounds of the house and the people within it. There is nothing for a few seconds and then there is the sound of a metal instrument clattering against enamel. There is a palpable sensation, then, that tingles against me like static. It is the sinking realisation that Sarah is here, that it is going to happen. I'm not sure if it's Jarek's feelings or my own. Perhaps it is both. I feel my heartbeat start to pick up as we advance down the corridor.

'Jarek, is that you?' a woman calls out from behind the glazed double doors. Jarek pushes them open and we're greeted by the smell of lemongrass and coconut. I hate Thai food. I can't bear the chunks of fiery ginger and the floral lining it leaves in my mouth. Sarah looks up at him, fleetingly aghast. The gleaming blade in her hand hovers over a half-chopped aubergine. This is the Sarah I recognise. She looks much the same as before, but she is slightly plumper, perhaps, and her hair is shorter; it's cut into a sharp bob around her jawline. After a moment, Jarek moves forward and lays a hand on her shoulder.

Sarah puts the knife down and rounds inwards slightly, curling her spine, as if she is protecting her heart from his touch. 'What are you doing here?' she demands, her shoulders tense. 'I thought you were coming over in the morning to spend time with the girls?'

'Just thought I'd stop by.'

Jarek moves awkwardly past the island of marble and sinks into an armchair by the wood burner, its insides battered with flames. Sarah's eyes follow his movement, and she presses her lips back between her teeth. I stay where I am, by the kitchen door, where I can see them both, although the outlines and edges of the room are vague. The kitchen knife begins to fall repeatedly against the chopping board again and I can't help but stare at the blade. I think about the splatter of blood from her face against the bed sheets. I think about how this is all supposed to unfold.

'You had your appointment with your Architect today?' Jarek mumbles. So, Sarah was planning to create her own Heaven, ahead of time, like writing a will. As with some of my old clients, she didn't want to wait until she was dying.

'Yes, I told you I was going. This morning, like I said.' The strain shows in her face as she tips the vegetables into the pan. Steam sizzles up into the wrinkles that underline her eyes, softening their years of worry.

'And you haven't changed your mind?'

Seeing them here, in their luxurious, warm home, it's almost impossible to believe that they aren't a happy couple. But then I catch a glimpse of his face as it turns from the fire. It's directed at Sarah's back and it burns with hatred. It makes me shudder and I wonder if she can feel it, too.

'Jarek.' Sarah puts down the knife and turns to face him,

folding her arms, standing tall. Even as outside observer, I'm not sure he wipes the expression from his face fast enough. I notice that she flicks her eyes towards the kitchen doors, as if she's checking that her exit route is clear. 'We've been through all this. We don't make each other happy. I don't think we ever did.'

'You don't think you owe it to me – after everything we've been through together – to be in my Heaven? For me to be in yours? You know I still love you, Sarah.'

And it crystallises. It was a smooth lie when he told me that he didn't want her in his Heaven. A lie that obscured his loss of control. A lie that concealed a motive.

'Love? Really? After what you've done to me?' Her voice wobbles with what I interpret to be fear, or anger, or both. My stomach turns as I wonder how much violence has been a part of her life. She must have kept it to herself for so many years. It breaks me to realise that not only did he not love me, but he also had no concept of what love is. Only obsession.

'Look, if you want to stay here tonight, I'll just go,' Sarah says. 'Mum will drop the girls back first thing. Don't worry, not late. I told her not to be late again. And I'll come back tomorrow evening as planned.'

The children aren't here. I wish she hadn't said that. I wish they were playing together upstairs. It might have changed everything.

'You don't have to leave,' he says, watching her closely as she picks up her Codex and lifts her handbag onto the work surface.

'Have the food if you want, it just needs stir-frying. I'll grab a takeaway or something.' She speaks quickly, stumbling over her words.

'I'm sorry to have surprised you like this,' Jarek says. 'It's just been a hard day. Every day is harder, now.' He speaks softly but there is none of the charm that I used to adore. There are no light-hearted jokes, no winks, no showmanship. He's used up all his energy on me. And what is left, he is conserving. He is withdrawing inside himself, centring his strength for one final task. There is perhaps one last thing to check.

'How are the girls?'

'They've been fine. We don't need to tell them anything about us yet. And I'll have a chat with Mum next week.'

I look back at Jarek, but there is nothing to disturb me in what I see. His isn't the face of a man preparing to commit such a heinous crime. He looks ill, yes, but he's relaxed in the radiance of the fire. His hands are loosely folded in his lap and his head rests against the back of the chair. And he is smiling – smiling over his love for his children.

Once more, he has tricked me, because, in the next beat of my heart, he has risen from the chair and is walking back across the kitchen. Sarah fumbles in her bag as I watch Jarek move around the kitchen, closing all the blinds fully. I watch him extract the lid of the canister from his pocket and lay it down on the work surface. He takes a wooden spoon from one of the drawers and pushes it into his back pocket, moving to stand right behind Sarah.

There are no recriminations, no reasons given. Jarek is what a barrister would call cold, calculating. It looks like the actions of a romantic husband as he takes the bag from her hand and lays it on the floor. With his other hand, he turns off the heat.

'You left the hob on, silly,' he says. I hardly recognise his voice.

He stands facing her. 'Where will you go this evening? Are you going to see him?'

'Who? I don't know what you mean.' She is a terrible liar.

'You've met someone else already, haven't you?'

'Jarek, please.' Sarah's hands curl into loose fists over her stomach.

He doesn't speak. His mouth is set as he focuses on what is next. He turns her around by her shoulders and presses her back against the oven. I am so close to them – a few feet away. I stumble backwards, steeling myself. He is wearing gloves now and I see Sarah notice that at the same time I do. *That's odd*, I see her think. And then she must see the look on his face because a veil of unbridled horror falls over her. It's too late for her to move because his hands are wrapped around her delicate neck, pressing.

'Why?' I hear him say. 'After what you've done, why is it only me that won't see our children grow up? How can you leave me now?'

Sarah vibrates. Her whole body is writhing and bucking against him. She scratches at the air in front of his eyes, but his arms are locked out straight and she cannot reach him. I watch his left arm shake, his knee buckle. He slips to the floor and drags her with him. She kicks out at his shins and thrusts her elbows towards his chest and face, and, for a moment, I rejoice in thinking he's too weak to carry on. As they lie side by side, bucking and twisting, it looks as though they could be making love. But I've momentarily forgotten that I know how this story ends. Jarek eventually hauls himself up and Sarah's body almost completely disappears beneath his.

'How's that fair, Sarah?'

Her choking gurgles crowd my ears. Her skin pales by the second, apart from the wrinkled pink half-moons beneath her eyes, which seem to crackle with blood. She claws at his arms but she can't reach his skin through the thick sweater he's wearing. What upsets me the most is the way that they stare at each other. She begs in disbelief and Jarek just stares back at her, through her, writing her oblivion letter by letter. I bring my hands to my own throat, feeling at its delicacy, trying to imagine how much strength it would really take to crush it.

He only loosens his grip when she stops making a noise, and then, with one hand, he swiftly extracts the canister from his pocket. Releasing her neck for a split second, he tips the contents into the back of her mouth. It happens at precisely the same moment she gasps for air. I imagine the sugar-coated pills fighting each other to sink down to her stomach as she tries to cough them up. I look down at the floor, even though I know Jess and Daniel will be annoyed with me. I can't bear to see any more, but the noises are worse on their own. By the end, Jarek's breaths shoot in and out of his nostrils in effort. Sarah moans from her stomach, chokes and splutters. I can almost hear the desperate thump of her blood. The whole room trembles. I must steady my own breathing to stay standing, gripping on to the door frame.

Eventually, it falls quiet. The vegetables are already cooling in the pan. The smell of burnt garlic and terror wafts around me. I brace myself before I look up. Jarek lays Sarah flat on the floor and pulls her mouth open with his gloved fingers. I sear with anger as I watch him pull something out from his other trouser pocket. I walk forward. The tangle of dark, wavy hair – my hair – sits like a storm cloud in his palm. He presses it on to the end of the spoon handle, pushing it to the back of Sarah's throat and jamming the spoon up and down like a plunger before letting it clatter upon the floor. There is no satisfaction on his face, but there is no sadness either. Only what I presume is a psychopathic emptiness. He stands up and looks down at her.

'You won't replace me,' he says, quietly, more calmly than before. Then he kneels back down and runs his fingertips around the outline of her body, as if he is checking for something. For about half a minute, he holds his index finger and middle finger against the side of her throat. He stands again, his back to me. I'm relieved not to see her eyes. We stand there for some time, just waiting, just looking.

Everything is fading and I notice that the last few minutes have been riddled by a sharp clarity in which I could see, smell and hear every little detail. The taste of the fried aubergine lingers on my tongue. As we walk out of the kitchen and into the hallway, the space around me pulses in shocked white. The walls are gone; the front door is vague, as if shrouded in mist. I stand still in the doorway as Jarek walks down the path and out on to the street. His hood is back up. He looks around once, twice, three times, and then he is gone. I wait here, guarding Sarah's body, wishing that someone other than her mother and two daughters could find her.

He is going to die in safety, where they will ensure he reaches his Heaven. This poor dying man, with a loving wife and a madly jealous mistress. But I've seen the truth. I've seen an obsessive dying man, with a wife who had finally found the courage to walk away from him, in both life and death, and a gullible, convenient mistress to whom he played the victim.

As I come around, I feel like I'm waking into either an

earthquake or a bomb until I realise that Daniel, Jess and Luke are holding me down to the bed. I am shaking with a violence that matches the pressure of Jarek's thumbs around Sarah's neck. I can't breathe in and I can't make any noise come out. I just gulp pointlessly at the air and let myself convulse until it starts to ease. I focus on the insistent pressing of Daniel's hands upon my upper arms. I let him lay me back on to the bench and, gradually, the oxygen returns to my lungs. I look around at their faces and they all stare back at me, wide-eyed, as if I'm a bizarre, unknown creature they've brought back from a deep and distant jungle.

Everyone is staring at me, open-mouthed.

'You got it, right?' I splutter. 'You saw it all?'

They nod in unison and I take several deep breaths. I listen for the beat of my heart in my chest. Bleary-eyed, I look around at the parts of the room I can see without moving my head. It is all a little darker then I remember, but it is here – it is real. I press my fingertips into the bench beneath me and draw comfort from its cool hardness.

'You did well,' says Daniel. 'Take your time.' And yet they continue to watch me, as if they are waiting for me to do something.

I slide my arm over my chest and face, to my head. It feels too heavy to lift.

'I want these gone,' I say, running my palm over my scalp.

'They're gone,' Jess says. 'I already took them out.' She gestures across the room to a bloody beaker. I see the metal against the glass at the same time as I realise I can't feel the cool circles beneath my hair.

Jess leans over me and slips her arms awkwardly around my

neck, squeezing me gently. She tells me how brave I am and how proud of me she is. I hum into her ear.

'You need to rest now, Isobel,' she says, then turns to Daniel. 'You need to let her go home.'

Daniel looks at me and then back at Jess. 'I need to take her back to the station first, but hopefully . . .'

'If she needs bail . . .' Jess adds.

'It's either charge or release, at this stage. But this . . . this should be enough.'

'If you need me to come down and talk it through, explain it to people . . . whatever, then I'm happy to,' Jess says.

I feel like a child standing between her parents as I look from one to the other, letting them discuss my future in front of me.

'And if you need somewhere to stay, Izz . . .' she says, squeezing me around the shoulders. 'Well, you know where I am.'

'I'm not sure I want to spend another hour in a lab,' I say. I feel a weak smile slink across my face as I realise I've made a joke.

'I *do* have a home, you know!' Jess rolls her eyes at me. She needs to rest, too. The pressure on her has been immense: taking responsibility for me, for my life, for the Heavens of the people she watches over. I don't know how she does it.

CHAPTER THIRTY-THREE

Six weeks later

All this technology and still something as simple as removing a tattoo is both time consuming and uncomfortable. I've been rubbing in the cream for weeks now, each morning and evening. With my little finger, I've pushed it into the lines until the skin of my ankle has paled beneath the pressure. The formula calls out to my white blood cells, asking them to come and clear away the ink that corrupts me. Particle by particle, the ink has been carried to my lymph nodes and erased. It's almost like it never happened. My angel has faded now, to a pale grey outline of what she once was – much like the memory of the past months in my mind. The time has come to get rid of it completely, to remove the lines that I have drawn through my life.

I'm walking the long way, I suppose. I've finished shopping, but the lights of Regent Street are too beautiful not to stroll beneath on such a dry, crisp winter's evening. I've just bought my last gift, and I feel in my pocket for the edges of the small box. Lela had always wanted this necklace. Maybe I'll wear it for her. I draw my hands into the cold air and clutch at the lapels of my coat, pulling it tightly around my neck. The faux fur tickles reassuringly on my cheeks, which are sensitive in the cold air. Despite the tears in my eyes, the atmosphere draws me into its frenzied grasp and it's easy to be swept along with all these other pink, wind-bitten faces, peeping out from thick coats and glowing with festive fever. I can smell the tempting aroma of the outdoor stalls which cluster at each junction, roasting sugary nuts and sweet chestnuts. Families and couples flow past me, loaded with bags and dazzled by the elaborate window displays that line the street. This year's lights hang above us, looking like an amped-up version of the night sky. Older children point out the constellations to their younger siblings, naming Orion and the Plough. Every so often, I pass under a planet. I almost feel the need to duck below Jupiter, which floats above my head, swirling in creamy reds and oranges like a giant bauble.

The London scenery that surrounds me is almost distracting enough for my purposes. But then I glimpse a man pushing back his red hair, I'm jolted into thinking it's Jarek, and I'm taken right back to that dark place. At one point, I pass a building with wide, grand stone steps and old, panelled wood doors, and it reminds me of the courthouse that's not too far from here, and never too far from my mind. If I find myself walking behind an old lady who holds the hands of two young, brown-haired girls, I'll always wonder if that's them – Jarek and Sarah's daughters – and whether I would recognise them if it was.

I would recognise Sarah's mother if I saw her again. She was petite and elegantly dressed each day in court. Her grey eyes were always calm, and that amazed me. She carried herself with such dignity. It was bemusing but admirable, how she held herself. I never saw her swearing under her breath, or letting tears slip down her cheeks – unlike me. She didn't gape in disbelief as she listened to the prosecution describe Jarek as a violent narcissist, rocked by sexual jealousy and unable to bear the idea that, in the last throes of his life, his wife, his property, was finally leaving him, escaping his mental and physical abuse to be with someone kinder. I had to stand up in that witness box and describe my understanding of how her daughter was murdered, but her chin never dropped. It might have done, though, had they shown the simulations in court. I was torn apart in the cross-examination. It was a character assassination, and yet I felt her eyes upon me, watching without judgement. I would have spoken to her if I had known what to say. I smiled at her instead, as we filed down the steps at the end. She was about to make a statement to the press, poised in her heels, but she smiled back with a warmth that my wishful heart sensed was forgiveness.

As we knew it would be, it was a landmark case. Jarek was found guilty, swiftly and unanimously, on the basis of his ghost memories, just days after the new law came into place. Despite being dead, he was posthumously convicted of murder and his punishment was the decommissioning of his Heaven: he would have to die a second time.

I glance at the time. By now, the systematic destruction of Jarek's Heaven is almost complete. Jess invited me to be there, which took me by surprise. I turned down the offer immediately, not even thinking about it for a moment. *I'm done with playing God*, I told her. I imagine her disconnecting everything in the Electric Lab as my feet hit the pavement and my coat flaps at my knees. She is taking his mirror neurons out of their tiny black cartridge and out of the solution that keeps them alive. They will be cremated and buried with the rest of him. Is this justice? I don't know. But it is over. At last, it is over and the darkness is no longer fathomless and engrossing but crisp like the night sky. I had built a career on delaying the inevitable, on pushing back that obscurity a little bit further, but now I don't know where to find the light to guide me. Is Lela's Heaven everything she was promised? *It looks stable*, said Jess. No ghost memories. Or, at least, none that she's spotted so far. I sigh in relief but it does nothing to soothe the ache I feel. Lela didn't want to die – she was young, happy – but I remind myself what matters is that she lived, and that she is remembered. That doesn't mean that grieving her is easy. Memories cannot fill her vacancy, or ease the sorrow that follows me throughout my days. People like Lela leave us forever, even though they can play in the meadows of their childhood holidays, and dance on a bar with their best friends, and kiss their husband goodnight again and again and again. They are still gone.

I cut down a side street, towards Cavendish Square. As I reach the end of Henrietta Place, I can see ahead that the grass is covered by tents and the trees are festooned with lights. As I get closer, the scent of spiced wine warms the air. I glimpse at the time in my vision and decide to cut through the market on my way to Harley Street. An old-fashioned carousel welcomes me, surrounded by parents waving to their little ones and encouraging them to keep their tiny mittened hands on the poles of their horses. There's an orchestral version of a Christmas song being played by a brass band somewhere. The throaty grumble of the tuba sounds live, but I can't see them or put my finger on the name of the song. I hum it in my head with forced jollity, hoping the words will come, but they don't. There are stalls selling gifts and food, and I stop at one to buy a mug of mulled cider. I watch people queuing up for the Belgian waffles opposite, letting the scent of melted chocolate and vanilla blend with the aroma of my drink. I sip at the hot liquid, sucking it back slowly over my tongue to let the spices coat my mouth. It tastes like Christmas. I feel rather alone, standing at the round bar beside the stall. But I shouldn't do. I'm spending the holidays with my sister's family this year. Some people have no one. I think of Lela's husband, and of Jarek and Sarah's two daughters, without their mother or father for the first time, and I feel an intense sadness gather at the back of my throat. I knock back my drink in a few more gulps to try to wash the lump from my throat, and leave the mug on the bar. Tightening up my coat, I head onwards, leaving the square behind me.

The clinic is a short walk up Harley Street. I've walked past it many times on my way to or from work. I've still got ten minutes before my appointment, so I decide to walk on further. Oakley Associates is two blocks away. I'm so damned sentimental these days. I walk past the tall, smart buildings, surrounded by black iron fencing. I look up at some of the windows and see the occasional cluster of fairy lights or green Christmas-tree branches. The old B.T. Tower flashes behind me like a beacon to warn passing ships. The streets here are tightly ordered. It doesn't take long for me to reach the Oakley Associates clinic and I stand across the street from the sliding doors, admiring the lime tree that frames the entrance with its branches. The protesters have gone for the day, but the lights are still on inside and, through the glass of the sliding doors, I can see a woman sitting behind the reception desk. She is wearing a dress the colour of Lela's lipstick and, as I stare, she swivels in her chair to reach for something on her desk. Stupidly, my heart falls when it's a face I don't recognise. I can see the window of my office from here – towards the back of the building. I wonder who is inside it now. Harry, perhaps. I hope so. I never told him, but he was really good at his job.

I wonder how something I once cared about so much can seem worthless to me. I put my soul into crafting Heavens. I fell in love with all my clients a little bit along the way. Is it wrong, what I did? I don't know. Looking at the clinic now, from the outside, its value has fallen. The slick lines of its architecture, the gleaming marble floors, the original artwork on the walls – it's all a sham. Life is the only thing of value in this world, especially when war is so imminent. I press my lips together in a silent farewell. I won't come here again. I could pretend not to care, but of course I do. I turn and walk back the way I have come, feeling the cooling air bite at my ears.

I still sometimes think that the past four months have been a dream, that none of it really happened. But Lela is gone, and that is a constant reminder that the conflict is real, and getting ever closer to home. Britain's airstrikes begin in earnest next week. Strangely, the more serious it gets, the better I sleep. It's been weeks since I've woken to the imagined sound of drones or bombs. Most days, I don't even think about it. Is it because I've seen what is beyond? My Heaven still taps me on the shoulder, whispers in my ear. It springs upon me when I'm feeling low. It offers me a crutch and it is tempting to think that I could fall back into that dreamlike oblivion. I have to speak firmly to myself. I have to remind myself that I have a life to live. And that the idea of Heaven is not as sweet as it appears.

I return to the Harley Street building and walk in through the revolving doors to a tiny Edwardian-era reception. It's carpeted and lined with wood panelling and bookcases. A display appears in front of the door that leads onwards. *Hello, Ms Argent,* it says. *Please sit down and someone will be with you shortly.* I do as it suggests and take a seat in the leather-effect armchair in the corner. I've barely sat down, and the hologram is still fading out, when a woman clad in a white tunic marches into reception to greet me.

'Please, this way,' she says, with polite efficiency.

I wordlessly follow her through the door, back into the building, and we enter the second door on the right. I find myself in a white clinic of claustrophobic proportions. She gestures for me to lie down on the bed that fills the longest edge of the room. Half of the space remaining is taken up by the laser machine that stands beside the bed, like a giant anglepoise.

'Please, if you could roll up your trouser leg to knee height and slip your shoes off?'

I kick my shoes off on to the floor and pull up the fabric, folding it above my knee. I peel off my socks and drop them on top of my shoes. The woman pounces upon my ankle.

'Now, let's have a look. You've been using the lotion for a month, correct?' she asks.

'Yes.'

'It's worked well!' She runs her finger over the remaining outlines. 'Yes, I think we'll be able to get rid of the last traces with one session. Please, lie back.'

She picks up a block and arranges it under my heel so that my foot is elevated. Then she angles the mechanical arm to face the tattoo.

'Just relax for fifteen minutes,' she says, before leaving the room.

The main lights dim and I close my eyes as the machine hums into life. I feel something pointed move over the skin on my ankle. The robot traces the lines on my ankle once, twice, three times, until it is sure and it's decided on the strength and thickness of the ink that remains. It whirrs briefly as the laser stutters into life. I can barely feel it tracing my skin, and I remember the pain that Brooke inflicted upon me. I could take pain then; I'm not sure I could be so brave now. But maybe I'm wrong. Maybe I'm stronger in different ways. I do as the woman suggested and close my eyes, feeling my body heat gather between my clothes and the bed.

If I am stronger, then no one would know it. I have found it hard to talk to anyone about what I've been through. My sister knows next to nothing, but then she wouldn't ask. There are few other people to tell, although I've had a lot of conversations with Lela in my mind – and even with Jarek, if I'm completely honest with myself. I've had coffee with friends in the past few weeks, but I've asked most of the questions. I've kept them talking. It's too difficult to know where to begin. They've asked me about work, which is the only thing I used to talk about. It's all they really know about me. And I've stumbled there, more than anywhere, for the first time identifying where my depression has stemmed from: this sudden lack of purpose. *What will you do next?* everyone asks. I've listened to myself come out with some bullshit about going travelling for a while, or doing some volunteer work, but only to fill in what would otherwise be gaping holes in our dialogue. I should admit to them that I don't know. I should ask them for help, but I don't. That's not the kind of person I am.

There is one skill I've taken from all of this. My ability to medi-tate is phenomenal. I let it happen now. I listen to my heartbeat and I imagine it slowing down. Perhaps it does. With every beat, my thoughts fade to the edges of my brain's vision, out of reach. I lie there, breathing, and for those moments it's enough to be alive. It's okay to be me.

'Right, let's have a look, then!'

I barely noticed the door open, but the woman is back beside me and the robot is withdrawing from the bed. The lights fade up and she leans down to inspect my ankle.

'I hope you won't miss it. It was beautiful.'

I pull myself into a sitting position and twist my head to look. You would never know there had ever been anything there. All I see is the bare skin, still darker than usual from the Goan sun. I decide that I will put my anklet on when I get home.

'No, I won't miss it,' I tell her. 'Thank you.'

I put my socks and shoes back on and make my way out into the crisp December evening. They are closing the clinic behind me; the hologram flickers into darkness and the lights go off as I leave. I stand in the entrance, buttoning up my coat and burying my chin into the collar. My breath warms my neck, only serving to drive the rest of me into a deeper chill.

'Hello,' a voice says, making me start. I didn't see him before, but he's leaning against the wall, wrapped up in a thick parka, pale grey fur framing his face.

'Daniel?'

He pushes back the hood as soon as I recognise him. I'm surprised, but not quite as much as I would have expected.

'Is it done?' I ask him, and it's as if I can feel Jarek's hand stroking the skin of my neck. I shake the image away. It reminds me that I am damaged and that there are lines carved into me that cannot be removed with a fancy cream or a laser. They will mark me forever.

'Yes, it's done. His mirror neurons have been returned to his family.'

I'm thankful for the gentleness in Daniel's voice. He drops his eyes and I can tell that, even after seeing what Jarek did, he respects the solemnity of what's happened today.

'But that's not why I'm here,' he continues.

'No?'

'You said you'd be in touch,' he says, softly. He sounds hurt. The street light shines upon his face and his smile is uncharacteristically full. I find myself returning it, against my better judgement.

'But I wasn't.'

'No.' He drops his gaze to the pavement. 'I thought your Codex might have corrupted my details, or . . .'

'Or?'

'Or I was wrong.'

'About what?'

'About you.'

He levels his gaze at me and I have to blink the intensity of his eyes away; they speak of things I've long left behind. When I look back at him, there is something of Jarek in his expression, behind the light in his eyes. I gulp back the shock and feel as though I've swallowed vodka.

'I wanted to check you were all right.' He shrugs. Exhaled air condenses into a mist in front of his face, softening it.

I narrow my eyes at him. He's as coldly logical as I usually am.

No, he wouldn't have come to find me without a good reason for doing so. 'Well, I'm fine, so I guess that'll be that!' I let out a little laugh and it comes out awkwardly, as if my diaphragm has forgotten how to hold itself or my throat is stunned by the sound.

I pull my hair out from beneath the collar of my coat and flick it over my shoulders, walking straight past him, down the street. He turns and walks next to me, of course. Our hands are thrust deep into our pockets but Daniel's shoulder rubs against mine as we walk. I hear him sigh. I'm supposed to hear it. I'm supposed to know that there's a part of me he's giving up on – for now, at least.

'I wanted you to know that there's a job for you, if you want it.' The softness has gone from his voice. He's only ever one Daniel or the other. I wonder whether the gentle half of him will always be retrievable or whether that sigh was final. Perhaps that was his last effort at an apology, at any hint of friendship. 'We could use you, Isobel.'

I make a very unfeminine grunt, which embarrasses me as soon as I hear it.

'You might not realise it, but you could be a great asset to a lot of people. To us, now, given single opt-in, given the coming changes in the law.'

'An *asset*.' I turn his choice of word over in my mouth, enveloping it with sarcasm. I can feel his eyes upon me. 'An asset in a witch-hunt? In tearing down people's Heavens?'

'You must be bored. Aren't you?' He smiles again now and it offers some kind of bridge between the two versions of him. For the first time, I can see both of him. 'I don't profess to know you well, but I know you're an intelligent woman, Isobel. You must be desperate to *do* something?'

I think about what the fallout from Jarek's trial will be in the media. I imagine a swollen crowd of protesters outside the clinic, jubilant with the evidence to bolster their hatred of an artificial afterlife. Who will want a Heaven now? I think about what might happen if Valhalla can't find a way to erase ghost memories. Worst of all, I wonder how likely it is that they'll find a way to simply tuck them out of sight, hide them from their simulations, so that only the dead will suffer them. It is conceivable. And if there's a risk of that happening, who will stop them?

We reach the junction and I pause, my toes pointing out into the crossroads. Daniel stops and stands beside me, our breath intermingling in the air between us.

'I'll think about it,' I say, with the same careful delicacy that I feel. And I mean it, because that's exactly what I do, how I help people. I think about things. I run them through in my mind, roll them over and over, shaping them, making memories from them before anything has ever happened. That is how you keep control. That is how you exact perfection.

ACKNOWLEDGEMENTS

When I committed myself to completing the first draft of this book for National Novel Writing Month in November 2015, I had no idea that it would come to be filled with such love and such loss. In the subsequent ten months, I would come to fall pregnant, sign with my literary agent, lose my Dad suddenly, give birth to my son, and secure a publishing deal. *The Memory Chamber*'s journey has been a whirlwind. At times, a tornado.

So, a huge thank you to the most amazing agent, Sue Armstrong at C+W, for not forgetting about me, and sending me the most exciting email of my life. Also, a big shout-out to the rest of the C+W/Curtis Brown team for their hard work, enthusiasm and entertaining tweets.

When I first spoke to my editor at Quercus Books, Cassie Browne, I knew this book needed her quiet confidence and razor-sharp insight. Thank you for making it the best it could be, and for making the process so enjoyable.

I'm lucky to have had the excellent parenting combo of my Dad, who always told me I'd be a writer, and my Mum, who instilled in me the confidence to make it happen.

Tim, my gem of a husband: if it wasn't for the path we've taken together – quitting our jobs, travelling the world, embarking on life-changing business ventures – I still wouldn't have finished a first draft of anything. You inspire me to keep my chin up and carry on dreaming.

And lastly, thank you to my biggest distraction, little Rafe. Every day, you open chambers in my heart and my mind that I never knew were lying empty.

The Memory Chamber

A Reading Group Guide

Reading Group Questions

1. *The Memory Chamber* is set in a world where you can buy and design your own afterlife. If Isobel was designing your Heaven, what would you choose to include?

2. Where would you side on the 'single opt-in' argument? When we explain death to children we often say that people will be reunited in Heaven; could a Heaven truly be complete if someone you loved was missing?

3. Isobel suggests that artificial Heavens are seen by many as 'morally dubious'. What issues around morality do they raise and is it the architect or the client who is compromised?

4. Do you object to the idea that the human afterlife is something we can control? Would you choose to have an artificial Heaven if given the choice?

5. Isobel asserts that she can never really know what her clients will experience. Is her handling of Heavens irresponsible, or is this just the nature of dealing with new and emerging technologies?

6. Isobel initially sees her job as the 'right thing to do, the kind thing to do' – are those two things the same? Is what is 'kind' always what is 'right'? Does Isobel always do the right thing throughout the novel?

7. Isobel's chemistry with Jarek is electric from the first scene and their passionate affair is a huge part of the first half of the book. Did you enjoy how the novel changed pace once a murder had taken place, and became about the search for a killer?

8. What were your initial impressions of Jarek? Did you trust him?

A Q&A with Holly Cave

Q: **The Memory Chamber has such a fantastic and original idea at its heart. Where did the idea of creating an afterlife made of memories come from, and how did you know this was going to become the premise of your next novel?**

A: I get most of my ideas whilst either walking my dog or brushing my teeth. This time, I was wandering the field edges with the dog, picking blackberries. It was a beautiful autumn morning and I was thinking to myself how perfect it all was, and how happy I felt. And then a line that's still in the book ('the footpaths of my Heaven are lined with blackberry bushes') just popped into my head. By the end of that walk, I had the beginnings of Isobel's character in my mind and I knew that she designed Heavens – I just had to figure out what happened to her.

Q: **Are there any writers who particularly influenced you in writing this novel?**

A: I love delving into a broad range of fiction. Margaret Atwood, Ali Smith, and Sarah Waters are a few favourites of mine – all female authors with something powerful to say about our world. Modern, memorable prose, smart ideas, and devious plotting, but never, ever, at the expense of character. A couple of books that I kept in the back of my mind while writing this story included Audrey Niffenegger's *The Time Traveler's Wife* and Kazuo Ishiguro's *Never Let Me Go*.

Q: **Do you have a specific place where you tend to write regularly? Is routine an important part of your writing life?**

A: When I first started writing *The Memory Chamber*, I was still living above the village pub that my husband and I used to run. When we moved into our house, I had a dedicated study for the first time, with a desk right in front of the window. I became a lot more productive! But then I had my son, who has stolen 'my' room for his nursery and I've been relegated to the spare room. Routine is probably more important to me than I care to admit. I try to start writing at the same time each day, always with a freshly made cup of tea and something on hand to occupy me during short breaks from writing (nail varnish, colouring book, small DIY job . . .).

Q: ***The Memory Chamber* is written in a first-person voice. Do you enjoy being inside a character's head when you write? What do you think it adds to the story, that we see the world through Isobel's eyes only?**

A: I started writing this story in the third person, but it just wasn't working because I kept hearing Izzy's voice in my head.

I also knew from the start that I wanted her character to feel complex, and for her actions to be questionable at times, so I knew the reader had to see right inside her head as she was making decisions. I loved writing from her perspective, and it allowed me to rip apart the romantic, idealised concept of artificial Heavens in front of her very eyes.

Q: *The Memory Chamber* raises a lot of complicated ethical and moral questions. Is that an important element of your work? Do you think that your novels going forward will continue to incorporate ethical dilemmas?

A: Absolutely. When I look back at my early notes and ideas for books, they are usually just a long list of 'what if?' questions, waiting to be answered. I seem to start with science-led, speculative themes and create the story from there. That said, I'll often change a plotline halfway through because my characters start behaving in certain ways, manipulating me and my best-laid plans. So, my writing is hugely character-led, which means that ethical and moral issues will always be a big part of my work; because how we behave is driven by what we believe.

Q: *The Memory Chamber* plays with the idea of choosing a certain ending for yourself by designing an afterlife and yet Isobel's future at the end of the novel is extremely ambiguous: she has lost her lover, her job, and her faith in the Heaven programme. The spectre of war looms large. Is there still hope for Isobel and her world?

A: Isobel clearly suffers a lot over the course of the book, but when I was writing the ending, I felt optimistic for her. Whatever she's been through, her life is now a blank canvas, and she can make of it what she will. She is stronger than she thinks, very able, highly informed, and in many ways the world is now her oyster. I know in my mind what Isobel does next and how she moves on from here. Maybe one day I'll write about it!

Q: **What would you like readers to take away from *The Memory Chamber*?**

A: It would have been easy when I was writing to get carried away with the idea of artificial Heavens. At times, it was a mesmerising thought. In Isobel's second meeting with Jarek, she suggests that he should include memories linked to negative emotions in his Heaven, to help frame the happy moments: 'True happiness is only cast from shadows'. The gist of this is something my mum always told me when I was feeling down, and I always carry it with me. I also enjoyed describing how Isobel tried to be such a perfectionist and never saw this as a potential flaw. Of course, she screwed up royally. There's a good reminder for us all there, I think. No one's perfect.